CAUSI\ INTERFER\

BY RICHARD LAWS

First published 2022 by Five Furlongs

© Richard Laws 2022
ISBN 978-1-9164600-5-8 (Paperback)

Cover photography © John Flanaghan

My sincere thanks for their ongoing help and advice:
John Flanaghan, Patricia Grant, Linda Cronk, Claire Dickens, and Mike Dunn.

One

Today wasn't the first time these two-year-olds had breezed up this particular turf gallop in Malton. Sitting in his car at the top of the gallop, their trainer, Dennis Smith, lifted his binoculars and focussed experienced and critical eyes onto his charges. They were jig-jogging impatiently at the bottom of the hill. One gave an impudent swish of its tail. Another was tossing its head, displaying his coltish eagerness. The third was swivelling his ears, alert, aware of his surroundings and perhaps expectant of the demands about to be placed upon him. The trainer's gaze dwelled on this horse the longest.

This trio of youngsters were early sorts, precocious sprinters who, all being well, could be starting their racing careers in a matter of weeks. They were young, fit teenagers, full of the exuberance of youth, exactly as they should be ahead of their debut flat season.

Dennis pushed open the door of his Land Rover and grimaced as the cold spring air stung his warm cheeks. He rarely came out to watch his first, early morning lot these days, but a touch of frost and a cool breeze pinching his skin wasn't going to dissuade him from watching this workout in person.

These youngsters would be expecting to canter for the first furlong and a half around a curved chute, straighten up and then breeze at three-quarter pace up the hill for a further three furlongs. In fact, this workout would be different to anything these unraced colts had previously experienced. This was going to be more than a three-quarter pace breeze; this morning Dennis would discover what sort of raw talent they possessed.

He'd bought all three youngsters at various yearling sales over five months ago. Two of them were moderately expensive purchases, colts with very decent pedigrees that belonged to a good, long term owner. The other he'd bought relatively cheaply for nine thousand guineas at Doncaster's Silver Sale. He was meant to be a fun horse Dennis would syndicate, but within hours of the horse arriving in the yard there'd been something about the colt. That indefinable feeling in his stomach had told the trainer he might be more than just a fun horse. He'd moved well once broken and ridden away, so Dennis had decided to retain ownership of him and run the youngster under his own name, until he knew for certain what he'd got.

Dennis raised his binoculars once more and peered down the hill. Despite having seen all of this many times before, he smiled to himself upon feeling a familiar tingle of anticipation. At fifty-eight, he'd spent thirty-nine of those years in horse racing and over thirty training under his own name. At one stage in the nineties, he'd had over a hundred and fifty horses under his control. Those days of striving for a hundred winners and a few million in prize-money each season had come and gone. He was now quite content to train around thirty-five to forty quality horses each season and delegate the early morning gallops, physically demanding yard jobs, and most of the travelling up and down Britain's roads to his loyal staff.

Leaning against his battered old Land Rover, he watched as the two-year-olds were led by an older horse around the circular warm-up area at the foot of the turf gallop. Danny, his Assistant Trainer, was currently giving the work riders their instructions and wouldn't be leading them onto the gallop for at least another minute. Dennis allowed his binoculars to drop to his chest, dipped into his weathered wax jacket and shook a cigarette out of its paper packet in one well practiced motion.

The trio of two-year-olds were accompanied by Danny on a four-year-old. The older horse was a decent sprint handicapper whose task was to lead the youngsters up the gallop. If any of the two-year-olds could get to the experienced horse before the crest of the hill Dennis would know he had a *proper* racehorse on his hands.

Dennis sucked in his first, most satisfying lungful of smoke of the day and examined the view over the Wolds, his expelled breath being whisked away by the light breeze. A sheet of impenetrable cloud had produced an unimpressive start to the day, however, the sun had climbed well above the horizon and was beginning to send shafts of light through the rapidly thinning cloud cover. He watched with a hint of a smile on his face as the beams of light raced over the hills, a scene he'd witnessed thousands of times and of which he never tired.

Sensing an alteration in the movements at the bottom of the gallop, Dennis lifted his binoculars once more. Allowing his cigarette to droop from the corner of his mouth, he followed the four horses' progress onto the turf gallop and felt his heart beat harder as they cantered around the bottom loop and straightened up for the final few furlongs up the gradually rising ground. The binoculars were now dispensed with, and instead, he removed a silver stopwatch from his jacket pocket and reset it with a click. In less than a minute he'd discover whether his choices at the sales had been the right ones. They'd been bought to do the specific job: being early, precocious two-year-olds capable of taking their owners to quality racetracks and if they were good enough, a tilt at a Royal Ascot race in June.

The four-year-old sprinter was given a touch of his reins from Danny and the gelding moved forwards purposefully as they met the rising ground. Momentarily left behind, the three youngsters were asked to lengthen by their riders; Dennis had ensured he had three seasoned professional jockeys to test this bunch out.

Whilst two of them responded, the third looked unco-ordinated and worryingly one-paced for a few strides, but eventually he got the hang of things and clung onto the heels of the other two. As instructed, the riders spread out until they were galloping upsides as the ground settled into a steady rise up the hill.

Dennis tensed, stopwatch in hand. There was no furlong marker, no stick in the ground to indicate when they were three furlongs from the top of the hill. But Dennis knew. He knew when that critical point would be reached on the gallop. Using the tree line behind the gallop, the trainer waited for them to flash in front of an oak tree in the distance and his thumb clicked the stopwatch. He breathed again, heavily enough to send out a flurry of ash from his cigarette. He was unaware he'd been holding his breath, being consumed by the quartet now being energetically ridden.

On the older, race-hardened horse, Danny took a two length lead. Together in second, two of the youngsters went after him, leaving the remaining two-year-old a length down, apparently struggling to go the pace. Danny began to push his gelding, and took another half a length from his pursuers, who in turn were encouraged to close by their riders. Another youngster dropped off the pace by a length.

Entering the final two hundred yards of the workout Dennis felt a thump in his chest, and then another. The youngster in second had just breezed past Danny's four-year-old. No amount of pushing down the older horse's neck was going to see him reel the youngster back in. The precocious young colt powered up to the crest of the hill and tore past Dennis with his pilot swinging off him. He clicked the stop-watch again and gaped after the two-year-old that had taken three lengths out of an eighty-five rated older horse in pre-season. Squinting at the time on the watch, Dennis's mouth dropped open and his cigarette fell, sending orange sparks bouncing off his chest.

As the four horses made their way over to him, Dennis tried in vain to wipe the broad smile off his face. His stopwatch had registered a time of thirty-one seconds for the last three furlongs. Not only was the front two-year-old potentially top class, the remaining duo had also proved their worth. Even the fourth home had made some good ground up the hill and finished off respectively well.

Danny brought his mount to a halt in front of his governor and grinned.

'What you reckon, Guv?'

Dennis raised his chin and peered slit-eyed at his Assistant Trainer, 'I reckon Greg Armitage is going to get a season of racing beyond his wildest dreams.'

Two

March 15th 2016

When his call was answered with silence, Thomas Bone decided to grasp the nettle and instead of introducing himself, tried a different tack.

'Miss Falworth? I'm so pleased I've managed to catch you. You *are* Miss Sophie Falworth?'

There was more silence from the other end of the line. He could tell he was still connected and someone was there, close to the phone, as he could hear a television or radio in the background and muffled scratching he presumed was a hand covering the mouthpiece. Although Thomas was relatively new to the business of being a solicitor, he'd already learned from previous conversations today that he must wait patiently until an answer was forthcoming and not jump in with more pointless words.

Presently, a soft voice replied with a disgruntled, 'Yes?'

'Ah, good. You're a difficult woman to track down, Miss Falworth!' he breathed lightly, 'I'm from…'

'Really?' the woman cut in.

'Oh yes, I've had to speak with a number of people before I managed to find your number.'

'That's strange,' said the voice, heavy with sarcasm, 'I'm deluged with sales calls. It seems my mobile number has been sold to every telephone marketing company in Britain. So what are *you* selling?'

'Oh no, Miss Falworth. I'm not selling anything, I work for Sedgefield…'

'It's six-thirty on a Tuesday evening!' the woman said, talking over Thomas, 'If you're not selling something then I assume you're after my bank account details so you can commit fraud. Either way I'm not interested…'

Sensing the phone was about to be disconnected, Thomas blurted, 'Mr Gregory Armitage…. has died.'

The woman fell silent.

'I'm er… a solicitor. Mr Thomas Bone.'

'Greg is dead?'

'Yes, I'm sorry to bring you this news over the phone, Miss Falworth, however time is of the essence. Can I just confirm I'm speaking with Miss… '

'Yes, yes. I'm Sophie Falworth. When… how did Greg die?' Sophie asked, all her earlier sarcasm replaced with an earnest concern.

'I'm afraid Mr Armitage succumbed to a rapid form of cancer just over a week ago. I believe it came on suddenly and it took him within weeks of his diagnosis.'

'That's…' Sophie said, her voice trailing away. There was a scuffling sound and the television background noise abruptly ceased.

'Why are you contacting me, Mr….'

'Bone. Thomas Bone, I'm so sorry to be bringing you this bad news, Miss Falworth.'

'Don't be too sorry, Mr Bone,' replied Sophie with a sigh, 'I haven't seen or spoken with Greg for seventeen years, and we didn't exactly part on good terms.'

'Ah, well that may be the case, however, there is a reading of Mr Armitage's will in two days' time and I have been instructed to ask if you would be able to attend.'

'I've got a mention in his will?'

'Yes. Mr Armitage has made certain provisions which relate to you. I'm afraid I don't have the exact details. This is an unusual situation and I've been asked to call you as it would be advantageous for you to be present in Alnwick on Thursday for the reading.'

'Alnwick… in Northumberland?'

'Yes. We're based in Alnwick. I see you live in York. I have a note here that tells me your travelling costs will be covered in full by Mr Armitage's estate, should you decide to attend.'

Thomas heard a short breath being expelled into the phone's mouthpiece and imagined Sophie had just gasped.

'Will his wife be there?'

'Ummm… one second Miss…'

'Call me Sophie,' she cut in, 'And you can drop the solicitor speak, just talk normally. You sound like you've got a rod stuck up your back.'

'Of course, erm… Sophie,' Thomas replied stiffly.

Sophie heard the sound of rustling as the solicitor checked his paperwork.

'Er… yes. Mrs Armitage is on the list of attendees. Is that a problem?'

'Is he… I mean, *was* he, er…Greg, still married to Clara?'

Thomas flicked his eyes back to the client brief. He couldn't see the harm in confirming the name, especially as Sophie had already mentioned it.

'Yes, a Mrs Clarabel Charlotte Armitage is due to be at the reading,' he replied.

The line fell silent once more.

'Can I put you down as attending, Sophie?' Thomas queried, inserting an expectant high note at the end of his question.

'No,' Sophie said with venom, 'I won't go within ten miles of that hateful woman!'

Thomas blinked a few times and recoiled from his phone,

surprised by the sudden collapse of Sophie's goodwill. A further icy blast of pent-up rage howled down the phone line for another thirty seconds until Sophie's rant finally drew to a shuddering halt.

Once she'd barked out her final mouthful of vitriol, Thomas took a breath and swallowed. He was tempted to try and engage her again, but it was now six forty-five in the evening and getting dark outside. He was dog-tired. He'd not left his small, wobbly desk stuck in the corner of the secretary's office since arriving at eight o'clock that morning, apart from being handed this poisoned chalice of a brief earlier in the day by his boss.

As he'd done previously over the course of his day, Thomas reverted to route one tactics.

'Sophie, I'm advised it could be *financially* worth your while *to attend*,' he said, purposefully placing undue stress upon the most impactful words in his statement.

With no answer forthcoming he added, 'You may not be aware that Mr Gregory Armitage recently sold his entire interest in his technology business for a cash offer of several million pounds.'

He waited for a few seconds and celebrated internally when Sophie's voice, wavering slightly and significantly calmer, came back on the line. After a short, pointed discussion, he took Sophie's email address, reminded her that the reading of the will was at eleven-thirty on Thursday morning, and rang off after promising to send her directions to the premises of Sedgefield Solicitors, Alnwick.

Three

March 22nd 2016

Not for the first time today, Sophie asked herself why she had even bothered to make this trip. It wasn't as if she could afford the time off work, and Monty, her faithful twelve-year-old Nissan Micra, had clearly suffered from the experience.

Tootling around her home city of York and the local country roads for the last eight years hadn't prepared her aging little car for the sustained speed required on the drag up the A1(M) North. Sophie had spent the final dozen of the one-hundred-and-twenty miles up to Alnwick in Northumberland nursing Monty up every incline. Each time she'd pushed the accelerator down her faithful servant had sounded more and more like an elderly gentleman clearing his throat.

Sophie was no stranger to the ancient market town of Alnwick. Greg had brought her here on several occasions to introduce her to his friends and family. Touring around the centre in Monty, trying to locate the solicitor's offices, she was reminded of her first visit to the town, over nineteen years ago. In 1997 she'd enjoyed a joyous evening with Greg, spent in a restaurant and then a couple of the town centre pubs before they'd stumbled drunkenly to a taxi rank and, to the driver's dismay, sung all the way to his parent's house on the outskirts of the town. It was in the early hours of the morning that they announced they were getting married. This was achieved by running around the huge house in a jolly, inebriated state and shouting out the news at the tops of their voices.

The memory soon turned sour in Sophie's mind and she determined that today, of all days, she would leave no room for sentimentality. She was here for one reason. Money.

Guiding the now loudly rasping Monty into a parking space opposite the entrance to the solicitor's office, she carefully ignored the glares from passing shoppers. She was pretty sure the car's exhaust had blown, but was in no position to fix it. She'd have to find a garage after the reading of the will.

The entrance to Sedgefield Solicitors was a grand affair, boasting a huge oak front door framed by ornate stonework within which the name 'Bradford & Bingley' was still chiselled. Sophie supposed they were the sort of premises that gave clients of Sedgefield's the same sense of solidity and trust the bank had once tried to convey with its grand facade. She grimaced inwardly at the irony; the bank had gone bust.

With growing nervousness Sophie frittered away a few more minutes watching the arched door across the road rhythmically open and close as a trickle of people she assumed were either clients, or Sedgefield staff, went about their business. She didn't recognise anyone. This pleased her, as she was secretly hoping that Clara might not attend.

Trying to kill time, she noticed her rear-view mirror was smeared with something and fumbling with a tissue, she gave it a wipe. The mirror suddenly dropped from the top of the windscreen, bounced off the gear stick and clattered into the passenger seat foot-well. Sophie spent the next ten minutes cursing as she tried to make the mirror adhere to the windscreen, without any success. At four minutes past eleven she locked Monty up and crossed the road, leaving the mirror on the passenger seat and wondering whether the solicitor's promise to pay her expenses would cover a new exhaust and super glue for her rear view mirror.

As expected, the inside of the building retained the hallmarks of its original purpose, with an abundance of oak panelling and a high ceiling propped up with stone columns. After giving her name to the receptionist, she was directed to a small carpeted waiting area further inside the building. A disgruntled teenage girl in school uniform slouched in one of the seats, arms crossed, glowering at a closed door across the corridor adorned with the name Edward B. Sedgefield. She treated Sophie to a wary glance as she passed. Presently, the door the girl had been watching opened with a jolt and a tall, elegantly dressed woman with a hard face and sharp features burst out in mid-rant.

'…and that's right, you *never* have time do you? Is it any wonder Alexandria has been excluded from school again! I really don't know why I put up with your pathetic excuses, but, of *course,* I do…'

The woman's diatribe came to an abrupt halt when her gaze fell upon Sophie and subsequently switched to her daughter. She sniffed and called over her shoulder, 'I'll see you tonight, Edward… and *don't* be late home, I have my Conservative Ladies arriving for a meeting at eight o'clock sharp!'

In the same breath she ordered the girl to stand properly, hitch her skirt up, and straighten her tie. She stalked off down the corridor dragging a protesting Alexandria with her, maintaining a firm grip on the girl's shoulder.

A podgy, doughy faced man that Sophie guessed was in his sixties, based on the silver hair combed slick to his head, appeared at the office door. Taking a handkerchief from his trouser pocket, he dabbed at his sweaty brow and glanced down the corridor to check the lady had departed before noticing Sophie and giving her an embarrassed half-smile. Disappearing back inside his office the solicitor soon emerged carrying a bundle of paperwork under his arm. He shambled off down the corridor and out of sight.

A couple of minutes later, a slightly overweight, dour faced young man in a dark lounge suit and black tie appeared. He initially looked relieved upon spying Sophie, although this seemed to wear off a shade when he took in her attire.

'Miss Falworth, I'm Thomas. We spoke on the phone. I'm so glad you could make it. I'm sorry you've had to wait. I wasn't informed you'd arrived through the town door – we have two entrances, you see. Please follow me, we're about to begin.'

He led Sophie down the poorly lit corridor and up a staircase and into a modern atrium with floor to ceiling windows facing out the back of the building. She noticed a car park below and a wide door with automatic sliding glass panels. There were three black cars parked close to what Sophie now realised was most probably the main entrance to the building. It appeared she'd entered through the back door to the solicitor's offices, despite it being on the high street.

Thomas stopped outside one of the meetings room and gave Sophie a watery smile, 'Erm… I should perhaps warn you that Mrs Armitage and the other interested parties have come straight from the funeral.'

'What?' hissed Sophie.

She looked down at herself. As if a thick, rainbow striped jumper wasn't enough, she was wearing light brown corduroy trousers that finished at her calves, and a pair of scuffed brown riders. To top this off, she had a bright yellow cloth bum bag tied loosely around her waist. Sophie had assumed it would only be herself and Clara Armitage in attendance, and she'd purposefully worn these specific clothes to telegraph her complete disregard for the woman.

With an apologetic smile, Thomas opened the door and gestured for her to enter. The meeting room was cosier than Sophie had expected, comprising three rows of five chairs facing a desk and a large flat television on the wall. It was windowless and she imagined it could be soundproof too. The moment she stepped inside, a dozen faces turned in their seats to examine the reason the reading of the will had been delayed. The Armitage family gave a collective sigh of frustration.

'You've got the wrong room, my little rainbow warrior,' a middle aged man told her with a snigger. The woman beside him inclined her head and whispered something to him. They smirked at each other before returning their disapproving gaze to the front of the room. Several of the immaculately dressed mourners seemed to agree with the man's assertion and lost interest, turning back to face the front.

The focus of the room was the rotund older man with a silver comb-over and sweat glistening on his forehead, seated behind a desk loaded with paperwork. Sophie immediately recognised him as Edward B. Sedgefield, the father of Alexandria and the husband of the forceful woman. He struggled to his feet and peered at her over a pair of small round spectacles. An expression of embarrassed recognition flitted momentarily across his face before he inquired, 'Miss Falworth?'

Sophie nodded and he smiled and gestured towards a vacant seat on the front row. Before she could take a step, a mourner on the front row jumped to her feet and spun round, glaring with disbelieving eyes at her. Sophie's stomach did a back flip as she was examined by the most treacherous person she'd ever had the misfortune to meet.

'What the merry hell are *you* doing here?' screamed Clara Armitage, her eyes bulging.

'I was invited... *by Greggie,*' Sophie retorted in a slow, defiant tone. She'd planned this moment for days and was delighted with Clara's response. She'd known using her own pet name for Greg was sure to infuriate her ex-best friend. Sophie was surprised Clara hadn't known she would be attending, but the shock had made her entrance and retort even sweeter.

As she locked eyes with Clara, Sophie noticed with a hint of envy that her one-time best friend had managed to retain her hourglass figure. That said, the Chanel dress Clara was wearing had clearly been tailored to her rather specific Rubenesque dimensions. Her voluptuous, blonde, five foot five inch nemesis was dripping in jewellery and had obviously made the most of her husband's success. However, if she wasn't mistaken, Clara's face was a shade taut for her age and her nose too straight; she'd definitely had work done. The thought made her lip curl.

'Don't you *dare* call my husband that horrible name you scheming little shyster!' Clara fired back.

'Oh, shut up you slovenly tramp...'

'Ladies. Please!' Mr Sedgefield called loudly across the two bickering thirty-eight year olds.

Sophie took a breath and scanned the room. Greg's brother, Simon, and his wife, Marion, were grinning at her, apparently enjoying the show. Greg's sister, Ruth, was staring at her wide-eyed and displaying the beginnings of a smirk. Sophie resisted the urge to reach out and flip the sour-faced little minx's mouth shut for her. An eight-year-old boy was staring up at Clara whilst idly fiddling with one of the brass buttons on the jacket of his suit. Sophie was betting the child had been bought the outfit specifically for the funeral. This had to be Jeremy, Greg's only child.

Greg's younger brother, Timothy, gave her a disinterested shrug when their eyes met. Sitting beside him was a woman Sophie didn't recognise. She surprised Sophie by offering a supportive smile. Beside her was Paul, Greg's best friend since University. He was craning his neck to see her, and nodded a smile her way.

The worst was saved for last. Greg's hard-faced mother, Gertrude, got to her feet. She looked her ex-daughter-in-law up and down with hard blue eyes, one of them unnervingly hooded, and began to shake her head, finally delivering her a look of pure disgust. Sophie returned her ex-mother-in-law as black a look as she could muster. Flicking her gaze back to Clara, Sophie looked down at the smaller women in amusement; she'd balled her hands into fists.

As if they'd anticipated this standoff, Mr Sedgefield and Thomas each took a lady in hand. Mr Sedgefield touched Clara's arm and quietly suggested, 'Perhaps Mrs Armitage could retake her seat?'

Thomas pulled one of the red moulded plastic chairs from the front row to the wall at the back of the room and raising both eyebrows, indicating to Sophie the seat was hers. Sophie eyed the chair and then glanced over at Clara and was relieved their seats were now out of each other's fist-swinging range.

With a final glare over at the now seated Sophie, Clara sat herself down, contenting herself with the knowledge that even at the age of thirty-eight the most hateful woman she knew still possessed no dress sense. Her clothes gave the impression she would be more at home in a hippy commune. Clara tried to concentrate on this thought in order to rid herself of the disturbing realisation that Sophie's complexion and long curly black hair looked as fresh and luxuriant as it had been when she last saw her in 1997.

As Mr Sedgefield started to speak, Clara was sure she could feel her heart pumping adrenaline around her, making her brain fizz with thoughts of what she'd like to do to Sophie. She began to bounce off the back of her plastic chair, staring ahead. Her young son reached over and gently placed a small hand on her knee. It was only then that she became aware her leg was jiggling involuntary. She took his hand in hers and smiled warmly at her son.

Sophie's attendance wasn't a complete shock to Clara, but nonetheless, annoying. It was something Greg had said on his last day alive. He'd insisted he would die at home and not in hospital. So, against his doctors' advice, they'd brought him back to the house by private ambulance for the last few hours of his life.

He'd been drugged up to the eyeballs and incredibly weak; a shell of the man he'd been only a month before. Greg had tried hard to tell her something, but he hadn't been able to maintain enough focus to be completely understandable. However, she had been sure Sophie's name had fallen from his lips before he'd drifted off into oblivion.

'I will make this as brief as possible, however, Mr Armitage insisted his will was to be read word for word,' Mr Sedgefield told the room authoritatively, dragging Clara's attention back to him.

Sedgefield continued, 'Mr Armitage created a wholly new will as soon as he discovered his condition was terminal and I can confirm that he was evaluated to ensure he was of sound mind by an eminent psychologist. I personally oversaw the creation of Mr Armitage's will and as the duly appointed executor, Sedgefield Solicitors are committed to carrying out Mr Armitage's instructions.'

Clara stared glumly at the carpet tiles on the meeting room floor as Mr Sedgefield continued his preamble. Greg had been excited about his will and told her so. She'd tried to discuss it with him in an attempt to ensure he didn't make any ill-advised grand gestures, but hadn't had the heart to insist; not this time. Greg had always been a dreamer. For sure he was creative, clever, and a step ahead of the game when he needed to be, especially when it came to running his software company. But in truth, Clara had always viewed her husband as a little boy, dreaming of wonderful things and retaining that childlike zeal that told him that whatever the odds, anything was possible.

Clara frowned. It was also why he'd previously spent time racing old minis, going fly fishing all over the world, and more recently, spent huge amounts of money owning those awful racehorses. Greg had recently become obsessed with the big, flighty, unpredictable animals, and she'd left him to it; just the thought of them turned her blood cold. He'd banged on about owning a racehorse good enough to become a sire. What that actually meant, and why being *a sire* was so important, she wasn't sure. However, horseracing had amused him each summer for the last few years and allowed him to dream his dreams, leaving her to pursue her own interests, which amounted to spending time with her son, clothes, and taking holidays.

Yes, grand gestures and dreaming had gone hand in hand where Greg was concerned. Her frown flattened into a sad smile as her mind was flooded with memories of past surprises. Greg had loved to spring a surprise and it hadn't seemed fair to rob him of his final chance to raise everyone's eyebrows. So when he became ill, she'd not protested when he altered his will, and didn't complain when he refused to share his plans with her. That was now looking like a bad decision.

Mr Sedgefield finished reading the heavy legal paragraphs of Greg Armitage's will and looked up at his audience. The solicitor noted with some satisfaction that his new recruit, Thomas Bone, hadn't taken a seat. Instead, he was standing at the back of the room, eyeing Mrs Armitage and Miss Falworth pensively. He was impressed. The lad must have taken the time to read the will in full and had the sense to predict there was more trouble on the way. With what he was about to be announce in the next few minutes, there was a good chance of fisticuffs before this eclectic bunch of firebrands were done.

Four

Mr Sedgefield cleared his throat once more and shuffled his paperwork, 'Ladies and gentlemen, this brings us to the most important section of today's reading. The following are the words of Mr Gregory Peter Armitage.'

Sophie noticed Mr Sedgefield glance up at Thomas, who was standing close by her chair. She couldn't be sure, but it appeared the solicitor had flashed the young man a warning. Young Thomas seemed to tense upon receiving the signal.

'My dear friends and family,' Sedgefield started, 'If I'm imagining this right, you'll be sitting on Mr Sedgefield's cheap plastic chairs in a small room without windows and dressed in clothes you hope you'll not have to wear again for many years!'

Well, they're definitely Greg's words, thought Clara. That said, they sounded strange coming from a balding sixty-five year-old with a strong Northumberland accent, rather than Greg's light Geordie.

'If you're all here, there should be eleven of you, if you include my son, Mr Sedgefield, and Mr Bone. I'll not keep you in suspense for too long; I'm going to run through you all, one by one.'

Mr Sedgefield paused for a few seconds and pushed his circular spectacles up his nose before continuing.

'As you all know, I sold my company as soon as I learned I only had a short spell to live. After death duties, and despite my life being cut short, I have managed to amass a little over eight million pounds. Quite a tidy sum, I think you'll agree.'

There was a hum of appreciation that circled the room.

'So, let's get to it. First of all, my wife and son will keep the family house, cars, and my possessions, and will receive fifty thousand pounds per annum from a trust fund which...'

'Whoah, whoah... just stop there,' Clara interrupted, holding up two flat palms, 'Say that again?'

Mr Sedgefield swallowed, pursed his lips and repeated '...will receive fifty thousand pounds per annum.'

Clara rocked back in the chair, stunned. Fifty thousand pounds wasn't enough. It simply wasn't enough! What was Greg thinking?

Making the most of Clara's silence Mr Sedgefield seized the opportunity to return to his script, 'A small trust fund of ten percent of my estate will be created by my executor for my wife and son. If managed correctly this annual income should be guaranteed for the rest of my wife's and my son's lives. A similar trust fund will benefit a variety of charitable causes.'

Mr Sedgefield kept his head down and ploughed on.

'The following sums should be paid immediately:
To my mother, Gertrude Armitage, £10,000;
To my brother and his wife, Simon and Marion, £10,000;
To my sister, Ruth Armitage, £10,000;
To my brother, Timothy Armitage, £10,000;
To my ex-wife, Sophie Falworth, £50,000.'

As Mr Sedgefield read the names and numbers the volume of his delivery gradually increased in order for his words to be heard above the mixture of exclamations, groans, complaints, and in one case, a squeal of derision from Ruth Armitage.

Sophie was jolted in her seat when her name was called. She hadn't known what to expect, and after the icy greeting from Clara had half wondered whether Greg was playing a seventeen-year-old joke on her. A disbelieving grin spread across her face. Fifty thousand pounds would wipe out her mountain of credit card and other outstanding debts, and might even allow her to finally retire Monty, or at least get him fixed. She might even be able to afford a deposit on a small house, rather than having to rent.

Clara spun around and glared at Sophie. Once they'd locked eyes Sophie realised she was still grinning, and felt no guilt in broadening it even further. Clara's face hardened into an expression of pure loathing. They remained like that for a few seconds until Jeremy began tugging on his mother's hand.

'The man says there's a video of Dad!'

Clara tore her attention from Sophie, her mind full of tawdry reasons why her husband should decide to reward a woman who had devastated their lives. Was Sophie behind his decision to leave her practically destitute? She wouldn't put anything past that woman. Sophie had already proved she was capable of *anything*.

'A... video,' Clara stammered.

'Look, on the wall, Mum,' the boy said, pointing a finger and ignoring the disgruntled comments his mother was receiving from his grandmother, friends, and extended family.

'I know he promised you more money!' Clara shouted above the clatter of complaints and recriminations, 'He did the same to me. It's not my fault!'

On the deep purple painted wall behind Mr Sedgefield the television screen, hitherto an inert black oblong, leapt into life and displayed a freeze frame of Greg sitting at a desk. Trying to ignore Greg's mother's grating voice and half-closed right eye, Clara peered at the television screen and immediately recognised their study at home.

The solicitor and his young sidekick were soon on their feet, trying to quell the outburst of dissatisfaction from the small group.

'Ladies and gentlemen!' called Thomas in a surprisingly deep and authoritative voice after several breathy requests by Mr Sedgefield had gone unheeded, 'The will reading is not complete! Mr Armitage recorded an addendum. He created a living will.'

This managed to bring the noise level down a few notches. However Ruth Armitage continued to harangue Clara and her sharp, insistent voice was still ringing out when silence descended, '... and it just shows what my brother really thought of you! You're not a *real* Armitage and Greg more than had the measure of you, you cheap nobody! He promised me a mill...'

Ruth's protest trailed off once she realised her shrill words were the only sound cutting through the stagnant air in the room.

Simon placed a hand on Clara's arm, 'Please, there's no need to react this way...'

Clara gritted her teeth. Simon was always the first to get involved in this sort of argument, falsely believing he was some amazing calming influence, when actually all he did was get on people's nerves. Clara flicked Simon's cold thin fingers away from her and cut him short.

'Get off me. And you can wind your neck in too, Ruth,' Clara spat back at her sister-in-law.

'Please, Miss Armitage?' requested Mr Sedgefield, indicating Ruth's vacant chair with his eyes.

The younger woman sighed loudly and angrily plonked herself down on her chair, making the backrest squeak in protest. Ruth's eyes had become slits. She crossed her arms into a tight, tense shelf under her bosom and glared at Mr Sedgefield.

Sophie hadn't moved in her seat. She was a little away from the others and had watched with growing amusement as the family turned on Clara. She'd particularly enjoyed Ruth's comment regarding Clara's relationship with Greg. Ruth had been a bad-tempered thirteen-year-old when Sophie had met her prior to her doomed wedding day. Apparently the intervening years had done nothing to temper Ruth's fondness for speaking her mind. And her mind tended to be in a state of constant disappointment with the world.

Greg's brother, Simon, was the last to retake his seat, after which Mr Sedgefield moved to the corner of the room and the video began playing with Greg smiling into the camera in his usual, easy-going, laid-back style. Sophie thought he'd put on a few pounds, but nothing too drastic. His brown hair was short, or at least shorter than he'd worn it at university, but he wasn't receding, and the few extra lines around his face only seemed to accentuate his smile. She glanced away from the screen for a moment, disgusted at herself; even after seventeen years his boyish good looks were enough to draw her to him.

'Good morning, everyone!' Greg announced with a gleeful pop of his eyebrows.

In the front row Clara shuddered, suddenly torn between sadness and disgust for her dead husband.

'I guess you're all suitably hacked off with me at the moment?' Greg ventured from the flat screen television, 'I imagine Clara is seething and my Mother's right eye is twitching?'

Greg waited, displaying a smug grin. His pause was well judged, as this comment set his family off into a round of grumbling and, in Gertrude's case, barbed comments aimed at Clara.

Greg continued, 'Sophie is probably gloating, Simon will be telling everyone to calm down, Timothy will be nonplussed, and is Ruth saying something spiteful?'

Sophie almost laughed out loud. Greg was correct on all counts, and she *had* been gloating – at least a little bit.

Greg's image on the wall paused again and he shook his head slowly, 'I get that most of you are disappointed, but if you give me a couple of minutes, I think you'll understand why the promises I made to each of you before I died, still have *every chance* of being fulfilled.'

Sophie noticed a couple of the friends and family lean forward in their seats once this statement had sunk in. She relaxed back into her seat and crossed her legs, waggling her ankle playfully over her knee, enjoying the spectacle once again. She was sure she was just a spectator now. Perhaps Greg had realised how much he'd hurt her back in 1997 and wanted to put things straight between them. Whatever his reason for giving her the money, she was glad of it. It was something of a bonus to subsequently watch the rest of the Armitage family self-combust as Greg's final surprise was revealed. There was bound to be a surprise; Greg did love delivering a big surprise.

'I've had a great life, and although I'm toddling off into what lies beyond a little earlier than I'd have liked, there are a couple of things I would have loved to have had a second chance at getting right.'

Greg had been smiling up to this point, but he now folded his lips together into a grimace, 'To be honest… there have been one or two hiccups along the way. Being informed you're about to die tends to focus the mind, and I've found myself focusing on my… regrets.'

He rubbed the back of his neck thoughtfully for a few seconds, got up from his desk and the camera panned out so that it could follow him. Greg walked to a huge floor to ceiling window that looked onto a three tiered lawn surrounded by mature trees, immaculate flowerbeds and below the last lawn the glint of sun on a slowly moving river.

'And the first is a big regret,' Greg said, a hint of sadness in his voice for the first time. He took in the view for a few seconds, then turned and approached the camera so that only his head and chest filled the screen.

'It's something that no matter how hard I tried, I could never work out a way to put it right. And foolishly, I gave up. The trouble is, it now haunts me more than ever. So, desperate times call for desperate measures. I'm going to create a second chance for myself. I'm going to have a go at putting it right.'

The camera began to slowly zoom in.

'Clara and Sophie. You were friends. The very *best* of friends. You spent seventeen happy years together before I met you both and largely because of me, you've now spent seventeen years apart.'

Greg paused, and with a small sigh told his audience, 'I'm going to try to ensure you enjoy at least another *seventeen years of friendship.*'

Five

Clara was feeling distinctly queasy and could sense a headache coming on. Greg was grinning maniacally at her from the television screen and try as she might, she couldn't make sense of what he'd just said. His dying wish was for her to suddenly be pals with a childhood friend who turned into a monster? It was ridiculous! She had a powerful urge to race from the building and be outside in the open air, to be able to breathe. But at the moment she wasn't sure her legs would cope with running. From the television, Greg began speaking again.

'My other regret is just as important, and concerns you, Ruth.'

Greg's younger sister bristled in her seat as everyone's attention switched to her. She didn't look around, choosing to stare fixedly at the television screen in stony silence.

'Ruth..., Ruth... *Ruth!*' Greg exclaimed despondently, closing his eyes and slowly shaking his head, 'When Father died, Simon was already married with children, Mother was as good as useless, and as it turned out, so was I. While you dealt with the mess our Father left behind, managing my Mother and a young Timothy, you were forced to place your life on hold. I ran off to university leaving you to cope with everything. It was incredibly selfish... in fact, we all were. You were only seventeen and had the world at your feet, and yet you never really got any credit for your sacrifice. And once you were ensconced at Armitage Hall, you not only missed the most important years of your life, you were then unable to break free of the role you took on. I'm ashamed I did nothing to stop this happening.'

To this point in the video Greg had appeared to be picking his words out of the air, but he now looked directly into the camera and wagged his index finger at Ruth, 'What's worse, I allowed you to become poisoned. I guess it was self-pity or resentment at the way things turned out – I don't know – either way, you got bitter and twisted... and became just like our Mother.'

'How *dare* you!' Gertrude protested shrilly.

She continued to squawk, addressing some of her anger to the television and the rest, inexplicably, at Ruth. Sophie had to smile, on the video Greg had stopped speaking and was waiting, drumming his fingers on the top of the table he was once again seated behind. He certainly knew his audience, thought Sophie, and his mother in particular.

Gertrude was shushed as Greg began speaking again.

'Please be quiet, Mother. This is about Ruth,' pleaded Simon.

Gertrude was silenced, although she studiously maintained a grumpy expression.

Greg leaned both elbows on his desk and clasped his hands together, 'So Ruth, I toyed with many ideas, projects... a way in which to make your next dozen years make up for the last dozen. In the end, I decided to team you up with Clara and Sophie!' he told his confused audience, 'I've told you time and time again that you should leave Armitage Hall and get out into the world. I don't know if its fear, laziness, or some insane sense of duty, but the way you're going, you will continue to lead a boring life of servitude under our Mother's toxic regime until one of you dies – and that's not good enough.'

He folded his arms flat to the desk, 'If you want the money I promised you, then you too will have to earn it.'

The camera panned out again and Greg stood and took a few steps around his leather-topped desk, picking up two sheets of printer paper from its surface in the process. He showed them to the camera.

'Ruth, Sophie, and Clara. Here's your task!' Greg announced, his eyes coming alive and a genuine smile gracing his face.

'These beautiful specimens are two yearlings I bought at the Tattersalls Yearling Sales last October,' he said proudly, 'That was back when I believed my disease ridden body might be able to last for another year. I've owned a number of racehorses over the last few years and to Clara's disgust, I've fallen totally in love with the sport. My trainer has sought out sharp, precocious horses this year in the hope that I could enjoy success in my last season alive. Now that delight will fall to... well, let's not get ahead of ourselves!'

Clara groaned and leaned forward in her chair so she could rest her throbbing forehead in her perfectly manicured hand. Greg's obsession with horseracing had annoyed and frustrated her in equal measure and she was becoming nervous about the direction in which his speech was heading. Her husband had that childlike excitement about him that usually meant a grand gesture was about to be unveiled. Greg's grand gestures usually came with a large dollop of embarrassment for her.

At the back of the room, Sophie was no longer relaxed. Greg's little video was beginning to suck all the fun from the situation and she was now nervously fingering the zip on her bum bag, unable to rip her attention from the screen.

'Here's the deal,' said Greg, his eyes sparkling with anticipation, 'After sorting out Clara and my charitable fund, there is just over seven million pounds of my money left up for grabs. I have instructed Mr Sedgewick to divide it equally among you... as I promised each of you… as long as Ruth, Sophie, and Clara can complete my task.'

Greg's smile broadened, 'Girls! The three of you have to do something very simple, *together*... I'm giving you my two colts and you shall be racehorse owners for the 2016 summer season.'

Clara gaped at her dead husband, completely unaware that her mouth was lolling open. On screen, he paused and shrugged theatrically, holding his hands up in a way that suggested he believed his task to be the easiest thing in the world.

'The three of you must visit your racehorses at the trainers' yard in Malton on a set day each month, and go racing together once a month. That's from the start of the flat season in April, until the end of August – just five months of the summer season. That means meeting up only twice a month for the next five months, once at the stables and once to go racing. What could be easier? If you fulfil my simple task, each of you will receive a share of the big money. I've already created a three-way syndicate in your names, and I've called it the 'No Regrets' syndicate.'

Greg smiled once more and the camera followed him back to his desk, where he shuffled ungainly into his seat. It was the first time his manner suggested he might be ill.

'Mr Sedgefield has all the details of this fun little jaunt for the three of you, and I wish you the very best of luck.'

He held this final grin for several seconds and as his gaze fell to his desk, the camera slowly began to back away. As it did, Greg again cast a critical eye over the two photos of the racehorses. His outline became a silhouette and the screen started to fade to black. At the moment he was about to pop out of existence, he suddenly called out.

'Oh! I forgot to mention!'

The greyness vanished and the camera zoomed back in on him at his desk, going right to close-up. There was a strange glint in his eyes that as one, Ruth, Sophie, and Clara recognised - and it made them go hollow inside.

'If *any* of you can't provide photographic evidence for all your visits to the stables, or the races, *all three of you* will forfeit your inheritance.'

Greg mouthed a mock, 'Oh no!' to the camera and placed his hand on his cheeks while rolling his eyes comically. Beside Clara, his eight-year-old son, Jeremy, laughed out loud.

'I'm going to be firm about this. If any of you miss one visit or one race then that's it. Finito!' he added with a half laugh, 'You see what I've done? It's one out, and you're all out. That's the *real surprise*! You'll either spend a little time together as a threesome, doing something I loved, or you'll all lose the jackpot!'

Greg fell silent and looked away from the camera, suddenly adopting a faintly melancholic expression, 'I think you know... I love all three of you. Clara and Sophie: I often wonder where you'd both be now if I hadn't... and Ruth, you had such a bright future... but there's no use reflecting on what might have been.'

He crossed his arms, the creases of a grin starting around his mouth, 'Now then, Timothy, Simon, and of course, my Mother! I bet you're wondering why I've still got you in the room!'

'Well now, Ruth, Clara, and Sophie, how can I make your task even more interesting?'

Greg rolled his eyes theatrically and then thoughtfully tapped his lips with his index finger. It was a gesture the whole family had witnessed before and it filled each one of them with further dread. Greg was more than capable of adding an outlandish, and on occasions, embarrassing twist to his surprises.

He smiled, his decision apparently made, 'If the three ladies manage to complete this little task of mine, every member of my family will *also* share in my money. I make that around a million pounds each... but only if the task of five stable visits and five race-day attendances are successfully completed. If Clara, Ruth, and Sophie fail, all the money will go into a trust fund and benefit a number of charities.'

It was like an electric current had just been run through the three people this statement affected. Gasps, groans, cries of delight, followed by a barrage of questions that ensured Greg's video ended in acrimony.

Sophie remained rooted to her seat. Numbness had crept over her, yet she watched the video to the bitter end. Only she and Greg's son, Jeremy, heard Greg utter his final words to camera. The jokey, over-acting Greg was gone. A stillness, heavy with disappointment, and possibly a touch of fear, descended upon the man who now stared out at his family for a few seconds.

'Ruth, Clara, and Sophie. I'm sorry it took the inevitability of death for me to try and put things right. All three of you, think hard and please, be tolerant and kind to each other,' he said quietly. Sounding sad, but not unhopeful, he added, 'Be assured that despite what you may be thinking now, I loved you all.'

Six

Sophie cast a final appraising eye over her living room and decided she'd done enough tidying. After all, it was only that young solicitor, Thomas, visiting her flat. There was no need to make too much of a fuss, even though what he had to say might help make her become a millionaire.

Two failed marriages had not only sapped her enthusiasm for men, it had also plunged her into debt, so the fifty thousand pounds that had hit her current account the day after her trip up to Alnwick had already evaporated; gone to pay off debts that had become even larger than she had imagined. It had been a liberating feeling, signing the last cheque, although being in debt had never worried her particularly. Conversely, the possibility of a further million pounds had given her a series of sleepless nights.

With both her parents dead, and a lack of close friends, Sophie didn't have many house callers. Belinda, her elder sister tended to call in once a week to moan about her husband and two grown-up boys. During her second marriage, Sophie had lost contact with many of her friends, being consumed by trying to keep her crumbling relationship with a controlling partner alive.

She didn't mind living alone. By the time she got home after a day of visiting her clients, all she wanted to do was walk along the River Ouse or across the Knavesmire with her rescue greyhound, Bella. She valued that time alone with her dog, it helped her unwind.

Her second floor flat on a Victorian terrace in Fulford, York, had no garden. Holidays and weekends spent inside could drag a little; however, the internet helped fill the void left by her lack of family and friends. Sophie was partial to a game of backgammon or bridge and thanks to her iPad she had an inexhaustible supply of virtual people to play against. Add a touch of Radio Four or Radio Four Extra in the background and she found an afternoon could fly by in a haze of dice throws, Just A Minute repeats, trick bids, and The Archers. However, this Sunday, only three days after her trip up to Alnwick, she was looking forward to a gentleman caller.

Thomas Bone entered Sophie's flat apologising for being a shade late due to a lack of parking spaces. He'd been touring the backstreets of Fulford and not found one free space within half a mile of her flat. Ignoring the doggy smell that wafted up toward him as he entered, he kept a straight face when confronted by the messy state of Sophie's lounge.

Stepping over dog toys and small towers of crime and romantic paperbacks, Sophie directed the twenty-four-year-old into her armchair. He noticed a stack of unopened cardboard removal boxes against one wall.

Various room names were scrawled on them in permanent marker. An open fire with an ornate floral tile pattern was the main focal point of the room as the large bay window had its curtains half drawn. Sophie herself was dressed in a mohair jumper, a busy ankle-length skirt and had her long hair pinned up. Thomas marvelled at how different this house was compared to Clara Armitage's.

Once he'd lifted about a dozen well-thumbed novels from the seat of his armchair and deposited them onto the floor he sat down and a cup of tea was immediately thrust into his hand. Sophie disappeared, presently returning with a tray containing, among other things, a plate of chocolate hobnobs.

'Sorry about the mess. I live alone,' Sophie announced abruptly as she settled onto the sofa. Thomas realised with a soft gulp that the other three-quarters of the sofa was taken up by a languid greyhound. The dog lifted its head and gave Thomas an appraising stare. Satisfied Thomas was low risk, Bella settled back, rested her head on her mistress's thigh and slowly closed her eyes.

'That's okay, it's fine. I er... guess it's tough living alone,' Thomas said awkwardly, before adding, 'There's never enough time to unpack when you first move in is there?'

'Actually, I've been here two and a half years,' Sophie muttered, 'I guess the boxes have become part of the room.'

Thomas immediately regretted his words and as an awkward silence descended he desperately scanned the room, searching for another topic. He eventually settled on, 'I see you read thrillers... er... crime thrillers?'

'Yes, I'm a regular customer at the charity shops around here,' replied Sophie over the rim of her teacup, 'I like a story with plenty of twists.'

'A bit like Mr Armitage's will?'

Sophie eyed Thomas steadily, 'You tell me, Mr Bone. Isn't that why you're here – to go through everything again because all hell broke loose after Greg's video finished?'

'Yes, and once again, we're deeply sorry for the abuse you had to endure from erm...'

Sophie waved his apology away, 'The Armitage family. Yes, they didn't take it too well, did they?'

'Mr Sedgefield did the right thing in allowing me to escort you out of the room...'

'And back to my car... and to the garage,' Sophie added with a smile.'

She studied the young man once more. When Clara and the Armitages had first turned on themselves, she'd sat back and enjoyed the show. However, they'd swiftly altered tack and launched a scathing attack on her, pressing towards her at the back of the room and making it quite clear what might happen if they didn't get their wedge of Greg's money. Thomas had acted with alacrity and an authority that belied his age. Once the Armitages, and especially Ruth Armitage, had become threatening - standing over her shouting all sorts of abuse and accusations - Thomas had stepped between her and the unruly mob and escorted her out of the building. He'd even stuck around to ensure Monty was roadworthy before waving her off to York. He had been the perfect, professional gentleman.

And yet there was something just a little... forced about him. She couldn't quite put her finger on the reason for feeling this way, perhaps it was the fact he rarely smiled, but she got the distinct impression the lad was trying far too hard. It was as if he were playing a role, or perhaps portraying a version of himself that didn't come naturally. Oddly, it was a quality Sophie actually found strangely endearing; a young man in a new job, perhaps his first ever job, trying to fit in and desperate to make his mark. She knew how that felt.

'I assume your car got you home okay?'

Sophie nodded, 'I still need to get Monty's exhaust fixed, but the patch-up the garage did worked fine. Oh, and the rear mirror hasn't fallen off again yet.'

'Good, good,' he replied, opening up his briefcase, 'And you received the fifty thousand pounds?'

Once he'd received another confirming nod from Sophie, he continued, 'Can I ask, Miss Falworth, whether you intend to follow Mr Armitage's instructions?'

'Please, call me Sophie will you? Miss Falworth makes me sound like an old maid.'

She watched him click his pen and write a note on the inside of a card folder now resting on his knees.

'Certainly, Sophie,' he said without a hint of humour, 'And returning to the requirements in the will – can I assume you'll be fulfilling Mr Armitage's request?'

Slightly irked by his chilly reply and the fact the solicitor's eyes hadn't risen from his folder, Sophie fired a question straight back.

'Has Clara agreed? And what about Ruth? I mean, it's all a bit academic if they haven't.'

Thomas clipped his pen to the folder and looked up, 'I met with Ruth and Clara Armitage yesterday. I can confirm both ladies have committed to being present at the training yard visits each month and attending one racecourse run per month from either horse within the No Regrets Syndicate... that's if you also agree.'

Sophie wasn't surprised. Quite apart from the fact that Clara had always been drawn to money, the Armitage's had been pressuring her to agree to Greg's demands in the solicitor's room, even before his video finished. If Greg's plan had been to expose his nearest and dearest as money-grubbing zealots, he had certainly succeeded. The Armitage family seemed determined to exact its full pound of flesh and didn't care who knew it. And Ruth, one of the worst of them based on her performance at the solicitors, would be the Armitages' woman in the thick of it, ensuring in her catty and disdainful way that Greg's money found its way into the family bank account.

Little else had occupied Sophie's mind since arriving back home on Thursday. Denying Clara her million pounds by refusing to participate in Greg's little task was enticing, and would more than satisfy her thirst for revenge. Even so, a million pounds would change her own life – and for what? – spending a few hours each month with someone she loathed and another woman who could sour milk with one glance. Greg was wrong to believe that a friendship so cruelly ripped apart could be rekindled, but the money... the money would allow her to stop working and perhaps help her sister out financially too. She could buy a place of her own, travel... for the first time in her life she wouldn't have to live hand to mouth; she would have *options*.

'Miss... I mean, Sophie, have you decided?'

'Remind me. What happens to Greg's money if we don't attend these appointments and race meetings together?'

Thomas shuffled his paperwork, found what he was looking for, and read, 'Should Miss Sophie Falworth, Miss Ruth Armitage, or Mrs Clara Armitage fail to complete the task, the balancing sum of just over seven million pounds will be placed into a charitable trust fund. It will be managed for profit and any annual income from the trust fund, will be donated equally to the following charities; Cancer Research UK, BPA, MU...'

'Okay, that's enough,' Sophie broke in, 'At least it won't be wasted. So what are the rules of Greg's little game?'

Again, Thomas riffled through his paperwork, cleared his throat and began reading.

'Miss Sophie Falworth, Miss Clara Armitage, and Mrs Ruth Armitage are to be given a thirty-three and a third percent ownership each in two horses currently owned by Mr Greg Armitage. They will race under the syndicate name of No Regrets, and carry Mr Greg Armitage's colours already registered with Weatherby's. All training and racing costs will be covered by Mr Greg Armitage's estate for the 2016 summer racing season. Together, you must attend the stables of Mr Dennis Smith in Malton, North Yorkshire on the first Wednesday in each month for a minimum of one hour to view your horses and determine forward planning for each racehorse.'

Thomas paused to allow the wave of heavy sighs and groans emanating from Sophie to subside. He cleared his throat and continued.

'The three ladies must attend together. All three ladies must attend one racecourse run per month from April 1st to September 1st, that's five runs. All three ladies must arrive before the race and remain at the racecourse for a minimum of half an hour afterwards. If a syndicate horse is not due to race in a calendar month, a substitute horse will be allocated by the trainer. The ladies must provide evidence of their attendances in the form of a group photograph, both at the stables and the racecourses. This evidence should be sent to the executor...'

Thomas continued reading the rules but Sophie zoned out. She was contemplating having to spend so much time with the woman who at the age of twenty-three, had sent her life spiralling out of control.

'...and failing to attend any stable visit or racecourse run for the length of time stipulated will make all the bequeathed amounts in schedule one void.'

Thomas took a breath and looked up at Sophie. She appeared troubled.

'Do you have any questions, or have you decided whether you wish to go ahead?' he ventured.

'Who decides whether Clara, Ruth, and I have done everything properly?'

'Mr Sedgefield is the executor and will determine that all the conditions of Mr Armitage's will have been met. Also, Mr Armitage made some other arrangements,' Thomas admitted, 'He, er... told Mr Sedgefield he has instructed an unnamed individual to report to the executor if any of the requirements of his task are not fulfilled.'

Sophie frowned, 'So we're going to be spied on!'

'Also, Mr Sedgefield has requested I attend the first stable visit in Malton to keep him abridged of your compliance...'

This appeared to be the lesser of the two evils, as Sophie waved it away, still reeling from learning she was signing up to being stalked by someone. Thomas waited a few seconds before asking his question for a third time.

'I think that's everything. Are you willing to accept Mr Armitage's terms?'

Blinking thoughts of being tracked away, Sophie gazed levelly at Thomas and once she thought she'd made him suffer the silence long enough, announced, 'Yes. I'm in.'

The young man smiled for the first time since he'd arrived. It was a shade forced, and only lasted a fleeting moment, but still, it was a smile.

'Good, then I need you to sign these documents and disclaimers,' he stated, passing over a bunch of papers.

'What are these?'

'The main one is to release Mr Armitage's estate from any blame, civil or criminal court case, or physical injury you and the Armitage's sustain during the racing season. The others are Weatherby's documents making you a racehorse owner, a member of a three-way syndicate and accepting the percentage ownership of the two colts.'

'Weatherby's?' Sophie said with an irritated sigh.

'They're a bank, but also act as the... well, they're like the civil service for racing in Britain. All owner registrations, race entries, and prize-money goes through them.'

Thomas offered his pen and Sophie quickly flicked through the pages, signing each one marked with small post-it notes and pencil crosses.

'So when do we start?' Sophie asked as she watched Thomas check each page and carefully pack the signed documents away. He then removed a bound A4 report from his briefcase and handed it to her.

'Eight o'clock next Wednesday morning at Mr Dennis Smith's racing yard in Malton. Everything you need is in there, addresses, telephone numbers, and dates. The rules of your conduct during meetings with the other two ladies are also provided.'

Sophie read the front cover, shook her head, and tossed the tome entitled, 'Greg's Task', onto the coffee table. Thomas clicked his briefcase shut and stood up.

'Greg always did love his paperwork,' she muttered, remaining seated on the sofa. Bella lifted her head to eye the nervous young man who seemed keen to be off.

'How did Clara react to all of this?' Sophie asked, gesturing at the report. Thomas pursed his lips and retook his seat. She couldn't decide whether he was irked at not being able to head for the door, or simply a little flustered by her question.

'Mrs Armitage used some colourful language,' he admitted, 'She is still quite upset.'

'I bet. And did she say anything about me?'

Thomas squirmed on the edge of the armchair. Sensing his unease, Bella unfolded herself from the sofa and dropped lightly to the floor. She shook herself and proceeded to stare levelly at the solicitor, her chin only a few inches away from Thomas's face.

Thomas swallowed, staring back at the dog with eyes wide.

'I'm not... good with large animals,' the solicitor stammered, flicking his gaze nervously to Sophie and back to Bella.

'Bella, basket!' Sophie ordered, suddenly realising why Thomas was holding his briefcase in front of him like a shield.

'I'm really sorry!' Sophie blurted, 'Bella's as soft as clart, she'd never do anything more than lick you.'

Thomas winced at this possibility, but relief flushed his face once the monster dog walked dutifully away and flopped into a large banana-shaped bed under the bay window.

'If it's okay, I'll be off,' the young man said, pushing himself back to his feet.

Sophie had been planning to pump him for more information about Clara, but decided that could wait. She led him to her front door and held it open. She was about to point out that he might have a problem when faced with horses at the trainer's yard, but once through the door he turned and spoke first.

'Miss Falworth, may I ask you a personal question?'

Sophie leaned her shoulder against the door frame and crossed her arms, 'I guess you want to know why Clara and I hate each other so much?'

Thomas returned a slow nod, 'Mrs Armitage told me you were violent towards her, but that's all she would say. It's just, if I knew what had come between the two of you, I may be in a better position to ensure you both successfully complete the task.'

The young solicitor held her gaze, waiting hopefully for a reply. Seeing no reason to refuse, Sophie drew in a deep breath.

'I grew up with Clara. Actually, we lived a few streets away from each other here in York. We were best friends even before we started infant school... we were inseparable. So much so, after our A-Levels we made sure we both enrolled at the same university up in Newcastle, so we could share a flat together. That's where we met Greg Armitage. A year and a half later, Greg told me on the dance floor of our wedding reception that he'd made a huge mistake marrying me, and admitted he loved Clara. The two of them immediately eloped. I was left alone, on my wedding day, to explain the situation to both sets of our family and friends.'

Seven

'This is the one and only conversation we will share before the task commences, Mr Bates.'

Bates waited, his mobile phone held to his ear. He sensed his client would favour silence rather than an interruption to his flow of words. Instead, he took a bite out of the vibrant red coloured meat stick he'd just squeezed out of its wrapper and quietly chewed.

'Our contact will be by text message. Keep your messages short. Only use this phone to send messages - the non-traceable one I sent you. Only send messages to the one number in the phone's memory.'

Bates swallowed, ran his tongue around his mouth to mop up bits of meat stuck between his teeth and said, 'Okay.'

The client continued, 'We will not meet until you have been successful. It's important we are not seen together… understood, Mr Bates?'

Bates thought for a moment, unhurried in his response.

'I will endeavour to carry out my activities without drawing attention to my team, or yourself.'

There was a short pause at the other end of the line, 'Very good. You understand that you're not to hurt her?'

Bates sighed inwardly, but replied with a level, 'Yes, I understand.'

'I want you to adopt a light touch. No publicity. No reason for any authorities getting involved.'

Bates remained silent. The client was beginning to irritate him. Besides, he wasn't about to agree to a course of action he may not be able to control or avoid. In his experience, no matter what a client might initially request, they didn't much care how he reached their goal once it had been achieved.

'The briefing document tells you about the horses and the details of each, er… *target*. Do you have it?'

'Yes.'

'There are three women, but Clara Armitage is likely to be the easiest to… manipulate. She's grieving, is prone to quick mood swings, and her anger may be her downfall. I estimate she would be most likely to crumple under prolonged pressure. She also has an eight year old son… you may wish to use this information to er... ensure she knows you mean business.'

'Noted,' said Bates, and resumed picking with his fingernail at a piece of the meat stick that had become lodged between two of his molars.

'And don't make contact until they've been racing for the first time,' the voice said in closing, 'There's a small chance the three of them will end up doing your job for you.'

Bates checked to make sure his client had rung off, then looked through the backdoor window of the terrace house in Byker, Newcastle he was standing outside. He slung a large canvas bag over his shoulder and entered the back room and one by one, took in the two young men, barely out of their teens, who were silently lounging in two crusty old sofas. Jimmy was watching a small flat television whilst Dylan was consumed with of all things, a heated blanket. He'd chosen Dylan and Jimmy specifically for this job, although studying them now, their talents probably weren't immediately obvious to most people.

He dropped the bag. It made a thump that hastened Jimmy to mute the television.

'I've spoken with the client. We go to work after the first run from one of their horses, but that won't stop us doing some groundwork in the interim.'

The wiry, sour-faced blonde boy looked up and nodded, before returning his attention to a tiny screwdriver he'd been using to dismantle the blanket plug.

Bates turned his attention to the much larger, dark-haired boy for confirmation and immediately realised Jimmy was confused.

'Interim,' Bates repeated not unkindly, 'It means the time before something starts, Jimmy. We'll be planning and setting things up for the next few weeks so we're ready when we make our first move.'

Jimmy returned Bates an open-mouthed nod. His bulk took up two thirds of his sofa and Bates reckoned by any measure the boy cut an intimidating figure.

Bates cast his eyes to a nearby coffee table and noted the scattered wires, electronic motors, and green plastic boards studded with microchips. A soldering iron lay in a small metal cradle and Bates sniffed. He thought there had been a whiff of smoke in the air when he entered the room.

'Is that thing on?' Bates asked.

Dylan flicked his eyes momentarily up to Bates and then the table, 'Yes.'

Bates sucked in one cheek and ground the flesh inside his mouth thoughtfully between his back teeth.

'Be careful,' he said presently, 'I don't want this place burnt to the ground.'

Dylan grinned, the act pulling the skin on his thin, bony face tight to his cheekbone, 'I know all about fire. Don't worry Mr Bates, I'm it's master.'

'I'm sure you are,' Bates agreed, moving to the wall, 'So am I.'

He bent over and flicked the old-fashioned sculpted switch up on the electrical socket. It gave a satisfying click and Bates pulled the soldering iron's plug out of the wall.

'Time to concentrate you two.'

Dylan tensed for a moment, then shrugged, placing his tools and a tiny electrical motor carefully onto the coffee table. He fell back into his sofa, his straggly hair flopping over his face as he bowed his head, partially hiding the hardening of his jaw; a reaction to learning there was work to be done.

'Good. Thank you, Dylan.'

'No problem.'

'It's a five month contract,' Bates continued in business-like fashion, 'You need to keep your noses clean and do as I say at all times, without question. If I encounter any backchat or either of you take it into your heads to counter my instructions, you're off the team for this and any other work... for good. That means you'll either be on the street committing petty crime, in prison, or in care. Living here rent-free is your best option by far. Do you understand?'

Content that both boys had indicated their acceptance of his conditions, Bates added, 'This will be a straightforward and lucrative... er, that's to say, it will be financially rewarding for both of you if we deliver for this client.'

He looked back at Dylan and saw the boy was now beaming at the mention of money, although the black gaps created by the lack of two front teeth lent his smile a disturbingly dark quality.

Bates smiled inwardly. It was as much the *impression* he and the two boys made that on their marks, along with their actions, that could determine their success. Luckily, Jimmy and Dylan's looks expressed an imminent threat in spades.

He spoke for a few minutes, relating instructions to the two members of his team : times, places, and actions. Finally, he gave the canvas bag a kick and spun around to face Dylan.

'This is for you. It's your living arrangements for the next few months.'

Dylan's eyes popped and he provided Bates with his first genuine smile of his visit.

'Is it...?'

'Yes. As you specified,' Bates replied, trying not to show his amusement.

The boy flew over to the huge bag and began to unzip various pockets and closely examine ropes, harnesses, and steel buckles, winches, and cogs. There was even a sigh of contentment from him as he rubbed the fabric of what appeared to be a coversheet.

Bates left the house a few minutes later, safe in the knowledge that Dylan would be salivating over his new toys for many days to come.

Eight

Thursday March 23rd 2016

The weather in Northumberland on this cold, March evening wasn't helping Simon Armitage's mood. His wiper blades were losing the battle to maintain a clear view of the road ahead due to the fierce combination of wind and rain. Despite knowing every twist and turn of this tight country road from Alnwick to Armitage Hall, difficulty in viewing the dark, greasy road ahead was forcing him into intense concentration. Risking a glance across at his wife in the passenger seat he noted that not only was her left hand gripping the door handle of their Volvo, she too was staring fixedly through the rain splattered windscreen. He hated being late for his mother. Even so, he eased off the accelerator and was satisfied when the tension in Marion's shoulders relaxed slightly.

'They'll all be there,' he muttered over the tinny sound of raindrops pinging off the roof of the car.

'You said,' replied Marion glumly, never lifting her eyes from the headlights striking the road ahead.

They drove the last two miles in silence, finally entering the Hall's grounds through two ivy encrusted stone columns and rusted gates to the sound of a distant thunderclap.

'To think, one day all of this could be yours,' Marion mused sarcastically, twirling her fingers at the poorly managed woods encroaching onto the muddy, potholed track.

'It could be *ours*,' Simon corrected.

Now they were on the laboriously long and winding approach to the house, Marion removed her hand from the door handle and flipped down the vanity mirror. She checked her make-up and hair, flicking a nail at a rogue eyelash.

'Leave your face alone, its fine... you're fine.'

'Huh, you think so? Gertie will no doubt find fault, she always does, the old battle-axe.'

Simon sighed, 'Please don't call her that, Marion.'

'What... an old battle-axe?'

'You know what I mean. Gertie was my Father's name for her, no-one else...'

'No-one else is allowed to call her Gertie,' Marion sang in a childlike voice.

'Just behave, will you? You never know, now that Greg is... gone, Mother might have called us here to hand over the reins of the estate to me.'

Marion looked over at her husband, ruminating on why a good

man like him would want so badly to save what was left of the barely salvageable Armitage estate. Two generations of steep decline had seen the farmland, various smallholdings, and forests sold off to keep the house going. And as the coffers had dwindled, so the upkeep of what was left had been ignored. A once generously proportioned Northumbrian country estate was now no more than a dilapidated money pit of a house surrounded by disused stables, barns, outbuildings, and twelve acres of wild woodland.

'You really want to take this on?'

Simon glanced over at his wife, slightly surprised by her soft tone, 'Yes. The older I get, the more convinced I am that the house and grounds deserve to be saved.'

Simon brought the Volvo to a stop on gravel that squelched rather than crunched beneath his wheels, parking neatly beside a line of three cars outside the pillared entrance. Switching the engine off, he turned to his wife and forced a smile.

'You know Marion, maybe today is the day when my Mother sees sense and I can get started.'

'Dream on, Simon,' she said, gently mocking him, 'You'll have to wrench the deeds to Armitage Hall from your Mother's cold dead fingers. She'll never give this place up while there's still a breath in her body.'

Marion looked up at the huge grey stone and slate mansion through the rivulets of rain pouring down the windscreen, 'I can't fathom why you'd want it. It's ugly and falling to pieces.'

'The Armitage family have lived here for four hundred years,' Simon replied reproachfully.

Exactly, Marion thought to herself, the place deserves some new owners.

The hall door swung open, casting a ghostly light onto the car and abruptly killing any further conversation. Simon squinted through the window at a rain-blurred image of a woman standing in the doorway. He instantly recognised the tall, flat silhouette of his younger sister, Ruth.

'Just stay away from my mother, will you,' he told his wife, 'Don't let her wind you up.'

'The council of war is in the library,' Ruth told them dully as she slammed the front door shut behind them and forced a large steel bolt into place with the palm of her hand and a tiny grunt of effort. She caught Marion giving the mechanism a quizzical frown.

'The lock's stopped working,' Ruth explained curtly.

Like everything else in this house, Marion thought, ignoring her sister-in-law's sharp tone.

'So fix it,' she suggested sweetly.

Ruth compressed her lips and shot Marion a filthy look as she brushed past without further comment.

Marion took a side-long look at Ruth as she swept across the dusty reception room, her slingbacks clacking on the parquet floor. Despite Ruth's lack of warmth, Marion felt a shade sorry for the thirty-four-year-old. Ruth had been relatively pretty in her mid-twenties, but was slowly becoming old maid material. Her tart comments had once come across as witty, when delivered with a bunched up smile. They now came spiked with vitriol, and tended to be backed up with a sneer.

And Ruth didn't help herself with the way she dressed. Everything she wore was a size too small, from the awful fawn cardigan that pulled mercilessly at the pearlescent buttons across her bust, to her fat feet that bulged out of the tops of her shoes. As they followed her into the library, not for the first time, Marion had the notion that Ruth's descent into bitterness seemed to correlate perfectly with her fading youth.

'You're late,' snapped Gertrude as they entered the library.

And this is what Ruth is destined to become, Marion thought dismally. Gertrude Armitage, the lady of the house, was standing in front of an impressive fireplace containing a sparingly fuelled coal fire and was flanked on either side by her two black Labradors, Hunter and Athena. The seventy-three year old had her silver hair balled up on the back of her head and was wearing a pair of gold coloured moleskin breeches, riding boots, and a hunt shirt, despite the fact the estate hadn't stabled a horse for at least fifteen years.

'Hurry up and sit down, Simon,' Gertrude ordered irritably, 'The dogs will want to be fed in half an hour.'

Simon nodded a silent hello to the rest of his family and did as he was told.

The library had a rich, fusty smell and was filled with horribly mismatched antique furniture, most of which had seen much better days. When Marion seated herself beside her husband on a scarlet chaise longue, a small puff of dust wafted up, the shimmering particles caught in the beam of a nearby lamp whose shade was broken. She resisted the urge to wipe the settling dust from her dress, given Gertrude was eyeing her intently, and instead cast her gaze around the dimly lit reading room at the Armitage family, doubting any of them had read any of the several thousand ancient texts that surrounded them.

Gertrude remained standing, dominating the room whilst Ruth settled into an armchair opposite Marion. Simon's brother, Timothy, the youngest of the Armitage clan, was leaning languidly against a bookshelf, sipping at a glass of wine while his young girlfriend, Alvita, was standing beside him examining her nails.

'Can we get on, Mother?' Timothy queried impatiently, 'Alvita and I have places to be.'

Gertrude's bony jaw tensed for a moment, then relaxed.

'What could be more important than the future of your family home?' she asked in a crackling voice, 'Come over here and sit down, Timothy. You too, Alvita.'

Timothy obeyed, but took a purposefully slow and circuitous route around the furniture, eventually flopping petulantly into an armchair yards away from anyone else. Alvita perched herself on the arm and leaned in towards her boyfriend until their arms touched.

Simon watched his brother's performance and fought the urge to remark on Timothy's childlike attitude. Timothy, like Ruth, had never seen the need to leave Armitage Hall, preferring as Simon saw it, to sponge off the estate. The eleven year gap between Timothy and himself had made their relationship difficult from the start. For a short while after their father passed, Simon had tried to be a father-figure to the boy, but his attempts had soon led him to view his sibling as a lost cause.

Timothy had suffered from ill health as a child and his sickness had continued right into his late teens, requiring many years of home nursing from his mother. As a result, he'd been allowed to miss school and exams, had no qualifications, and most importantly, lacked a group of friends. He'd become aloof and silent in his early twenties, unwilling and most probably unable to work, and most importantly, accustomed to being cosseted by his mother.   Gertrude had doted on her youngest child, excusing Timothy's idleness and rudeness, and ignoring his poor social skills and predilection for throwing things at the walls when he became frustrated. He spent most of his time in his rooms on the top floor, only venturing out into Alnwick when absolutely necessary.

Having parked herself on the arm of Timothy's chair, Alvita crossed her long dark legs and proceeded to do what Simon believed was the girl's sole purpose in life; to be physically there... and pretty much nothing else. Any hope that this first woman in Timothy's life might help him to grow into a rounded individual had been discarded when Simon had met her just under a year ago. She hardly spoke, and when she did, Simon was always puzzled by her. At eighteen, she was a full four years younger than Timothy, and seemed drawn to him simply because he'd put up with her strangeness. She worked part-time in a nail bar in the town and the latest word from Ruth was that the girl now appeared to be living with Timothy at Armitage Hall.

Simon exchanged a sullen glance with Timothy and, not for the first time, wondered what on earth his brother and his girlfriend must talk about.

Gertrude cleared her throat, a tried and tested method of silencing her children and gaining their attention. Even her dogs took a pensive look up at the old woman.

The sound of heavy rainfall filled the silence in the library. Behind the thin curtains, lightning flickered momentarily providing an unflattering illumination of Gertrude's craggy face. A roll of thunder followed and one of the Labradors gave a small whine.

'The fate of the Armitage estate has been wrenched from our grasp,' Gertrude began, hoping her utilisation of the angry elements outside would heighten the impact of her opening statement.

'I had hoped Gregory would listen to me and his will would favour the Hall and estate,' she said, taking a few steps and eased herself into a high-backed chair closest to the fire, 'However, we Armitages have never backed away from a fight.'

She looked up at her audience and whilst her children were variously smiling or nodding their approval, Marion looked perplexed and Alvita was poking at her mobile phone. The old woman paused. She was resigned to her family's poor choices in partners, after all, her own marriage, whilst fruitful in terms of offspring, hadn't been a joyous or fulfilling union. As far as Gertrude was concerned, her husband's only redeeming quality had been to promptly succumb to a heart attack in his late forties, once his job of siring successors to the Armitage line was complete.

'I know you'll all be disappointed with the contents of Gregory's will,' she added to the continued sound of heavy rainfall on the roof tiles two floors above them. She noticed Ruth raise her eyes to the discoloured cornice on the ceiling and wondered whether her daughter was worrying about that leaky roof in the guest bedroom, or the damp patch of green mould that appeared on the ballroom wall every time there was anything more than a light shower. She doubted it; in her opinion Ruth only worried about herself.

'Why would we be disappointed?' queried Marion.

'Yes dear, disappointed. Gregory has let us down – the estate comes first.'

Marion sighed, 'Greg's been propping up this crumbling dinosaur of a building for years. He's the only reason you lot can still live here.'

'Will you control your wife, Simon,' called Timothy, 'She's just called Mother a dinosaur!'

Ignoring Timothy's asinine comment, Marion continued, 'Greg obviously thought long and hard about how he was going to use his money, and if...'

'Yes, dear!' Gertrude cut in sharply, 'And in a roundabout way it will end up where it should be, invested in the estate. But we have to *ensure* that's where it ends up.'

There was an uneasy silence while the Armitage children checked each other out, wondering who would speak first. Eventually, Simon sighed and looked over at his mother.

'I don't see how we, or Ruth, can influence what Greg's wife and a woman we barely know...'

Gertrude's ever-deepening frown sucked Simon's words from him. He shrugged and looked away.

'Gregory was always a bit of a joker,' Gertrude continued, 'He's having his last laugh. We must ensure that last laugh isn't on us.'

She paused again for a few seconds, allowing this thought to settle on her little gathering, 'It's in all our interests to ensure the money in the family comes back to the estate.'

A small, heavily South American accented voice said, 'Isn't that up to him, Greg, I mean? He was ever so nice when I talked with him. He had such lovely ideas. I think he saw things... clearly. Maybe knowing you're dying helps to free the mind from petty squabbles.'

A more distant crack of thunder outside helped to punctuate Alvita's speech, during which time even Timothy stared up at her. She smiled down at him from her perch on the arm of his chair, displaying a perfect set of bright white teeth, her glossy black hair falling into curls around her shoulders as she self-consciously bowed her head upon realising she was the centre of attention. He smiled back at her, uncertainly at first, but then scanned the faces around the room wearing an expression mixed with surprise and pride.

'Yes, thank you for that, my dear,' Gertrude said, wafting a derogatory wrist in the girl's direction, 'Now, moving on, I have a plan that should ensure Clara and the Falworth woman deliver the funds for us. I will...'

'Did everyone else speak to Greg alone before he died?' Ruth asked.

'Ruthy, my love...' started Gertrude.

'Seriously, Mother. Did he give you a task and tell you what you should do with your share of the money if Clara and Sophie complete his wretched task?'

'And you, darling *Ruthy*,' Timothy interjected smoothly with a mirthless grin, 'Don't forget that he chose *you* to keep them in line.'

Ruth scowled at her brother, 'I'll do my bit. There's no worries on that score. I want to know what Greg said to you all...'

Gertrude leaned back in her chair and unconsciously fondled the collar of the dog sitting beside her as she considered her answer.

'Yes, I believe Greg spoke with everyone here. In fact, I know he did. He told me.'

'Really? I thought it might just be me. So what did he tell you?' pressed Ruth.

'He wasn't thinking straight,' Gertrude said carefully.

'Mother!'

Gertrude rounded on her daughter, her bottom lip curled up in anger, 'My son wasn't in his right mind. The money from Greg's task must come back into the estate to secure its future.'

Marion stared over at the old lady, momentarily lost for words. She finally found her voice, addressing Gertrude in exasperated breaths.

'Hold on. You're expecting... all of your children to plough any money they get from Greg into... this dreadful hell-hole?'

Gertrude turned slowly to face her daughter-in-law and fixed her with a menacing, almost maniacal glare. The dog she had been petting whimpered and pulled away as she inadvertently crushed its ear as she made a fist.

'If you don't agree, my dear,' she whispered, pausing to lick her lips and swallow, 'I will endeavour to make sure all of you receive absolutely nothing.'

It may have been a roll of thunder, but Simon could have sworn he heard the joists in the roof of Armitage Hall creak alarmingly in response to his mother's ultimatum.

'And how will you manage that?' Marion spat back scornfully.

So forced was Gertrude's attempted smile her lips lifted above her teeth to create a snarl, 'We can help... or we can hinder the completion of their task.'

Marion rolled her eyes and looked to her husband for support. Simon didn't react, he had his eyes closed and was kneading his forehead as if attempting to ease a headache.

'Now to business,' said Gertrude in a lighter tone, 'We need to work out how we will ensure Gregory's two ex's can't screw up their task!'

Everyone looked towards Ruth.

'No pressure then...' Ruth moaned, her words dripping with antipathy. She provided the room with a sour expression for good measure.

Nine

Wednesday 5th April 2016

Dennis Smith could safely say he'd never experienced anything like these three women. Since their arrival the atmosphere in the yard on this first Wednesday in April had turned icy cold and the air was crackling with derision as all three of them continually fired verbal pot-shots at each other, separated by the bonnet of their solicitor's car. What made it worse was that the young man seemed to be frightened of his own shadow and was losing the battle to control them. It was bad enough that these three now co-owned two very decent young horses, but the prospect of putting up with this sort of performance for an entire summer season was filling Dennis with deep-seated apprehension.

They'd all arrived in separate cars. The two older women currently trading insults hadn't even left the car park yet, so he'd not been able to introduce himself. However, due to the shouting and ripe language, every member of staff in the entire yard knew they'd arrived and several stable lads and lasses were currently staring at the warring women from the entrances to his three large barns that dominated the yard. The other, taller woman was standing close by, arms crossed, grinning waspishly as the argument escalated, expertly injecting spiteful comments in order to fan its flames.

Dennis stopped twenty yards away from them, closed his eyes, and squeezed the bridge of his nose between thumb and forefinger. Having composed himself, he strode up to the women and cut across the bickering pair with a piercing shout of 'Ladies!'

Clara and Sophie immediately recoiled, reduced to a stunned silence by the sudden male scream coming from the six-foot, ruddy-cheeked Yorkshireman dressed in a filthy wax jacket, jeans and gumboots. Thomas gave Dennis a faintly relieved smile but immediately cringed when a lean German Shepherd trotted up. The dog sat down at the trainer's heel and lolled its tongue out.

'I only have two rules for owners in my yard, ladies,' Dennis rumbled, allowing a touch of anger to sharpen his words, 'The first is, don't feed the horses. The second is, don't get in the way of us training your horses.'

He paused for effect, before hoisting a thumb over his shoulder, 'Your argument has managed to distract my stable staff, got several two-year-olds climbing their stable doors, and you're nowhere near a horse yet!'

'Well, this is a fine way to...' Clara began, but was halted by Dennis's raised flat palm.

'I'm not interested in your arguments and neither are the horses...
although they hate you two screaming at each other. While you're in my
yard, you'll keep your differences to yourselves and keep quiet. If you
don't like it, then feel free to leave and I'll take your horses to the sales.'

Clara, red-faced and hackles raised from her argument with
Sophie, opened her mouth to return a cutting remark, but Thomas jumped
in first.

'Mr Smith, I'm Thomas Bone from Sedgefield Solicitors, Mr
Armitage's executors. We spoke on the phone. This is Mrs Clara Armitage,
Miss Sophie Falworth, and the other lady, over there, is Miss Ruth
Armitage,' he said, rushing his words out.

Dennis nodded, shook Thomas's hand, but immediately turned to
eye Sophie and Clara once more.

'I was warned about you two,' Dennis stated with a wry smile that
helped to warm the atmosphere, 'Conflicts between once close friends live
long in the memory, eh?'

Sophie caught the trainer's eye as he was looking the two of them
up and down in the pause that followed. His gaze lingered on her.

'Take a breath,' he told her.

Sophie frowned but soon realised her heart was still racing from
the argument with Clara. She was taking short, quick breaths. Drawing in
a few longer, steady breaths immediately made her feel better.

Ruth ambled across to join the group as Dennis shook hands with
Clara and Sophie. She gave the trainer an unimpressed sniff as she took his
hand and shook it with her thumb and forefinger, examining her fingers
afterwards for evidence of dirt, or worse. Dennis noticed the slight, but
ignored it; he was used to dealing with her sort.

Sophie and Clara traded a scowl. They'd agreed not to speak, and
basically ignore each other for the duration of this yard visit and those that
followed over the next five months. Unfortunately, Sophie hadn't been
able to stop herself from commenting on Clara's perfect, baby blue three-
piece outfit and matching high heels. By pointing out her clothes were
more suited to an ambassadorial reception than a visit to a racing stable,
Sophie had set Clara off on a tit-for-tat rant. It had admittedly got out of
hand, but Sophie felt strangely better for it, having discharged some of the
pent-up pressure she'd felt building during the car journey.

Clara looked back over her shoulder and once again rolled her eyes
in contempt at Sophie's colourful ankle wellies, torn jeans and fisherman's
jumper. With her blood still boiling, she marvelled at the sheer cheek of the
woman to poke fun at her immaculately pressed outfit.

'My condolences, Mrs Armitage,' Dennis announced, making her
spin around and examine the trainer's disarming smile, 'Your husband
was a good man and a valued owner here at Middlefield Stables. Everyone

here was shocked when the news came through; he'd become a prominent figure in the stable.'

Dennis locked eyes with Clara and continued, 'He had a razor sharp mind and could... read people. I've never seen anyone grasp the nuances of thoroughbred pedigrees so quickly. He was on course to be an important player in the sport.'

Clara blinked a couple of times, unsure how to react to this insight into her husband's character. When she thought about it, there had been a healthy number of messages of condolence from the Malton area, most of which she'd only given cursory glances. She eventually managed to choke out a muttered thank you.

Sophie was bursting to point out that Greg's knowledge of pedigrees couldn't have been that good, as evidenced by his choice of wife. However, she managed to quell the urge to be catty, and instead crossed her arms and took on a look she hoped signalled impatient disinterest to those around her.

'Right, ladies,' announced Dennis authoritatively with a clap of his hands. The noise made the dog at his heel immediately tense, flick its ears forward, and become alert, which made Thomas freeze, his eyes appearing to be on stalks as he nervously assessed the large dog.

'This is Kilroy,' the trainer said, noticing the solicitor shrinking away, 'Ignore him, he's as soft as clart.'

He turn to the ladies, 'As we now understand each other, let's get on with the tour.'

Dennis spun on his heel, shouting 'Show's over, get back to work!' to the half a dozen staff still milling around at the three barn doors, some clutching rakes or brooms, hoping the ladies might kick off again. They immediately melted away.

Dennis stopped momentarily to light a cigarette taken from a soft packet of Marlboro's. Once he'd taken the first puff, he led Sophie and Clara, separated by the solicitor, and then Ruth, to the first barn door where he gestured for them to peer inside. Clara made a point of turning her nose up and wafting the cloud of cigarette smoke away with a gloved hand. Behind her, Ruth gave an amused snort.

Sophie had been impressed with the racing yard so far. Located on the edge of Malton and Norton, a winding single-lane track had led off the main road through high hedged paddocks and past a rambling old farmhouse surrounded by trees and a well-kept garden, to a parking area for about a dozen cars beside three huge brick built, steel roofed barns. The mixed perfume of horses, leather, and linseed oil had come to her in waves, along with the sound of metallic shoes on concrete, the odd snort from a horse, and the buzz of stable lads and lasses chattering. Even at eight o'clock in the morning, the place seemed alive with activity and to

Sophie's surprise she experienced a spark of genuine interest as Dennis led them into the first long, oblong building. He stopped his little entourage once they were out of the glare of the morning sun.

'My mares barn,' he declared. He sucked on his cigarette with slitted eyes and added, 'Three-year-old fillies and older mares.'

'You keep the girls separate?' Sophie queried as she peered down the barn. It had to be eighty to a hundred feet long, and consisting of steel and wooden stables lined up on each side of the barn, separated by a concrete walkway littered with bales of wood shavings, feed buckets, shovels, rakes, and hand carts. There had to be thirty or forty stables, although the bottom third of the barn appeared to be unused.

'Oh, aye, just the lasses,' Dennis replied without further explanation.

'Hell's teeth!' Clara suddenly complained, dancing around on one foot. She'd managed to spear a large clump of drying horse dung on the tall heel of her shoe.

Wearily, Dennis remarked, 'I'd save your heels for the races, love. Around here you're better off with boots.'

Ruth was about to guffaw, but stifled it upon realising her flats were just as inadequate. Under orders from her mother to listen and learn whilst keeping her mouth firmly shut, she felt this was best achieved by hanging back from the other two women.

With his cigarette still in his mouth, the trainer bent over, grabbed Clara's foot, pulled the offending material off her heel and tossed it casually into a nearby muck cart.

'We like to keep the place clean, but where you've got horses, you're going to get horse muck.'

'This is ridiculous,' Clara muttered viciously, 'For two figs I could walk out right now!'

'Never mind a couple of figs, how about a million pounds?' offered Sophie cattily.

'It's just horse muck, love,' Dennis noted genially.

Clara scowled at Dennis's back as he led them out into the morning sun, and then cast a dark look Sophie's way, daring her to comment. Sophie pursed her lips in an, 'I told you so,' expression, but remained silent.

'Come on then, I'll show you your youngsters,' said Dennis, sending another plume of cigarette smoke over his shoulder.

They were passing the central barn, which Dennis pointed out was for the older colts and geldings, when he noticed something just inside the barn and suddenly drew to a halt. Dennis called over to a lean, fair-haired lad in his late twenties who was bent over inside a nearby stable, inspecting a horse's foot. The lad bounded over athletically and Dennis introduced him to the group.

'Danny Smith, no relation,' Dennis told them in a single breath, 'He's my Assistant Trainer and Head Lad.'

'What does that mean?' Ruth queried.

'It means I do everything the Guv'nor tells me to,' grinned Danny. He looked around the group and finally received a warning stare from Dennis and the grin faded.

'Just joking, I'm in charge of the barns and the staff. I also travel to the races and represent the yard when Dennis is away racing or at the sales.'

'He's my right-hand man. If I'm not around, he's the man to turn to,' Dennis added.

Danny nodded his agreement and treated the ladies to another grin.

Leaving Danny to deal with re-bandaging a horse's ankle, Dennis continued the tour. When he reached the last building he announced they'd reached the 'juvenile barn.' He walked straight in and down the central aisle, Kilroy tailing his every step.

Ruth and Clara were last in, but both of them noticed Thomas holding back at the barn door.

'I'll stay here and wait,' he told Ruth in answer to her questioning frown. Ruth shrugged and headed off after Clara, whose steel tipped heels were clacking on the concrete and echoing down the barn.

Passing several stable lasses and lads, all of whom greeted the trio with a hello, they reached the centre of the barn and Dennis stopped, shooed a couple of stable lads from the nearby boxes and waited with a patient smile for Ruth to catch up. Sophie noticed her sister-in-law had not responded to any of the stable staff, preferring to glare contemptuously at each of them.

'Where's the legal eagle?' asked Dennis.

'He stayed up there,' Clara replied distractedly, pulling at the hem of her skirt that had risen over her knees during the short walk, 'I guess he's outside.'

'Lad's frightened of animals,' the trainer sniffed, taking a final drag from his cigarette and blowing a cloud of blue smoke above his head before grinding the butt beneath his heel, 'We'll tread clever on that, but for now, you need to meet your brace of two-year-olds.'

Carefully flicking the bottom catch up with the toe of his boot, Dennis unbolted the metal door to the stable in front of him. Speaking lightly to the horse, he approached slowly, rubbed the colt's long neck and busied himself undoing the horse's coat. Whisking it aside he revealed a gleaming chestnut rippling with muscle and beckoned the three women to the stable door.

'Blimey, he's beautiful!' Sophie exclaimed, her words having left her mouth before she'd had chance to sense check them. She stepped into the stable and took in the magnificent animal.

Dennis beamed, 'He should be, he cost Mr Armitage an arm and a leg.'

'How much of an arm and leg?' queried Clara from the stable door.

'Seventy-five thousand guineas. Come over, you can give him a pat if you like, he's a sensible lad.'

Glum faced, Clara swallowed hard but remained by the stable door. Ruth watched on from behind her. Sophie didn't need to be asked twice and was by Dennis's side almost immediately. She placed her flat palm slowly onto the colt's neck and was surprised at the heat beneath the thin layer of waxy golden hair. Looking up into the horse's soft eye she stroked his neck, completely taken with the majesty of the young animal.

Ruth had purposefully hung back, remaining aloof, and only casually glancing past Clara through the stable's open door. She'd not had any contact with horses for a long time, not since her father had died. Her preference was for art galleries, theatre, and socially acceptable indoor pursuits. She didn't consider herself a prude, but getting down and dirty with large animals wasn't her idea of fun.

And yet... Ruth found herself pushing past Clara and entering the stable. She picked her way across the shavings on the concrete floor to touch this... noble beast that was partly hers. Something clicked into place, a long forgotten memory aroused by the strong aroma of horse. She was atop a huge gelding, holding onto its mane and pushing back into her father's chest as they cantered together, his strong arms making her feel safe. They were laughing.

When Ruth arrived beside her, Sophie noticed the sour expression the Armitage woman had been holding onto all morning, had disappeared. She too stroked the neck of the colt and even giggled slightly when the animal turned its head and breathed hotly onto her, tickling the hairs on the back of her hand.

'Oh, sorry Guv,' said a young female voice behind them, 'I didn't know you were busy.'

Dennis didn't look around, 'It's okay, Martha, we're almost done. This is Martha, ladies. She's the stable lass who looks after both your horses and rides them out most days. She'll be giving him a workout in a few minutes.'

'You're getting to know Frankie, eh?' the girl said, stepping past Clara at the door to the stable and smiling at Ruth and Sophie.

'He's such a darling. I love him to bits. Are you the new owners?' she asked brightly.

Ruth looked up and nodded, a genuine smile on her lips.

'Tickle him behind his ears, he loves that,' Martha added encouragingly, as she deposited the bundle of saddle and tack she'd brought with her against the back wall of the stable.

It was difficult not to pick up on the girl's enthusiasm as she chatted away about how she'd been with Frankie since he'd arrived from the sales. She pointed out where he'd had a touch of ringworm that had left a missing few inches of hair on his back. She told them about an abscess that had cracked his hoof on his front fore, and how she'd had to poultice it for several weeks. He'd also been over-exuberant in the paddocks one day and bumped into a fence, catching his mouth and needing a couple of staples in his bottom lip.

'He's a little terror,' Martha chuckled, 'But he's got a massive personality – you can see that for yourselves!'

Sophie and Ruth grinned at the girl, unable to disagree. They petted Frankie a little longer and then stood back to watch Martha diligently prepare the colt for his morning exercise.

'How fast is he?' Sophie asked.

'Oh, he's quick, a sprinter. I'm sure he'll win a race.'

'So says the girl who practically lives with the horse every day of her life,' said Clara in a sarcastic and partially bored tone from the stable door.

Martha looked up at her and to Sophie's delight, without a shred of dissent the girl beamed at Clara for a second before telling her, 'You're absolutely right. I know I'm a bit biased, but this chap is a proper little racehorse.'

'He should be plenty of fun for all three of you,' Dennis chipped in, keen for Clara not to challenge his stable lass further, and surreptitiously moving to position himself between Clara and Martha.

'Both your horses will need racing names,' he continued, 'So what do you think for this one – he could be racing in a matter of weeks?'

'He's called Frank isn't he?' Ruth queried.

'Frankie,' Martha confirmed, giving the colt's mane an affectionate rub.

Dennis wrinkled his nose, 'As a stable name, but I doubt it will be available when we come to register him to race.'

'How about Fun Frankie?' Sophie suggested, 'You said he'd be a fun horse for us.'

'Fun Boy Frankie, would be nicer,' Ruth said quietly.

Sophie studied Ruth for a moment and found her gazing at the horse, an unexpectedly warm smile on her face.

'I agree with you, Ruth. Fun Boy Frankie it is! I'll check it's not already taken and register it for your syndicate,' Dennis promised, clapping her lightly on her back. Ruth and Sophie shared a nod of approval and stepped forward to stroke the colt's neck once more.

Presently, Sophie looked over her shoulder to check on Clara, a grin on her face, momentarily caught up in the thrill of stroking the youngster's warm and silky neck. Her grin faded once she realised Clara was leaning on the stable door, her face lit up with the artificial glare of her mobile phone.

'Clara! At least show a bit of interest, will you? You could be petulant when you were younger, but this casual rudeness you're inflicting on everyone around you is getting rather tiresome.'

Clara tapped at the little screen for a few seconds, then raised her head and locked eyes with Sophie, 'Unlike you, I have a social life. And to be honest, it's far more exciting than petting a dumb animal.'

Sophie turned to face Clara, eyes narrowed.

'Right, Tinkerbell! Let's get a few things straight,' Sophie growled in a deliberately low, threatening voice.

She'd first used this nickname for Clara when they were fourteen, and at regular intervals through their teenage years. Sophie had employed the 'Tinkerbell' handle when Clara was being unreasonable, or to be more accurate, pig-headed. The comparison to the sulky young fairy as depicted in the Disney Peter Pan movie had tended to make Clara stop and consider; a trigger word that helped to cut arguments short and more often than not would eventually put an end to Clara flouncing off in a huff when she didn't get her own way. Sophie hadn't meant to use it. It had just been there, on the tip of her tongue.

'I'm not a teenager any more, Sophe!' Clara responded cattily, dredging up her own pet name for her ex-friend.

Sophie's face hardened and leaving Fun Boy Frankie's side she strode over the deep layer of wood shavings on the stable floor and forced Clara from the door frame and out onto the barn's central walkway.

Ignoring Clara's fierce stare, Sophie paused to run a critical eye over the woman's face. At one time she had fanaticised about punching it until it was red-raw.

Sophie dropped her tone to a flat whisper, 'I want the money and you want the money, correct?'

Clara jerked her head in resentful agreement and crossed her arms.

'So we'll be seeing each other on a regular basis, something neither of us wants. Greg was wrong, we know we will *never* forgive and forget.'

'Agreed.'

'So let's not make this any more difficult than it needs to be,' Sophie pressed, 'You stop being such hard work and I'll... try to stop winding you up.'

'Try?' questioned Clara scornfully.

'Okay, I *will* stop. It'll be difficult, but I'll stop.'

A heavy silence fell on them, eventually broken by a sigh from Sophie.

'Ruth's got the right idea, let's keep our mouths shut and go through the motions. Greg's instructions didn't say we had to get on, or speak to each other, we just have to spend time in each other's company. That way, *all three of us* will be winners at the end of this.'

Clara surveyed the woman in front of her and shivers of remembrance travelled down her spine. They'd been here before. Could they really be playing out exactly the same moment in Sophie's bedroom when they were teenagers? She could see the room, with its painted cream woodchip wallpaper and the yellow and blue flowered curtains through which they could look down on the tree-lined street; a street much nicer than her foster mum's, three-bedroom council terrace. She could smell the Mr Sheen polish Mrs Falworth used on the banister, touch the photos of Duran Duran and Madonna cut from the pages of Smash Hits. And Sophie was even brokering a similar agreement to the one twenty-five years ago, only that one had been a pact; they'd sworn never to lie to each other.

Clara looked through the white painted steel bars that started half-way up the wooden outer wall, suddenly aware she was the centre of attention. Dennis was watching her closely, staring without a hint of embarrassment as Sophie waited for her reply. Ruth and Martha were quietly petting the horse, listening intently, but not overtly watching her like the trainer.

Clara sighed inwardly. Sophie was annoyingly right. She had arrived in a bad mood and decided to be a bitch about everything today.

'Okay. I agree,' Clara said quietly, 'I'm only doing this for Jeremy, for his future. You keep your clever comments to yourself and I'll...'

'You'll shut up and stick a smile on...' Sophie's words caught in her throat as she realised how hectoring she sounded. Under her breath she whispered, 'Force of habit. I'm er... sor...'

'No, you're not sorry. Not really,' Clara cut in abruptly, 'It's okay. We're agreed. We'll both keep our thoughts to ourselves, put on a brave face, and get on with it.'

Clara returned to the stable door and contrived to produce a plastic smile. Whilst Dennis accepted it with a non-committal nod, Martha returned her a troubled frown.

'So, what about our second horse?' Clara asked, wishing she was elsewhere and unable to keep a dash of irritation from muddying her question.

Dennis nodded, instructed Martha to continue saddling Frankie and took the three women a short way down the barn. He stopped outside an identical stable with an open half door and indicated a taller, less furnished horse. The colt eyed his owners warily from the back of his box.

'He's nice, probably classier than your other one, but will take longer to come to hand. I won't take you in, he can get a bit fretful. But he needs a name, just like Frank... I mean Fun Boy Frankie.'

'I'm sure Martha will still call him Frankie,' said Sophie with a smile, 'The girl is smitten.'

'So, come on,' Dennis said, nudging Clara, 'Your turn to name one.'

Clara gave the horse a cursory glance before turning to stare at the square of light created by the open gates at the bottom of the barn, 'If it was a girl, I'd tell you to name it Tinkerbell. As it's a male, you can call the horse whatever you want. I've had it with men.'

There may have been a smidgen of petulance in Clara's tone, but if there was, Dennis ignored it. Sophie shook her head, but said nothing, half expecting Ruth to weigh in with a derogatory comment. However, she too remained silent, seemingly in a world of her own, judging by the wan smile on her face.

Dennis looked thoughtfully at the colt for a good while before turning to Clara and nodding.

'No problem, Mrs Armitage, I'll get him named.'

Ten

They never got to enter the stable of the second horse, as a diminutive twenty-year-old wearing riding garb and a thick protective jacket arrived carrying a saddle and tack.

'Mornin' all!' the lad called brightly in a heavy Irish accent, touching his helmet. The deferent gesture amused Sophie, as much as it impressed Clara.

'This is Mitch Corrigan. He's our stable jockey,' Dennis explained, 'He's come in to ride some gallop work this morning. Come on, we'll get gone to the gallop and wait for 'em up there.'

Following a bumpy fifteen minute ride up a rough track on the outskirts of Norton, Dennis brought his Land Rover to a halt at the top of the gallop, jumped out and immediately lit another cigarette. Kilroy landed with a thump on the turf beside him once the back gate of the car was opened.

In the rear seats, Clara noticed Thomas's knuckles were white and the boy looked terribly pale.

'Try to relax. It's just a dog,' she told the solicitor as they all tumbled out of the car.

'It's a very... big dog, and it was breathing on me all the way here,' said Thomas, 'I'm not good with er... large animals.'

'Why's that then?' asked Sophie as the four of them adopted a position upwind of Dennis's cigarette smoke.

Thomas paused. He seemed to be debating internally whether he should share this information.

'There was an incident when I was thirteen... with cows,' he offered.

'Cows?' Clara scoffed.

'I got trampled,' Thomas continued, ignoring Clara, 'I was on a walking weekend with... umm, my mother, and we went through a pasture and for no reason, a herd of cows attacked us. I tripped up trying to run away and ended up spending a week in hospital and, er... got this.'

He lifted a hand to his forehead and brushed his thick black fringe back to reveal a crescent of scarred skin.

'Harry Potter has his magical scar, I've got my cows hoof,' he told them with a faintly embarrassed grimace.

'Impressive,' Sophie commented. She saw Clara had her hand over her mouth, stifling a laugh, and shot her a warning glare.

'I think I'll stay in the car if that's okay,' Thomas said, and he made off.

Dennis shook his head, but soon announced to the remaining ladies that the jet black horse on the nearside of the four coming towards them up the grass gallop was called Norman, an older horse. He was followed by Mitch on Fun Boy Frankie, Martha on their unnamed horse and finally another two-year-old not in their ownership.

'Frankie, your unnamed colt, and one more two-year-old will be doing a swinging canter. I've put Mitch on Frankie, as he'll be the first of your two to race. Mitch has the experience to know exactly where we are with Frankie's fitness and readiness to race for the first time,' the trainer explained.

Sophie watched transfixed as the small blurs in the distance below them reached the rising ground and the sound of hooves slapping moist turf could be heard. It became louder as they approached, until the noise was suffused with the breath, snorts, and creak of the saddles as the four horses streaked past them only fifteen yards away.

'And that was only, what, half speed?' asked Sophie, unable to take her gaze from the group of horses as they continued to the top of the hill.

'About three-quarter pace,' Dennis corrected.

'Why call a horse Norman?' asked Clara, tugging at her thin heel that was working its way into the soft turf.

Sophie looked over at her, trying to detect whether the question was laced with sarcasm, but it seemed it was genuine. However, she did raise a smile at the fact Clara appeared to be shrinking before her very eyes. She was already two inches smaller! Sophie satisfied herself with an internal smirk but with their recent deal still fresh in her mind, she made no comment.

'Norman tried to do everything at once when he first came from the sales,' Dennis explained, 'Ran away with a couple of lads in his first week on the gallops. There's no malice in him, he's just high-spirited and full-on. So we called him Stormin' Norman. He's much better now, he's calmed down a lot since we gelded him. It did Frankie a lot of good too.'

'Frankie is no longer an entire?' Ruth asked.

Dennis gazed thoughtfully at her, 'So you know a bit more about horses than you let on.'

'I did ride when I was younger. In fact, I quite enjoyed it,' Ruth replied defensively.

Dennis grinned, 'Good for you.'

Ruth felt her cheeks grow warm.

Presently, Dennis said, 'Greg Armitage's instructions to me were to train the horses this season as I see fit and make all the racing decisions as to where to place them and when to race them. Frankie wasn't showing enough on the gallops to be a potential sire and it warranted the vet being employed to calm him down. He recommended gelding him, so I had him cut.'

Clara visibly winced.

'Gelding is a standard procedure these days, we do them standing up in the yard. The horses don't feel too much and they benefit from a much better standard of life,' Dennis explained, then changed tack, 'Come on, we'll walk up and have a word with Mitch about Frankie. He could be getting entries in less than three weeks.'

When they met Mitch walking back down the hill, he slid off Frankie and stood the horse so that his owners could admire him. The gelding was smaller than the other colts, but was thickset, and being a flashy chestnut, he was no less impressive to look at.

'Does that mean Frankie's not as good as our other horse?' Ruth asked, tentatively patting the young horse's neck and trying not to recoil when her hand picked up a covering of Frankie's sweat and wax from his coat.

Dennis pulled on a cigarette whilst considering his answer, 'The other lad is classy and has more scope, but this chap will be running in April and has the speed to win a sprint Maiden.'

'Frankie gives a good feel,' Mitch chimed in, 'He should be a fair handicapper once he's run a few times, as he likes to put his head down and run for fun. Lots of 'em go through the motions, but this lad likes the competition. He wasn't for lettin' any of this bunch past him today.'

Frankie closed his eyes and seemed to drift into a standing slumber as Sophie rubbed her palm up and down his bowed head. Ruth had been standing back, but she now stepped forward and tentatively reached out. Sophie backed away and watched as Ruth's lips parted in delight as the horse pushed his forehead gently against her palm

'Look at his long black eyelashes,' Ruth marvelled, continuing to rhythmically rub the gelding's forehead, 'He's beautiful.'

Dennis shared a knowing look with his work rider and thirty seconds later he legged Mitch back up onto Frankie's back. The gelding blinked a few times and slowly lifted his head so that despite being the smallest of the four horses he towered above Ruth like an equine Adonis.

Dennis looked down the hill and told Mitch, 'Get him back to the yard, we're heading there now.'

'You're not watching the other lots?'

Dennis shook his head, 'Things to do.'

As they began to cross the rough turf back toward the Land Rover, the sound of hooves once more thundered behind them. Dennis kept his stride, head down, but the three women looked around and found another group of four horses making determined progress up the gallop. About half-way up the hill a large, black horse with four white socks pulled to the front and careered away from his workmates, the lad on top barely moving.

'Was that one of yours?' Sophie demanded of Dennis when she

caught up with him at the car.

'Aye, that's one of mine. One of my best horses,' the trainer replied coyly.

'Who owns him?' asked Thomas from the window of the car. He leaned forward to hear Dennis's reply.

'He'll run in my name, but he's actually owned by a really good owner of mine who likes to keep his involvement in racing under the radar. He doesn't have a racing name at the moment. Oh, and best lean back, son.'

Dennis opened his driver's door and Kilroy jumped up and over the trainer's lap and sat down beside him in the footwell of the passenger seat, close to Ruth's legs. She gave him an amiable pat. Instead of looking at Ruth, the dog turned its big head and regarded Thomas between the seats with judgement in his eyes and saliva hanging from the corners of his mouth.

Thomas pushed himself into his seat back as far as he could go.

Eleven

On their arrival back at the Middlefield yard, Dennis invited the syndicate into his farmhouse for a coffee. Sophie was the first to accept, having warmed to the trainer's gruff exterior, dry sense of humour, and whiff of nicotine, and to her surprise Ruth did the same. Even more surprising was Ruth, backing up her acceptance with a smile for Dennis, which amused Sophie no end.

With the group having stayed the statutory sixty minutes required by Greg's task, Thomas produced a copy of the Daily Mail and gave it to Clara, telling her he wanted to take a photo. Clara examined the newspaper, holding the corner between thumb and forefinger as if it were soiled rag.

'It helps to establish provenance, as well as a date,' Thomas explained as he snapped the three women he'd grouped together.

'Yes, but the Daily Mail!' Clara complained. Sophie and Ruth rolled their eyes.

Photos completed, Thomas advised that ideally, they should do the same at the races.

'A photo of yourselves together in the parade ring with your racecards will be enough proof,' he told them, catching the eye of each woman to be sure they understood, 'Send the proof of attendance photos through to me by email as soon as you can afterwards.'

'So you're the one keeping score,' Sophie noted.

'Yes. But it's Mr Sedgefield who will determine whether you've successfully completed Mr Armitage's task following your final racetrack attendance in August.'

Clara sighed irritably, 'So are we done for today?'

'Almost,' Thomas replied, 'You should know that I won't be attending any further stable visits or any run from your horses. This was a one-off to get you going. You're on your own now. Just remember to keep emailing the photos through to me as proof. Oh, and Mr Sedgefield asked me to remind you that should any of you miss a stable visit or run from either horse, every beneficiary will forfeit their inheritance.'

Clara had been tapping her foot throughout Thomas' answer and she was now giving him a 'wind it up' signal by petulantly twirling her finger at him.

'Are we *done*?' she barked.

Thomas shoulders slumped a little, 'Yes, Mrs Armitage.'

Upon receiving this confirmation, Clara headed straight for her big SUV, stumping off without another word to anyone.

'Mr Sedgefield will be pleased,' Thomas told Sophie as he watched Clara's car leave in a cloud of dust, 'I spoke with him last night and he was concerned none of you would turn up today and that would be that.'

The boy delivered this news in his usual plain, almost downcast tone. However, she noticed that currently his attention was entirely taken up with Kilroy, who was sitting watching the solicitor intently.

Sophie went over to the dog, who had planted himself on some rough grass between the parking area and a small, but densely populated wood that bordered the northern edge of Dennis's property. With the trees only just in bud, a two-bar fence and a country road were just visible through the jumble of sycamore, brambles and birch.

'He really won't attack you,' Sophie said, bobbing down and scratching the large dog behind his ears, 'You should give him a pat. It might make you less frightened of him.'

Thomas looked over at the dog. Kilroy had his mouth open and his tongue lolling out one side. The solicitor shivered, recalling the tongue of the cow… as it trampled him. He gave Sophie a troubled glance and replied, 'Maybe next time, Miss Falworth.'

With that, Thomas jumped into his car. Sophie caught him examining his rear-view mirror a number of times as he exited the yard, presumably to ensure Kilroy wasn't running after him. She heard the German Shepherd give a small whimper as the young solicitor departed and she stared quizzically at the dog as if expecting him to explain. Instead, Kilroy stood up and set off walking slowly toward the barns.

Sophie watched Thomas indicate right at the end of the private track and slowly pull out onto Beverley road, heading into Norton. She could just catch the movement of his car behind the hedge and would have turned away if it wasn't for the fact that his indicator continued to flash right. The car slowed and at the end of the hedge marking the boundary of Dennis's land, Thomas turned right, his car appearing in flashes behind the trees in the wood that ran along the edge of the trainer's property, slowly climbing up the hill. Sophie deduced a small country road ran between Dennis's and the next property. She watched Thomas's car for another hundred yards and lost it behind the farmhouse and other outbuildings as the road wandered northwards towards Norton.

'You coming?' Ruth asked impatiently.

Momentarily distracted, Sophie didn't reply straight away, but eventually murmured her agreement.

The farmhouse was stone built, covered in ivy and protected on all sides by a waist-high privet hedge clipped perfectly symmetrically. Situated a hundred yards away from the training barns, Dennis's home stood solidly at a right-angle to the remainder of the yard buildings. Sophie wondered why this might be, but soon worked out that anyone looking through its six forward-facing windows would have an uninterrupted view to all three of the barns.

As they approached, Ruth noticed a further row of terraced cottages that had been partially hidden behind the farmhouse and pointed them out to Sophie.

'Accommodation for some of his staff?' Ruth wondered aloud.

'It's a deceptively big place,' Sophie murmured as they opened the garden gate and ventured up the short path to a large front door that had been left ajar. Boot cleaning equipment sat to one side of the large concrete front step and a large hessian mat ordered them to 'Wipe Your Feet!'. Before they could do so, Dennis called them in from somewhere in the bowels of the house.

Both women hurriedly did as the mat told them and as one, they pushed the door back and stepped into a dark, spacious hallway. Sophie got a waft of something earthy; possibly furniture wax or polish mixed in with flowers and… dog. She looked down and discovered Kilroy staring dolefully up at her, tongue, as ever, lolling out.

'Wow!' Ruth exclaimed under her breath, lifting her chin and rotating to take in the full effect of the entirely oak panelled walls and impressively wide staircase that led to a gallery above, 'I wasn't expecting this.'

'No,' Sophie agreed quietly, her eye caught by the intricate lighting fixture high above her, 'I didn't have Dennis down as a chandelier sort of chap.'

A parquet floor, only slightly discoloured in places from over a century of foot traffic, led off towards a brighter room at the end of the hallway, twenty yards distant. Dennis's silhouette appeared in the rectangle of light and he beckoned them in with a, 'Come on through, the kettle's on.'

Passing framed photographs of horses racing, horses winning, horses in mid-jump out of stalls and what appeared to be original paintings with similar equine subjects, Sophie led the way. Ruth stopped to inspect one particularly large portrait of the head of a bay colt set in an ornate gold frame and, upon reading the inscription punched into a brass plate at its base, realised it had to be over a hundred years old.

Presently, the two women stepped into a bright kitchen-cum-sitting room at the back of the house with a high, bare oak beamed ceiling. It revealed itself to be a large, yet sympathetic extension boasting a barn conversion feel without losing the grandeur provided by the main house. Sophie calculated the floor space of this room alone outstripped her entire flat. In contrast to the entrance and hallway, morning sunlight poured into this room due to several windows being set in the roof and an uninterrupted arc of larger ones facing out onto a terrace and the garden beyond. It gave the impression of a pavilion rather than a room, and when Ruth looked around she realised Dennis must spend most of his time here;

there were areas for preparing food, eating, sitting, working, and relaxing in front of a large flat screen television. The only thing missing was a bed. Ruth could smell flowers and noticed a large vase on the kitchen table stuffed with brightly coloured blooms. Beyond a central set of doors was a mature rose garden in the early stages of budding.

'Have a seat,' Dennis said, nodding to a large kitchen table as he readied a tray with a teapot, milk, and sugar.

Ruth continued to look around the huge room with hands clasped to her chest and her mouth open. Sophie smiled inwardly, but didn't comment. She was used to walking into her clients' houses, be they grand or grubby, large or small, and had long since stopped judging the person by their surroundings.

'This is a wonderful country house, Mr Smith,' Ruth said as she angled her backside into a less than generously proportioned leather padded kitchen chair.

'Please, call me Dennis,' the trainer replied, placing the tray onto the sparkling black marble table. It now included a plate of chocolate digestive and bourbon biscuits that Ruth cooed over as they were offered. Sophie noticed Kilroy lifting a paw onto her knee under the table and Ruth surreptitiously drop half a biscuit onto the floor beside him.

At the other end of the table Sophie caught sight of a folded newspaper. She recognised the layout. It was a Yorkshire Post, left open on a page with a half-completed cryptic crossword. Lying beside it was a laptop computer and a thick spiral bound folder studded with a multitude of brightly coloured post-it notes.

'The Racing Programme Book,' Dennis said in explanation, having noticed her peering quizzically at his pile of paperwork. Sophie's gaze jumped back to the trainer and caught him with a curious half-smile on his lips.

'It's my bible,' he continued, nodding towards the thick tome, 'Getting horses fit and well is only half the story. Placing them in the right race is just as important when you're looking for winning opportunities.'

'So owners don't choose their horses' races?'

'Some will suggest races, but there's more to race planning than meets the eye. Bringing the horse to the peak of fitness is never enough on its own. Not only do you need to know your racehorse back to front and the idiosyncrasies of the racecourses, you must match the race conditions to your advantage. Then there is the going and the draw. Both are out of your control and can have a huge effect on your chances. You can take an educated guess at whether it will rain when you declare to run two days before the race, but if you're handed a bad draw in the ballot it can mean you'll be giving away lengths to better drawn competitors.'

'It sounds terribly complicated,' said Ruth.

Dennis grinned.

'We trainers would like you owners to think so,' he rumbled amiably.

'I was going to ask… or rather, request something regarding the runs from our racehorses,' started Sophie.

'Oh yes?' Dennis replied, realising he'd been led down this path of questioning for a reason.

'I'm assuming you know we, that is the three of us, have a task to complete, set by Greg Armitage?'

One corner of the trainer's mouth crept upwards slightly, 'You have to land here once a month and go racing each time either of your horses run, or at least once a month until the end of… August I think.'

'Mmm…' Sophie hummed, 'Well, I was wondering whether you could limit our horses to a single run from one of them per month?'

Dennis leaned back in his chair, his gaze shifting from one woman to the other as he considered his response. Following an uncomfortable pause that Sophie found difficult not to fill with an explanation of her original question, Dennis spoke.

'Racehorses need to race,' he said, capturing Sophie's eye and staring fixedly at her, 'When they come to hand, or rather, when I'm ready for them to race, they are bursting with energy. To not allow them that release on a racecourse can make them boil over at home. And if I don't train them to get fit and ready to race, they may as well stay at home, as they'll never produce a winning performance on the track, especially with young horses like yours. You have to run them when they're ready, not when an owner suddenly decides they fancy a day out.'

Sophie opened her mouth, but never got to voice her rebuttal.

'Besides,' Dennis added swiftly, 'It's not really in the spirit of Mr Armitage's task… is it?'

This neatly nipped Sophie's intended response in the bud as a pang of guilt rippled through her.

'You must have to manage *all sorts* of owners. Surely our request isn't *that* difficult to work with?' Ruth suggested. Sophie winced, feeling Ruth might be attempting to spread her womanly charm a little too thickly.

'Oh, aye,' Dennis stated with a poker-face, 'I'm used to working with difficult, wealthy, and often opinionated people who have little knowledge of horses or racing.'

Ruth looked shocked for a moment, but to Sophie's surprise the woman tossed her head back and broke into one of her low, rumbling, desperately contagious laughs. Dennis seemed to appreciate this, beaming back at her. He placed his elbows on the table and clasped his hands together, studying the two women.

Once Ruth's laugh had subsided, she composed herself and asked, 'Did you know my brother well?'

'Ah! So you're his younger sister. I got a little confused with being introduced to a number of Armitages and your, er… disagreements. Yes, Greg was a good owner and I liked him a lot.'

Ruth frowned, allowing her eyelashes to flutter ever so slightly and asked, 'What makes a good owner?'

Dennis rubbed his chin as he locked eyes with Ruth. This was probably the question she'd wanted to ask earlier, before he'd refused to discuss his owners. Sophie thought Ruth had overdone the dramatic flutter of her lashes, but it seemed Dennis was amused by her cat and mouse tactics, his eyes twinkling slightly as he contemplated his answer.

Speaking in a deliberate voice, Dennis replied, 'A good owner is one who is patient, empathetic to a horse's needs, celebrates a win when it comes along in the knowledge the next one may be some time in coming… and pays his bills on time.'

Sophie grinned but Ruth was irked by this answer. She leaned back on her chair, cocked her head to one side and fixed Dennis with a troubled stare, 'Surely it must depend on an owner's motivation. It can't all be about winning a race?'

'How so?' Dennis prompted.

Sophie was sure he was tempting Ruth and sure enough, she waded in and attempted to answer her own question.

'Racing is about gambling. Surely owners simply want their horses to win in order to bet on them. The horse is just a means to get inside information on its chance in a race.'

'I don't wish to offend, but that's a very jaundiced view of horseracing, Miss Armitage.'

Ruth's eyebrows climbed her forehead and pinpricks of red began to pepper her cheeks.

'Many of my owners *never* place a bet on their horses. Some will spend thousands of pounds a month on keeping their horses fit and healthy, but will baulk at placing a bet of more than a fiver when it races. Others will own no more than a hoof in a syndicate, yet will stake eyewatering amounts on their horses. I suppose I'm suggesting that a good owner is one who finds joy in their involvement in the sport, be it from the experience, the days out… or even the gambling. The question is, what sort of owner will you be?'

Ruth eyed the trainer carefully. He was holding his chin in his hand, his forefinger tapping his bottom lip and staring at her expectantly. He displayed no inkling of an emotion. Sophie held her breath and didn't move.

Ruth stuck her lips out in contemplation, playing for time, but not for a moment dropping eye contact with Dennis.

'You have a point,' Ruth conceded, 'Made somewhat crudely I might add.'

Evidence of amusement curled up one side of her mouth, 'I shall endeavour to experience ownership, have days out racing… and I shall gamble. I'll tell you what sort of owner I am at the end of the season, Mr Smith.'

'I look forward to it,' Dennis said through a toothy grin.

'Is it always like this around here?' Sophie asked breathlessly.

'Oh, aye,' Dennis confirmed happily, 'Although this house has been somewhat lacking in the cut and thrust of informed argument like that for some time.'

There was a short pause, but Ruth soon directed the conversation back to Dennis.

'You live here alone?'

He blinked rapidly for a second or two, bemused by the sudden change in topic.

'I'm in the house alone, yes. But look out there and to the right,' he said, pointing towards the back garden, 'Four members of my staff live in that line of terrace houses, so I'm never alone really. The house is too big for me, but I've been here for so many years I can't ever see myself moving.'

Sophie had noticed when they first shook hands that Dennis didn't wear a wedding ring, but wasn't going to ask the question that immediately leapt to mind. Ruth, however, was reliably blunt.

'Do you have family, Dennis?'

'Divorced eight years ago,' he returned without hesitation, his concentration not wavering from his pouring of the tea, 'I got the yard and the house, she got everything else.'

He waved a hand skyward, 'No children, more's the pity, but I love the house and the work. Actually, this room was her idea when I come to think of it. I still see her – we parted good friends. Elaine is a successful trainer of Eventers and Dressage horses down Lincoln way now.'

Sophie watched Ruth's reaction to this titbit and tried to keep herself from grinning. From the engaged look on Ruth's face, it wasn't only the racehorses the spinster was impressed with this morning.

Sophie immediately scolded herself. After all, Ruth was only thirty-five and if there was anyone around here who was a spinster, it was herself, being three years older. She guessed Dennis was in his mid to late fifties, although he moved like a younger man. When she thought about it, Ruth had every right to be interested in him; for the most part she looked and acted like a much older woman.

They chatted for a while, Dennis showing enough passing interest in the ladies' private life without drilling into too much detail. Sophie had expected Ruth to dominate the conversation once Dennis asked about her, but was pleasantly surprised when she deflected the question and seemed far more interested in his training methods, feeding and exercise regimes, and race selection strategy. There was definitely more to Ruth than her sniping and sour looks.

Dennis eventually cast his eyes to his wall clock and realising the time, apologetically told the ladies he needed to head off and catch his farrier before he left the yard.

Sophie and Ruth made to get up with him but he insisted they stay to finish the pot and 'hoover up the biscuits' as he put it. He left them, promising to let them know when Fun Boy Frankie would be making his debut.

Sophie only realised when she'd driven a few miles towards York that the house hadn't smelled of cigarette smoke and Dennis hadn't lit up inside. As far as she could remember, she'd not seen an ashtray either. It appeared Greg had befriended a house proud, professional single man who possessed that rarest of qualities, a decent sense of humour. He'd also handed him on a plate to his sister, Ruth.

***

It was early evening when Martha set off walking into Norton. At a touch over a mile, she could make it a brisk pace and arrive in the town centre within twenty minutes, but she took it easy tonight, enjoying the sight of snowdrops in full flower and daffodils in bud on the roadside.

Living on the yard was enjoyable, however Martha had found that never leaving there day after day, especially in winter when there was hardly any flat racing, made her feel claustrophobic. A walk into Norton, or even continuing into Malton if sunlight hours allowed, gave her a sense of scale. Sometimes she would walk with friends, or she would cadge a lift off one of the stable lads with access to a car, but this evening she walked with Kilroy.

The German Shepherd lolloped happily beside her, staying well away from the verge, beyond which cars on Beverley Road could often scream past at annoyingly high speeds as they dropped into Norton from the surrounding hills. However Martha was lost in thought, paying little attention to the road. Her mind was full of her meeting with the new owners of Frankie.

They were a strange bunch, those three ladies, the girl decided. Apart from that awful Clara woman, the other two had shown sparks of interest in their horses, which puzzled Martha. She would do almost anything to own one, never mind two such wonderful animals. The more she thought about the three women, the greater her confusion became. And the first faint whips of anger, an anger Martha couldn't explain, began to lash at her insides.

With her mind occupied and eyes firmly set on the roadside path, Martha didn't notice the car that slowed to walking pace beside her until a young man's voice called out to her through the driver's window.

'Is it Martha?'

'Yes?' she replied, swinging round, expecting to see a lad from one of the local stables. She'd often be offered a lift if they saw her walking into town.

This wasn't any stable lad. He looked like a young professional, wearing a suit, although there was no sign of a tie.

'Hi there?' he said, looking slightly embarrassed, 'I... um, wondered if I could have a quick word with you?'

Martha peered into the car's interior, remaining several yards away on the path, Kilroy at her side. The young man gave the dog a quick look.

'Big, isn't he?' he commented, nodding at Kilroy, 'I reckon he must need a long walk every day, but if you're going into Malton I could give you a lift?'

'It's okay, thanks. Kilroy needs the exercise,' she lied, not so sure she wanted to get into a stranger's car, even if it was driven by a well-spoken young man with a friendly face and a decent job. That said, when she looked closer, he was younger than she'd thought, no more than a boy really.

The young man met this refusal with a glum expression.

'Actually, I wanted to ask you a few questions about the horses you look after,' he admitted sheepishly, 'It's the only chance I'll get, as I'm just about to drive back up to the North East. I've just visited my Grandmother over in Hull and was on my way back when I happened to see you. I've seen you leading up the Dennis Smith horses at the races you see.'

The boy's mouth curled up at the edges into a hopeful half-smile, 'I like a bet, just on a Saturday, mind you. Perhaps if I pull over and park up, could we walk the big chap together for a bit and you can fill me in on some of the horses you ride out? I actually know some of your owners. They have horses at your yard. It would be nice to know how they're getting along.'

Martha screwed her lips together. The boy's request seemed fair enough. She didn't mind discussing her horses, and the boy did have a sweet smile when he tried hard.

'Yeah, okay then,' she agreed, unaware she was digging her hands deep into her jacket pockets, mirroring the boy's embarrassment.

Minutes later, the young man was hanging on every word Martha spoke as she chatted away, swinging Kilroy's lead in her hand. They walked together for half a mile, stopping to sit on a bench just outside Norton-on-Derwent to continue their discussion. Martha noticed that throughout their conversation, her new companion kept a wary eye on the German Shepherd, careful to maintain a fair distance from Kilroy.

They returned to his car half an hour later and Martha waved the boy off in thoughtful mood. She jogged back to the yard with Kilroy, her mind full of thoughts of the cute young professional instead of the No Regrets syndicate.

Twelve

By the time Clara had arrived back home in Durham, she was in a foul mood. She'd hoped to enjoy an uneventful return journey up north, simply listening to the radio or some music, but instead, her drive had been interrupted by Gertrude Armitage.

Gertrude was, if anything, direct. The old woman had asked whether Ruth had turned up and then demanded a report on 'that Falworth woman'. Was she reliable? Would she turn up at the races? Clara had given her mother-in-law one word answers that had only served to make the old battle-axe more determined to ping even more queries at her. If it wasn't for the Armitages' being the only family Jeremy had, she'd have cut her off without a second thought. Clara viewed the Armitage family as nothing more than an annoyance. Yet she couldn't just ignore them – she knew what it felt like to have no family, and she didn't want that for her son.

Greg had been the Armitages' golden boy; the middle son who made good and propped them up financially. His father had died relatively young, leaving the family in poor financial shape, forcing Gertrude to slowly sell off chunks of the estate in order to stay in Armitage Hall. Greg had occupied a pedestal at which his mother and siblings were happy to worship, although Clara had always thought it could come tumbling down if her partner's money hadn't been available to bail his family out from time to time.

Greg wouldn't countenance any disparaging comments about his family. Ruth's dark looks and rudeness were overlooked. He'd been blind to Gertrude's sharp tongue, ignored Simon's foolishness, and refused to acknowledge his younger brother, Timothy, who was work-shy and possessed a sly streak a foot wide. Clara had been sure Greg knew his family's shortcomings, and his comments on his living will video had confirmed this. However, any salacious comment Clara had made to her husband about his family had been met with astonishment and an unwillingness to accept her version of events. After a few years, Clara had learned to keep her views to herself and put up with the Armitages' snide asides, rudeness, and self-deluded lies when Greg was around. Privately, she'd happily told each of them exactly what she thought of them, so instead of being part of Greg's family, she'd remained an outsider.

Funny how things work out, Clara thought as she let herself into her house, tossed her jacket aside and kicked off her heels. The Armitages had treated her with considerable distain over the years; always the butt of a joke here, or the subject of a cruel comment there. For the last seventeen years they'd treated her like Greg's mistress, and Jeremy like a bastard son: an embarrassing footnote in the Armitage family tree that deserved to be ignored. But now… *she* was in the driving seat.

Since Greg's funeral the Armitages had altered their allegiances, and as was their way, they'd done so immediately and with a complete lack of subtlety. Clara was currently being smothered with sugary-sweet attention by the Armitage family, and hated every second of it. Gertrude had been the first to call her to get a report on what happened at the yard in Malton. Clara had almost laughed at her; she was a symphony of narcissism. Every one of Gertrude's questions or comments revolved around one thing; what was best for Gertrude. Then she'd had an excruciating fifteen minute conversation with Simon Armitage, who had smarmed and slithered his way around the subject of his inheritance, probably believing he was being charming, when in fact he'd come across as downright creepy.

Hurrying over the thirty-foot-square marbled and mock pillared entrance to her executive home, Clara continued on, padding barefoot into the vast open-plan kitchen diner. The back of the house had a perfectly landscaped garden and a position on the valley side that overlooked the River Wear. The room felt too big, the view too impressive. Without Greg and Jeremy here, it all felt so vast… and empty.

Clara crossed to the kitchen area and smiled inwardly as she poured a large glass of white wine straight from the fridge, telling herself that a few drinks at lunchtime were allowed. Her first swallow was made before the liquid had the chance to settle in its glass.

Ruth had often referred to her behind Greg's back as 'the husband-stealer'. Clara let out a crackle of laughter as the wine sent a welcome shot of warmth around her body, dulling the headache she'd developed listening to Simon fawn over her. Now that their future wellbeing depended on her delivering their inheritance, she was going to have a bit of fun with the Armitages, and especially Ruth. At least it would take her mind off having to constantly bite her tongue when she was in Sophie's company.

Clara took a seat up on a high stool at her breakfast bar and after pouring more wine, studied her glass, running an index finger down its sculpted stalk to the flat crystal base. Only one thing was bugging her, and it wasn't the Armitages or Sophie Falworth; she'd soon leave them all behind. The real source of her headache was what she and Jeremy were going to do now Greg was gone.

For the last fifteen years she'd been an archetypal Managing Director's wife, which primarily consisted of arranging the odd dinner party or event for Greg's business partners and clients. She hadn't worked for the last fourteen years, once Greg's business took off. It hadn't been a demanding lifestyle, filling her days with shopping, gym sessions, hair, nails, facials and massage appointments, regular foreign holidays, and of course, doing lunch. Lunch had been the highlight of her day, but even that small pleasure managed to ebb away to nothing in her late twenties. For no apparent reason, she'd been left at the age of twenty-nine bored, and wholly dependent on Greg, who was too busy building his software empire to notice.

Thank goodness, Jeremy came along a couple of years later, Clara thought. She lifted her gaze to a range of photos on the far wall and a quickly fading smile graced her face when the images of her son as a toddler sparked the memory of his years at home with her. Now he was eight and she was already losing him to his pals at school, video games, and his collection of comics.

The chimes of the doorbell rocked her from this disturbing thought. She took another swig of her Pinot Grigio and tramped back through to the front of the house. A well-dressed, lean man in his late thirties with a long, smiling face appeared through the door's spyhole. His arrival managed to place a momentary smile on Clara's face and she pulled the door open. At least this visitor was on her side.

'Hiya, Paul, come on in. Want a glass of wine?' she called over her shoulder, allowing the door to swing wide open, already on her way back to the kitchen. Paul closed the door behind him and followed.

'I'll pass,' he replied, watching her replenish a half finished glass, 'It's quarter to eleven, I'll take a coffee'

It was so Paul. Non-confrontation and non-threatening was his way, and yet… she knew there was a query bubbling under his words.

'Really… only ten-forty-five,' she reflected, checking the tiny gold watch on her wrist but not really reading its dial.

'I was up and out so early today…' she said, her voice trailing off. She wasn't used to being out of the house before ten o-clock. She would get up to see Jeremy off to his private school at eight and often go back to bed once he'd left. Clara frowned, she'd imagined it had to be one o'clock in the afternoon by the time she'd got back; she seemed to have crammed plenty into the morning already, including becoming a shade tipsy.

Paul provided her with a warm smile and clicked the kettle on, 'You went up to Malton to meet Dennis Smith this morning, didn't you?'

'I had to get up at five-thirty to meet a nicotine-stained man, a woman I detest, another woman I detest, and a bunch of sweaty horses.'

'Oh, Dennis can be a bit curmudgeonly, but he's a decent chap I think. Greg told me what Dennis doesn't know about horses isn't worth knowing.'

'So you've met him?' Clara queried, pouring the remainder of her glass of wine into the kitchen sink.

'Greg took me. I've been to the yard once and I went racing a couple of times too. I don't know too much about racing, but it was always fun. Why didn't you come along?'

'You know Greg, he likes his… he *liked* his time alone.'

Paul didn't take the conversation any further. Instead, he busied himself searching for a second mug in the kitchen cupboard. He made Clara a black coffee and brought it over to her at the breakfast bar.

Clara sighed, 'Greg made it quite clear that racing was *his* thing and I wasn't welcome… he made a lot of things very clear to me in the last couple of years.'

Paul remained silent, preferring to lean against the breakfast bar a yard away from Clara, rather than take the seat beside her.

'Come on, Paul. You knew him better than anyone, perhaps even me. If Greg hadn't got cancer I think he'd have left me anyway. Instead, he's got his revenge by putting me through this stupid rigmarole with the two horses, Ruth, and Sophie blasted Falworth.'

Clara took a sip of her coffee and although wincing at the initially bitter taste, went on to take a deeper draft.

'The cancer made him see things differently. His priorities altered,' Paul stated softly once it became clear Clara had said her piece, 'I think he tried to fit a lot in once he was forced to accept he only had a short time to live.'

Clara snorted and shook her head, 'After receiving his diagnosis he lived for just five weeks. As far as I can see, the only thing Greg concentrated on in that time was how he was going to screw with me and my son.'

'He had to sell his business and sort out…'

Clara spun round in her seat and met Paul's eye, 'Don't you dare defend him. Greg wasn't here for the first three of those five weeks. He spent them at work, sorting out his precious company instead of being with his wife and son. When he finally came home for good he was already ill and then he insisted his family watch him grow weak and die. It was like Grand Central Station here in the last week. That was Greg; selfish right to the end.'

Clara spat the last few words at Paul with such venom he took an involuntary step back. The shock must have registered in his face, as Clara's expression immediately softened.

Cupping her coffee in both hands, Clara closed her eyes and sighed again. When she opened them again she cast her gaze out of the huge patio windows and down to the trees hugging the River Wear, 'I guess you're here to make sure I'm still going through with Greg's task.'

'I'm not here for that at all,' he objected, 'I came to see you. Of course I'm interested in how you got on, but that wasn't the main reason for calling round.'

Clara gave a faint, disappointed smile. Even Paul, Greg's greatest friend and with whom she'd been friends for almost twenty years, had been caught up in Greg's sticky web. She was certain he was here to check she'd done her job this morning and he'd called around in person to do it!

'The money's safe,' Clara murmured, 'I was a good little girl and did what Greg wanted; I put up with Sophie, and gave Ruth a wide berth.'

Paul frowned, 'I don't care about that.'

Clara slid a disbelieving look his way, slowly raising an eyebrow.

'I wondered if you wanted me to come with you to the races when the horses start running? There's nothing in the will that says you and Sophie can't have a guest for lunch, or you have to wander around the parade ring alone.'

Everything Paul did was measured. He never judged... he made his short, often insightful and honest comments and left the decision up to you. That's why Greg had insisted he join his company once it had started to grow. He'd been the perfect foil for Greg, who was often inspiring, but also dangerously impulsive. Greg had often referred to Paul as his calming influence; his voice of reason.

Clara's lip quivered and her eyes became glassy as Paul's words swirled around her. She sagged in her seat and grumpily leaned forward, elbows on the granite work surface, holding her cheeks in her hands.

Paul hadn't moved, remaining standing stock still, his hands by his side. He contemplated the woman in front of him with concern, unsure what to expect next. His pulse quickened when Clara kicked her feet from the stool and straightened. They locked eyes and he suddenly feared a further tirade against Greg and himself. Without a word she lunged forward from her high chair, wrapped her arms around him and hugged him tight, her cheek flat to his chest. She squeezed him for a few short seconds before releasing.

'Thank you,' said Clara, touching a tear away from the corner of her eye, 'It would be lovely to have you there at the races with me.'

Thirteen

April 7th 2016

'Yiv brokin' me sneck!'

'Shut up.'

'An' you stink of pepperoni, man...'

The youngster's voice was beginning to get on Bates's nerves, so he bounced the thief's head against the external brick wall of the pub and supported the boy as his eyes rolled back in their sockets.

The sound of heels clacking on cobbles came from around the corner of the pub.

'You feeling okay, lad?' he said, loud enough for the two young women to hear him as they passed the entrance to the side alley. Bates smiled over at them, noting they were suitably dressed for a night out in Newcastle; glittering crop-tops, short skirts, big hair, and high heels. The girl nearest to the alley glanced his way and Bates indicated his slumped friend was drunk by means of a shrug. She stopped to peer into the poorly lit alley.

'Need to get him home. The lad can't hold his beer.'

She nodded, giggled knowingly, linked arms with her companion and carried on walking toward the quayside.

A thick line of dribble exited the corner of the boy's mouth and joined one of the rivulets of blood from his nose. Together they dripped onto his fake Lacoste polo shirt. The lad – Bates reckoned he was no more than seventeen – took a few seconds to come around, but when his iris's flared and then contracted to focus on him, Bates released his grip and allowed him to lean against the pub wall unaided.

'Where you from?'

The boy began to raise his hand in order to deliver a rude gesture, only for Bates to batter it away. The boy whimpered, not knowing whether to clutch his newly injured wrist or his throbbing nose. His shoulders fell a few inches and he was immediately subservient, his eyes staring fixedly at the floor.

'Wallsend.'

'You been caught thieving in the pubs there?'

'Only once.'

'But they've all barred you in the area. Thought you'd try the city, eh? Easy pickings where no one knows you...'

'Sort of. Look fella, I divn't knaa...'

'Okay, give me 'em,' Bates ordered.

The lad lifted his chin and produced a sorrowful look, then in one swift movement transferred all his weight onto his right foot and pushed off, intending to bolt into the darkness of the alley. He enjoyed two paces of freedom before his accuser's boot swung into his legs, ensuring he crashed onto the cobbles. The boy lay there groaning and nursing his shin.

Bates shook his head, grabbed a fistful of polo shirt and wrenched the boy to his feet once more. He heaved him head first against the wall and kicking the pickpocket's legs open, Bates removed three mobile phones from his jeans pockets. He popped two of them into his jacket pocket and spun the lad around.

'If you weren't so thick you might be useful,' Bates told him, 'You might also realise I'm actually helping you. See this?'

He held up the third phone, a slim, expensive looking device with an equally lavish leather case. It was deeply monogrammed with the letters FRF and he waggled it intimidatingly in front of the lad's face.

'Francis Roger French,' Bates stated slowly.

The boy's eyes popped and he ran the back of his hand over his lips as he flicked his gaze between the phone and Bates.

'I nicked Fat Frankie French's phone?' he gulped.

'I admire the alliteration, but as soon as Fats finds it's gone, I fancy clever talking won't save you. He'll skin you alive. Considering he's done time for armed robbery, Fats is pretty black and white when it comes to his own property being stolen.'

'Tak it!' the lad pleaded, the pain in his nose and wrist forgotten, 'Tak it awa!'

Bates regarded the lad for a long moment.

'I'll put this right if you tell me your name. Your *real* name.'

The lad hesitated and for the first time took a proper look at the man who had ruined his night. Early forties, a whisker off six foot, and fit. He couldn't find an ounce of fat on him, and yet there was that peculiar smell on him - a fatty, acrid aroma. His shaved head accentuated his lined forehead, which dived into forgettable facial features except for his craggy chin. He wore a white t-shirt and brown leather jacket, dark pants and matching boots, and based on the throbbing coming from his shin, they were almost certainly steel toe-capped.

'Give me a false name and it'll take me longer to find you when I need my favour returned. I don't like wasting time. And if you think I won't find you, think again live wire. I know every corner of this city and move among people who make it their business to know who walks the streets on their turf.'

'Mike… Mike Tyson,' the boy stammered.

Bates stared at him.

'Really, I'm Michael Tyson,' he added bitterly, 'Blame me Mam, she'd never heard of the boxer.'

From the inside of Bates's jacket a phone buzzed but didn't ring.

He whipped it out without taking his eyes off his prisoner. Satisfied Michael wasn't in fit shape to run again he released his grip, tapped the answer icon on his phone and asked the caller to wait and placed them on hold.

He studied the lad once more.

'Go home, Michael. You've got good, soft hands but try pickpocketing in the city again and you'll get them chopped off. First rule; know you mark.'

As the lad began limping away into the comforting darkness of the alley, Bates called out after him, 'I'll be in touch, Michael.'

'Yes?' he said quietly into the phone.

He listened for thirty seconds, said, 'Soon. We've been following her for the past fortnight. Timing is everything.'

He waited another ten seconds and rang off without speaking again. So much for only contacting me by text message, he thought.

Bates strolled around the corner, entered The Bridge pub, reacquainted the phones with their initially surprised and subsequently delighted owners, and headed home, satisfied with his evening's work.

Fourteen

Saturday, 23rd April 2016

'Can't this rust bucket go any faster?' Clara moaned at Sophie from the back seat. Beside her, Ruth swore and told Clara to stop wriggling.

Hunched over the wheel of her car, Sophie ground her teeth for a moment before barking a reply.

'We'll get to Ripon on time, just calm down. Monty is going sixty five miles an hour, any faster and things start to drop off him.'

Dennis Smith had been in touch. As promised at the yard visit, the horse formally known as Frankie, now given a racing name of 'Fun Boy Frankie', was to have his debut run at Ripon. In accordance with Greg's wishes, all three of them had to be there.

Clara had set off from Durham with Ruth and Paul accompanying her, whilst Sophie had been making her own way there in Monty from York. She'd received Paul's call for help as she tootled up the left-hand lane of the A1(M). It seemed Clara's car had developed an engine problem at Scotch Corner services. With the recovery services unable to reach them for at least an hour, Paul had persuaded her to go out of her way continuing up the motorway to pick them up – in order to ensure Clara and Ruth didn't immediately fail Greg's task.

'Huh! Monty!' Clara snorted derisively, 'What is it with you and naming cars?'

'Don't start again, Clara!' Sophie warned, 'My Dad always named his cars. I do the same. If it wasn't for Monty you'd still be stranded at Scotch Corner services, desperately trying to find someone to repair your flashy SUV.'

Clara rolled her eyes dramatically in the hope Sophie might be watching her through the rear-view mirror. When it became clear she wasn't, Clara demanded, 'Stop the car and let me out then, I can't be doing with your sanctimonious blithering.'

'I'd happily leave you by the side of the road if we weren't on the motorway,' Sophie fired back, 'In fact, to hell with the law, I'll pull over now and you can walk back home to Durham up the hard shoulder!'

From the passenger seat, Paul gave a loud, exaggerated sigh and shook his head.

'This takes me back,' he complained, allowing a modicum of amusement to shine through his disappointment, 'I'd forgotten the two of you were experts in the art of bickering. At university it was sharper, and possibly contained more swear words, but you've both still got it. The big difference now is that you don't end by laughing at each other.'

He paused to shift in his seat and study the women one by one, hoping his statement might spark some distant memory of their lost friendship. He decided it hadn't - both of them were still simmering with barely concealed rage. Clara was staring grumpily out of her rain-splashed rear window and Sophie was concentrating fixedly on the slow lane of the motorway and gripping the steering wheel so hard her knuckles were white. Ruth was sitting primly in the back seat, staring disinterestedly out of her own window.

'Seriously, can't the two of you get on? We've only been in this car for ten minutes and I've had to listen to three separate arguments and endure two awkward silences. For heaven's sake, it's been seventeen years since the wedding. When will the two of you wake up? You are still perfect friends for each other and now Greg's gone you have the opportunity to bury the hatchet.'

'She stole my husband, reported me to the police, and...' Sophie started. At the same time Clara piped up with, 'She wrecked our flat, and beat me up, and...'

'I *know*!' Paul butted in above the whingeing, 'I was there, remember.... So you both did some... stuff, but look at the two of you. You're experienced, mature women, yet you argue like you're still teenagers! It's stupid. You're both *stupid*.'

Paul had raised his voice to a pitch where his final words seemed to reverberate around the cabin of the little car, forcing the two women to take a breath.

'You've changed, Paul,' Clara pointed out, once the hum of the car's engine had returned, 'You used to be so quiet and unassuming.'

'And you're treating us like spoilt children,' Sophie added reproachfully.

Paul looked over from his passenger seat and regarded the driver with an exaggerated comic grimace, 'I think you know what my response to that statement will be... Then stop acting like...'

'Yes, alright, Paul,' sniffed Sophie.

'Just think about it the two of you. You made a great team when you were friends. Both Greg and I thought the same. He knew you couldn't be reconciled whilst he was still around, but now he isn't. It might be a bit ham-fisted, but this... *task* is his way of trying to get you two back together.'

'Yes, we got that,' Clara grumbled from the back seat, 'It's just a shame he's made me into the Armitage family financial saviour in the process.'

Ruth cocked her head toward her fellow passenger and glared at Clara, hissing, 'It's *always* about you, isn't it?'

Clara ignored her, 'And I don't like the thought of us being followed around by some sort of undercover detective. Just the idea of being watched makes my flesh creep.'

'Agreed,' chimed in Sophie.

Paul leaned back in his seat, happy in the knowledge that he'd at least managed to get the two women united in their criticism of Greg's will. He could hear Greg speaking to him only weeks before from his sick bed: 'Small wins, Paul. That's the way with those two. Small wins along the route to reconciliation.'

***

When Sophie finally pulled the handbrake up in the Owners car park at Ripon racecourse, Monty's clock read one-thirty. The traffic had become heavier as they approached the racecourse, which Sophie had noted with some relief was actually on the outskirts of the North Yorkshire town; she hadn't fancied having her passengers judge her ability to navigate a busy town centre. She was at best, a cautious driver, even on streets she knew well. And she'd been lucky, managing to avoid an accident close to the racecourse that could have made them terribly late.

On turning into Ripon racecourse, Sophie was struck by the majesty of the mature trees that lined the entrance road, and the sheer volume of cars parked on the neatly clipped grass car parks. Long rows of cars stretched into the distance to her right, and she was pleased when Paul advised her they would be parking on the left, in a smaller, less busy area reserved for owners and trainers. She was directed by the race-day staff onto the grass and a chap in a fluorescent tabard waved Monty into a space beside a Porsche. A brand new Range Rover followed her into the next free spot and Sophie thought she glimpsed a snigger from the driver when he looked down at her little car, many feet beneath him.

'Have any of you been racing as an owner before?' asked Paul as he unfolded himself from the Nissan Micra. He was well over six feet tall, and even in her passenger seat, Sophie had noticed he'd had to travel with his knees awkwardly pulled close to his chest.

All three women shook their heads.

'At least, not recently,' Ruth qualified.

'No worries! Follow me.'

They'd driven through several sharp showers on their way, and the grey sky promised there was more to come. Grabbing coats, bags, and brollies, the women allowed Paul to lead them through lines of expensive vehicles in the owners car park, across a white fenced walkway for horses, and over to one of several single level red brick buildings linked by a tall wall. More than likely built in the 1930's, they reminded Sophie of army mess huts, but when they entered the double doors emblazoned with an 'Owners and Trainers' sign, they were greeted with a smile, rather than a salute, from the lady and gentleman situated behind a small counter.

'I took the liberty of ordering us Owners' Badges for today,' Paul explained after giving their names and Fun Boy Frankie's to the lady, who busied herself checking several sheets of printed paper attached to a clipboard.

'Ah yes, Mr Paul Corbridge plus three,' the lady confirmed, running her biro through a line on her printout. She handed each of them a racecard and a thick card ticket cut in the shape of a shield. The word 'Owner' stood out, being printed in bold black ink. Each badge came tied with maroon coloured string and once the elderly chap protecting the open door into the racecourse had conscientiously punched a small hole in each shield, Paul helped the ladies attach them to their buttonholes.

'You'd better hurry,' the doorman warned them as they edged past him, 'You're in the first race and the horses are already entering the paddock.'

Stepping into the premier enclosure of a racecourse for the first time, Clara was surprised with how relaxed and... well, *nice* everything appeared. It was as if she'd walked into a well-kept garden, from the lawn she was standing on, to the myriad of spring flowering plants. A champagne bar to her left was serving happy people sitting at tables out in the open. To her right the winner's enclosure and weighing room bustled with officials and the odd jockey, and in front of her a large oval parade ring was spotted with impressive trees that shaded racegoers and horses, alike when the sun broke through the clouds in short bursts. The sound of a distant brass band came to her above the hum of the crowd and staring past the parade ring and into the distance, Clara managed to pick out a bandstand. There was colour everywhere, even in April. A multitude of beds, hanging baskets, and window boxes full of flowering plants adorned every building as well as the parade ring itself.

Men wore suits or refined country wear and the ladies, despite the cool day and the threat of showers, had clearly made an effort to dress to impress. There was also a sense of anticipation in the air, and that little buzz of controlled excitement was strangely intoxicating. It wasn't quite what she'd expected.

Clara's only experience of horseracing had been a trip to York racecourse with a hen party when she'd been twenty. They'd spent the entire afternoon drinking in a large marquee at the back of the stands whilst being leered at by large groups of drunk young men. She'd never seen a horse in the flesh all day, nor in a race for that matter, as she and her pals had drunkenly staggered out of the racecourse gates late in the afternoon. The scene before her promised a completely different experience and she had to admit to being mildly curious of what the afternoon might bring.

Clara was still enjoying the scene when she became aware the sleeve of her coat was being tugged. She found Sophie urging her to get a move on. Without thinking, Clara smiled back.

'Come on!' insisted Sophie, ignoring Clara's smile, 'We have to be in the parade ring before the race; it's one of the requirements of Greg's task! Otherwise we might as well go home now!'

Clara snapped back into the present, lost her smile and followed Sophie and Ruth, who in turn were tracking Paul as he picked his way around the parade ring. Dennis had told them Fun Boy Frankie would be running in the first race on the afternoon card, and the race was due off at 2-05pm. Clara checked her watch; it was a quarter to two.

Paul stopped half-way around the parade ring and waved them between two sets of concrete steps filled with race-goers watching a line of horses walk around the parade ring with their stable lads and lasses. A steward doffed his cap as they squeezed past.

'Come on, into the ring,' Paul called hurriedly, 'Before the horses come this way.'

Sophie and Clara did as they were told, walking over a spongy red walkway, presumably kind to the horse's feet, and found themselves on the manicured grass inside the parade ring. Ruth followed, holding back slightly. Several hundred sets of eyes followed the foursome as they walked under the trees looking out for their trainer.

'Now then you three,' Dennis called out as he strode across the grass. It appeared he'd entered the parade ring earlier and had been waiting for them.

'Four actually,' Sophie pointed out as they shook hands.

'Ah! Good to see you again,' Dennis said, catching Paul's eye. He turned his smile on Clara, Ruth, and Sophie then nodded toward the gelding, 'So what do you think, compared to the others?'

'Greg was the one interested in horses, not me,' Clara admitted, 'You're better off asking Paul.'

'Nonsense,' Dennis replied directly.

The trainer bowed his head and beckoned the women to come closer.

'Frankie won't be winning today, he'll need this run. You see that colt over there?' he indicated a tall, mostly bay horse with a splash of white on its forehead being led around by not one, but two handlers, 'It's already had a sighting run and is probably a ninety rated horse in the making. At this time of the season racing experience is worth a couple of lengths. He's headstrong, but he should be winning this. See how he uses his walk, he's got a natural swagger...'

The three women listened attentively as Dennis proceeded to provide a similar commentary on several of the other runners, pointing out which of them were light, carrying condition, needed to fill out, were too angular, hadn't come in their summer coats, or were like Fun Boy Frankie; in need of a run and likely to run 'green'. None of the ladies understood the entire conversation, as Dennis managed to sprinkle his words of wisdom with phrases and racing terms that meant very little to the first-time owners. Paul soon caught their blank expressions and silenced Dennis by suggesting it was time to take the photos that would prove all three of them had attended this April run.

As Paul declared he was happy with the resulting photo, he was interrupted by the arrival of their jockey who held the tip of his cap in deference and shook the ladies hands firmly. Despite wearing a helmet that covered much of his face, and wearing brightly coloured green and orange silks, Sophie recognised their rider from their morning at the yard. Mitch Corrigan had a big grin on his face, mirroring the one he'd given them on the gallops.

'Today's the day, then ladies!' he announced pertly in his soft Irish accent, slapping his thigh enthusiastically with his whip, 'This fella's first day at school, eh?'

Ruth nodded her agreement but once again, both Clara and Sophie didn't quite see the relevance of the reference.

Realising the two women were a little lost, Paul stepped forward and asked, 'How's he been going at home, Mitch?'

'Frankie ain't no world-beater, but he's got a big heart. He'll probably run around a little, especially on the undulations, but I imagine we'll still be beating a bunch of this lot home.'

Before Sophie could query what 'undulations' might be, a bell rang out from the centre of the parade ring and the grin fell from Mitch's face.

'Time to go, ladies. Don't worry, I'll bring the lad home safe and sound.'

'What does he mean, why would we be worrying?' Clara asked Paul urgently once Mitch and Dennis had left them to walk to the edge of the parade ring in order to intercept Frankie and his stable lass.

Paul explained, 'These animals are athletes, and just like human athletes they sometimes suffer injuries. Mitch was letting you know that he's not going give Frankie an unduly hard time and will look after him during the race. After all, he has his entire racing career ahead of him.'

They watched Dennis flip Mitch onto the gelding's back and the rider dug the toes of his shiny black boots into the steel stirrups high on the gelding's sides. Walking to the end of the parade ring Clara and Sophie followed Frankie's progress down a chute that led to the racetrack. He got lost behind the crowd, but Sophie caught sight of Mitch bobbing up and down on the gelding's back as Frankie turned to his right and kicked off down the track at a canter. Horse and rider disappeared behind the side of a building. She looked again and realised it was the back of a grandstand.

'Come on, we'll find a vantage point to watch the race,' said Paul, once again setting off with the three women in tow.

They found a position half-way up the large steps of the lower stand, almost in line with the winning post. In the centre of the course, a large television screen showed the horses milling around in front of the starting stalls.

'Where are they?' Sophie asked.

'Right down at the bottom of the straight,' replied Paul, pointing to the brightly coloured dots in the distance to his right.

'How many times do they go around?' Sophie queried, having noticed that the track was a large oval. After the finishing post it continued around a sharp bend, past a caravan site and around the edge of a huge lake.

Paul chuckled, opening his race card to the 2-05pm race. He spent the next two minutes pointing out all the race details, with Clara peering over his shoulder, also taking in the information. On the step above, Ruth consulted her own racecard throughout, appearing to ignore the conversation but secretly making mental notes.

'The youngsters like Frankie start racing over five furlongs at this time of year. That's the shortest sprint distance – so they jump out of the stalls and run straight for a little over half a mile until they reach the finish over there,' Paul said, gesticulating towards the track and a pole topped with a red circle, it's stem fitted with mirrors.

With all this fresh information still swirling around their minds the racecourse commentator announced the stalls handlers were starting the loading process and their attention was drawn to the huge screen once more. Clara wouldn't admit to it, but she held her breath when a stalls handler led Fun Boy Frankie forward. To her horror, she suddenly realised she was trembling with excitement. Her heart was pounding and she felt genuinely nervous. To her relief, the youngster slotted into his stall with the minimum of fuss.

'Follow the race on the television screen for the first couple of furlongs,' Paul advised, 'But once they're in range, switch to looking up the course to spot your green and orange colours – it's far more exciting when it's live in front of you instead of on a television screen.'

'Shouldn't we have a bet on Frankie?' asked Sophie, casting her gaze down on the line of bookmakers on the concourse in front of them. Their electronic boards advertised Fun Boy Frankie as an eight-to-one shot. Perfect Shot, the horse Dennis had pointed out to them was showing odds of eleven to ten, which Sophie assumed meant he was the well-fancied favourite.

Paul glanced at the television screen in the centre of the course, 'It's too late, they'll be off in a few seconds.'

When he saw Sophie deflate slightly, he quickly pointed out that in a way, all three of them were already backing Frankie.

'As owners, you've paid a fee of about forty pounds to enter him for this race, and if he manages to come home in the first four, prize-money will be credited to your Weatherby's account. You'll all share about three thousand pounds if Frankie wins, and a few hundred if he gets placed.'

Clara frowned, 'That's all it costs, thirty pounds to run a horse in a race?'

Paul gave a soft laugh, 'Hardly, it's another two hundred for your jockey fees, fifty pounds in lead-up fees, plus transport, which could be anything from fifty to a few hundred pounds, depending on the distance and the type of transport. Then there are the registrations and monthly Weatherby's fees for managing your account, Dennis's training fees, and not forgetting the gallop fees.'

'You seem to know an awful lot about the costs involved,' Ruth challenged.

Paul nodded his agreement, 'Greg got obsessed with the commercial side of racing. He was amazed at the money involved and would talk about it endlessly when he first got involved a few years ago. He didn't want his finance guys seeing the details, so I used to help him sort out his business and personal expenses – some of the vets bills made my eyes water! Oh, hey, watch out, they'll be off any second.'

Clara turned to face the huge television screen on the inside of the course with Paul's words ringing bells in her head. Greg had bored her with all this nonsense about training fees and race fees – even the cost of a set of clothes for the jockey, insisting they were referred to as 'silks'. It was in stark contrast to how he managed his own personal wealth, as he'd always kept the state of their finances a closely guarded secret. She'd never known exactly how well his business was going, and he'd always insisted on managing all the household bills himself.

'And they're off,' called the commentator over the public address system.

Clara and Sophie scoured the image on the screen for any sign of Fun Boy Frankie's green jacket with an orange spot on the chest and an orange cap. She hadn't made the link before, but Clara suddenly realised the jockey's silks were the same as the corporate colours of Greg's software business. And there they were; Frankie was towards the back of the field.

'He was slowly away,' Paul noted.

'Three furlongs to run and the warm favourite, Perfect Shot, has taken a two length lead,' called the race commentator. He listed the other eleven runners in their order and completed the synopsis with the words,

'... and Purple Fields and Fun Boy Frankie are still in rear.'

'Oh dear,' Sophie muttered.

'Hold up,' said Paul, 'Mitch hasn't started pushing him yet.'

As the field reached the two furlong pole, one by one the jockeys started to pump their hands up their young mounts necks as they urged them forward. A few pulled their whips through, but Mitch Corrigan wasn't one of them. He was threading his way through toiling competitors without resorting to his whip.

'Frankie's passing them!' Clara called out excitedly. She quickly glanced round at Sophie, Paul, and finally Ruth, who was standing behind and above her. Beside her, Sophie and Paul appeared equally excited, but, she was forced to take a second, longer look up at Ruth. Her usual resentful scowl had evaporated, replaced with wide eyed, ruddy-faced trembling as she focused on the horses. Along with her dress, shoes and cardigan all being too tight for her, it seemed to Clara that Ruth was trying hard to keep from exploding.

Perfect Shot was already in splendid isolation at the head of the field, three lengths clear of his nearest challenger as he flashed past the furlong pole. However, the women were oblivious to what was happening at the front of the race, they concentrated solely on Frankie and Mitch, and how the gelding was cutting through the pack under a hands and heels ride. From a seemingly impossible position in the rear of the field, Frankie had gone past three horses in a matter of two strides, then into eighth, seventh, then suddenly fourth as the volume of the packed crowd in the grandstand swelled in the closing stages of the race.

Frankie took a definite third with half a furlong to run and started to chase down the horse in second who in turn, was a length and a half behind the leader.

Unable to hold in her excitement any longer, Ruth bellowed, 'Come on, Frankie!' at the top of her lungs.

Laughing at Ruth, Clara soon found herself screaming Frankie's name, and holding both her fists up in front of her. She was aware Sophie and Paul were making similar noises, but couldn't tear her eyes from the race. In the last two strides her horse flashed past the winning post alongside his weakening rival for second place. *Her* horse she thought, contemplating what that meant for a moment, through a mixture of pride and excitement.

Paul had already hopped down two of the massive grandstand steps and turned wide-eyed to face Sophie, Clara, and a red-faced Ruth, 'He's in a photo for second place. Come on you lot, you need to be at the winners' enclosure!'

Ruth was breathless, with a silly grin plastered to her face. She'd not shouted that loud for years and could feel a few pinpricks of soreness at the back of her throat, but ignored it, setting off after Paul. Sophie was buzzing and inadvertently glanced at Clara. It was only a fraction of a second, but the two of them enjoyed a returned smile for the first time in seventeen years.

Horrified to realise she was grinning, Clara forced her features to harden. It wasn't easy, it seemed her cheeks had set and suddenly, producing a smile was far easier than a frown. She rubbed at her cheek bone as she followed Sophie down the steps, through a forest of chattering people, and joined a small stream of race-goers who, like Paul, seemed to know where they were going.

The trio of ladies managed to make it to the winners' enclosure just before Frankie and the other two horses were led in, during which time the public address system announced Fun Boy Frankie had finished third, with the winning distances being a length and a quarter, and a nose.

Dennis greeted them under the third placing pole in the winners' enclosure with a nicotine-stained smile. Having delivered Clara, Ruth, and Sophie as quickly as possible to Dennis, Paul hung back once they started speaking to their trainer, patting Fun Boy Frankie's neck, and sharing a few comments with Mitch and especially Martha, whose smile lit up the winners' enclosure. Paul noticed the trainer's smile subtly change from something rather set and practiced, into a pleased beam when he realised all three ladies were genuinely thrilled with the gelding's performance.

Fifteen

Once Ruth and Sophie had given Frankie a final pat to say well done, he and the first two finishers departed the winners' enclosure. Clara's eyes lit up when Dennis suggested they all meet up at the champagne bar once he and Martha had seen Fun Boy Frankie safely back to the racecourse stables. He promised to rejoin the three of them, plus Paul, in a matter of minutes.

Thanks to a cool glass of Pimms and a rather indulgent prawn salad sandwich, Sophie was still experiencing the high from the race fifteen minutes later. She wasn't used to being profligate with her money, but when Paul pointed out that Greg was paying for everything, she allowed herself to indulge. The group discussed the start of the race, Frankie's progress through the field, and especially his finishing spurt in the dying strides.

Sipping at her quickly dwindling glass of champagne, Clara let the racing conversation wash over her, preferring to sit back and allow her drink to relax her. She watched Dennis approach their table and was surprised when Ruth jumped up from her chair to greet him. She'd never seen her sister-in-law move so fast, or with such grace, and was momentarily fascinated to see how things developed. Ruth immediately engaged Dennis in earnest conversation, pulling the trainer's sleeve to ensure he sat down beside her. To Clara's continued surprise it seemed Dennis was more than happy to be captured. Clara's natural reaction was to butt into their heart to heart, simply to rile Ruth, but discovered she couldn't be bothered. Instead she drained the last of the bubbles from her glass.

Refreshing her champagne from the bottle Paul had bought for the table, Clara leaned back in her chair and closed her eyes. This was... nice, she decided, wondering why Greg had only ever taken her racing once. She tried to recall the evening at Newcastle races almost three years ago, but frustratingly the memory was dominated by an argument they'd had. She couldn't even remember what it was about.

Sophie was drinking mineral water, yet she was enjoying a warm, hazy state of mind. As Paul was drawn into a conversation with Dennis and Ruth, she allowed her gaze to wander from the glorious display of flowers around them to the paddock, where the runners for the second race of the day were beginning to be led around by their handlers.

Despite the warm afternoon, Sophie shivered. It was the way he'd been standing that made her look back to confirm the strange déjà-vu moment she'd just experienced.

It was the tall man with his back to her. He was dressed in a mustard coloured linen suit with scuffed trousers, badly wrinkled around the back of his knees, and had a closely shaved head. He might be young, she couldn't be sure of that until he turned around. However, it was the manner with which he held himself that struck a chord. He was bowlegged. Not desperately bandy, but the sort where the knees turned out to give him a notably wide stance. Sophie probably wouldn't have recognised him from his side profile, but from behind she had little doubt. She'd seen the same man some days earlier.

So she'd seen the bandy man just recently, but couldn't quite place him. At least, she thought she recognised him... Sophie looked away towards the winners' enclosure, mulling over the conundrum of where and when. By the time she'd doubled back to stare quizzically in the man's direction he had stepped between race-goers milling around the paddock and she'd lost him.

'... so I was thinking we'll head to Scotland with Frankie next,' Sophie heard Dennis say whilst shaking the bandy man's image from her mind.

'That'll suit me,' Clara enthused as she polished off her second glass of champagne.

'Me too!' added Ruth.

Paul leaned back and allowed himself a congratulatory grin as he sipped on his sparkling mineral water. The girls were having a good time.

Dennis went on to explain that the next race, at a racecourse called Hamilton, located south-east of Glasgow, would be a lower class event and he expected Frankie would be more than capable of putting in a winning performance.

'He'll come on a bundle for today's run and Hamilton is a similar five furlongs to Ripon. The racing will be less competitive and he can hopefully get a win on the board,' enthused Dennis.

'It's about four weeks away, and will give him a week's rest on Doc Green and then we'll build him back up again.'

Clara frowned, 'Doc Green?'

'Doctor Green. Green grass,' Dennis grinned, 'Nothing better for a horse than fresh spring paddock grass. Settles their nerves, builds them up, and drives all the impurities out of their system. It's like giving them a full medical without the vet getting involved.'

'I get the same effect when I drink Red Bull,' Sophie said without thinking and was surprised when the table erupted in a crackle of laughter.

After the second race had run and the winner and placed horses had been led past them, Dennis left to saddle his second runner. It was a handicapper in a later race that would, he claimed, 'badly need the race' and not to pin any hopes on it getting placed. He'd walked a few paces away from the table before stopping, and turning back.

'I almost forgot. I've registered your second colt's racing name for you,' he told Clara. She stared back at him, none the wiser.

'Name it whatever you want, you told me last time we met,' he prompted with one eyebrow raised.

'Right. Yes, of course. I remember,' Clara blustered uncertainly.

'So it's been named. I'm told is quite appropriate, given he's known as 'Quo' in the yard. Certain members of my stabling team told me so, although I've no idea why.'

'I'm sorry, Dennis,' Clara pleaded, 'I don't quite understand. What's the horse's name then?'

Dennis gave her a yellow-toothed grin.

'We've called the colt 'Whatever You Want'.'

Clara stared back at the trainer, trying desperately to regain the thread and make sense of their conversation.

'I think Dennis took your naming instructions quite literally,' Paul interjected smoothly.

It took a few seconds, but eventually Clara's face crinkled into a smile of understanding, 'I get the Quo reference now,' she nodded.

'Actually, I like the name,' she added, looking up at Dennis with a sparkle in her eye, 'I'm glad I chose it.'

Dennis beamed, 'Oh, and do you remember that black horse that you saw on the gallops a few weeks ago? It worked in the lot after Frankie.'

Clara and Sophie nodded.

'He's been named Charlie Soap, and he runs his first race in twelve days' time at Chester in a Novice race over five furlongs. You might want to keep an eye out for Charlie,' Dennis said with a wink before departing for a second time.

'I wonder why the owner chose Charlie Soap as a name,' Clara pondered out loud as she watched their trainer duck under the white railings of the paddock chute and follow the unplaced horses to the stabling area at the back of the racecourse.

Paul tapped on his mobile phone for a few seconds before announcing, 'According to Google, Charlie Soap was the well-known husband of an American Indian activist. I'm guessing the family pedigree must have some reference to them.'

Clara tipped the last of her champagne into her mouth and enjoyed the bubbles as they fizzed on her tongue before swallowing, 'Wasn't he the boy in Charlie and the Chocolate Factory?'

Paul laughed, 'That was Charlie Bucket!'

From the other side of the paddock, Simon Armitage played with the zoom function on his camera until he achieved a sharp image of the table as Paul and the three women shared a joke. He took several quick photos, lowered the camera and maintained his gaze over at the champagne bar from under the rim of his hat. That was enough photos now. He'd got plenty of them in the parade ring.

Simon was pleased the three women were getting on. He'd always felt he hadn't done enough to support Sophie on her failed wedding day – none of his family had. They'd rallied around Greg; it was the Armitage way. He still carried that guilt with him. Somehow there'd never been the right opportunity to tell Sophie how sorry he was for what went on that day.

It was also pleasing to see Clara with a smile on her face for a change. Her outspoken manner and snobbishness was a little hard to take on occasions, however, she'd stayed loyal to his brother despite his failings as a husband and father. She'd always been an outsider, and remained so, despite her son bearing the Armitage name. Simon reflected that he seemed to be the only member of his family who respected Clara for placing the youngster first.

However, the majority of his attention had focused on his sister Ruth. He'd been watching her closely when she'd been speaking with her trainer, their heads bowed closely together. She'd suddenly thrown her head back and laughed, and the older man had done the same. He'd stared at Ruth through his lens for a long moment, remembering the strange shiver that had run through him at the sight of his sister enjoying the man's company.

He squinted harder through the view-finder, still watching his sister. There was a confident stillness about her now the trainer had left. Simon lowered his camera and stared down at the concrete step on the parade ring viewing gallery he'd chosen for its elevated position. He checked some of the images and was pleased to find he'd captured that moment of his sister's joy.

He decided his task was complete, and against the flow of race-goers, Simon headed for the exit. He walked slowly, so as not to raise attention to himself, tilting his Fedora downwards to place most of his face in shade. With each step he took, a feeling of betrayal grew within him. His fervent hope was that the pictures he'd taken would never need to be used. No matter how many times he ran this thought through his mind it did nothing to assuage a gnawing sense of foreboding.

Sixteen

May 5th 2016

Whenever people asked, Sophie would tell them bereavement counselling was a vocation that had found her, rather than a career path she had planned from the start. A few months of volunteering for the Samaritans after university had been followed by twelve years working in numerous roles for a charity supporting victims of crime. Those years had given her the grounding, and experience of working with deeply traumatised, vulnerable people, very often in difficult situations. However, it took the loss of both her parents in quick succession to make her realise how suited she was to supporting people suffering from a bereavement.

She seemed to have the right balance of empathy, understanding, and strength, combined with the ability simply to listen… allowing a grieving person to describe how they were feeling and what thoughts were running through their mind.

After returning to her local college as a mature student, Sophie had completed the relevant courses in her early thirties and became a self-employed bereavement counsellor. Drawing upon her charity connections she managed to pick up referrals from several charities, government bodies, and with a growing number of private clients, she made just enough money to keep a roof over her head and Bella supplied with her favourite dog food and treats.

There were good days and bad days. On the good days she would return home to her upstairs flat and cook; she'd become a bit of a 'foodie' in recent years. However, on the bad days, she and Bella would hit the streets, parks, and pavements of York. Whatever the weather Sophie could walk for miles with her greyhound trotting happily by her side. On this particular night, the dark skies and persistent rain were a reflection of Sophie's state of mind. She was concerned for a client, a woman in her late twenties who had lost her six-year-old son in a traffic accident.

The key to maintaining her own sanity was not to continually dwell on her clients' problems. Her dog walk might start with her mind full of issues, but she would methodically address each one and settle on a course of action. It was rare to completely solve an issue, grief didn't present any easy options. But once each problem had a next step, a positive action, Sophie would file it away in that part of her brain that was ring-fenced for work. The rest of the walk would provide her with the opportunity to release the pressure, concentrate on other things, and clamber down from the dizzying heights to which her working day had taken her.

Sophie was trudging down Tadcaster Road in the unrelenting

spring rain when she hit upon an idea; a possible course of action that could aid her client. Having committed this solution to memory, she sensed the pressure of work lift. Her breakthrough acted like a release valve. Sophie raised her head and looked around. She'd hardly been aware, but had reached a path opposite the Knavesmire, the huge expanse of flat common land that was home to York Racecourse. Bella was drenched, but the dog still returned a look that held anticipation for a run off the lead.

Two minutes later the greyhound was careering across the vast flat mire that in past centuries had hosted the hanging of convicted criminals; the 'knaves' of the mire. A smiling Sophie watched as Bella cavorted in huge circles around her, her paws splashing through newly created puddles in the undulating ground, pleased she'd decided to wear her wellies this evening.

Sophie had no reason to feel vulnerable. The moon was almost full, so despite the rain clouds scudding overhead, its reflected rays lit the Knavesmire in short bursts. Besides, there were plenty of streetlights, a couple of other dog walkers were also braving the rain, and she was surrounded by busy roads and suburban sprawl in virtually every direction.

So when a lone man with a strangely familiar, open gait left the path that led to the racecourse and started to head towards her across the dark green expanse of the Knavesmire, Sophie took notice, but initially wasn't concerned. At thirty yards away, Sophie took a long look at him, and purposefully changed direction as a precaution. He altered his course and broke into a run.

Sophie called Bella and took a look around her, taking in the position of other dog walkers. She could probably scream and be heard…

'Missus Falworth,' called the man, stemming Sophie's imminent scream for help. It was a young, thin voice. Early twenties, perhaps younger she guessed. He dropped to a trot and covered the last twenty yards at a walk. Of moderate height and thin, a hoodie masked his face. Sophie noticed his knees poked out sideways with each step, giving the young man an angular feel as he approached. A mental image of the thin, bandy man at Ripon races flashed across her mind.

'Stay there!' she called out as he came closer.

The man obeyed, coming to rest in a puddle five yards away. He wore muddied trainers and tan cord trousers that had a tell-tale ridge at the bottom, indicating they'd been let down. Yet they were still too short for him; an inch of red sock was displayed. Bella must have sensed the fear in her voice as the dog came to her side, touching her shoulder to Sophie's thigh.

'Don't worry, Missus. I'll not touch ya,' he said, burying his hands in the pockets of his increasingly sodden hoodie.

Sophie squinted into the black recesses of his hood. He was holding his head slightly bowed, only the tip of a thin, bony nose poked out. He coughed without removing his hands from his pockets, 'You ain't gotta go to the races, ok?'

'What did you say?'

'You ain't gotta go racing. You thick or somethin'?'

Sophie's eyes narrowed for a moment, but then she took in the figure again. The arms of his hoodie had shrunk to stick to his skin, revealing terribly thin limbs. His clothes were cheap and threadbare, in several places she could see holes that hadn't been repaired. He was probably cold. A gap in the clouds allowed moonlight to shine down on him for a few seconds.'

'Have you eaten today?'

The boy looked up in surprise and Sophie stared unblinking into the face of what she was sure was a teenage boy. He was pale and his skin seemed to cling paper-like to his cheekbones. She was struck with how unwell he appeared, a look that wasn't helped by the lack of two front teeth.

'I... yeah, I...'the boy stammered at first before his mouth curled into a snarl, 'Get stuffed, lady,' he growled, removing a hand from his hoodie pocket and pointing a bony finger at her, 'You stay away from the gee-gees, alright!'

'Or what? Are you going to shout at me again and try to scare me?'

He bared his gap-toothed teeth in a wicked grin, enjoying Sophie's response. It was time to show this frumpy old woman he meant business. Tearing the hood from his head, he revealed a shaved head and several blue tattoos of what appeared to be dragons on both sides of his neck. Sophie took in his skeletal face and tried not to show her shock. The boy had to be ill.

'If you try goin' racin' I'll stop you,' he said, weaving his head from side to side, as if preparing himself for a fist fight.

Bella didn't move from Sophie's side, regarding the boy carefully, only blinking when a raindrop fell onto her eyelashes.

'Okay, I get it. You don't want me to go to the races.'

'Or you'll be sorry,' the boy sneered.

He paused, as if it was Sophie's turn to speak and he was uncertain what to do without a feed line.

'Okay,' Sophie repeated, a little louder this time, 'I promise not to go racing.'

The boy coughed. His whole body shook in response. He restored his hood, forcing the sodden material over his scalp. Digging his hands deep into his pockets, he turned to leave.

She didn't know where the thought came from. It just popped into her mind, swam around for a couple of seconds and seemed to make sense. He was wet, cold, and as far as she could make out, ill. Was it pity? More likely, a reaction to being accosted and demands made of her... but what she was about to do made sense to her in that moment. She didn't feel frightened of this boy, she felt sorry for him. Maybe empathy might soften his heart...

Sophie let the teenager take a few steps through the mire before she called out to him, 'You've got a cold. Here, take this and get yourself a meal and a hot drink.'

The boy stopped and spun around. Sophie was holding a twenty pound note out at arm's length and smiling expectantly.

'Summut's wrong with you.'

The smile didn't leave Sophie's face, 'You think?'

He flicked his eyes to Bella, then back to Sophie.

Sophie took two steps forward, continuing to hold the banknote out at arm's length, 'At the moment, I think you need this more than I do.'

The boy moved slowly within snatching range, but didn't reach for the note. Instead he kept his eyes on Sophie, as if he expected a trick to reveal itself.

Sophie dropped her arm to her side, 'Who sent you?'

He studied her for a few seconds with a quizzical expression that folded his brow downwards. As if reaching a decision, he backed off.

'Do as I tell you,' he warned.

'Who? Who wants me to fail Greg's task?'

The boy didn't answer. He had already turned his back and broken into a jog. Sophie watched him splash through puddles in the grass, reach the pavement beneath the line of trees, and get into the passenger seat of a waiting car that immediately pulled away. She tried to read the number plate, but couldn't make it out in the gloom. From its shape, she thought the car was an Audi. It took the bend beside the racecourse entrance and was immediately lost from view.

Sophie didn't move for a short while, preferring to simply breathe. Once her heartbeat had returned to something approaching normal, she stuffed the money back in her coat pocket and putting Bella back on her lead, she started for home. For the second time that evening her mind was consumed with a problem. However, this time her thoughts didn't concern a client. This time they were wholly centred on herself.

Seventeen

13th May 2016

Clara had worn sensible footwear to Dennis Smith's yard this time, although she still automatically kicked the boots away and peeled her socks off the moment she unlocked the front door and entered her house. She'd also taken a half-drunk bottle of white wine from the fridge and poured herself a generous glass before she realised she neither wanted alcohol nor needed it.

Sloshing the wine into the sink, she wandered over to the lounge area, dropped into her favourite sofa and flicked the television on. Five minutes later she turned it off again, having found the noise a distraction and realising she'd not listened to a single word the morning chat show presenter and his chef interviewee had uttered. As they had been during the car journey back to Durham, Clara's thoughts were full of her morning out at Dennis Smith's yard.

It had been totally unexpected. Her early morning in Malton had generated a genuinely warm feeling in her. Clara reflected on a thoroughly enjoyable time with Frankie and Quo, watching the two of them breeze on the gallops, then afterwards following them back to the yard and chatting with their stable lass, Martha, as she washed Frankie down. Dennis had been his usual convivial self and although Ruth had annoyed her by monopolising the trainer's time, she and Sophie had managed to remain civil.

However, there was something quite different about the yard on this visit. It now possessed an exciting atmosphere, a vibe that you could almost reach out and touch as soon as you reached the barns. The whole place had been buzzing with the news of Dennis's new stable star, Charlie Soap. Dennis had proudly told them that 'Charlie' had won his debut race at Chester and didn't seem upset or surprised that neither she nor Sophie had backed him. Ruth had smiled smarmily and announced she'd won over a hundred pounds from her twenty pounds investment. Apparently Charlie Soap waltzed home 'like an old pro', as his jockey, Mitch Corrigan had put it, and then the statuesque black horse had run his competitors ragged nine days later at Newbury in a six furlong contest.

Even though Charlie Soap wasn't their horse, there was a real feeling of being part of the yard, or 'A member of the gang,' as Ruth had put it. Clara had found herself becoming excited as the trainer talked about taking the colt to some of the more prestigious race meetings. Dennis's team were now all looking forward to a race in less than a week at Sandown, where the trainer expected to, 'really find out what Charlie's made of!'

All Clara knew was that the tall, dark Charlie Soap was extremely partial to carrots, crunching through them with reckless abandon, unlike Whatever You Want, who insisted on spitting bits of them at her and making a mess on the barn floor.

She'd also found herself engaging with Sophie, and this time it hadn't been so awkward. They compared notes on the horses, spoke of upcoming races and how they would ensure they would be there at the next race meeting together to fulfil Greg's requirements. They'd seemed to be able to steer their conversation away from the more contentious issues that remained between them, even sharing a few stories from their childhood and gently ribbing each other over their past exploits together. It had been a lovely morning - Sophie had said so.

Clara shuddered. She was loathed to admit it, but Greg may have been right. She and Sophie did appear to share a strange, immutable bond. Her stomach had done a back-flip every time her brain attempted to come to terms with this possibility.

On the journey home, Clara had found herself trying to quantify her current friendships. She had a couple of coffee shop friends, and a small clique of mothers she saw from time to time as a result of Jeremy's school friends, but with no parents of her own, and the Armitage family for in-laws, she had no one she could call her 'best friend'. Sophie had been the only woman she'd ever totally trusted, but even a relationship that strong hadn't been able to withstand the anger, sense of betrayal, and grief that surrounded those few days around Greg and Sophie's wedding.

When the doorbell bongs sounded Clara was so relieved to be able to concentrate her mind elsewhere she scampered to the front of the house and flung the door open without adhering to her normal security checks. Before she'd laid eyes on her caller, she sang out a bright, 'Hello'.

'Hello, Mrs Armitage,' said a gravelly, flat voice, 'May I come in?'

The man immediately stepped into the house and onto her inset door mat, suddenly coming within an inch of Clara's face. Before she could take a step backwards he breathed on her. As Clara backed away, she was forced to slam her eyes shut as a waft of an eyewateringly strong aroma stung the inside of her nose and addled her senses for a moment. She automatically gripped her nose between thumb and forefinger. It was a pungent, meaty smell. A strong, spicy stink that put her teeth on edge and was making her eyes water.

Ignoring Clara's muddled complaints, the man settled his hard blue eyes onto her whilst clicking the front door shut behind him. He crossed his arms and looked around, casting a critical eye over the house.

'It's like the lobby of a hotel in here,' he commented, apparently impressed.

'Get out!' Clara ordered, 'Before I call the police.'

'Really?' he smirked.

Standing in bare feet on the cold marble floor Clara suddenly felt vulnerable and began fumbling in her jeans pocket for her mobile phone. As she dug it out, the man closed the small gap between them and calmly plucked the device from her grasp in one swift movement, waving one distracting hand and purloining the phone with the other. Clara, recoiling from the cloying odour once more, howled in rage.

Without touching her, the man guided her back out of the hall and into her kitchen. He indicated Clara should take a seat on one of the high breakfast chairs.

'Don't struggle or argue Mrs Armitage, just listen,' he told her in a commanding and slightly patronising tone.

'Take what you want, just take it and go!'

'I don't want your stuff!' the man insisted scornfully. He spoke with a watered down Northumbrian accent and seemed disgruntled that by implication he was nothing more than a common thief.

'Seriously, I've got some expensive stuff...'

'Okay, shut up,' he ordered as Clara began trotting out a jumble of items he could help himself to, 'Listen carefully, Mrs Armitage. When I'm content you understand me, I'll leave.'

Clara thought better of her intended retort and instead, bit her tongue. Suddenly aware her heart was pounding, she took a breath and rested her eyes on her foul-smelling uninvited guest. Her nose wrinkled as she caught another strong whiff of him. He reeked of meat; a meat man.

He was probably in his early forties, perhaps younger; his azure eyes made him look younger than the creases around them suggested. He was wearing a cheap, shiny suit. His head was shaved and apart from his striking eyes, his defining facial feature was a rubbery set of lips that pouted naturally when he wasn't speaking.

'Look at the floor,' he demanded, as if he didn't like her studying him. Clara gave another squeak of shock and obeyed immediately, bowing her head. She stared at his shiny black boots and noted the dusting of short white hairs clinging to the bottom of his suit trousers. It makes sense, Clara deduced, smelling of meat he must attract plenty of dogs, this... this, *Meat Man!*

'It's very simple, Mrs Armitage. You're not to go horse racing this summer.'

Despite his warning, Clara looked up and frowned at her tormentor.

'What the hell-type of stupid demand is that?'

The Meat Man slammed his fist down onto the breakfast bar, eliciting a gurgled apology and instant subservience from Clara.

'If you go racing in the next few months I will find you,' the man hissed, raining spittle onto her granite worksurface, 'And it won't be your table top I'll be smashing my fist into next time. Understand?'

Clara nodded, her teeth gritted.

'Understand?' he repeated, his gaze unflinching.

'Yes, I understand,' Clara blurted angrily. She was becoming short of breath again and a cold sweat was pouring from her forehead. Worried she was having a panic attack, she wrapped her arms around herself.

The man slammed a flat hand onto the breakfast bar once more, his blubbery lips curling into a contorted smile as Clara jumped in her seat. His hand shot out and grabbed her wrist. She tried to pull away, twisting her arm, but his grip was solid.

He pulled her closer to him and whispered into her face, 'You understand you cannot attend *any* race meeting?' he repeated.

The sickly meaty odour on the man's breath forced Clara to reflexively gag. Tears began to flow freely, scoring black lines of mascara down her cheeks.

'Well?' he growled expectantly.

'Yes,' she groaned, 'I won't go racing.'

'Eyes down,' he told her, releasing her wrist. She immediately clamped her hand to her chest and once again dropped her gaze to the marble tiled floor.

Reminding her not to look up, he casually walked through the hall to the front door and opened it.

'I'll be watching you Mrs Armitage. Go racing, and I'll be back... only it won't be *you* I'll be looking for...'

Clara raised her head slightly and caught a glimpse of the Meat Man standing in the doorway, ready to pull the door shut. He'd paused to inspect a small group of family photos on her hall wall.

Satisfied with his decision, the man cast his gaze back to the woman. She was hunched over with a curtain of hair shielding her face.

'Don't misbehave Mrs Armitage,' he sniffed, 'I see you've got yourself a good looking son...'

Eighteen

Thursday 25th May 2016

Not for the first time on this journey, Clara muttered a string of indecipherable complaints under her breath as the car juddered once more. Paul glanced over at his disgruntled passenger and decided against saying anything to her this time. His last placatory remark had elicited a small explosion of anger, plunging the atmosphere inside the car into an icy cold silence.

Paul sensed someone squirming in his back seat and a glance in his rear view mirror confirmed that the other two women were also wearing concerned expressions. Ruth was drumming her fingers on her armrest and it seemed Sophie was unable to settle, emitting a tutting sound from the roof of her mouth each time she adjusted her sitting position.

They were late for Frankie's race at Hamilton and there was something really wrong with his car. It had started losing power as they crossed from Newcastle over the A69 to Carlisle. The only reason he was still bothering to nurse his poorly vehicle up the A74(M) into Scotland was because he feared the verbal, and possibly physical backlash from the three women if he pulled over and called the recovery services.

'It sounds to me like you've put petrol into a diesel car,' Clara sniffed.

'You're only saying that to sound clever,' Sophie commented before Paul could shape an answer.

'Drop dead, Sophie!' exclaimed Clara, 'Try being clever yourself some time, instead of self-righteous.'

From the back seat of the Range Rover, Sophie issued a dramatic and irritated sigh, then barked, 'Leave Paul alone. What is it with you today, Clara? You're in a stinking mood.'

Paul's heart sank. Clara wrenched her head around and the two women tore strips off each other for the next few minutes until he was finally forced to pull over.

'What are you doing?' Clara demanded as the Range Rover finally gave up and drifted to a silent stop on the hard shoulder, 'We need you to get us to Hamilton races! You're doing exactly the opposite of what I want you to do!'

'It's not me, it's the car,' Paul replied miserably as he scrolled through menus on his phone. He checked the time; it was a quarter to one in the afternoon and Frankie's race was due off at two o'clock. Even if his car had been in perfect order they would have been cutting it fine.

Right from the get-go this morning, it seemed as if the universe was determined to ensure he didn't get the women to Hamilton races on time. The gates to his driveway had been closed by someone overnight and the joker had gone to the bother of placing a heavy duty U-lock on them. It had taken forty-five minutes for him to saw his way through the metal lock whilst being watched by his amused wife and children. He wasn't a handyman – a fact his family had been delighted to point out at great length. It hadn't helped that the only implement he could find was a junior hacksaw he'd found in his garage, left by a previous owner of the house.

The mechanical issues with his virtually brand new car had begun to manifest themselves within a few minutes of issuing his apology to Clara, Ruth, and Sophie for being late. They'd crawled along the A69 West and finally broken down just North of Lockerbie.

'We should call a taxi,' he told them, wincing as an articulated lorry swept past, making the car wobble violently in its backdraft, 'And I think we should get out and sit on the embankment, just in case.'

This brought more protests from Clara, but he managed to hustle the three women out of his car and up the slope, out of harm's way.

'Cars breaking down seem to be your thing,' Sophie pointed out as she shaded her eyes from the midday sun, 'This is the second time in two trips to the races.'

When he didn't reply, Sophie looked over at Paul and felt a shade guilty when she saw she'd embarrassed him; his normally pale cheeks had turned crimson.

Thankfully, the taxi arrived less than five minutes later and Paul waved the ladies off, promising to catch them up once his car had been fixed or rescued by the recovery services. Sophie wasn't too surprised to detect relief in Paul's face as the taxi pulled away.

In the back of the taxi she told Clara, 'You didn't have to be so harsh with Paul. It's hardly his fault we're late. These things happen.'

Sophie watched Clara's reaction. She could tell her ex-friend was seething for some reason. She was sure Clara wanted to scream and shout, but instead she sat silently for the entire hour-long journey and smouldered. She really was in a foul mood, which wasn't like her. In their teens Clara had always tended to dip in and out of grumps, rather than entrench herself. This had to be something serious. She considered whether it could be delayed grief. It was possible, but Sophie wasn't so sure.

Clara's demeanour hadn't improved by the time they reached the Owners and Trainers entrance at Hamilton Park. They'd managed to get to the track only a few minutes before the race and burst into the small, empty owners entry booth and announced themselves and the fact they had only seconds before their horse was running, only to be told that Miss Sophie Falworth, Miss Ruth Armitage, and Mrs Clarabel Armitage had already entered the racecourse.

'It has to be a mistake,' Ruth told the two ladies behind the counter, slapping her drivers' license down as evidence.

The manager of the booth sniffed at the pink oblong of plastic and gave Ruth an unimpressed stare over her bi-focal spectacles. She looked the three English ladies up and down once more and in an accent reminiscent of Miss Jean Brodie said, 'On this occasion we will allow you to enter, but...'

Ruth didn't need to hear any more. She'd been ready to burst waiting for the answer. Skipping through the entrance doorway she got her bearings and headed for the parade ring, pursued ten seconds later by Sophie and Clara clutching badges, meal tickets, and race cards.

'Two to go,' announced the public address system.

'This way!' Sophie called to Clara and Ruth, peeling left toward the white stick with a red circle she presumed was the winning post, 'We've missed the parade.'

They rounded the grandstand and found themselves on a large paved concourse beside a deep green racetrack bordered by bright white rails. The track stretched uphill into the distance to where a line of starting stalls straddled its centre. Clara was mesmerised by the view for a second, fascinated by the fact that after a few hundred yards the track rose up a steep hill. She'd assumed all racetracks would be circular and flat. This was certainly nothing like that.

The stands were busy, without being full, but with only seconds before the race was due off, Sophie gestured to Clara and Ruth to follow her. Dodging between race-goers they took up a position near to the winning post, on the rails.

Sophie came to an abrupt halt. Looking over her shoulder with a puzzled expression she attempted to peer between the forest of people waiting for the race to start.

'What's up?' Clara gasped, out of breath following their short sprint.

'Simon... I'm sure I saw Simon Armitage.'

She frowned at Ruth, 'Are you expecting your brother to be here today?'

For a long moment, Ruth was lost for words. When she finally shook her head Sophie's frown deepened. For a split second she could have sworn that Ruth had shown a flash of embarrassment.

Sensing Sophie wasn't going to let this lie, Ruth turned away from the rails and peered into the mass of faces, 'Do you mean him over there?'

They all stared into the crowd, but Clara soon gave up.

'Simon's got that sort of pale, hangdog face. It would be easy to think you'd seen him if you only caught a glimpse of someone similar,' she commented, 'Greg was always poking fun at him. He said his brother got his sullen bad looks from his mother, whereas he'd got his smile and stature from his Father.'

Ruth stared quizzically down at Clara. She was a good seven inches taller than her sister-in-law and had towered over Greg, and indeed her father, since the age of fourteen.

'So where does that leave me?' she demanded.

Clara shrugged, 'Somewhere in the middle,' and turned back to lean her arms on the rails. She had been close to pointing out that Ruth had Gertrude's height, looks, and that nasty edge to her personality, but there was only so much bad news you could heap on someone all at once.

Sophie gave up trying to spot the Simon Armitage look-alike and turned back to the racetrack. She spent a few seconds ruminating over Clara's little speech, and decided it rang true. Greg's smile had been an attractive quality, and unlike his brothers and sister, he'd displayed it at every opportunity. She'd never met his father, although she'd been told he was a jolly chap, and very similar in height and build to Greg.

'The stalls handlers are placing a blindfold onto Golden Dragon, and she will be the last to be led forward,' the commentator boomed through the public address system.

Clara got a tap on her shoulder. She spun around half expecting someone to be complaining about them taking their place on the rails.

'What the... Oh!'

Martha, Frankie's stable lass, was grinning at her, clearly amused by her reaction.

'Just got here?' she asked, her boyish grin never leaving her face, 'Mitch and I were looking for you in the parade ring, but couldn't see any of you.'

Martha now caught sight of Ruth and Sophie.

'I'm so pleased you made it, Frankie's in super shape.'

Ruth couldn't help it; the girl's excitement and genuine enthusiasm for her horse was infectious, and she allowed a smile to bend her mouth upwards. It felt good.

'We had car trouble,' Ruth replied with a roll of her eyes.

'Did Frankie travel here okay?' Sophie asked over the commentator telling the crowd about a horse backing away from its stall.

'He kicked the hell out of the partitions again!' Martha chuckled, 'I think he likes being a bit of a naughty boy and loves the attention. Dennis will be mad!'

'Should I be placing a bet on him?' asked Ruth.

'And... they're off,' called the public address system.

Martha shrugged, 'Too late for that I'm afraid! I'd better go – I need to lead him in afterwards. I'll see all of you after the race.'

The eighteen-year-old waved and jogged away to take up a

position well beyond the winning post alongside a gaggle of other stable staff watching the race via a large screen on the inside of the racecourse.

Clara watched her go, suddenly reminded of how exciting and carefree life had been at that age. In the late May of her eighteenth year she and Sophie were just finishing their A-Level exams and both of them couldn't wait to set off for university after summer. They'd received confirmation of their shared room in halls, and for the first time ever she would be free of foster parents. That feeling of freedom and becoming her own woman had been intoxicating.

'...and Fun Boy Frankie is whipping them in, with the slow starting Golden Dragon the last of this field of ten two-year-olds in this six furlong Novice Auction stakes race,' called the commentator.

The mention of Frankie's name prompted Clara to snap back from her trip down memory lane and transfer her full attention to the huge television screen. She was surprised at how nervous she was. Dennis had told them by telephone on their journey up that the good to firm ground may not be to the two-year-old's liking, but otherwise he fancied his chances. She located Frankie's colours at the back of the main bunch. He was almost obscured by the rest of the runners, but Clara was able to pick out his orange cap bobbing along in rear. God, she really hoped he would win. That would help show that horrible bully, that... Meat Man, that she wouldn't be intimidated.

Clara felt her heartbeat quicken as the runners reached the three furlong pole. Frankie's orange cap had moved up closer to the head of the field, and for the first time she caught a full view of Mitch's green and orange silks, poised in behind the front rank. Beside him, a fellow jockey was low in his saddle, already pumping his mount along, yet Frankie was floating over the turf with the merest of nudges from Mitch's knuckles.

Clara was aware she'd been in a reckless mood ever since waking at five o'clock in the morning, drenched in a cold sweat. He'd invaded her dreams: the man who had entered her house uninvited was now inside her head, threatening her boy. It was important she was here today and ideally, Frankie would run a big race. Clara wasn't going to be intimidated or scared out of hers, or Jeremy's rightful inheritance. Paul's late arrival and the issues with his car had only served to compound her bad mood, but Frankie could be the release valve she needed. Whoever it was who wanted her to fail Greg's task would have to realise she'd never give in. If she boldly refused to be intimidated, they would surely cease bothering her and she'd be able to put the whole sorry episode behind her.

At the two furlong pole a horse on the far side of the pack struck for home and went a length and a half clear. The entire field was under pressure now, riders asking for maximum effort from their charges... except Frankie. Mitch eased the gelding into a share of second place and waited another three strides before he crouched lower and flicked his whip, barely touching Frankie's flank, but indicating to the youngster that it was time to get the job done.

As Fun Boy Frankie surged forwards, leaving all but one horse behind, three screams of banshee-like quality rose into the air together from the ladies on the rails. They entwined into one powerful bellow of, 'Come on Frankie!'

Clara was only dimly aware that Sophie and Ruth were screaming at the top of their voices too, the three of them lost in willing the horse they co-owned to reel in the leader. The leading horse had just flashed past the furlong marker a length up on Frankie, the rest of the runners no longer a threat.

Now in the drive position, Mitch asked Frankie to close up with hands pushing, feet squeezing. The gelding responded immediately by lowering his head and lengthening, eating into his competitors' lead with every stride. The volume of the small, but feisty midweek crowd swelled as Fun Boy Frankie ranged up beside the horse Clara, Ruth, and Sophie would soon discover had been backed into favouritism.

Fifty yards from the finishing line, Fun Boy Frankie drew level with his competitor and the two horses eyeballed each other, rolling around and bumping as their riders urged them forward, trying to elicit that extra effort that would produce the difference between being the victor, or the runner-up. They flashed past the post as one, their heads dipping together, jockeys at full stretch, synchronised with the final roar of the crowd and the screams of delight from the three ladies in their late thirties, jumping up and down on the other side of the rails.

'That's too close to call,' were the last words from the commentator as a different voice cut across the public address system to announce 'Photograph, photograph.'

Martha, dodging between race-goers appeared breathless and excited in front of the ladies for a moment. She was forced to pause, surprised to be witness to Clara beaming back at her and in a state of euphoria. She was shocked further when Clara inquired, 'You don't think he'll have been hurt when they bumped into each other, do you?'

A trembling ball of nerves herself, the girl bounced on her heels, calling, 'No, he'll be fine. Come on! I think he won,' and with a quick wave she shot off. The women grinned at each other and set off after the teenager, back the way they'd come, toward the parade ring that doubled as the winners' enclosure and the placed horses' unsaddling area.

Sophie felt the buzz of excitement coursing through the people around her as she hurried to the parade ring. She imagined that like her, they were listening out for any crackle of static over the public address system: an indication the result was about to be announced. However, by the time they'd reached the winner's enclosure and Mitch had slid off Frankie's back, the public address system had remained obstinately silent. Phrases such as, 'It's taken too long, it must be close,' and 'Dead-heat,' began to circulate among the crowd that had gathered behind the arc of rails at the end of the parade ring.

'I thought he just got up,' Mitch told them, still slightly out of breath, saddle and straps bent over his arm.

Before he could say any more a three note chime rang out and as one, hundreds of people looked up into the air expectantly and a hush descended as they waited for an announcement. Sophie couldn't help smiling to herself, it was as if God were about to pronounce judgement upon his creation. However, it wasn't the announcement she expected.

An officious male voice with a light Scottish accent said, 'There is a Stewards Enquiry. Members of the public are advised to retain all betting tickets until...'

'What does that mean?' Clara queried.

Mitch bunched his lips together and his brow furrowed under the rim of his helmet.

'It means I've got to speak with the Stewards. We got a bit close to the favourite in the last few strides, but he bumped me back after I straightened my lad up.'

'Oh, okay,' Clara responded, still none the wiser.

Mitch tipped his cap, thanked the ladies for the ride, apologised for having to go and weigh in so quickly due to the enquiry, and hurried away towards the weighing room.

Martha was still holding Frankie away from the winners' position in the enclosure, as was the horse that had battled him to the line. She now moved forward to allow the gelding take a drink from a plastic bucket. The three ladies watched as the impressively sweat-ridden gelding buried his head in the bucket and drank noisily.

'Here is the result of the photo-finish,' crackled the voice once more over the public address system, 'First, number three, Fun Boy Frankie...'

A small cheer and clapping rose from the spectators around the winners' enclosure. Clara, Ruth, and Sophie squealed like schoolgirls and forgetting themselves, hugged each other. Martha looked on, smiling. Frankie responded to the sudden outbreak of emotion by tossing his head backwards out of his bucket and simultaneously snorting a fine spray of saliva and water over his owners.

It was as Sophie was laughing and backing away from behind Frankie's flanks to wipe the water from her cheeks that she glanced across the paddock. She stopped in her tracks and her mouth dropped open as she tried to make sense of the strangest of sights; three terrible replicas of herself, Ruth, and Clara posing for photos a few yards away.

Nineteen

Sophie blinked a few times, making sure the spray of water hadn't fooled her eyes into seeing something that couldn't... and *shouldn't* be there. But no, there they were, as bold as brass... the Armitages.

From beside her Clara exclaimed, 'What on earth...'

Frankie had his head buried in the bucket of water once again and having been left to stand alone, Ruth sidled over to Clara and Sophie.

'What is it?' she asked as she circled behind them, 'What's more important than our horse... Oh!'

Simon Armitage was taking photos. An awful lot of photos. Taken from many angles. Behind him was Timothy Armitage, looking on with a disinterested, but critical eye. However, it was the subject of those photos that had Sophie and Clara lost for words.

Clara took a few steps forward, a frown carving deep furrows into her face. Gertrude Armitage, Marion Armitage and Timothy Armitage's girlfriend, Alvita, were posing with a racecard.

'Ruth?' queried Clara, 'Is it just me, or is your mother wearing the same dress you wore to Ripon a few weeks ago?'

'I'm afraid so.'

'And she's wearing a wig?'

Ruth's cheeks flushed red, but she didn't reply.

'The young girl has your outfit on, Clara!' Sophie added, 'And... oh my word, is Marion supposed to be...'

'Come on!' growled Clara. She stumped across the paddock toward the group of Armitages', an incandescent rage emanating from her entire being.

Timothy was the first to spot the three ladies approaching and from being half asleep he was suddenly very much interested in what was occurring. He pointed silently but urgently in the direction of Clara, Ruth and Sophie and the rest of the Armitage's swung around.

'What in God's name are you doing?' Clara demanded as she arrived in front of the three women, for the first time taking in the full effect of the Armitage family's attempt to produce a copy of each of them. She noticed that as well as Gertude's black wig to ape Ruth's long hair, Alvita's dress appeared to be stuffed with something to fill out her bust and Marion was standing on a small wooden box to ensure she was the same height as Sophie. All three of them were wearing a strange array of make-up and had their hats pulled down at jaunty angles, presumably to cover as much of their faces as possible.

'We're making sure you don't screw up our future!' hissed Gertrude, 'You weren't here, so we've been covering for you.'

'By dressing up in our clothes and pretending to be us?' Clara hissed back, still staring the three women up and down, 'You look like something out of a horror movie!'

'God, this is embarrassing,' Ruth muttered, 'Mother, when you said you were going to make sure we turned up at the races I thought you meant you'd be *helping* us with transport or something... this is just stupid. None of you look anything like us.'

'I think we can all agree on that,' Marion said sourly, looking down at her ill-fitting outfit then glaring at her husband, 'I can't believe Simon talked me into this.'

Simon was diligently perusing the photos on his digital camera and doing his best not to become a part of the conversation.

Gertrude pursed her craggy lips, 'Don't start... *Marion.*'

The old woman pronounced her daughter-in-law's name like it was an expletive and flicked her eyes around her co-conspirators, daring them to add to the criticism.

'I'm protecting everyone's interests,' she continued, pointing a crooked finger at the real owners, 'If just one of these three unreliable types hadn't turned up we'd lose everything!'

'Well we *are* here, you crazy old woman,' Clara told her, unable to conceal her contempt any longer.

Sophie winced at this, fully expecting Gertrude to explode. She cast her gaze around the parade ring as the old woman's face began turning purple and discovered they were the only owners left in the large oval of green grass. Martha and Frankie had gone, as had the other placed horses. However, their strange little gathering and hot exchange of words had ensured a smattering of onlookers outside the ring had remained to enjoy the fun.

'Let's get out of this ring,' she said urgently, 'I admire your tenacity Gertrude, but it's not necessary to wash our dirty linen with all and sundry watching. I'm sure we can discuss this somewhere with a bit more privacy.'

'Very well,' Gertrude snorted after cocking her head and scowling at the small crowd of amused onlookers. She led the way to the parade ring exit, shuffling awkwardly in the same dress Ruth had worn at Ripon.

Twenty

'I still can't believe it,' Clara said morosely from the backseat of Paul's car forty minutes later.

Ruth gave a weary sigh, 'Believe it.'

'Causing interference... as if! That horse... what was it called... Good Knight? *He* was the one that caused the interference to Frankie!'

'It could have been worse,' Paul called over from the driver's seat, 'At least Frankie was placed second, the Stewards could have disqualified him completely.'

'But the replay showed that Good Knight gave Frankie a much bigger bump!' Clara stated in a whiny voice.

Sophie sighed again. They'd been over this ground several times and yet it seemed Clara was still unable to let go of the unfairness of the Stewards decision to demote Frankie to second place. The race officials had found Mitch and Frankie guilty of causing interference in the last furlong to the horse placed second. The result had been amended and Frankie had been demoted to second place, and that was that.

'I wouldn't have minded, but that jockey on Good Knight got a four-day ban for using his whip too many times!' Clara continued, 'How can a jockey cheat, finish second, and then be handed the race afterwards... what sort of sport rewards someone for breaking the rules?'

Sophie zipped her lips and waited, knowing what was coming next.

'It's because Good Knight was the favourite and the Stewards must have backed him!' Clara declared in a hurt tone.

'I'm not so sure about that,' Paul said in a soothing voice, 'Whilst I think Frankie has been harshly treated, I doubt the Stewards were influenced by the runner up's starting price. Anyway, I don't think they are allowed to bet on a race at a meeting where they are an official. Frankie won by a nose, if it had been a head or a neck they probably wouldn't have swapped the result.'

'I imagine Frankie believes he won, as he got that many pats and photos taken of him. It's Martha I felt sorry for. She was really cut up that he lost the race after getting up to win,' Ruth pointed out.

This brought a thoughtful silence to the car as it sped on down the A1(M) towards Durham. Even Clara, whose cheeks had turned scarlet with rage upon learning that Frankie had been demoted, calmed down as she pictured the stable lass desperately smiling in order to hold back tears of disappointment before she returned to the racetrack stables.

'That girl is a bit special,' Clara finally croaked, 'She's certainly in the right job.'

Compared to their outward journey to the racecourse, the return home was completed with alacrity. Paul had managed to get his car fixed at the roadside and had arrived at Hamilton a few minutes before the second race - just in time to encounter Clara's wrath and Ruth and Sophie's disappointment after the result was revised. He'd also learned of a rather misguided attempt by Gertrude Armitage to try and fool the solicitors with doctored photos.

'How did you leave it with your family, Ruth?' Paul asked.

Ruth didn't respond. Having refused a lift home with her family, the combination of the disqualification and embarrassment caused by her mother was weighing heavily on her. She was lost in her own thoughts and Sophie took pity on her.

'Once we'd all calmed down we thanked Gertrude and her clan for their novel idea. Then Clara suggested that if we needed their help over the next five months we would ask for it,' said Sophie on Ruth's behalf.

'Sophie's gilding the lily,' Clara told Paul, 'I advised them to get lost and leave us alone. It was a total embarrassment.'

'It does explain why our Owners Badges had been used before we got to the track,' Ruth said dully.

'Oh, yes!' Paul declared once he'd thought about it, 'They'd have needed your Owners' Badges to tie to their lapels to make it look as real as possible.'

Ruth snorted mirthlessly, 'Fat chance. They looked ridiculous. Simon's photos wouldn't have fooled anyone, and especially not an eagle-eyed solicitor.'

Clara looked across the back seat at Ruth. She was staring out of her window and appeared desperately unhappy. Ruth had been unusually quiet during the conversation with her family once they'd left the parade ring and were waiting for the result of the Stewards Enquiry. Gertrude had been her normal, bombastic self – a way of being that Ruth had modelled herself on. And yet Ruth had remained silent. It was most peculiar, and Clara couldn't help wondering what was going on behind those sad eyes.

Clara said, 'Timothy Armitage is a whizz on Photoshop apparently. He was going to doctor the photos and insert images of our faces from Ripon into the photos from today and then send them through to Thomas Bone. Gertrude and the rest of her minions genuinely thought we'd decided to not to turn up today.'

'You weren't that late,' Paul said with a half laugh that jarred with Ruth. She shuddered, wondering what they would have done if they'd arrived another ten minutes late and missed the race completely, failing Greg's task. Paul had taken the photos needed in the parade ring after the race, complete with race-cards on show, but she was going to make sure he sent them to the solicitors.

'Can you copy me in on those photos you email to Sedgefield's,

Paul?'

Paul glanced at Ruth in his mirror, 'Of course,' he replied. She stared out of the window. Had that been a questioning glint in Paul's eye?

'I don't know,' Clara said a moment later, having noticed Ruth pouting, 'I kind of have a grudging admiration for Gertrude. Greg's refusal to accept defeat and his determination to overcome every setback or hurdle had to come from somewhere. I'm guessing he had his mother to thank for that.'

Clara's little speech effectively bookended that conversation. She was pleased to see Ruth's chin subsequently rise from her chest and her general demeanour improve for the rest of the journey home.

None of them had been able to stomach any further racing after losing Frankie's win in the Stewards room, so they'd left whilst the third race was underway. It was late afternoon when Paul dropped Ruth off in Alnwick before continuing to Durham.

As they approached Clara's house, she checked the time and was pleased she was in time to pick Jeremy up from school herself, rather than him spend time at a pal's house. As Paul drew to a halt outside Clara's house he noted that the steel gates were shut and locked with a padlock; the first time he'd known them to be anything other than wide open. Greg had hated anything that slowed him down. Clara left the car without another word.

'I forgot to ask because of all the kerfuffle with Frankie. What was wrong with your car?' Sophie asked as the two of them drove to Durham railway station.

'Water in the petrol tank,' he told her as they pulled into the station, 'Apparently it can build up and cause the engine to misfire.'

Paul turned his attention back to the road. After giving Sophie a wave goodbye he tried to generate a genuine smile, but in the circumstances found it difficult. The recovery mechanic flushing his car's fuel system had reported that someone had introduced at least a gallon of water into his petrol tank, causing it to gradually lose power and eventually the car's engine had failed.

Once he was alone, a phrase Clara had repeated began to bounce around Paul's mind as he drove through Durham. *Causing interference...* the reason Fun Boy Frankie lost his race; stopping his rival from achieving the best placing possible...

His family home was on the outskirts of Durham and it took over ten minutes for Paul to make it across town. When he pulled into his drive and killed the engine he was shocked to discover he'd been so consumed with the events of the day he couldn't remember any of the drive home from the station.

***

On the other side of Durham, Clara let herself into her house and kicked off her shoes. She changed quickly, pleased to be able to pick Jeremy up from school. Pulling on a thin, chic jacket that would go down well with the other fashion-conscious mums at the private primary school, she noticed a small off-white envelope lying on the marble floor near the door. She frowned. She was sure it hadn't been there when she'd come in a few minutes ago.

The envelope was hand-written with her name on the front in small, neat writing. Ripping the missive open, a single piece of lined A4 torn from a pad had the words, 'Last chance. Do as you're told,' written in angry red biro.

Without thinking Clara unbolted the front door and flung it open in time to catch a glimpse of a man clambering over her garden wall. Once he'd dropped to the other side she ran down the drive in her bare feet and peered through the vertical twisted steel bars of the gates. The man wore tan trousers, trainers, and a dark blue hoodie and was loping in ungainly fashion across the road. He pulled open the passenger door of a non-descript family car that immediately pulled out into the road, did a swift u-turn and drove away.

Pushing her face against the bars of the gate Clara watched the car disappear down her suburban tree lined street, scowling when she couldn't make out the registration plate. For the second time that day her heart was pounding, and once again, she felt cheated with the way the world was treating her.

Twenty-One

5th June 2016

The school run was a twice daily routine that gave Clara's day shape. She actually looked forward to it, particularly picking Jeremy up from his school in the late afternoon. It was within walking distance of the house and Clara enjoyed the leisurely stroll along the leafy streets, chatting with the mums outside the school gates, and welcoming Jeremy when he careered out of his classroom at a run and flew into her arms.

Since Greg's death he'd not been quite as exuberant, preferring to walk out of his classroom, but his delight upon finding her among the gaggle of parents was just as heart-warming.

It was a Friday and Clara spent the fifteen minute walk to school thinking about her meaty-breathed caller and the subsequent note she assumed was also his work. Despite the warnings not to go to the police, Clara had visited her local station to report the unwelcome caller. The officer had dutifully taken the details but she'd been left with the impression that because nothing was stolen and the man hadn't physically threatened her, from a policing point of view he'd been a nuisance caller, rather than anything more serious.

What bothered Clara most was that the man who delivered the note wasn't the same man who had entered her home. The note deliverer had moved across the road to the waiting car in a notably strange way. It bothered her because she felt the number of men working against her had just doubled.

Jeremy was in high spirits. When he came out of school he was full of the news that his teacher had arranged for a blind lady called Grace and her guide dog, Jerry, to visit the class today. Swinging his hand in his mother's, Jeremy told Clara how the teacher had said *he* could call himself Jerry, and how the black Labrador had guided some of his friends around the classroom blindfolded!

Clara smiled down at her son and raised her eyebrows as his story drew to a close.

'Really?' she said in mock astonishment, 'A black Labrador!'

She judiciously failed to mention the name 'Jerry'. Greg had suggested shortening Jeremy's name to Jerry or Jez, pointing out that she was named Clarabel on her birth certificate. However, she had resisted and eventually he'd dropped the subject.

The dog, to which Jeremy had taken a shine, dominated the conversation for the next five minutes, until the boy, having exhausted his queries about dogs, fell silent for a short while. Clara wondered whether he was going to ask for one as a pet, but instead, Jeremy surprised her.

'Do you think I look like a 'Jerry', Mum?' he asked earnestly as they turned right into a thin one-way street that tended to be free of traffic and was shaded by mature trees above high brick walls on both sides.

Clara pretended to give the question some thought, frowning theatrically and humming. Presently she asked, 'What made you ask that?'

'My friend Peter said I look like a Jerry and he's been calling me it all day.'

'No, Jerry doesn't suit you. You're a Jeremy,' a man's voice suggested from behind them. His statement was delivered with cold certainty and in a light Northumbrian accent. Pulling Jeremy to her, Clara swung around, fully aware of whom she was about to encounter.

The Meat Man grinned at them, his blue eyes blazing despite being in the shade of the trees. He was wearing the exact same suit from a fortnight before. Beside him was a much younger, larger man who loomed over all three of them. He seemed to block out what was left of the light, his presence almost as intimidating as the smaller Meat Man. The huge teenager stared blankly at Jeremy, tossing a football lightly from hand to hand. Clara glanced up and down the street; they were alone. She considered grabbing Jeremy's hand and running, but had no doubt the men could chase them down with ease. Screaming would scare Jeremy and could quite possibly scar him for life. No, she had to play for time and hope that another mother or father would walk around the corner of the street and be good enough to help them. Holding onto Jeremy's hand tightly, she straightened defiantly.

'What do you want?'

'Hey kid, fancy a game?' rumbled the young man with the football. He continued tossing the ball from hand to hand without taking his eyes off Jeremy.

Jeremy backed into his mother's side. Staring up at the two men he shook his head.

'That's a great idea,' agreed Meat Man, nodding enthusiastically and pursing his rubbery lips, 'Then I can have a quick word with your Mum, Jeremy.'

Clara looked up and down the street again. They were still alone. This street was close enough to the school walk routes that another family or even a lone pupil could happen by, but it wasn't guaranteed. Both men looked relaxed, confident, and weren't being threatening... so far.

'He stays with me,' Clara insisted, 'Say what you have to say and then leave us alone.'

The younger man abruptly tossed the football into the air with his left hand. A long thin blade appeared magically in his right, and he stabbed at the ball as it descended. It instantly popped and hissed, making Jeremy jump and push himself further into his mother. The man moved a thumb and the flick knife blade sank soundlessly back into his palm. He crossed his arms, and settled his sullen eyes on Clara.

The Meat Man snorted derisively at the boy, 'You're not a Jerry! A Jerry wouldn't hang onto his mother like that.'

Clara felt Jeremy push away from her. He turned and faced the grinning man. Balling his small fists by his side, he shouted angrily, 'You're a bully! I stand up to bullies!'

Clara allowed a moment of pride to wash over her before she quickly gathered her son back in, her arms pulling him to her and she backed up to a brick wall, placing Jeremy behind her. There was still no-one on the street and she considered her options again. Perhaps a scream would be best.

Meat Man crackled with a forced half laugh. He reached into the inside pocket of his suit and Clara tensed, ready to fill her lungs and belt out the loudest scream she could muster. Instead of an instrument of violence, he pulled out a thin, shiny green wrapper with black writing printed vertically down its side, accented with a red dot. She recognised the brand immediately as a popular meat stick. Expertly tearing the top of the packet and pushing the red meat out of its greasy plastic sleeve, Meat Man took a bite of his salami sausage and chewed thoughtfully whilst examining his cornered prey.

That explains his meaty halitosis, Clara thought, unable to stop the corners of her mouth turning down in disgust.

Meat Man swallowed and stepped up to Clara, nonchalantly waving his salami stick around as he spoke.

'You didn't do as you were told.'

'How much do you want?' Clara demanded.

This elicited another snort, 'You think this is about money?'

'Isn't it?'

Meat Man smiled, breathing pepperoni fumes over Clara as he placed a hand on the brick wall behind her and leaned in, waving his meat stick in her face.

'I'm all out of patience. No more racing, Mrs Armitage,' the Meat Man warned, his relaxed demeanour apparently spent. Tiny blobs of salami coloured spittle danced on his bulbous lips and Clara couldn't help but turn her cheek and clamp her mouth shut in disgust. Behind him, his young partner actually sniggered.

For some reason she couldn't fathom, the boy's giggling maddened Clara. A rush of anger pulsed through her. Pursing her lips she whipped a flat hand around and slapped the Meat Man's hand hard, sending his meat stick flying. He followed it's looping trajectory, frowning when it landed among the dandelions growing in the layer of dust and dirt at the base of the wall.

Over the Meat Man's shoulder Clara caught sight of a woman and her child. They were crossing the junction thirty yards to her left. She took her chance.

'Hi Elizabeth! Could I have a word?' she shouted, even throwing in a little wave for good measure.

The woman looked up, a confused expression on her face. Clara wasn't surprised in the least, she'd never met the woman, or her child. But it was enough to alter the Meat Man's demeanour. He and his now non-giggling cohort backed away. Grabbing Jeremy's hand tightly Clara set off walking towards the woman who had crossed the road, but was now, thank goodness, waiting on the pavement, ready to tell Clara she had been mistaken.

'Don't go racing with your racehorses,' the Meat Man hissed as Clara and Jeremy hurried away from him.

A few steps before Clara reached the woman on the corner of the street, she chanced a look over the shoulder. The Meat Man and his partner had vanished.

Twenty-Two

Sophie frowned when her doorbell buzzed at seven-thirty in the evening. Muting the television, she patted Bella's head reassuringly on her way to the wall-mounted intercom. She could count the number of genuine callers she had each week on the fingers of one hand and so picked up the handset, either expecting her sister, or a cold caller. With the second option being far more likely, she added brusqueness to her answering tone.

'Yes? Hello.'

A short silence developed and Sophie wandered to her front bay window, pressed her nose to the cold glass and peered down to the small red-tiled entrance to her second floor flat ten yards below. A small boy with black hair was standing alone, feet together, arms by his side, facing her front door.

'Is that Sophie?' said a mature female voice from her handset.

A shiver of recognition ran from the top of Sophie's head through her neck and pulsed down her back.

'Yes?'

'Sophie... it's Clara... Can we come up?'

Sophie found it somewhat unnerving when Clara and Jeremy entered her lounge. Until recently this woman had featured as the main character in her nightmares. To be offering her a cup of tea, her son a glass of lemonade, and inviting them to have a seat on her sofa felt downright weird. What was even more bewildering was Clara's state of being. She was unreasonably quiet, poorly made-up, and had a nervous desperation about her.

'The biscuits are for you,' she told Jeremy warmly as she put the tray of beverages down on the coffee table in front of her unexpected guests. The young boy produced a hardly audible thank you and continued to hold on tight to his mother's hand.

Sophie had seen the boy at the reading of his father's will, but this was the first time she could really study him. His thick black hair was cut into a rather severe fringe that accentuated the pale white skin on a glum little face. Bella took a few steps toward Jeremy but stopped and sat down when he shied away from her, gripping his mother's hand so tightly Clara had to loosen his fingers one by one in order to place a comforting arm around him. The boy and the dog locked eyes, both uncertain of each other.

'This is Bella. She might lick you to within an inch of your life, but she won't bite,' Sophie assured him, 'She's just interested in you. We don't get too many children calling on us and she probably just wants you to give her a stroke under her chin, like this.'

Sophie gave Bella a scratch and watched bemused as Jeremy twisted his ankles together and clamped his arms to his sides.

'He's not good with dogs,' Clara pointed out, 'Especially ones this big.'

Sophie nodded, suddenly understanding. She checked Clara's body language and it confirmed it was the adult who was unsure of the dog, her son was simply following his mother's lead. Sophie ordered Bella back to her basket and Jeremy relaxed as the greyhound loped over to the ragged old cushion, hopped on, circled her bed several times then folded herself into it and rested her head on her front paws.

Clara also relaxed, taking a sip of her tea and examining the room above the rim of her cup. Forcing a weak smile she said, 'It's um... a nice flat you've got here.'

'No, it isn't. It's small and pokey, but it's all I can afford,' Sophie replied with a confused frown, 'Look Clara, let's get to the point of this visit. What's wrong?'

'Why should there be something wrong?'

Sophie rolled her eyes, 'We spent seventeen years living in each other's pockets, I can still tell when something's wrong! It's almost eight in the evening and you're here in York with your eight-year-old son, miles away from your million pound home. Besides, your face has the same look it had the day your foster parents caught us red-handed skipping school. I seem to remember we were testing perfume at Brown's in York city centre when they caught up with us.'

Clara took a sly glance down at Jeremy, partly to see whether he'd registered this revelation about his mother's childhood, but also to make sure he wasn't sucking his thumb. He'd started this habit again recently, particularly when she wasn't close to him, and was keen he didn't do it in front of Sophie. However, his hands were clamped to his chest and he seemed to be engaged in a staring match with Bella.

'Yeah, I remember.'

'So why are you here, Clara?'

Clara hesitated, 'Have you had a visit from anyone in the last week or so?'

Sophie closed one eye, as if concentrating; 'Yes...'

Clara's lips parted and she froze.

'... Gertrude Armitage dropped in unexpectedly with her daughter, Ruth, about a week ago,' Sophie continued.

'Oh, right, Gertrude,' Clara breathed, 'What did she want?'

'Not much. I got the impression they were just sounding me out to make sure I was going to follow Greg's instructions and deliver their share of the inheritance.'

Clara had endured a similar visit from the two Armitage women on what sounded like the same day. In her case, she'd bundled them out the door within a couple of minutes, after Gertrude had upset her by referring to Jeremy unkindly.

'So no-one else has called on you asking about you going horseracing?'

An image of the shockingly thin teenager she'd met on the Knavesmire swirled around her mind for a moment. She quashed it, deciding Clara didn't need to know.

Sophie shook her head, 'No, nothing like that. Come on then, tell me why you're here! I can't imagine for one minute you'd actually choose to be sitting on my sofa on a Thursday evening unless you absolutely had to.'

Clara insisted the television was switched on, Jeremy was placed in front of it, and the two of them went into the kitchen at the back of the flat. Sophie couldn't help noticing Jeremy's eyes nervously following his mother. She reassured him that they were within shouting distance and Bella would protect him. The boy squirmed a little, fetching his legs beneath him on the sofa, and stayed put.

'Once we got home after meeting these men for the second time, I packed a bag, locked the house up, drove to York, and we stayed in a hotel last night,' Clara concluded ten minutes later. They were leaning against the units in the narrow kitchen, facing each other but being careful not to lock eyes. Clara sighed expressively, relieved her story was told. It seemed to Sophie that her friend from the past lost inches in height as she exhaled.

A multitude of questions about Clara's two run-in's with these mysterious men were raging in Sophie's mind, but she remained silent, thinking hard. If she had doubted Clara for a second before they entered the kitchen, she didn't now. Her ex-friend was capable of many things, but she couldn't believe she would make up such a detailed story, never mind feigning shock and being frightened for the safety of her son.

When the silence extended beyond what Clara felt was comfortable, she filled the void by saying, 'You were always better than me when it came to handling a crisis.' She'd half expected this mute reaction from Sophie; unlike herself, she was a thinker… and looked before she leaped. Clara looked down at her calf length leather boots and admired the Cuban heel whilst wishing she could take them off – they were killing her feet.

'Kick those off,' Sophie said, nodding curtly at Clara's feet, 'I know you want to. You've been rocking on your heels for the entire time we've been in here.'

The boots were duly unzipped and the socks were dispensed with too. Clara wiggled her toes against the cool beige linoleum, enjoying its numbing effect. For a full minute the only sound in the kitchen was from the open door to the lounge; an old episode of Only Fools and Horses. It was only now that Clara noticed Sophie was wearing a bathrobe, a pair of fluffy outsized slippers and her hair was damp. She wondered how she'd missed this and was trying to stop herself from making a sarcastic remark, when Sophie's chin raised from its bowed position.

'Do you still want to claim your inheritance?'

'Of course I do. But...'

'You either do or you don't,' Sophie said sternly, fixing her with a stony faced stare, 'Which is it, Clara?'

'I do... I mean, I'm not going to let some intimidating little lowlife stop me getting what's mine.'

Sophie filled her lungs and held her breath for a few seconds before breathing out whilst saying, 'Good. Then you better stay here tonight so we can work things out.'

'No, that's okay... I wouldn't want to... We'll go back to the hotel, I mean, what if the Meat Man comes here!' Clara blurted.

'Meat Man?'

'His breath, it stank of meat. He was eating one of those horrible sticks of processed meat!'

Clara glanced through the open kitchen door, suddenly aware she had raised her voice, worried Jeremy might have heard. Dropping to an urgent whisper she added, 'Look, Sophie, I came here to warn you. That's all. I didn't know what to do, other than run - I guess I panicked. I thought York was a good place to go because I grew up here and know the area. I also thought you should know you might get a visit from the same man.'

'And I'm grateful, but why not go to the police, or a friend in Durham? I'm sure Paul would have...'

'Paul's married with three kids and his eighty-year-old father lives with them. He's got enough on his plate. The Meat Man told me not to go to the police or he'd hurt Jeremy, and...'

Clara ran out of words, she'd wanted to say, '...and I haven't got any real friends in Durham,' but that wasn't a truth she was ready to share with Sophie.

'... and I just wanted to get Jeremy away from Durham.'

Sophie looked up at the ceiling tiles and shook her head.

'We've spent plenty of hours together over the last few weeks and you've not taken in anything new about me, have you?' Sophie said without malice, 'What do you imagine I do for a living?'

Clara frowned and a kernel of resentment began to grow inside her - until she realised Sophie was right. She was fairly sure Paul had mentioned Sophie did something for the council...?

'I'm a Bereavement Counsellor.'

'So what? Clara snorted, waving her open palms at Sophie, as if pushing this useless piece of information back at her, 'You reckon I'm grieving, do you, and you can put me right?'

Sophie slowly crossed her arms and keeping her voice low and level she made a show of looking away to her right, 'No. Not you,' she said deliberately, 'But, you need to believe me, Clara, when I tell you that staying in an unfamiliar hotel room is the last thing *you both* need tonight.'

Momentarily confused, Clara followed Sophie's gaze to where Jeremy was standing in the kitchen doorway, watching her intently. He held a tight little fist to his mouth, a thumb inserted between his lips. The other hand was resting on the head of the large greyhound beside him, and his fingers appeared to be scratching the dog behind its ears.

'Oh, there's something else as well,' Sophie added with a grimace, 'I've had my own run in with a teenager who was keen for me not to go racing.'

Twenty-Three

By the time Jeremy had been tucked up in Sophie's bed it was nine-thirty and pitch black outside. Clara was careful to leave the bedroom door slightly ajar and joined Sophie at the bay window in her lounge, looking down on the lamp-lit street below.

'Thank you for taking us in and giving up your bedroom,' Clara whispered.

'Now there's a sentence I never expected to hear this evening.'

'Nor me.'

Sophie gave Clara a tight smile and led her over to the sofa in front of the lit fire, indicating for her guest to take a seat. She didn't join her. The small sofa had a broken spring and tended to dip in the middle. Sophie had no wish to find herself knee to knee with Clara; that would have been far too cosy. Instead, she chose to sit in her armchair.

The two women sipped their coffees in silence for a minute, listening to cars passing on the road outside and the distant squawk of a television from the flat below. Clara relaxed into the sofa and closed her eyes. The flat had an earthy perfume, presumably a mixture of the bowls of potpourri scattered around all the surfaces, combined with the whiff of dog, and she was reminded of the countless sleepovers she and Sophie had shared in their teens. She'd jumped at any chance to be out of her foster parents' house for a night. The blow-up mattress placed between Sophie and her younger sister's bed had been far preferable to the chaotic and sometimes aggressive atmosphere she endured at home, living with a constantly changing group of foster kids, each with their own combination of hang-ups and issues.

Sophie's parents would watch television in their tiny front room below until ten thirty (after News at Ten) and then go to bed, leaving a wonderful quiet to descend on their happy little house in the Clifton area of York.

'How are your Mum, Dad, and your sister these days?' Clara asked, her mind still full of the woodchip walls dominated by posters of George Michael, INXS, and EMF.

Sophie blinked away the tiredness that was starting to take hold and steeled herself, as she always did when this question was asked.

'Mum died of a stroke in 2009 and Dad followed her six months later. He sort of gave up without her around.'

Clara's shoulders sagged. She waited a few seconds in case there was any more, but presently mumbled, 'That's... a shock. They always seemed so fit... and happy.'

'My sister Fiona's okay though,' Sophie sniffed, 'She's still in York and only lives a few miles away with her husband and two kids. He's decent enough, and Joey and Nora think I'm a pretty cool Auntie, mainly because I spoil them rotten.'

The silence returned, as did the sound of canned laughter, rising up through the floor.

'Mr Lewis is going deaf,' explained Sophie, keen to change the subject.

'Who?'

'The chap downstairs. He can't hear his TV, so instead of getting a hearing aid he listens to everything on full volume. I've gently suggested he gets his hearing tested, but he's the sort of man who doesn't like being told what's good for him.'

'You always were fond of telling people what to do,' Clara agreed.

The corners of Sophie's mouth turned wryly upwards for a moment, but she didn't reply.

'That's quite a job you've got, talking to desperately sad people day after day. It must get... depressing.'

When Sophie responded with nothing more than a faintly amused smile, Clara ploughed on, 'So, Jeremy... you're certain he's grieving for Greg?'

'I'm sorry if my advice cut across you being his mother. I can't help it; the working side of me kicks in and I seem compelled to get stuck in.'

'No, no, that's okay. Actually, he hasn't been himself recently. It's just... I hadn't considered he would actually miss Greg. In the last few years he hardly saw his father, never mind spending any quality time with him. He was upset at first of course, but after a bit of a cry the day he died, he seemed to get over it quickly.'

Sophie frowned at her house guest, received a shrug in return and made the decision not to investigate Clara's comment further. Greg had often spoken of having children and made no secret of the fact he was set on a big family with plenty of kids around. That hadn't happened, but she couldn't believe Greg would ignore his only child.

'Jeremy seemed happy enough when you tucked him in. I think he quite liked the lamp on and Bella sleeping at the foot of his bed. Children deal with the loss of a parent differently to adults. Jeremy's showing classic signs of grieving,' Sophie said matter-of-factly, 'The thumb sucking, following you around, and being generally clingy. They're all coping mechanisms; he's suddenly lost one parent and is frightened of losing you too.'

'So him wanting to sleep in my bed with me is normal?'

Sophie nodded, 'He's lost a parent quite quickly. His instinct as a child is to keep his other parent right beside him at all times so it doesn't happen again.'

'It wouldn't be so bad if he didn't kick me half to death every

117

night,' lamented Clara, allowing the women to share a brief smile.

Sophie's experience with bereaved families told her the next question she asked should have been, 'And how are you coping?' but she couldn't bring herself to plumb the depths of her ex-husband's relationship with the woman who usurped her. Besides, as far as she could ascertain, Clara wasn't exhibiting any of the classic symptoms of grieving. So instead, she turned to more pressing matters.

'We need to discuss how we're going to get through the summer's racing with this... 'Meat Man', as you call him, pursuing you.'

Clara gathered herself, trying to appear more alert than she actually felt, 'I'm not giving up without a fight! That nasty little bully isn't going to stop me getting what is rightfully mine.'

'The question is, why does he, or whoever sent him, have so much interest in us not completing Greg's test of endurance?'

'That's how you see this? An *endurance* test?' Clara snapped.

Sophie gave a heartfelt sigh, 'Oh, stop being so defensive. I need you to be the brave, impetuous, life-and-soul of the party girl I knew in my twenties, not this... rich, bored, and spoilt housewife.'

Sophie knew she'd gone too far well before Clara's face began to flush. In their teens they'd gone through a fiery period of love-hate, tearing each other's hair out one minute and the closest of pals the next. Based on past experience, Sophie tensed, half expecting a hair-tearing episode. It proved somewhat confusing when Clara didn't instantly jump up and go for her. Instead, she burst into tears and buried her face in her hands.

With the notion that Clara wasn't exhibiting any signs of grief cast aside, Sophie took herself off to the kitchen in search of a bottle of Riesling. She'd always had one at the back of the cupboard, ready for the next time her sister, Fiona, called in unannounced and needed to offload her worries and frustrations onto her.

Twenty-Four

Clara's phone rang first. It started with a loud jangling noise coming from the bedroom that made Sophie wake with a jolt, despite having slept on the sofa in the lounge. From somewhere in the back of her mind a little voice told her she was being accosted by Wham!

She swung her legs off the sofa and blinked bleary-eyed around her lounge, struggling to get her bearings. George Michael hadn't even reached the chorus before the caller's patience wore thin and the music abruptly ceased. A few seconds later Sophie's own phone started to vibrate angrily against the veneer of the coffee table. She picked the device up and started jabbing at the screen, managing to connect the call and navigate it to her ear successfully, albeit the wrong way up.

Being the sort of person who bothers to label everything, she knew before she heard his smoker's cough that Dennis Smith was about to speak.

'Sophie? It's Dennis Smith. I'm afraid I've got a bit of bad news about Quo.'

'Hi Dennis, fire away,' she said, stifling a yawn.

'Sorry, love. Have I woken you up?'

'Sort of, but it's okay,' she replied, trying to use a brighter tone. Clara stepped quietly into the lounge from the bedroom wearing silk pyjamas and looking annoyingly perky. Sophie beckoned her over to the sofa, tapping her phone onto loudspeaker and placing it face-up on the coffee table once Clara was sitting beside her.

'Clara's here with me and you're on speaker. I guess you tried to get hold of her first?'

'Clara's with you. Really?' Dennis retorted, unable to suppress his surprise.

The two women traded an amused look. Clara could imagine the trainer's eyes rolling and his cigarette getting stuck to his bottom lip as his mouth opened of its own accord.

Clara said, 'Yeah, I'm here, Dennis. Sophie and I have... reached an understanding. So what's up with Quo?'

'Ah, that's good. Well, we worked him this morning. He went really nicely for the first couple of furlongs up the All-Weather gallop and showed plenty of speed up the hill, but he's come back to the yard with sore shins and a slightly swollen knee joint on his off-fore.'

'Sore shins?' Clara queried.

'A common issue in two-year-olds,' Dennis assured her, 'We asked him to breeze a little faster than he's ever been before and the pressure on his legs has caused his shins to heat up, as they're still quite pliable in a youngster his age. It's nothing that time won't fix, but he won't be racing

119

in the first week of June as I intended. I'm now looking at late July or possibly August for him to have his racecourse debut.'

'But he'll be okay?'

'Oh, aye.'

Clara turned to Sophie and shrugged, 'That suits us I guess. It's one or two less trips to the races.'

Sophie didn't look so sure, 'Sort of... Clara, have you actually *read* the instructions Greg provided with his will?'

The uncertain expression Clara's face adopted told her she hadn't.

'Dennis, are you aware of the err... *expectations* Greg has of Clara and I?'

A croaky laugh made the phone vibrate, 'Aye, lass. It's a strange do, and no mistake!'

'So if Frankie can't run in each calendar month from now until September, do you have another horse we can go racing with?'

'If you need one, I'm sure I can find something for you,' Dennis confirmed.

Sophie caught Clara bunching her face up and scratching her forehead. She's obviously unaware of the stipulations in Greg's will, she decided.

'Thanks for the speedy update Dennis, I suppose we'll see you next at Newbury in two days' time?' Sophie asked.

'That's the other thing,' Dennis said after a short pause, 'I won't be declaring him. The ground will be too firm for him down there. We'll have to wait for the rain and go racing with him later on in June, if that's okay.'

'Oh, okay,' Sophie responded, a shade disappointed, 'But he's okay?'

'Aye, he's in grand shape. I'll call you when I find another race for him.'

'I was looking forward to going down south on Saturday with Frankie,' Clara moaned as soon as they'd both called goodbye to the trainer and finished the call.

Sophie jumped up and held out a hand, pulling Clara to her feet, 'We agreed we're going to see out Greg's wretched little project to the end and claim our reward, didn't we?'

Clara sucked in a deep breath, 'We did!'

'Good, so the first thing we need to do is get dressed, then I'll get you to read the full instructions, so you understand exactly what we can and cannot do. Then we'll get a plan together for the next few days.'

'Could we jemmy breakfast into that plan?'

Sophie rolled her eyes, 'I suppose so... are you still a fan of Weetabix with milk and golden syrup?'

Clara hadn't made herself this teenage breakfast for years, yet the thought of it now made her mouth salivate.

'Absolutely!'

Sophie started towards the kitchen but stopped and turned back.

'By the way, Clara, if you want to live beyond lunchtime you'll change your ringtone from 'Wake Me Up Before You Go-Go'. That song drives me insane.'

Half an hour later Clara tossed the printed pages of Greg's instructions aside, hugged a mug of coffee to her chest, and settled back in her armchair.

'Greg really did think of everything, didn't he?' she sighed dejectedly, 'So even if both our horses couldn't run in any one of the five months, he had Dennis agree to send us racing with another of his horses.'

Sophie slowly nodded her agreement, 'I was mulling it over the other day. Greg was a software designer, and those instructions in our task read like a computer program. I guess a programmer spends a lot of time telling a computer, 'if this happens, do that. If another thing happens, do something else'. A programmer must have to think of all the possibilities and make a case for each alternative, which is exactly what he's done with our task.'

Clara considered this for a moment, 'So if our horses can't run in a particular month, Dennis has to allocate us a substitute horse.'

'That's right.'

'And if we don't attend the races together at least once a month, we fail the task.'

'Right again.'

'Or if any of us don't attend the stable visits when we should, we fail.'

'Greg made absolutely certain his task was watertight,' Sophie confirmed, 'Miss one stable visit, or our monthly run, and we fail the task completely...'

Clara watched Sophie get up from the sofa. She was deep in thought.

'What is it?' Clara queried.

Discarding her half-eaten bowl of Cheerio's, Sophie slowly paced the length of the room three times, from kitchen door to bay window with her head bowed and the fingers of her right hand pulling at her bottom lip. She paused frequently, either to shake her head, or to navigate around the mess on the floor, an immoveable frown creasing her brow. Clara waited, not bothering to speak. To try would have been pointless; she'd either be shushed or receive a flat hand thrust at her to blank her query. She'd seen variations of this behaviour from Sophie plenty of times before. Whether it was deciding to date a boy, a decision on what outfit to wear, or even something as banal as whether to go to a nightclub or attend a party, it was

Sophie's way of working through a problem.

Clara closed her eyes and leaned back into her armchair. Whilst it was irritating, she had to admit that on the whole, Sophie's decision making was far better than her own. However, she flicked her eyes open with a start when Sophie barked a question at her.

'What's Greg's objective?' Sophie demanded. She was standing in front of her, hands on hips. Her expectant expression worried Clara.

'I don't know. To make my life a misery?'

'No. That's the pitiful little housewife in you talking again. Come on, think! What's Greg really after?'

Clara pursed her lips in concentration, 'I suppose he wanted us to... meet again.'

'Yes, and...'

'Get us to go racing?'

Sophie raised an eyebrow, asking herself whether Clara could really be this thick.

'Oh alright! I'll say it,' Clara snapped, 'He wanted us to rekindle the relationship we had before I stole your husband from you.'

Sophie recoiled, staring at Clara slack jawed. A vexed Clara shot her a disgruntled glance, leaned back in her armchair and crossing her arms grumpily, concentrating her gaze on the fireplace.

'Yes, I... um... the point I was trying to make was that his goal is... *was* to resurrect our friendship. If that's true, then it's kind of worked.'

Clara continued to stare into the ashes of last night's fire, a perplexed look on her face. It was too early in the morning for her to wrap her head around the complexities of her husband's last request.

'The racehorses are a blunt tool,' continued Sophie energetically, 'They're a means for Greg to ensure we have to spend time together.'

'Okay, I get that. It's pretty obvious.'

'But what if Greg thought we needed... more of a shove...? What if he thought we might need to be *forced* to get together?'

Clara scrunched her face up and shook her head.

'No way. You're suggesting Greg arranged for the Meat Man to scare the living daylights out of Jeremy and me, just so we'd get together?'

Sophie thought for a few seconds, desperate for the threads of her argument to make sense. Eventually she sighed dejectedly, 'No. Not really. I'm grasping at straws. The problem is I can't work out who stands to gain if you don't go racing and fail to complete Greg's task.'

'A bunch of charities?'

'Exactly... charities that don't even know they are in line for a big windfall if we fail to satisfy the conditions of Greg's will. Besides, I reckon Greg really wants us to finish the task, not fail it.'

Down on the road outside, the morning traffic was starting to build, with the rhythmic swish of passing cars becoming the predominant sound in the lounge.

Sophie sighed; she'd lost her line of thought. The old-fashioned Micky Mouse clock sitting on her mantelpiece told her it was almost eight o'clock. It brought a sad smile to her face. The trashy plastic clock was one of those possessions she'd impulse bought in her late teens and could never quite throw away, despite the case being scratched and tarnished. Following the failure of her second marriage it had turned up in an old university junk box and had made her smile, so she'd plonked it on top of her fireplace the day she'd moved into this flat. And there it had stayed, looking incongruous, but making her smile from time to time.

Sophie pulled a dressing gown around her and shuffled over to the bay window. She drew her curtains back and took long look down at the busy road whose pavements were dotted with people on their way to work.

'Why does the Meat Man want us to fail our task? Who benefits?' Sophie wondered aloud.

She ran everyone concerned with Greg's will though her mind, looking for anyone who could profit from a failure to complete their task. The list was worryingly short. There was the Armitage family; Timothy, Ruth, and Simon were in line for large payouts if the task was completed, and so was Gertrude. There was Simon's wife Marion, and Timothy's young girlfriend, Alvita, but both of them would also benefit financially, albeit indirectly. The only other person who knew about the will and the task was Paul...

Sophie's reaction was to shake her head and smile at the same time. From her experience, Paul wouldn't hurt a fly. Paul and Greg's friendship had started in their first year at Newcastle University. They'd become inseparable, mainly due to an unquenchable love of beer, women, and video games – in that order - and a shared, slightly warped sense of humour.   A straight-talking Yorkshireman, Paul had been a steadying influence on Greg and as far as Sophie knew the two of them never had a crossed word. One look between them settled any dispute. The four of them had often gone out as a foursome, but neither she nor Clara had ever been interested in Paul romantically.

Sophie turned to eye Clara, 'Why was Paul at the reading of the will? He didn't get left anything did he?'

She thought for a moment, 'No, I don't think he did. Wasn't he Greg's executor?'

Sophie frowned, 'No, that was the solicitor, Mr Sedgefield.'

'Maybe Greg asked him to be there. After all, they were terribly close. And he was at the funeral. Perhaps he just came along to the reading and no one questioned it,' suggested Clara

'What did Paul do for Greg, in his business I mean?'

'He was something to do with accounting I think... he left when Greg sold the company. You can't think that Paul is mixed up in all of this? He'd never do anything to hurt Greg, or me and Jeremy for that matter!'

'But we both know he idolised Greg. Maybe being left out of his will has made him angry, hurt...'

Clara shook her head, 'No. I just can't see it. Paul was the one person who would keep Greg grounded. Besides, becoming a rich businessmen was Greg's goal, not Paul's. I always got the feeling he wasn't that bothered about money.'

Sophie bit her lip in contemplation. She knew Clara was right. Paul didn't fit as a vengeful type. He was reliable, staid... and in truth, a shade boring.

'It was just an idea,' she said, wafting a dismissive hand, 'It's... frustrating. I'm struggling to see who benefits from scaring you like that and forcing us to fail Greg's task.'

From inside the bedroom, Jeremy called out.

'Mum?' he repeated, in a higher register this time.

'We'll have to try and work these things out later,' Clara said as she made her way towards the bedroom, 'I also need to sort out whether I'm going back to the house in Durham. There's only a bit of the term left, even so, I'd rather Jeremy didn't keep missing school.'

Sophie scooped up her printed copy of Greg's task and his will, beginning to skim-read them once more. From his commanding position on the mantel, Micky's mechanical hands told her it was now eight-thirty. She only had the one counselling session today, late morning at a client's house in Doncaster, so she could spend another hour trying to dissect who was behind a plot to ensure she and Clara, and the rest of the Armitage's didn't collect Greg's inheritance.

The sound of suitcases being unzipped in the bedroom, the young boy dressing under instruction from Clara, and curtains being drawn back, took her thoughts elsewhere. As the mother and son everyday conversation filtered through the open bedroom door, Sophie listened, a tinge of jealousy creeping into her. Being single at the age of thirty-eight, she'd begun to accept the fact she was unlikely to ever have child of her own. She smiled, but only inwardly, at her propensity to be jealous of Clara. She only had herself to blame for screwing up her second marriage. Besides, since her divorce ten years ago she probably hadn't tried too hard to replace the deadbeat misogynist she'd spent three years trying to change.

'Sophe... Sophie?'

Sophie snapped back; it was the type of call that she knew only too well. Clara wasn't *requesting* attention, she was demanding it.

'Sophie!' Clara called again, her pitch increasing.

Inside the bedroom she found Clara looking through the back window. Meanwhile, Jeremy was busy cleaning his teeth in her small en-suite bathroom. He was giggling, having just offered Bella his toothpaste foamed electric toothbrush. The greyhound was bending her long tongue energetically around the rotating spearmint offering, much to Jeremy's amusement.

Clara was standing cross-armed, looking out onto her back garden. Well, Sophie *called* it her back garden; it was more a walled yard with a solid wooden door leading to the thin cobbled alley that separated them from the next line of terrace houses. At one time the backyard would have boasted a privy and a coal shed, but the concrete square was now filled with a number of potted plants tended by her half-deaf neighbour downstairs, Mr Lewis.

Clara glanced over her shoulder and beckoned for Sophie to join her. Speaking under her breath, she told her, 'The Meat Man knows I'm here.'

High up on the backyard wall, above Mr Lewis's newly planted tubs of geraniums and wallflowers, someone had spray painted a message in yellow, foot-high capital letters that read, 'GO RACING AND SUFFER'. Underneath in smaller, lowercase letters were the words, 'the consickwences'.

Sophie read the words three times before turning to Clara. Without hesitation she gave her a hug. When they broke, Clara used a knuckle to dot a tear from her eye.

Sophie grinned mischievously at her, 'Not only are we being threatened, but what's worse, we're being threatened by criminals who can't spell! Do you remember our English teacher, Mrs Smart in the fifth year...? She'd be horrified. She'd make them spray the whole wall white and start again!'

Clara's shoulders began to bounce uncontrollably and laughter followed soon after.

Twenty-Five

Ruth Armitage stared uneasily at the envelope bearing her name. Propped up against her open laptop, it was written in shaky capital letters. She'd left the computer closed upon leaving for the swimming pool two hours ago – she was sure - but now the laptop was flipped open on her writing desk, and the envelope placed prominently against its screen. The item had been carefully positioned, staged in such a way to be discovered as soon as she entered the first of her three adjoining rooms on the second floor of Armitage Hall. This thought brought Ruth to a halt in the middle of her sitting room.

Looking around, a sense of vulnerability invaded her throat and lungs with a hollow shortening of breath. Someone had been in her rooms, despite them being locked. Could they still be here? Spinning around she scanned all the places a burglar could potentially hide; the curtains, furniture... the open door. But this surely wasn't the work of a burglar. Burglars didn't tend to leave calling cards.

The sitting room was silent except for birdsong coming through the three sash windows and the tinny sound of her mother's television filtering down through the ceiling from the floor above. Whilst Ruth didn't place herself into the 'bright' category her mother reserved for brothers, Greg and Timothy, she believed herself to be quick-witted. The computer screen was dark; it had automatically entered its sleep mode. That meant it had been left open for more than fifteen minutes. Quarter of an hour was more than enough time for whoever had left the envelope to be long gone. Just the same, she opened the door to the landing to give any intruder a clear exit path, then making plenty of noise, checked her bedroom and the en-suite bathroom before returning to lock her sitting room door and finally, approach her desk.

Ruth swallowed hard. She had a feeling the contents of the envelope might be similar to the other curious messages she'd started receiving by email and text message over the last few days. The thrust of the communications were all the same; they instructed her to stop going racing or face some sort of unspecified peril or retribution. She'd ignored them up to now, despite their tone becoming increasingly blunt. She'd imagined it would be Timothy messing with her. He enjoyed a sick joke.

The odd silly text message or spam email dropping into her Hotmail account was easy enough to delete and block the sender, however, breaking into her private rooms and leaving a letter was quite another matter. As anger replaced her fear, Ruth snatched up the envelope and ripped it open, determined to phone her brother immediately, read his own message back to him, and castigate him for playing such an inane mind game.

Unfurling the badly folded single sheet of paper inside the envelope, Ruth read the note in her left hand. In her right lay her mobile phone, index finger ready to tap the redial button for Timothy. Seconds later, the device slipped from her fingers, clattering onto her writing desk.

The shadow of vulnerability returned, only stronger. She slowly lowered herself into the writing desk chair, sagging as she read the note for a third time. Ruth knew one thing for certain; Timothy wasn't the author of this message.

She didn't know how long she'd been sitting, staring at the note. The muffled television noise from upstairs combined with the blackbirds chirping outside, but gradually, and with difficulty, Ruth concluded she needed help. Searching around her desk, she found her bound copy of Greg's task under a couple of discarded romantic fiction novels. They were a guilty secret, but necessary. She found the contact list, dialed the number and immediately hit the call icon so as not to allow herself to contemplate her decision any longer.

Her doubts set in immediately, and she considered ending the call after the third ring. The digital clock on the desk blinked the seconds at her and was a reminder that it was late afternoon. Perhaps she wasn't there...

'Hello?'

Ruth took a calming breath, 'Sophie, it's Ruth.'

The line went quiet.

'It's Ruth, Ruth Armitage.'

'Hello Ruth. Yes, I get it's you, I'm just a bit surprised you're calling me.'

'You and me both,' Ruth said miserably.

There was another few seconds of silence before Sophie, in a markedly less abrupt tone asked, 'So... what's up?'

Ruth closed her eyes and started to talk. She kept going without taking a proper breath for more than a minute before saying, '... I considered other people, but on balance...'

'You should come and see us, Ruth,' Sophie cut in purposefully, 'Clara is here. Pack, and come this evening.'

'Clara is *with* you? You mean *staying* with you?'

'Look Ruth, I can go through all the reasons why you should come down to York, but I don't think that's a great idea as I'm walking my dog around the streets at the moment and anyone could hear me. Besides, by the time I've finished, you could be here. Jump in your car...'

'I don't have a car of my own...'

'Then get on the train. You can get a taxi from Armitage Hall,' replied Sophie somewhat exasperated, 'Just get yourself down here so we can work this out.'

'I'm not so sure,' Ruth argued, her voice hardening.

Sophie sighed, 'Clara and I have been threatened too. Both of us, but in different ways. It sounds like the Meat Man is targeting you too now.'

'Who?'

'I'll explain when you get here. So are you coming?'

Ruth scrunched her face up, trying to clear away all the questions that were now pressing for answers.

'Yes, okay. I'm coming.'

Twenty-Six

11th June 2016

From the caravan steps, Sophie watched Jerry and Clara for a short while as they kicked a football backwards and forwards to each other through grass that was longer than ideal. The ball kept getting caught in tufts of uncollected grass clippings. However, the boy was gleefully scooping up hay with every kick and laughing as the stiff breeze blew the dried grass around him.

Jeremy had insisted on being called Jerry from now on, despite his mother's protests, informing her tearfully that his dad had called him Jerry when Clara wasn't around. Clara had stood her ground at first, but it was difficult to argue against the clandestine wishes of a dead husband, especially when her son was so adamant. Sophie thought the nickname suited him and had said so, much to Clara's disgust, and Ruth's amusement.

As Sophie had spent time around the eight-year-old, the deeper she was convinced Jerry had inherited Greg's quiet intelligence, combined with his strength of purpose. That said, the boy also exhibited a refreshing stillness and a willingness to reflect and freely admit when he was wrong; a quality neither of his parents possessed. Jerry was undeniably a credit to Clara, and their mother-son bond was strong, a situation that Sophie could not solely attribute to Greg's sudden death. Clara had made a good fist of bringing the boy up, a fact that Sophie had grudgingly admitted to her on their second night at the caravan. It made the subsequent discovery that Jerry wasn't Greg's son all the more bewildering.

For the last three days Jerry, Clara, Ruth, and Sophie had been living together on a country campsite a few miles away from the east coast seaside town of Whitby. The caravan belonged to Sophie's younger sister and was a twelve-year-old six-berth static that served as a family holiday home, and more importantly, a bolt-hole for her sister when she needed a few days to re-establish some perspective on her home life.

Sophie spent the odd weekend in the caravan, using it as a base to walk the moors with Bella and to simply slow down and enjoy some quiet time. There was no television, and the nearest house was a few miles away, although the site thankfully boasted a workable mobile signal.

Now that the Meat Man had made his presence felt in each one of the women's daily lives, Sophie had hit upon the idea of going 'off the grid', and suggested the caravan as a short term base for the three of them. It was currently empty, and it was unlikely the Meat Man would know it even existed, which meant there would be little chance of him knocking on the caravan door to threaten them further. Quietly disappearing for a week or two to work out what on earth was going on, and to decide how they were going to deal with the Meat Man and his sidekicks, had seemed a sensible option.

On their arrival at the caravan site, the women had complained and argued interminably as they'd all adjusted to living in close quarters. Many of the sharp words dealt with the lack of amenities, not least the use of a communal toilet and shower block. Neither Ruth nor Clara had ever spent a night under canvas or caravanning, so they hadn't been prepared for the rudimentary facilities offered by the aging caravan and rather rustic campsite. Sophie had been sure Clara was going to walk out on the first evening after a bust-up with Ruth, having accused her of stealing her towel from the shower block – necessitating Clara to make a sodden, and rather bedraggled dash from the showers to the caravan. As the two had argued, Jerry had disappeared and returned with the lost towel in hand, telling his mother he'd found it draped over a chair at the end of the line of shower cubicles, exactly where he'd seen his mother leave it.

Ruth had laughed victoriously and announced, 'The boy may not be an Armitage by blood, but he's sharper than most of the family, and a good deal more honest!'

Under minimal questioning, Clara had revealed she and Greg had adopted Jerry at the age of two. It was clearly not a great secret, with Jerry thankfully aware of his parentage, given Ruth had made her statement with the boy within earshot. Sophie tried not to seem surprised, although she'd subsequently noted Clara eyeing her intently to judge her reaction. The conversation had soon spun away from Jerry and back to Ruth mocking Clara for her shower mishap and the three of them had gone to bed that evening not so much as friends, more as acquaintances with an understanding.

The next morning had brought a bright, sunny day and with little to do, they'd lazed around. That experience had been useful. It had helped them to drop into a routine that meant the trio, along with Jerry and Bella, rubbed along tolerably well together, taking things slowly. There were the inevitable sharp words every now and again, driven by underlying tensions but Sophie had noticed that having a third person around to break up the arguments when they erupted between the other two gave this strange arrangement a weird kind of balance.

Having already put Clara's past misdemeanours to one side in their pursuit of Greg's task, Sophie had been somewhat surprised to find herself warming to Ruth. The shock of the Meat Man invading her personal quarters at Armitage Hall had taken the edge off Ruth's appetite for scorn and derision. The upshot had been fewer dark scowls and her desultory attitude had brightened to a point where conversations with her didn't come barbed with stinging little asides.

Once it had become obvious that the Meat Man and his two younger associates were capable of invading their lives easily and seemingly at will, the three women had visited Sophie's local police station. Sophie had named the Meat Man's sidekick 'Skeletor' - to reflect the young man's pale complexion and drawn facial features. It seemed only right that the large, powerful lad Clara had encountered should therefore be nicknamed 'He-Man'.

Their experience at the police station in York hadn't filled them with confidence. Suggesting the local constabulary might provide them with round-the-clock surveillance to ensure they made good on a mad-cap task set by a dead relative was met with barely concealed mirth by the desk sergeant who listened to their story. Whilst the production of a knife by He-Man was enough to raise one of the policeman's eyebrows, the fact its use had been to pop a toy ball, rather than seriously threaten, was the clincher; he kindly advised renewing the locks on their houses and not coming back until a crime had been committed.

Remaining together, whilst irksome, had made sense to each of them when Sophie suggested it. Having one or two people constantly watching your back was certainly preferable to being alone, which is how the three women usually spent their days. When Sophie mentioned the caravan idea Clara and Ruth had reacted positively. So the three of them, along with Bella and Jerry, sneaked off in Clara's car very early in the morning - having toured twice around the York ring road to make sure they weren't being followed - before heading to the east coast.

The campsite itself was tiny, with only half a dozen caravans tucked away in what was better described as a small, east sloping paddock cut into the southern side of a valley. Mature woodland filled the view below the caravan, and above them they were surrounded by the rolling hills of the North York Moors National Park. Running alongside the site were some small paddocks, containing a veritable menagerie of farmyard animals that Jerry had found fascinating.

The caravan park owners, a friendly retired couple in their late fifties, lived in the nearby farmhouse and as far as Sophie could make out, spent half of their day caring for their smallholding and the rest of the time chatting to whoever happened to be on the campsite. They also ran a small shop with minuscule opening hours, keeping a supply of essentials available at understandably extortionate prices. With a mile-long single track road leading to the farmhouse, and eight miles to the nearest convenience store, the campsite was suitably remote.

Sophie had spent the last two days at the campsite scouring all sixty pages of Greg's will and the appendix containing the details of the task he'd set them. Determined to work out why anyone would be interested in making them fail, she had searched for every possible angle and reason, no matter how ridiculous, for the Meat Man and his sidekicks to be bothering them.

As Sophie watched Jerry forsake his football in favour of picking up a handful of grass clippings to throw at his mother, she asked herself for the umpteenth time: Who benefitted? If they failed his task, Greg's money would head into a trust fund that would finance a long list of nominated charities. However, all these potential candidates could be ruled out of any wrongdoing. None of the good causes would know anything about their windfall until their cheques arrived in the post.

Perhaps it was a personal grudge, Sophie reasoned. Someone filled with enough spite to condemn an entire family to never claim their inheritance. But who would want the Armitage family, Clara and Jerry, Ruth, or even herself to fail to benefit from Greg's money?

Later that evening when Jerry was curled up with Bella at the other end of the caravan, once again, the topic was revisited.

'If someone is doing this for sheer devilment, they'd need to have a pretty big chip on their shoulder to be that vengeful,' Clara had pointed out as they'd relaxed with a glass of wine around the fold-away table, 'And they'd have to know Greg's task in detail, where we all live, and be motivated enough to send the Meat Man after us.'

'Could the Meat Man be the one with the grudge?' Ruth suggested, 'Maybe Greg has... or *had* enemies we know nothing about.'

The women pondered this until Clara spoke up, 'I suppose Greg did have to sack employees from time to time...'

The three women continued to discuss their predicament over what became one too many bottles of red wine. Thanks to their alcohol slackened tongues, the conversation become a loud, lively discussion.

'What about the Armitages?' Sophie suggested with a querying look at Ruth, 'Maybe one of your bunch is willing to forfeit their slice of his fortune for some reason?'

'Nope. No. No way, Jose!' Clara replied before Ruth got chance, shaking her head firmly, 'Greg was their little ray of sunshine. You couldn't say anything bad about Greg to any of the Armitages.'

Ruth remained silent.

'So it's still the same,' Sophie said, looking to Ruth for confirmation, 'Greg was the golden boy when I was around, and I'm guessing it was still the same when he died?'

Ruth sighed irritably, 'We all might have been a little jealous of his success. Even so, he was generous with his money. He always saw to it that we were well looked after.'

'Don't I know it,' Clara muttered dejectedly.

Ignoring Clara, Sophie continued, 'What about Marion and Timothy's girlfriend... I forget her name?

'Who, Alvita? That little leech?' Ruth scoffed, 'She may have Timothy wrapped around her little finger but I can't believe she's anywhere near capable of arranging for people to go around threatening us on her behalf, besides, she thought Greg was wonderful and depends on any money that filters through Timothy. Marion blows hot and cold, but again, she and Simon are just as desperate to land the money. Speaking as someone on the inside of the family, all of us need the money, especially my mother.'

'Ah, yes, Gertrude,' Clara said, holding her wine glass aloft in a mock toast to the matriarch, 'As Lady Diana once famously said, there were three people in my marriage. There was Greg, me, and an ever-present spectre called Gertrude!'

All credit to Ruth, Sophie thought. She'd actually grinned at Clara's outburst.

'But Gertrude and you have Armitage Hall, so I assumed you're okay for cash?' Sophie queried.

'Naaa. The Armitages are absolutely desperate for money, all of them,' Clara declared, once again answering a question intended for Ruth, 'Well, apart from Simon. He's the only one of them who holds down a steady job. They're all counting on getting their hands on a chunk of Greg's cash to continue living their selfish little lives.'

Ruth pushed her lips out and stared ruefully at Clara. Sophie had waited for her to burst forth with a torrent of vitriol, and was surprised when it failed to arrive.

Seizing the moment, Sophie asked, 'So, Clara, I'm guessing you don't think any of the Armitages' will be willing to forfeit their windfall to ensure you don't get anything more?'

Clara stared out of the caravan for a short while, 'I've never been treated as part of the family. Not really. And that extends to Jeremy too. They've always been cold towards us; I was never good enough for their Gregory. But you're right, they're far too money-minded to be giving up a single penny on my account.'

Sophie thought for a moment, trying to build up a picture of each member of the Armitage family and what possible reason they might have to see Greg's money go elsewhere. She soon admitted defeat. A seventeen year hiatus in her relationship with the family meant she simply didn't know any of them well enough. So she deferred to Clara.

Clara grinned when asked to go through the family, rolling her alcohol-reddened eyes.

Clara said, 'Every single Armitage is far too self-obsessed and money-minded to give it up.'

Counting on her fingers, she continued, 'When the money arrives Gertrude will play lady of the manor. That old house will continue to fall down around her as she's so miserly, and the old crone will continue to delight in making her entire family's life miserable with her cruel comments.'

Without taking a breath, Clara's tirade continued, 'Timothy will be a weirdo recluse in his rooms at Armitage Hall, doing whatever it is he does up there. Meanwhile, his very odd girlfriend will be egging him on, and Simon can... well, Simon will keep being boring old Simon with his boring wife. He will allow himself to still live in Greg's shadow and be continually henpecked by his wife and never amount to...'

'So what about me?' Ruth cut in, her hand becoming a fist around the stem of her wine glass, 'You must have a pigeon hole for me too, Clara.'

Clara hesitated, her finger tracing the ring left by her wine glass on the flip-up table. She shrugged, swallowed another mouthful of wine and swaying slightly, cocked her head at Ruth, speaking slowly and deliberately.

'Ruth will hoard her money and spend every hour of every day getting ever more bitter and twisted. If she allows it, Ruth's mother will continue to crush her heart by reminding her she has no husband and no children, until eventually Ruth will *become* her mother: a cruel, lonely old woman, obsessed with a ramshackle building filled with the ghosts of her ancestors, and full of regret for not having had the gumption when she was younger to take a chance on a different life.'

Clara and Ruth stared depressingly at each other across the flimsy table, their eyes locked and unblinking. Sophie dared not breathe. The standoff lasted for what felt like an age.

Eventually, Ruth took a deep breath, 'So you, the queen of the quick put-down and clever, cutting retort is accusing me of being unfulfilled, bitter and twisted?'

Clara lifted her glass, saluting her sister-in-law, 'Yup, welcome to my world!' she said, slightly slurring her words. Gulping her wine, Clara set her glass down on the table and fixed Ruth with a faraway stare.

The only sound to punctuate the scene was from the owls outside the caravan, calling to each other from the trees in the bottom of the valley.

Sophie wasn't sure whose lips twitched first. She missed whether it was Ruth or Clara who initially found their standoff funny. But suddenly, they were grinning at each other, then snorting, and within a few more seconds the two women were in gales of laughter. This was swiftly followed by drunken shushing of each other so as not to wake Jerry, sleeping at the far end of the caravan.

Sophie joined in the laughter, more out of relief than anything else. Of course it was the wine that had tipped their conversation into the ridiculous, but Sophie was glad for it. The release of tension seemed to cover the caravan in a blanket of wellbeing.

'That's not funny. But it's so funny!' Ruth had managed to squeeze out between fits of barely suppressed giggles.

The next half hour consisted of more pulling of legs, and a slow reawakening of the gossipy conversational style the three women had enjoyed as girls in their late teens, only now their conversation was tinged with the benefit of experience. Together they enjoyed a rush of warm memories from those few years of youthful vigour.

'What about upsetting people, the Armitage family must have some enemies?' Sophie had eventually asked when others were drawing breath after another of Ruth's anecdotes about her mother.

'Oh, there's plenty of them,' Clara agreed, 'Ruth and I alone must have upset half of Alnwick over the years with our sharp tongues!'

This elicited another bout of laughter. Ruth had such a low, rumbling growl of a laugh, it alone was enough to ensure you wanted to join in. Sophie wondered why Ruth didn't laugh more often, it altered her face completely and injected life into herself and the people around her.

Presently Ruth asked, 'If it's someone with a grudge, how would they get to know about Greg's will?'

'Unless one of your lot let it slip,' Sophie pointed out, 'I've not told a soul.'

Ruth pondered this, but didn't offer a reply. Her family could be an unpredictable bunch at times, but she couldn't see any of them sharing intimate details of their potential windfalls. The one characteristic each Armitage possessed was an old-fashioned, class-ridden view of their position in society, and she doubted any of them would bring themselves to associate with the likes of the Meat Man, He-Man, and Skeletor.

'So, what about Clara and me. Come on Ruth, what does the Armitage family really think of the two of us?'

'Ha. What about the two of us,' Clara repeated in a silly voice. Ruth smiled, but an answer wasn't forthcoming; besides, Clara had more to offer.

Clara continued with staring eyes and a deep, doom-laden voice, 'Sophie… You're like Voldemort! You're 'She who shall not be named!' and I'm…'

Clara paused for a moment, closed her eyes and became strangely serene, 'I'm the embarrassment,' she said in a flat tone, 'I'm the woman that lived with Greg… out of wedlock.'

Sophie had started a laugh, expecting Clara's signature big finish; she was so good at comic storytelling when she was tipsy. Instead, her laugh was shelved, replaced with shock over witnessing Clara's admission that Greg had never actually married her.

'Depressing isn't it?' Clara told her with a slightly drunken slur, staring at the last remnants of her wine as she swirled it around her glass, 'After everything he went through with you, Greg said he couldn't face getting married again. I thought he'd eventually come around, especially when Jeremy came along… sorry, *Jerry*! But, he never did. In the end I had to change my surname to Armitage by deed poll to keep up appearances.'

Sophie gulped down a slug of her wine and tried not to react. After the initial shock, an unexpected sadness set in; she tumbled into bed that night with a rotten feeling inside. Ruth seemed subdued as well, disappearing to bed with a curt, 'Night all.'

Sophie knew that Clara had always wanted her day in the sun – marriage in a church with roses above the door and flowers adorning the end of every isle, with the perfect dress, a horse drawn carriage… and Sophie had imagined that's exactly what Greg had provided her with, once their own annulment had come through. Instead, it emerged Clara and Greg had lived together for two years in a small, one-bedroom flat close to Leazes Park in Newcastle and he'd started his software business sitting on their single bed with a laptop propped up on his knees. A bigger house in Heaton had followed, and finally the house in Durham five years ago. Clara had never got to enjoy her day in the sun.

The last thing the three of them agreed to before they turned in was that they needed some help. And out of all their friends and acquaintances, Paul was the most trustworthy. They'd all known him the longest and as Clara had pointed out, none of them could countenance him defrauding Greg, his life-long best friend. He certainly wouldn't be involved in a plot to intimidate the three of them.

Clara fired off a text message with an invite to the caravan and Paul responded immediately, promising to be with them tomorrow. They turned in, hopeful that Greg's greatest supporter would help them decide how to proceed.

Twenty-Seven

Sophie heard a rattle coming from inside the caravan and realised her phone was vibrating against the fold-away table. She dodged inside and checked the caller ID before answering; it was Paul. She was still supporting her clients by phone, but only answering calls when she was sure who was calling. All three of them had received calls and text messages from 'unknown numbers' in the first few days of the caravan adventure and had been sure they were from the Meat Man. She now let virtually every call go to her answer machine.

'Where on earth is this blessed campsite?' Paul complained as soon as they'd swapped greetings, 'I've followed your instructions to the letter and ended up at a pig farm!'

Sophie smiled, 'You should have waited for the next left turn. Go back to the B-road and look for a blue three-bar gate with a hand-painted, 'Borrowby Caravan Park', sign.'

Twenty minutes later Paul's car pulled up next to their caravan. As soon as his feet landed on the grass he was accosted by Jerry who challenged him to a game of football.

'Oh, I've got someone much better than me to be goalie!' Paul assured the eager eight-year-old. From the other side of the car, Stephen, Paul's youngest son jumped down from the Range Rover. Jerry's eyes went as wide as saucers when he caught sight of the nine-year-old, with whom he was already friendly, despite the two boys meeting up on an infrequent basis.

Paul, Sophie, and Clara watched Jerry fire penalties at Stephen for five minutes and, when Ruth appeared from the direction of the farmhouse with milk and bread clasped to her bosom, they left the boys to it, decamping to the table inside the caravan.

Deciding to let Paul in on their secret location hadn't been an easy decision. Having had two run-ins with the Meat Man, and one with He-Man, Clara was of the strong opinion that they should contact no-one with knowledge of Greg's task. She reasoned that they could only trust themselves, and she didn't want her son to encounter either man ever again. Sophie could sympathise with her view, as the Meat Man sounded like a nasty piece of work, but she'd pointed out that her encounter with Skeletor had been less intimidating. She also argued that they wouldn't be able to complete Greg's task without outside help, not if they also wanted to discover why their three pursuers were so intent on them failing.

Paul was well over six feet tall, and at university had towered over all of them, as well as Greg. Sitting in the caravan, his knees were jammed up against the table top. It had been a bit of a running joke that he stood almost a foot above Greg, who hadn't measured more than five foot five inches tall. Together they'd looked rather incongruous, not that either of them had been faintly bothered by the difference in height, to them it had been a tried and tested source of jokes and when they'd been single, a double-act that had incorporated chat-up lines.

Feeling a little awkward behind the small table in the confined space, Paul said, 'Good to see you're all …erm, getting along. It's all been a bit quiet. I guess you've been out here... on holiday together?'

Sophie ignored Paul's poorly worded intimation that the three of them were the best of pals. They were all nursing hangovers from the night before and a faint aura of embarrassment hung around the caravan. She cut to the reason for inviting him and set about explaining why they were holed up in East Yorkshire, with Clara and Ruth joining the story to share their experiences of meeting the Meat Man, He-Man, and Skeletor.

Paul's manner changed from convivial guest to one of concerned recruit to their cause as they told him about the message on the backyard wall, as well as Ruth's unwelcome letter. Clara's run in with the Meat Man both at home, and with He-Man in the street, and Sophie's conversation with Skeletor on the Knavesmire had been the clinchers and as they'd hoped, he immediately offered any assistance he could give.

'My sister isn't too chuffed that I've block booked the caravan for the next few weeks, but it's either that or face increasingly threatening behaviour from Meat Man and his mates,' Sophie told him.

Paul grinned at the nicknames the ladies had come up with. Labelling the three men was *so* Sophie and Clara. It was good to see the two women getting on and sparking off each other, as they had done all those years ago. Ruth also seemed somehow different, far less confrontational. Paul was surprised Ruth had jumped at the chance to join the ladies and assumed she must have received a significant scare.

'I'm so pleased you've asked for my help. I was worried when you disappeared and weren't answering your phones. To be honest, I've thought there was something strange going on since the day we went to Hamilton races.'

'How do you mean?' asked Ruth.

'Oh, just the car breaking down like that,' he replied, deciding not to mention the problems he'd had with his gate earlier that day. There was no need to make the three ladies more worried than they already were.

'You think someone sabotaged your car?'

Paul leaned back as best he could, trying to get comfortable on the thin foam cushion covering his seat. His knees scraped against the table and made it rise an inch. He nodded and returned to his original hunched position that didn't make the table wobble.

Clara was frowning, 'My car broke down on that first day racing when we went to Ripon. That was weird too! You don't think…'

Paul took on a sheepish expression, 'Erm… no. That was me I'm afraid…'

All three women leaned closer. Clara noticed Paul's cheeks had flushed a little.

'How do you mean?' inquired Sophie, a note of disquiet in her voice.

He indicated Clara and Ruth, 'I removed a spark plug while the two of you were in the services at Scotch Corner. It was just a way to get the three of you together for longer. It meant Sophie had to pick us up. Greg asked me to…'

'Hold on a minute,' Clara said sternly, 'Greg has something to do with this… I knew it! Him and his insane surprises – and you're in on it, aren't you!'

Holding up both his hands, Paul 's brow furrowed and he closed his eyes as if fending off an invisible wall of pain as all at once, the three women began to demand answers.

A troubled silence eventually fell, with much crossing of arms, rolling of eyes between the women and intent accusatory stares directed at Paul.

'Greg wanted you to… well, *be like this…*' he said quietly, '…being able to talk to each other… to communicate meaningfully without past history getting in the way. He told me the task he'd set you would bring the three of you together and asked me to try and… help it along if things got a bit rocky. And he was right to ask. I reckoned you needed a helping hand to work together, after all the arguments at the reading of the will. So I manufactured a way for your first visit to the racecourse to be… *managed* in order to get your arguments out of the way before you reached Ripon…'

Paul ran out of words and stared miserably around the table, taking in one disgruntled face after another.

'Paul…'

It was more of a controlled explosion than a spoken word. He turned toward Clara and immediately shot back against the caravan wall, his eyes wide. She was trembling with rage, and despite the considerable size difference, she looked about to leap across the caravan and throttle him. Ruth and Sophie didn't move a muscle; Clara held the room.

'Tell us…' she snarled, 'Tell us that you and Greg aren't responsible for sending these men after us. Tell us that this whole mess isn't just another of Greg's surprises being directed in his absence… *by you.*'

Paul was already shaking his head half-way through her sentence, but when Clara spat out her last few words his easy-going charm fell away and his face contorted into a riot of emotions.

'I… no… no, no, no! It's not like that at all! It was just the car.

Really! Greg said I was to try and get the three of you to start enjoying each other's company. I don't know anything about this Meat Man and his accomplices.'

Sophie had been the least vocal so far, but there was something about the way Paul's eyes flitted between them that made her feel uneasy. Despite his protests, she was sure he was holding back.

'What is it?' she asked softly.

Paul gave her a questioning look.

'There's something else isn't there. Something gnawing away at you. Perhaps something Greg wants you to do that you're not happy with… or not sure about.'

Ruth and Clara leaned in closer. For Clara, this meant practically kneeling on her foam cushion.

Paul looked like a frightened rabbit in a set of car headlights. His eyes dropped to the table, and with shoulders hunched, head down and hands clasped together on his lap, he began to speak between heavy breaths.

'Greg called me three days before he died. I went to the house and… he was weak and looked… awful. He was my best friend and he was dying, and it crushed me. He was so unafraid and brave. He actually smiled. He smiled throughout. And he told me about his surprise and asked for my help. He knew I would do *anything* for him… but asked for so little.'

Paul flicked his eyes up at Clara for a split second before returning to doggedly examine the edge of the table.

'He told me about the task and said everything was in place and that he wanted to bring his family together, something he'd ignored for far too long. But he needed me to keep an eye on the three of you and make sure you gave it a proper chance.'

For a man well over six feet, Paul suddenly seemed small, head bowed, hunched over the table. A palm wiped nervous sweat from his forehead and he frowned in concentration.

'Greg asked me to help you two to start talking,' he said, indicating Clara and Sophie with a finger, but not looking at them, 'They'll do the rest, he said. And make Ruth experience more than Armitage Hall, she's forgotten how to have a good time. He said that he'd realised life was over in far too short a time and it was family, and friends like me, that gave it depth and offered fulfilment.'

Paul was almost in tears. When Clara checked, both Ruth and Sophie were welling up too.

'That's all very touching,' Clara said sternly.

Paul blinked, sighed and looked up, appearing somewhat abashed.

'What else Paul,' Clara added, allowing a harshness to enter her tone, 'Come on, what else did Greg ask you to do?'

'Nothing,' he replied blankly.

'You're lying. There's something else.'

Sophie shot her a quizzical look. Clara ignored it and went back to concentrating her gaze on Paul. His eyes were darting round the caravan, but eventually came to rest outside the window where the two boys were playing football.

'Greg didn't tell me everything,' Paul said resignedly, 'He could be secretive at times. But, you don't spend almost twenty years around someone like Greg without being able to know when something isn't right.'

Paul closed his eyes and breathed out raggedly, 'I'm sure Greg was planning more than just your task around the racecourses in order to reignite your friendships. There was that... *something* about him the last time we talked. It's bugged me ever since.'

He bit his lip and slowly shook his head.

'It's infuriating. Greg was up to something, and he wouldn't tell me what it was. I asked him again and again – he refused point blank to answer, he just... smiled. All he would say is that he'd be killing three birds with one stone.'

'Oh, wonderful!' Clara exclaimed, 'I guess we're the three birds then.'

'I'm not so sure. I asked him what he meant, but he wouldn't say. I'm worried he may have made some bad business decisions... and upset the wrong people.

'Is that it? Ruth asked, aghast, 'Has Greg got enemies we don't know about, who are taking their revenge on us?'

Paul shook his head again, 'I really, truthfully don't know,' he pleaded, 'All I could get out of Greg was that his only regret was...'

Paul paused, keen to quote Greg word for word, '...that he'd not get to see the look on their faces when he finally showed his hand.'

***

They'd been sitting around the caravan table for a further half an hour before Clara said the words, 'Okay, Paul, that's enough. I think you should leave.'

Sophie and Ruth nodded their agreement and Paul offered the table a sheepish smile.

'I don't think any of us are impressed with you,' Sophie said sadly, causing Paul's smile to immediately fade. Clara and Ruth nodded their agreement.

She continued, 'We asked you here for advice, but I think we're even more confused. What's worse, I don't know if we can trust you.'

Stricken with remorse, Paul launched into a bunch of reasons why they should place their faith in him. His remonstrating was cut short by Ruth.

'We can't be sure you're on our side, Paul,' she said, delivering her words with cold, hard steadfastness.

It was a simple statement that brought his flow of words to a shuddering halt. Less than a minute later, Paul's car quietly trundled off the campsite. He'd not uttered another word.

As his car disappeared down the single-track lane, Clara's thoughts turned to Greg. He'd loved to reveal a big secret. Secrets that allowed him to spring surprises, she thought mournfully. She didn't know why, but a particular surprise bubbled up from her memory.

It had been a warm summer evening. She could remember there had been swallows swooping and diving along the tree-lined road in Durham. Greg had driven her there from Heaton on the pretence of taking her to a fantastic new restaurant he'd discovered. Without warning, they'd pulled into a driveway and Greg had announced she was sitting outside her new home.

Yes, it was a beautiful house, but she'd wanted to scream at him. Yet she hadn't... screaming at Greg was useless, he'd just ignore you and flash his boyish smile. Before you knew how he'd managed it, you'd be apologising for screaming. It made her wonder how many times Paul had apologised to his best friend...

Twenty-Eight

9th June 2016

Sophie always looked forward to visiting her sister's caravan. It was the perfect place to regain perspective. Although you had to be careful; its simple, quiet style of living could become strangely beguiling. It was all too easy to lose touch with the outside world. If you allowed each day to melt into the next, you could easily succumb to its charm and forget there was a life beyond this pretty little valley enclosed by the thick wood on one side and endless bracken covered hills on the other.

The No Regrets syndicate had been on the campsite for ten days when Dennis called to confirm Whatever You Want was still suffering from sore shins. However, Fun Boy Frankie was preparing to race at Carlisle later in June, ahead of contesting a Sales Race down at Newbury in July. The trainer had chosen to call Ruth, but she was preparing lunch for everyone, so Sophie sat on the caravan steps and answered her phone on her behalf. Sophie had to catch herself. Ruth Armitage, the woman who up until recently could only contribute sneers and barbed comments, had offered to make ham salad sandwiches for everyone's lunch… *in the tiny galley of their caravan*!

Dennis gave Sophie the impression he was ever so slightly peeved that he wasn't speaking with Ruth. This notion brought a smile to her face. He went on to explain what a Sales Race involved and the fact he'd entered the horse many months before. To her surprise, it didn't mean that Fun Boy Frankie was going to be sold if he won, it actually sounded like an excellent chance for the gelding to win a considerable amount of prize-money. It was after he'd imparted this racing information that Dennis pointed out amiably to Sophie, 'I got the feelin' yer all enjoyed yer yard visit here last week?'

'Yes. Far more enjoyable than our first visit,' Sophie confirmed.

'I'd have to agree,' replied the trainer amiably, 'They're gettin' better. But then you set the bar low on your first visit.'

The date for their third visit to Dennis' yard had fallen only a day after their calamitous meeting with Paul at the caravan site. This stable visit had meant all of them, plus Jeremy and Bella squeezing into Clara's car for the forty minute cross-country trip to Malton. They'd spent another interesting and pleasant hour and a half with Dennis. Once Sophie had taken their obligatory photo with a newspaper, and she'd emailed the evidence of their attendance off to the solicitors, they'd headed straight back to the campsite.

'Is Martha feeling better?' Sophie asked.

There was a pause from Dennis.

'To be honest, I wasn't aware she was ill,' he admitted.

Sophie explained that Martha had been feeling unwell when they'd returned to Frankie's box after watching his morning gallop. Once she'd guided the gelding into his box the stable lass had excused herself. No-one had seen her for the rest of the visit.

'I'm sure she's fine now,' Dennis assured her, 'Martha's been riding out three or four lots a day since you were here.'

Sophie allowed herself another half-smile. It was perhaps typical of a man like Dennis that his method for calculating whether an employee was fit and well should be determined by their ability to ride a number of horses each morning.

'Will it just be you three going to Carlisle?' Dennis inquired.

'Yes, just us ladies. Paul won't be with us this time.'

As a result of his visit and subsequent revelations, Paul hadn't been considered for their trip to the North West with Frankie. His apologies had been heartfelt, but ultimately hadn't helped his cause. Clara had been his greatest critic, being intensely annoyed that he'd manipulated her at a time when she was feeling vulnerable after the Meat Man's visit, as well as during the visit to Ripon races.

However, neither the Meat Man, nor either of his two accomplices had put in an appearance since Paul's departure. As Ruth had pointed out, if Paul was in cahoots with them, the Meat Man would surely have been knocking on the caravan door within a day or two reminding them of the dire consequences of completing Greg's task.

It had also placed a question mark against how they should attend the stables.

'These men know about the task and that we have to go racing,' Sophie had pointed out, 'We have to assume they also know we have to attend the stables on the first Wednesday of every month. Going to the trainer's yard could mean... well, they could be waiting for us.'

None of them had considered forfeiting the task. Instead, they'd taken a tour around the B roads of North Yorkshire, ensuring they weren't being followed either to or from the stables.

'Anyway,' Dennis went on, 'Ruth's family turned up after you'd left. About five of them I reckon. They only stayed for a few minutes, had a look around and went home again. Was all a bit odd, but that's owners for you.'

'The Armitages?'

'That's them. The old woman ordered the others about for a bit and then they left. Was a bit of a rum do.'

Sophie filed this information away for discussion with Ruth and Clara later. She'd had one or two important questions to ask Dennis.

'Have you read Greg's document, Dennis?'

The trainer paused, 'You mean that task thing of his, telling me how I have to train and race your horses?'

'Yes, that's the one. In fact, I've been studying it.'

'Have you now,' said Dennis, his words tinged with trepidation.

'Would you have another horse running this month that might allow us to attend as owners? I mean, other than Fun Boy Frankie?'

Again, the line went silent as Dennis considered her request.

'I might have, why?'

Sophie explained that after reading Greg's task document at length, she'd come to the conclusion that if Dennis was to give them explicit instructions, they could go to the races with another racehorse from his yard, as long as it was a racehorse of his choosing.

'Based on recent experience we have a… umm… potential *security risk* if we go racing with Frankie at the moment,' she said, hoping Dennis would allow this nugget of information to pass by without any further investigation. It was no surprise when he didn't.

'You mean someone's after you? Tryin' to stop you gettin' your money from Greg?' he immediately deduced.

'Erm… yes, that's about the top and bottom of it.'

'Blummin' money and family. It makes people go daft,' the trainer rumbled, seemingly happy to leave the matter there, 'Yes, of course. Charlie Soap runs next week, two days before Frankie, would he do you?

Still holding the mobile phone to her ear, Sophie did a gleeful leap from the steps that made the caravan wobble on its mountings. It had taken several days of immersing herself in Greg's task document, but she'd managed to tease out the smallest of holes - in reality no more than a hairline crack in its text. Nonetheless, it was there, and she had been determined to take a claw hammer to the crack and make it work for the three of them.

She thanked Dennis, arranged the Owners Badges with him for Charlie Soap and rang off.

Sophie's working life was ruled by paperwork - interminably long, detailed forms that required filling and filing on a timely basis with the relevant authorities. In a job where a client's depression and mental instability often combined to create hugely complex cases of grief, you couldn't afford to get the paperwork wrong. As a grief counsellor, Sophie was fastidious when it came to documenting her clients' state of mind. She had to be. If she missed, or mis-recorded a suicide risk… well, the consequences were unthinkable.

Greg, on the other hand, had been an ideas man - it was always the big picture with him, the short term strategy and the long term roadmap which needed to be imparted, or sold to people around him. It was always the people around him who would place the meat on the bones of his idea and actually make his plan a reality. Sophie knew that Greg wouldn't have written the task document, he may not have even read it through… he'd have left it to his solicitor. And in Sophie's experience, solicitors could get things wrong, sometimes with unintended consequences.

She'd read a particular paragraph in Greg's task dozens of times, sensing there was something awry. It had been so subtle she'd missed it several times, just as Mr Sedgefield or one of his minions had done when drafting the document for Greg. Yet upon that one word hung a way for Clara, Ruth, and herself to complete Greg's task whilst keeping the Meat Man and his two associates guessing.

'It all comes down to one central issue,' Sophie told Clara and Ruth later that evening. They were sitting outside the caravan, their barbeque long since finished, watching the fire send short-lived sparks into the star-filled blackness.

Sophie continued, 'We are stuck with being at certain racetracks at specific times. The Meat Man knows our syndicate name and by association, our horses names, so all he has to do is wait for either Fun Boy Frankie or Whatever You Want to be declared to race and make his plans to stop us.'

'The daily runners are printed in virtually every newspaper, and on hundreds of websites,' Ruth agreed.

'So that's how he knows where and when we're going racing,' Clara said gloomily.

Sophie grinned into the gathering darkness, 'I may have found a way to outfox him. Or maybe send the Meat Man on a wild goose-chase.'

Greg's task document had been explicit – it stated the three ladies *must* go racing together at least once a month. However, the task recognised that racehorses could be flighty, unreliable creatures, as could the weather. If either horse was unable to race in a given month, Greg had an agreement with Dennis that the trainer would allocate the ladies a substitute horse of his choice. Clara, Sophie, and Ruth would then attend the races to complete their monthly task, albeit with a horse they didn't actually own.

Ruth and Clara squinted at Sophie from their lawn chairs as she explained.

'Because Quo is unable to race, we can swap!' Sophie pointed out excitedly, 'And there's no way the Meat Man and his accomplices will know!'

Clara screwed her face up, 'For heaven's sake Sophie, what the heck difference does it make if we go racing with a different racehorse?'

Sophie tossed her head back and let out a cry of frustration before ploughing on, 'It means we can go racing without The Meat Man knowing where we're going to be!'

146

Unconvinced, Ruth queried, 'Are you sure?'

Sophie beamed at her, 'I've spoken with Thomas, you know, the young solicitor who was at the reading of the will and who came with us to the first stable visit?'

They both nodded.

'He's confirmed it. The way the task document is written, we can go racing with Frankie *or* another horse Dennis chooses for us!'

She quickly added, 'He admitted it wasn't quite in the spirit of the task, but he checked with Mr Sedgefield who also agreed I was right.'

Grinning from ear to ear, Sophie leaned back in her lawn chair, knitted her fingers together and extended both her arms above her head and declared, 'Oh, yes!'

Ruth and Clara both wriggled to the edge of their chairs, not an insignificant achievement for Ruth, whose hips had a habit of getting wedged into the light, thin seats.

'We can do this because the task was written incorrectly?' she boggled.

'Yup!' Sophie confirmed gleefully, 'At last, my grade E in A-Level English Literature has come in useful!'

'So you spoke with Dennis. What did he say?' Clara demanded, beckoning urgently to Sophie for her to give up the rest of her story.

Sophie leaned forward and confirmed again that her discovery meant they could go racing without telegraphing where and when they would be racing.

'Yes, but how did Dennis react?' Clara complained, her patience wearing thin.

Sophie cast her mind back to the conversation with Dennis and began to relay it word for word.

'That would be great, Charlie Soap would be perfect. Where's he running?' Sophie had asked Dennis excitedly.

'Aye, well, there's a thing,' he'd replied, 'Charlie Soap's running at Ascot next Tuesday...'

'That sounds okay. I'm sure we can make that date. It's a bit of a trek in the car, but it'll do us fine.'

Dennis had pressed on, 'Charlie Soap is running in the Coventry Stakes at Ascot, that being *Royal Ascot*. It's one of the top two-year-old races of the season.'

'Ah... that's... nice,' Sophie had fumbled, as the importance of the race and the meeting slowly dawned on her. She'd been unsure whether to be excited or daunted, in the end settling for a thoughtful silence.

'You three lasses can find somethin' nice to wear. I'm told it's a bit of a thing for the ladies...' Dennis had added before breaking into a chuckle.

Twenty-Nine

'I've got two days to find an outfit for Royal blummin' Ascot?' Clara shrieked for the third time, 'You must be insane!'

She was strutting up and down the caravan's thin corridor, hands either on hips or thrown in the air as she continued her tirade.

'...and what will we do with Jerry? We can't leave him here!' she added, striding unthinkingly over Bella who lay flat out on the caravan floor. The greyhound swivelled a wary eye at her but otherwise remained immobile.

'We've been through this Clara,' sighed Ruth, 'I mentioned Jerry and to Dennis. He said he can stay at the yard. There will be plenty of people there to look after him for you.'

'Yes, but just two days warning!' Clara moaned, 'It takes me two days to choose a new pair of shoes, never mind an entire outfit! And what about my hair, my nails, and my make-up?'

'You and I have very different priorities these days,' Sophie noted airily from the other end of the caravan.

Clara stared unimpressed down the corridor to where Sophie was sat cross-legged, reading on her bed. She was wearing a faded white t-shirt two sizes too big for her that informed the world in bold black text that 'Frankie Says Relax'. A pair of baggy, stripy red and white cloth shorts were topped off with a pair lurid green fluffy slippers.'

'Says the woman whose idea of chic is to give her hair a brush through with her fingers before she leaves the house each day!' called Clara irritably.

'I only did that at University.'

'Really?' Clara returned petulantly, 'You're still wearing the same clothes you hung round in when you were eighteen! Look at yourself – you're a symphony of late eighties fads.'

'Give us a break, Clara,' Ruth chimed in behind her, 'It's only a race meeting.'

'It's *Royal Ascot!*' Clara bellowed, so loud Bella got to her feet and trotted down the caravan, flopped down beside Sophie, and looked at her with worried eyes, 'It's one of the society events of the year. Do you two live under stones in a cave?'

Clara waved a hand dismissively at Ruth, 'Don't you ever aspire to wear anything more than an undersized cardigan that's constantly in danger of pinging a button across the room?'

Ruth's lips pushed out into a pout and she wrapped a self-conscious hand protectively around her bosom. Clara continued her rant, but Ruth was too busy looking her sister-in-law up and down. Until recently, she'd have torn into Clara with a vengeance, trading insults with her until the two of them were close to clawing each other's eyes out. She didn't know why, but Ruth felt the caravan was doing her good. There was no more waking up and dreading the day ahead, she'd started to *enjoy* the banter between her and the two women. And so, she didn't scream and rant. She didn't stamp her feet and shape her face in to a ready scowl. Instead, she smiled sweetly. Clara glanced at Ruth and immediately her brow dipped into a frown.

'What?' she asked, looking down at herself, unsure why Ruth wasn't firing insults back at her.

'Clara,' Ruth announced with an even broader smile, 'I have three words for you.'

'Oh, here it comes,' Clara said with a roll of her eyes.

'Shopping trip to Leeds.'

'That's four words,' called Sophie from the other end of the caravan.

Clara had her mouth open, ready to whack a scathing rebuke back at the taller woman, only to find she had no response to give. She cocked her head to one side and examined the now beaming Ruth for a few seconds.

'Are you feeling alright?'

Ruth said, 'I want you to take me to Leeds and help me buy an outfit for Ascot. It's Saturday tomorrow, we can drive over and spend the day. I doubt the Meat Man will be looking out for us in Leeds city centre.'

Clara eyed her uncertainly.

Ruth continued, 'And you can get yourself sorted at the same time. Call it…'

'Can I come too?' Sophie interrupted, having walked the length of the caravan to witness first hand Ruth acting peculiar and for her, completely out of sorts, 'On reflection, my clothes may not quite cut the mustard at Ascot.'

'A girls shopping trip…' Clara queried uncertainly, 'With you two?'

Ruth caught Sophie's eye and raised both eyebrows in a silent salute, 'Yes, I think that's what we're saying, and I'm asking for you, Clara, to act as our erm.. *advisor* on what would be the appropriate fashion for Ascot… within my budget.'

Clara started to laugh, all her anger and frustration having fizzled out like a wet firework, 'Sod your budget, Ruth, I'm paying for everything – all three of us. Greg is going to buy each of us an outfit fit to meet the Queen!'

Thirty

Bates was alone. That's why he came to Scotland. He liked being the only human for miles in every direction. He valued the freedom a solitary existence offered and actively sought it out. To be truly alone in the United Kingdom you had to work harder and harder to seek out these places. Few of them still existed. People had infested everywhere in Britain as far as Bates was concerned. So he came to Scotland to be alone.

Leaning back in his lawn chair Bates tugged at his cap, pulling the brim just over his eyes. Despite sitting under the cover of a beech tree, the afternoon sun was still bright enough to cut through the branches and invade the darkness when he closed his eyes. In front of him, Loch Awe lapped listlessly at the sandbank he had been casting from for the last few hours in a vain search for a trout supper. A fishing rod and tackle lay beside the chair along with the remnants of a sandwich wrapper and several empty plastic processed meat sleeves. A little way away, his motorbike leaned on its stand close to a pitched one-man tent.

Bates was in the process of dozing off when one of the four phones in his rucksack chimed and began vibrating. He grumbled as he pulled the pack towards him and located the offending device. He read the first message.

UNKNOWN: We need to move quickly. Where are you?

BATES: Scotland. What's up?

UNKNOWN: The syndicate has a horse running at Royal Ascot tomorrow. Ownership altered overnight. Forms part of their task. Horse called Charlie Soap. Opportunity for you.

Bates grimaced.

BATES: Not enough notice.

UNKNOWN: Opportunities running out. Ladies proving more resilient than expected. Statement of intent required.

Bates looked out across the empty loch and a hawk screamed in the distance. He took his time, made a call and finally composed his reply.

BATES: Leave it with me.

UNKNOWN: Let them know we mean business.

BATES: Yes, I will.

He dozed for a few minutes, waiting for a further message. No second thoughts came through. Twenty minutes passed and he'd received no indication that the client had any reservations. He made another short call.

Bates jumped to his feet and started to collect his gear. He smacked his lips – they were still greasy from his last meat stick – and smiled. He'd waited for this moment for two months. He'd just been let off his leash.

Thirty-One

14th June 2016

Dennis would rarely display nervousness before a race. Over the years he'd carefully nurtured a reputation for level-headed stoicism, erring on the side of cautious optimism. Even when he was at the height of his training success in the mid two-thousands, it would take a special horse and a high profile race for him to reveal the turmoil bubbling within him.

The Coventry Stakes was due to be run in twenty-five minutes time and Dennis tried not to dwell on the fact he had a proper contender and expectation was high. With a perfect race record of two wins from two runs, both executed in tantalizingly impressive style, Charlie Soap would be giving Dennis his first crack at a Group race in nine long years. That alone was enough to make him nervous.

However, Dennis' current state of unease had nothing to do with Charlie Soap – at present the colt was the least of his worries. He had another, far more pressing reason to be nervously shifting his weight from foot to foot in the Ascot parade ring. Dennis watched as Sophie, Clara, and Ruth floated over the pristine grass of the parade ring in jaw-dropping summer dresses. They would be joining him in a moment... meaning he would need to launch into his prepared speech.

It was the perfect day for it. It was warm without being too hot, balmy without too much of a breeze. Sophie scanned the Ascot paddock again. It was heaving with men in top hats, middle aged women in elegant outfits and younger women showing plenty of skin. Amongst the people connected with runners she noticed a TV camera crew was running around after a chap with a microphone – there was someone to avoid if at all possible. She spotted Dennis on the fringes of the hubbub and allowed her amusement to show, the corners of her mouth turning up. Used to seeing him in his yard clothes, she'd almost passed him by. He looked out of place in his morning suit and shiny top hat. Her smile broadened as recognition registered on the trainer's face, quickly followed by genuine astonishment.

Clara had certainly delivered on her promise to deck the three of them out appropriately for Royal Ascot. They'd had an absolute ball in Leeds at the weekend.

Sophie had been reminded during their shopping jaunt that Clara had always insisted on being well dressed as a teenager, despite having precious little money. She would save for weeks, and sometimes months, to acquire a piece of clothing that she rated perfect for her, rather than compromise with a more affordable, but lesser item. She'd spend what Sophie at the age of eighteen, considered eye-watering sums on some of her clothes. Her wardrobe was small, but high quality, and when Clara was done with an item of clothing she would sell it, because as she pointed out, quality always retains its value.

And yet Clara hadn't been a brand snob. It was the cut, the feel, and most importantly, the style that she looked for, not the name. That said, when Clara had discovered a perfectly fitting Chanel jacket in a second-hand clothing shop in Newcastle for under ten pounds in their first few weeks at university, she hadn't shut up about it. That jacket had formed the basis of an outfit she'd worn to all manner of events throughout all three years of her university degree.

As she and Ruth had been escorted around Leeds by Clara, Sophie remembered just how critical her friend had been of her own wardrobe at university.

'You dress sloppily,' Clara had once told her, 'That's as enthusiastic as I can get. If only you'd allow me to clothe you and cut that lank hair of yours into something resembling a style, you'd make a much bigger impression. You've got the body and face of an English rose and yet you wrap yourself in baggy clothes and enough make-up to pass as a circus clown!'

Given the urgency, and the fact Clara was paying, Sophie had swallowed her protests and allowed her teenage friend to act as her style consultant for the day. She had to admit, the result was pretty impressive. However, if her own transformation turned heads, it was completely blown out of the water by Ruth's new look.

For the first half hour of the day, spent in an eye-wateringly expensive boutique, Ruth had rediscovered her scowl, rejecting every piece of clothing Clara had suggested. As Clara searched for that key item to build Ruth's 'look' around, she'd become increasing frustrated with the younger woman's intransience. Inevitably, the two strongly opinioned women had argued. The argument had turned into a spat and the spat into a screaming match that had brought the incredibly posh-sounding sales assistant to their fitting room at a run.

'Ladies, please! A little decorum!' the mature, impeccably dressed woman had demanded sharply, silencing the altercation immediately. Her bosom heaving due to her hasty arrival, she had glared at the three of them over the rim of her spectacles with thinly veiled disgust and declared, 'Really. This is simply too much. Your caterwauling is upsetting Mrs Ponserby!'

The woman's chest rose again as she sucked in another breath, adding in a less strident tone, 'I trust my ladies will refrain from any further outbursts?'

The three of them had nodded back at the woman, desperately trying to keep a straight face. Clara had been the first to giggle when the thick cloth curtain had been drawn behind the woman, ensuring Ruth and Sophie followed suit soon after. Ruth's deep throated chuckle was entertaining to say the least. It extended their mirth to such an extent Sophie had eventually needed to shush the other two in fear the woman would return and insist they leave.

'Was I mistaken or does that sales assistant have a touch of the Dowager Countess from Downton Abbey?' Clara had said in a conspiratorial whisper.

'Yes! Maggie Smith,' Ruth agreed.

Sophie had allowed the renewed soft giggling to ebb away before saying, 'More like Mrs Slocombe from Are You Being Served, if you ask me!'

When they'd all regained control and Clara had dabbed away a few tears from the corner of her eyes, she'd turned to Ruth, bobbed down in front of her and said, 'Do you want to dress like your Mother for the rest of your life? And what is it with all your clothes and shoes being two sizes too small? There are women out there who would die for your hips and backside, let's make the most them. The men will come running!'

Stunned, Sophie had waited for Ruth to explode. But, as is often the way with Clara, she'd picked her moment perfectly. Ruth took a breath and nodded.

From that moment, it had turned into the most enjoyable, entertaining, frustrating, tiring, and exhilarating day's shopping of their lives.

Dennis did a double take, the roof of his mouth suddenly becoming dry. Ruth was wearing a dress that appeared to be sculpted to her body, emphasizing and smoothing her feminine shape. She now had a defined waist, and small heeled boots that seemed to be part of her, raking stylishly into her calves, rather than bulging like a pair of trotters. Her hat was stunning, with a wide brim that somehow managed to cast a softening shadow across her face.

The three women came to a halt in front of Dennis and, although Clara and Sophie were equally well turned out, the trainer was unable to prise his stare from the youngest of the three women.

'Put your tongue in Dennis, people are starting to stare,' Sophie joked.

Dennis blinked hard and grinning, replied, 'Well aren't you three a sight for sore eyes.'

His comment seemed to go down well, being received with a trio of smiles. He noticed Ruth's smile was tempered with a dash of relief. It was a crying shame he had to drop his bombshell. As excited casual conversation broke out between the four of them, Dennis decided he could afford to let the ladies enjoy the atmosphere a little longer.

The walkway around the outside of the parade ring was almost full of runners when Charlie Soap entered, led up by Martha. The terraces surrounding the parade ring thronged with race-goers, creating a bubbling amphitheatre of conversation. Sophie pointed Charlie Soap out, and when Ruth self-consciously looked up for the first time since entering the ring, she was shocked at the number of faces peering down at her. Her cheeks flushed and nerves jangled through her for a moment, but she fought them off by reminding herself of Clara's words. Ruth had been replaying that moment regularly that morning, as a way of bolstering her wavering confidence. Clara had been adamant.

'If you wear that dress to Ascot, men will want to be around you and women will want to *be* you,' Clara had said admiringly when Ruth had swept the changing room curtain aside and with a glum look, displayed the outfit Clara had insisted she try on. They'd argued for several minutes before she'd capitulated and donned the pale blue sleeveless dress. Once Ruth had realised the comment wasn't a cheap sarcastic crack, and that both Clara and Sophie were staring wide-eyed at her and clearly *did* think she looked good, she'd felt ten feet tall. It had been a number of years since she'd been complimented on her appearance, and she certainly couldn't remember any other women *ever* having done so.

Ruth swallowed hard, tilted her chin upwards toward the terraces of race-goers and settled her gaze on Martha leading Charlie Soap around the oval walkway. Ruth caught the young girl's eye and stepped across the paddock towards her. Martha smiled back, slightly questioningly at first, as if she couldn't quite place Ruth. Martha's smile broadened as she realised exactly who the tall, elegant woman was, and took in the transformation in its entirety. Her jaw dropped, her eyes popped.

Martha mouthed, 'Wow!'

As the stable lass passed with Charlie she called over a oneword description to Ruth: 'Stunning.'

Ruth mouthed, 'Thank you!' in return.

Clara and Sophie looked on, amused smiles on their faces.

'Do you think the hot pink works?' Clara asked, referring to the thin accent of colour running through the sash around Ruth's white boater. The same shade of pink was reflected in different ways through the outfits all three ladies wore.

Sophie didn't have chance to reply, as Ruth rejoined them and Dennis began to speak with an air of urgency, beckoning them all closer to him and lowering his voice.

'Ladies, there's something I need to share with you,' he announced in a very un-Dennis like manner. He paused, and starting with Ruth he looked each of the ladies in the eye, before returning to her and emitting a heavy sigh.

'Thing is, Charlie Soap is your racehorse.'

This revelation didn't result in the sort of reaction he was expecting. Instead of anger, demands for an explanation, and dark looks tinged with sadness and betrayal, Dennis met with three blank expressions and silence.

'I mean, the three of you own him,' he said with a shrug.

Sophie scrunched her face up, 'You mean we own him for today. You've altered his ownership for us so that we're not bending Greg's rules too much?'

Dennis shook his head.

'No. The three of you own him. He's yours.'

Sophie crossed her arms, and peered at Dennis with one eye almost shut, 'Eh?'

Dennis almost rolled his eyes, but caught himself. Instead, he spoke softly and slowly, whilst giving them a pained look.

'Look here, I bought him at the sales for Greg last year. Greg bought him – so he's your second horse. You own Frankie and Charlie Soap, not Whatever You Want.'

Clara asked, 'Why would you tell us he was owned by someone else?'

Dennis sucked in a breath and held it for a few seconds, rubbing his chin in an awkward fashion as he exhaled. In that moment Sophie was reminded of primary school and her teacher extracting a confession from one of the boys at the front of the class. Unfortunately, from the look on Dennis's face this tale of woe was going to be more serious than pulling girls' pigtails.

'Do you remember when you first came to my yard?'

Clara nodded and spun her index finger to hurry him along.

'I got given my own set of instructions from Greg's solicitors,' Dennis explained, 'They included having to immediately halt training and selling both Greg's horses the moment you failed his task. I already knew that Charlie Soap was pretty special and so when you all started arguing before we'd even got into the yard… I was worried the task would fail there and then, and I'd lose one of the best horses I've come across in the last fifteen years.'

Dennis dropped his gaze to his feet and dolefully scuffed one of his shoes through the top of the perfectly sculpted parade ring grass.

'I hadn't planned it, but when I went to show you the horses I… It was selfish. I didn't want to lose him, and it looked very probable the way the three of you were at each other's throats. He could be a very, very good horse. Possibly Group class – the best there is. When I took you all into the barn something came over me and I found myself showing you a different colt.'

The women shared a three-way look that managed to combine bewilderment with a touch of amusement. Sophie turned her back on Dennis and the three ladies shared a few short words before facing their trainer again.

'We weren't at our best that day,' admitted Sophie after Dennis had lifted his eyes from his shoes to inspect the ladies, keen to judge their reaction to his admission of guilt. Clara and Ruth nodded back at Sophie in silent agreement.

'It's… unexpected, but I suppose this news will put an edge onto today's race.'

'You won't lose any of the prize-money he's earned,' Dennis assured them, the signs of relief beginning to show in the trainer's face, 'And if you check the racecard, you'll see I've already altered him into your ownership.'

'I suppose we'll have a chat and discuss this with you after the race,' Sophie added, checking with her co-owners.

'Thank you, ladies,' Dennis said solemnly, 'I thank you for your understanding in this matter.'

Ruth beamed at him. She was not only pleased to officially part-own a horse running at Royal Ascot, but the way Dennis had dealt with his misdemeanour had impressed her. He bunched his lips together and gave her a determined smile back, but she noticed his eyes were dancing with what she assumed was the anticipation for the race.

'Why did you name him Charlie Soap?' she asked.

Dennis's frown returned.

'It's slightly embarrassing,' he admitted.

Sophie and Clara edged closer and cocked their heads.

'You named the other colt Fun Boy Frankie, he said, indicating Ruth, 'So… I though this one should be named after Sophie and Clara.'

Ruth and Clara returned a blank stare. Sophie frowned, but within seconds she was grinning at her companions.

'What?' Clara demanded.

Sophie turned back to Dennis, 'You like your cryptic crosswords in the Yorkshire Post, don't you?'

A sharp nod and an amused smile from Dennis indicated she'd worked it out.

'It's an anagram,' Sophie declared, 'Charlie Soap is an anagram of our names - Clara and Sophie.'

Ruth studied the trainer's weathered face for a long moment. Running the tip of her tongue along her bottom lip, she raised a newly shaped eyebrow and suggested, 'You're something of a dark horse, aren't you Mr Smith?'

Thirty-Two

Mitch rarely got rides in Group races, especially on horses with realistic chances. This was only the second time in three years he'd snagged a ride in such a high profile race and had no doubt the knot of nervousness in the pit of his stomach was due to the weight of expectation.

Martha released Charlie Soap onto the racetrack, called out a final, 'Good luck,' and Mitch calmly waited for his nervousness to be washed away. Finally being alone with his mount was a blessed relief. He looked forward to this moment every time he went racing; just him and the horse as one. He would sense whether the animal was keen and playful, or flat and workmanlike. Even a moody and intransigent partner would help steady his nerves, and in turn he would telegraph his own confidence to the horse through his reins during that first few strides and together they would strike up a relationship, a bond for the duration of the race.

But as Charlie Soap broke into a trot to follow his rivals up to the six furlong start, the twist in Mitch's stomach remained. Runners were scattered around the Ascot straight, some of them reduced to dots, shimmering in the heat haze developing around the starting stalls. This was very different to the provincial racecourses where Mitch tended to ply his daily trade and the enormity of the task ahead was threatening to overcome him.

This icy touch of self-doubt travelled onto the nape of his neck as he rose in the saddle. It had been a simple hand on his boot once aboard Charlie Soap in the parade ring that started it. The effect of that pressure from Dennis's fingers squeezing his foot and staring up into his eyes, so full of silent pleading, had remained with Mitch until he'd passed the last grandstand full of racegoers. He was a few strides into the country when he awoke from his stupor. It was as if leaving the noise of the crowd behind broke Ascot's soporific spell.

Mitch cast away thoughts of the parade ring, the perceived importance of the race, and his trainer's anxiety, and instead, concentrated on Charlie Soap. He felt strong and fluid under Mitch as he cantered, his daisy-cutter action stroking the tips of the turf. This colt had always been a cut above every other two-year-old he'd ridden up the Malton gallops this year and his first two wins had been nothing less than exhilarating. Charlie Soap had gears, plenty of them. His rivals had flattened out or faltered at Chester and Sandown, unable to cope with Charlie's relentless injection of speed. Horse and rider continued to slowly draw the starting stalls to them, every stride further away from the mêlée in the enclosures delivering another injection of confidence into Mitch.

They reached the stalls and stood behind them for what felt like an age, but finally a stall handler stepped forward. As the handler looped his lead rope through Charlie Soap's bit, a smile crept onto Mitch's face. He was led forward and the colt immediately slotted into his allotted bay, stall one of eighteen, standing tensed, ready for the gates to open. At least the decision as to which side of the course he would race on was already made; he'd run up the inside rail.

Mitch ran a gloved hand down from the colt's ear to the base of his neck.

'This is your league, Charlie,' he whispered, 'We're in the premiership now and you can be top banana. Let's show 'em what you've got.'

Mitch gave his mount a pat and felt Charlie Soap's ribs expand as the horse sucked in a deep breath. A pawing of the ground with his right foot was followed by a sharp snort from the colt that fired his hot breath into the plastic padded stall gate, inches from his nose.

It was Mitch's turn to tense; however, his nervousness was soon forgotten. A second later the gates split open and horse and jockey surged forward as one.

***

Sophie, Ruth and Clara had chosen to stay in the parade ring. Uncertain where to watch the race from, and noting that many of the other connections had remained there, the ladies joined their rival owners in watching as a long line of horses simultaneously jumped from the stalls. Unwilling to fight their way through the crowds and risk not finding a suitable vantage point before the off, around fifty people including the television crew and paddock officials were glued to the large portable screen at the back of the parade ring.

'Look for the orange cap,' Sophie reminded them.

'I know!' Clara complained.

A few seconds went by, the booming race commentary drowning out everything else around the course.

'Blast it!' Clara grumbled loudly, 'I can't see Charlie anywhere. Where on earth is he? On the far side or the near side?'

Ruth and Sophie share an amused look.

Ruth said, 'He's on the far side, in about third position in that group.'

'Why have they split in two?'

'The ground. Some of the jockeys must think it's faster ground up the stands side.'

'Shush you two, just watch the race!' Sophie scolded.

The camera position suddenly changed, showing only the nearside group. A grey horse called Silver Stone was leading, a line of five horses a length down and more in behind.

'Show us the far side!' Clara ordered angrily after a few seconds.

It seemed the director was listening, as a close up on the far side group soon showed Charlie Soap up against the rails in a share of third place, his green and orange silks standing out against the white rails.

'Mitch has him up there,' Ruth said excitedly as the camera position changed again, showing the entire field reaching the junction with the round course. At the bottom of the screen the two furlong pole came into view and within a few strides every jockey was pushing, issuing reminders, and urging on their mounts.

'He's in the lead!' exclaimed Clara.

***

Mitch had been niggling at Charlie Soap, but knew he still had more to give. The colt was stretching out beautifully, grabbing the ground and with the rail to run against, had remained perfectly straight throughout the first four furlongs. When the pacesetter in his group started to be scrubbed along over two out, Mitch had no choice, he had to go on. It was a shade early, but Charlie Soap was rolling now, he couldn't take the chance of holding onto him any longer. Taking a length out of his nearest rival, Mitch stole a quick glance over to his left - the grey horse leading the other group was beginning to falter, and a new contender was making ground with ominous ease. The horse was almost black, his jockey wearing the instantly recognisable dark blue silks of his rich and powerful Irish owners.

'Let's show 'em, Charlie,' Mitch called into the wind and he asked the colt for the extra gear he knew he'd never used before. Charlie Soap drew away from his group... two, then three lengths.

***

Sophie heard a scream when Charlie Soap suddenly shot clear of his field and assumed it was Clara, but something about its pitch wasn't quite right. Spinning round for a split second before returning to the television screen, she was delighted to discover the excited scream had come from Ruth!

There were shouts coming from several of the owners in the parade ring now, but none as loud as Clara, Ruth, and Sophie. Charlie Soap was careering away, one, two... now three lengths clear of the opposition... until he wasn't.

'Oh no,' said Sophie, the first to notice the danger.

A single horse from the nearside group had broken clear of its rivals and was making eye-catching progress. Seizing upon its target, the jockey in dark blue edged left under a two handed drive, drawing closer and closer to Charlie Soap.

'Come on, Charlie!' Clara yelled.

Beside her, Ruth screamed once more.

***

The final three strides of the 2016 Coventry Stakes lasted a lifetime for Mitch. Charlie Soap had given him everything and despite having to take up the running further from the finish than he'd have preferred, for one, glorious moment he had the race won. They'd beaten off their group, and there was clear ground to their right.

Tinteretto, the short-priced favourite came at him, moving inexorably closer with every stride. A huge roar from the Ascot stands over a hundred yards out from the finish signalled the race wasn't over. Yet Mitch knew his fate well before the explosion of noise from the crowd reached him. The challenger had the finishing pace and Charlie had done his running.

The chestnut horse swept majestically by and opened up by a length, the champion jockey on his back punching the air and standing up in the saddle the moment the finishing post was a flash of red to his right. Charlie Soap gave everything and had strained to go with the new leader for a stride, but secure in second, Mitch eased Charlie over the line and gave the colt a series of congratulatory slaps down his neck.

'Thanks, Charlie. Hard luck boy,' Mitch said quietly into the colt's ear as they slowed to a walk. The horse tossed his head back and snorted, forcing a smile onto Mitch's lips. They turned and cantered back toward the parade ring chute.

***

Mitch's smile broadened when Dennis and Martha rushed up to him and he could read the mixture of delight and excitement on their faces, and the greeting from Charlie Soap's newly informed owners could not have been more excitable and chaotic. By the time Mitch tore himself away from the three ladies, he was covered in lipstick, a fact not lost on the television anchor when a roving cameraman caught him jogging back to the weighing room.

'And here we have Mitch Corrigan returning to weigh in,' said the anchor, 'Always popular with the ladies, and judging by the colour of his face, Mitch has added a few more admirers after that ride in the Coventry!'

Mitch blessed the camera with an amiable smile and replied, 'If you think this is bad, you should see the state of Charlie Soap.'

In the parade ring the ladies heard the exchange and watched as Mitch winked cheekily into the camera before heading for the weighing room. It wasn't long before they began reliving each furlong of the race, telling the story of the race like excited schoolgirls.

Areas of green space started to appear in the parade ring as winning connections filtered back into the public areas, and the terraces emptied. Martha had long since disappeared back to the racecourse stables with Charlie Soap. Dennis had regained his colour, and his breath, and once the ladies excitement abated, he began to brief them on where he would take the colt next.

'There's the July Stakes at Newmarket, and the Richmond Stakes at Glorious Goodwood in late July. Assuming he comes out of today's race well, you have plenty to look forward to, ladies.'

Their trainer continued to discuss the race, his audience still on a high from shouting Charlie Soap home, questioning him excitedly. Dennis was explaining that the second placing at long odds, three lengths clear of the third horse home, represented an astounding achievement for the youngster. It was then that Ruth noticed the large, powerful looking man standing alone on the parade ring terrace nearest to them.

He was wearing a lounge suit that was too small for him, the sleeves tight around his muscular arms, cuffs finishing three inches up his forearm. His off-white shirt was unbuttoned and a red tie with an impossibly small knot hung like a noose half-way down his expansive chest. Ruth could have dismissed the man's image from her mind if it wasn't for two, far more disturbing attributes. He was staring, no... smirking horribly at her, his flabby, evil grimace making her shudder... His cold blue eyes stared unblinkingly at her. Again, she could have ignored him and gazed elsewhere, if it wasn't for what he was doing with his right hand. This really worried Ruth. The man was holding a metal cigarette lighter at arm's length. It had an inch high yellow flame and the man was waving the lit instrument from side to side.

'Clara... Sophie...' Ruth began, cutting across the ongoing conversation with Dennis. She touched Clara's arm, unable to take her eyes off the young man mountain, 'Can you take a look at our friend over here on the terrace please.'

Clara swung around and all the joy was washed from her face once she spotted the young fellow on the other side of the white parade ring railings.

'It's the Meat Man's side-kick, He-Man,' she croaked, her voice still rough from screaming Charlie Soap home.

The man seemed pleased he'd garnered the full attention of all three women, lifting his upper lip slightly to bare his teeth as the lighter continued to burn.

'Do you know him?' Dennis queried, moving in front of the three ladies and peering at the strange man half-way up the almost empty terrace. The man sniffed at Dennis, extinguished his lighter and called out to the women in a rasping tone.

'Last chance, ladies. You know what you must do.'

He leered at the group, turned his back, and strode confidently up the terrace, the pockets of his undersized suit jacket flapping behind him. He disappeared among the wave of race-goers returning to view the runners for the following race.

Dennis spun around, 'What on earth was all that about?'

Sophie looked the least shocked and so he settled his frown on her. She shrugged, flicking her gaze between the other two.

'It's a long story,' she said with a sigh, 'It's even more complex than your reason for deceiving us about Charlie Soap!'

Amid the excitement of being placed second in the Coventry, Dennis had forgotten he might still be in the doghouse. However, he still pressed his owners for an answer.

'Let's find somewhere to sit,' Sophie suggested, aware Clara was as white as a sheet despite Ruth offering a comforting arm around her, 'Then we can explain.'

Dennis agreed and the foursome began to make their way across the parade ring. A few yards before reaching the exit Sophie came to a halt on the carpet of grass and dug her jangling mobile phone out of her clutch bag.

'Just my sister,' she called to the others, 'I'll catch you up.'

Dennis nodded, and taking Clara by the arm escorted her across the horse walkway and into the public area of the course where he halted and began looking around for a suitable place to find a seat. Ruth was about to follow but hung back when she saw Sophie's mouth drop open and an expression of consternation spread across the co-owner's face. The next moment she was craning her neck over to where the Meat Man's accomplice had disappeared.

Ruth strode up to Sophie's side and anxiously asked what was wrong.

Sophie swung back to face her and for the first time since they'd met, Ruth thought she could detect fear in her friend's eyes.

'It's the caravan,' Sophie told her.

Swallowing hard before continuing, she added, 'It's on fire.'

Thirty-Three

'All my clothes are gone?' Clara complained bitterly.

Sophie sighed, 'Yes, everything went up. Apparently there's nothing left apart from a blackened caravan chassis. My sister is hopping mad.'

'Not as mad as I am!' Clara assured her.

Sophie took another slug of Pimms and almost choked, grumbling as she chewed on a sour tasting mixture of diced fruit. Forsaking the Owners and Trainers bar, Dennis had managed to find a table for them in one of the paddock-side restaurants. He parked Clara with her back to a wall so she could look out for any sign of the chunky young man with the lighter, and ordered drinks. She was now sipping at her own Pimms and regaining some of the colour in her cheeks, although complaining about the fire seemed to be doing that on its own - the alcohol was only helping the process along. Ruth had ordered a glass of mineral water, but hadn't touched it.

'At least we had the sense to leave Jerry with your sister,' Ruth pointed out, 'He could have been...'

Sophie swiftly directed a warning stare Ruth's way.

'...Yes, well. We won't dwell on that,' Ruth finished off lamely, going on to ask after Sophie's dog.

Sophie nodded positively, 'Yes, she's fine. I've spoken to the site owners and it turns out Bella was the one who warned them. She was barking and pawing at the farmhouse door. They came out to calm her down and saw the flames down on the site. They were too late to save our caravan, but stopped the fire spreading to the others.'

Up to speed on why the three ladies were living together in a caravan out in the wilds of North Yorkshire, Dennis had been relatively quiet for the last fifteen minutes, only posing the odd question. The trainer seemed to be ruminating about everything they'd discussed. However, a beep from his phone prompted him to speak up.

'Martha's going to join us,' he said, beginning to tap out a short reply, 'Are you ladies okay with that?'

'Sure, but perhaps we'll not burden her with our story and the er... difficulties with the caravan?' Sophie suggested.

Ruth and Dennis immediately agreed, but Clara replied in a faraway voice, 'He was giving us a final warning.'

'He was trying to scare us, just like the other times,' Sophie corrected.

'No, it was definitely a proper threat. I've worked it out you see.'

'What have you worked out, Clara,' Sophie asked irritably, her patience beginning to wear thin.

'The fire in Borrowdale must have been lit just before the race went off. Straight after, the Meat Man's side-kick is here holding a lighter...'

'Yes, we get the connection!'

'But don't you see?' said Clara, staring from face to face around the table, 'We thought we were safe, untouchable. No one knew where we were apart from Paul and Sophie's sister. She wouldn't burn her own caravan down... so it has to be Paul...'

'Paul Corbridge?' Dennis checked.

Sophie shook her head, 'I was as disappointed as both of you that he was keeping things from us, but Paul has nothing to gain from stopping us collecting Greg's money.'

'Yeah, he's already minted anyway,' said Clara, in a tone that suggested she thought everyone would be privy to this information, 'Paul doesn't need the money. He owned part of Greg's company and got twelve million when it was sold.'

Ruth gasped. This was news to her and it would be to the rest of the Armitage family. Greg had kept his own affairs very much to himself, but learning he'd not owned his company outright would come as a shock. However, it did explain why the amount in Greg's will didn't tally with the figure reported in the online media reports when he sold his business.

Clara continued, 'Perhaps Paul had a grudge against Greg and wants to see the money going outside the family. After all, he was always Greg's number two, the lesser light. He must have got terribly frustrated walking in his best friend's shadow for so long.'

This brought the table to an uneasy silence as everyone considered this possibility.

'I told my mother where I was,' blurted Ruth.

Three sets of eyes stared at her and she flushed, 'I've been telling her where I've been since I left Armitage Hall.'

'What on earth for?' Clara demanded.

Ruth shrugged, 'She insisted - she's my mother!'

'I suppose my sister might have told someone I was in her caravan, or Paul may have said something to someone without realising,' suggested Sophie.

'Maybe someone saw us shopping in Whitby,' Ruth added, 'Or they traced our phones, or your car, Clara. If they had access to our bank accounts they could...'

'Oh yeah, and maybe the Meat Man consulted Mystic Meg and asked her when would be the best time to burn our secret hideout to the ground!' said Clara, opening up her arms and waving her hands. This earned her a sorrowful pout from Ruth.

'Paul is still our number one suspect in my book. He lied to us, and I got the impression there's more he's not telling us.' Sophie concluded, crossing her arms resolutely across her chest and staring at her untouched glass of wine.

Dennis took in the three unhappy faces around the table and offered, 'Only met him a few times, but he seemed a straight-up sort of chap to me.'

Sophie unwound her arms and gave Dennis a weak smile, 'Truth is, we really don't know why this is happening, or who's behind it. One thing is clear though. As we get closer to finishing Greg's task, the attempts to intimidate and actively stop us are becoming more serious. We are running an increasing risk that one of us, or the people we love, are going to get seriously hurt. I keep imagining what would have happened if one of us had decided to stay behind at the caravan today.'

This sobering thought cast a thick cloak of gloom over the table. Their dark mood was still in evidence when Martha reached them and her smile was immediately downgraded to a concerned frown when she took a seat. She looked around the table uncertainly. It seemed no one wanted to share their reason for the strange atmosphere.

'Charlie's fine. He walked straight into his stable,' she said in a bright voice, 'He recovered quickly, I've given him a pick of grass and he drank gallons of water.'

'That's good to hear. Thank you, Martha,' said Sophie, forcing a smile, 'He's given us an amazing thrill.'

Galvanized by this statement, Clara and Ruth quickly added their own thanks, echoing Sophie's sentiments. Yet they were all tinged with shadows of nervous concern.

'Please, tell me what's wrong,' Martha said worriedly, 'Charlie hasn't been demoted or something like that has he? Or is it me... have I...'

All three ladies immediately assured Martha she wasn't the cause of their low spirits. Martha looked to Dennis, her eyes imploring him to place her mind at rest.

'You've done nothing wrong!' he assured her, 'The ladies have just received some bad news.'

'What bad news?'

Martha immediately slapped a hand to her mouth and winced, 'I'm sorry, it's none of my business.'

'Nonsense,' Dennis replied, with a trace of a smile, 'They've come second as owners in the Coventry at Royal Ascot, one of the top juvenile races of the year, but have also learned their erm... holiday home is no longer...'

'The caravan we've been living in was burnt to the ground while Charlie's race was running,' Clara announced.

Ruth put an exasperated hand to her forehead and Sophie sighed deeply.

'What?' Clara protested, her brow knitting together, 'The caravan is a gloopy black mess, why should we keep it a secret? It's not as if we can go back there.'

Neither Ruth or Sophie could find a counter argument and settled for rolling their eyes at each other.

'So that's why we're a bit glum,' Dennis said quietly, 'The ladies are in immediate need of a place to stay.'

'Oh dear, I'm so sorry for you. Where will you go?' Martha asked.

Clara almost shot back a dark, sarcastic reply, but the girl's inquiry was so genuine and heartfelt, her own words suddenly felt trite and selfish. They stuck in the back of her throat and she remained silent.

'Ah, it's funny you should ask,' Dennis answered before any of the ladies could form a response, 'You see, I think I may have the perfect location.'

He turned to face his owners, 'And it could earn me a reprieve for my lack of faith in these three fine ladies.'

Thirty-Four

Friday, 8th July 2016

'Come on Clara!'

Not for the first time that evening, Sophie pounded on the door to Clara and Jerry's cottage. The door swung open.

'Yes, I'm here. Keep your hair on!' Clara remonstrated, standing with one leg bent, trying to pull on a shoe.

'We're late. Or to be more precise, you're making us late.'

'It's fifty yards away! Dennis lives *fifty yards away*,' Clara complained, 'It'll take a whole minute to get there.'

Sophie leaned against the door frame, lifted her eyes skyward, and with an exaggerated sigh said, 'That's why we should be on time. We've no excuse to be late!'

When Sophie and Clara entered Dennis's kitchen-diner through the French windows at the back of the house, he and Ruth were already sitting down at the table, discussing something. Sophie only caught the back end of their conversation, which included a mention of Weatherbys and the BHA and she assumed they were talking about race entries.

Clara pulled out a chair and plonked herself down, still in a fluster. Noticing the other three all had pads and pens, she groaned and made to get up.

'Don't worry, you can sit down,' Sophie smiled knowingly, 'Here. I brought plenty,' she said, ripping a dozen sheets from her pad and pushing them across the table.

Clara's shoulders relaxed and she returned a grateful half-smile, 'Thanks. As Jerry told me the other day, I'm currently a rabbit with negative euphoria.'

Sophie laughed, but Dennis and Ruth frowned.

'Not a happy bunny,' Clara explained.

Once they'd both broken into a smile of understanding she continued, 'I had another call from Gertrude.'

The others grimaced. Even Ruth didn't try to hide her sympathy for Clara.

'She calls on the pretence of wanting to hear about how Jerry, sorry, 'our dearest Jeremy' is getting on, but really she's checking up to make sure we're not going to foul up her inheritance.'

'Think yourself lucky,' Ruth said gloomily, 'She calls me *every single day* for an update. I know she's my mother, but I'm getting heartily sick of it.'

Clara caught Sophie's eye and they shared a look that managed to combine surprise and a silent cheer. Since the three of them had come to live at the Middlefield Stables, Ruth's character had undertaken further subtle changes, and encouraging ones at that.

After Charlie Soap's thrilling second place at Ascot Dennis had suggested that the three ladies, plus Jerry and Bella take up residence at his yard. Clara had been dubious, despite having few other options. There was nothing left of the caravan except a smouldering wreck, and they all recognised that returning to their own homes was at best, reckless. When Dennis made it clear that there were two empty, fully furnished cottages available, and he'd be delighted if the three of them, plus Jerry, made use of them. Clara had still been uncertain.

Clara had imagined small, filthy rooms, previously occupied by young stable staff who had treated them like an eighteen-to-thirty campsite. She'd made it crystal clear she wasn't in the mood for any of that nonsense. Meanwhile, Sophie had cheekily suggested an eighteen-to-thirty holiday atmosphere might be just what they needed.

'What could we possibly gain from living with a bunch of teenagers?'

Sophie had pointed out that being surrounded by healthy, fit young people might act as an effective deterrent to the Meat Man, which only partly placated Clara.

Clara had assumed there would be no carpets, bare walls, and olive or orange bathroom suites out of the seventies, plus a kitchen to match. She'd been wrong. The ladies were pleasantly surprised to find the cottages in excellent order, clean, and modern. Sure, they were on the small side, but at the moment it was more important everyone felt secure. And there could be little doubt Dennis had that aspect covered too.

He'd given them a peek at his security system the evening they'd arrived. Following a spate of burglaries a few years previously, Dennis had invested heavily in a network of cameras and motion detectors attached to lights that covered the entire yard, from the private driveway, all around the barns and staff cottages, and even into the lunging pen, ménage, and turn-out paddocks at the back of his property. Clara had noticed the small devices, some with LED lights, attached to the walls on her first visit to the stables, but had been far too busy arguing with Sophie and Ruth to give them anything more than a cursory glance. Dennis had assured his new residents that, should the Meat Man come calling, they'd know about it well before he'd made it into the yard. An alert would sound on Dennis's and his head lad Danny's phones, and everything the intruder did would be captured on surveillance video.

A flying visit into Malton allowed them to buy new clothes and within a few days the three ladies, Jerry and Bella had settled into their temporary new homes. Whilst each of them discovered living in a racing yard had its drawbacks, they were heavily outweighed by the benefits.

Dennis ran his yard like a finely tuned machine, with each part of the day structured around the care, training, and down-time of his horses, and the same for his staff. It had taken Sophie and Clara a few days to tune into the frenetic early mornings, afternoon lulls, and then evening activities around the yard. All of this punctuated by horses coming and going, to the races, the vets, or to and from other yards. Meanwhile, Ruth had welcomed the routine and embraced it immediately. As the days and weeks had passed, she had not only got back in the saddle, she'd become a de-facto member of the staff, and both Sophie and Clara were convinced it suited her.

'What did Ruth do all day at Armitage Hall?' Sophie had queried one morning as she and Clara had leaned against a three-bar fence watching Dennis take Ruth through her paces riding a large gelding in the ménage.

Clara replied, 'I always imagined she would get up late, scowl, and complain in unison with her mother for a few hours, start drinking mid-afternoon, and watch TV in bed into the early hours until she fell asleep. I know Greg was worried she was sleeping, or at best, drifting through her life.'

Following Ruth as she guided her mount around the ménage another two times, Sophie noted, 'I think Greg's task has managed to wake her up.'

Clara snapped back to the present. She stared blankly at her notepaper and allowed her thoughts to stray once more to her own future with Jerry. She'd been thinking of little else recently. She started to write 'Schools?' on her pad...

'Redcar next Tuesday,' Dennis repeated in a louder voice, successfully shaking Clara from her daydream this time.

'Yes, Redcar!' she reacted, looking around the table from face to face.

'Come on, Clara, don't be zoning out. We need to make sure everything goes smoothly, and you're a big part of that.' Ruth pointed out.

'Yeah, sorry. I'm a bit distracted I guess. It's just... well, I'm thinking of moving down here. York probably. There's nothing keeping me and Jerry in Durham, and I don't know if I can go back to that house now, or take Jerry back to school at the start of term knowing the Meat Man could be waiting for him.'

'Okay!' Dennis announced drily with a clap of his hands, making Ruth jump slightly in her chair, 'I'm sure you ladies can discuss this outside our meeting?'

Sophie was dying to follow up with Clara, but instead said, 'Yes, of course,' then silently mouthed, 'Why didn't you tell me?' across the table and gave Clara an expressive questioning shrug. She received an 'I don't know!' shrug in return.

With Dennis now fully aware of the ladies task and appreciative of the fact that someone was trying to stop them completing it, he had acquiesced to the ladies request that he only run one of their horses in July and one in August. Frankie would go to Redcar in July and August would see Charlie Soap racing again.

As Sophie had pointed out, by burning the caravan down the Meat Man had shown he was becoming increasingly willing to place people in danger. Completing Greg's task with the bare minimum of race meeting visits would minimise the chances of him doing any further damage. All three of them had agreed that getting Dennis to meticulously plan the remaining two runs was an excellent idea. It also allowed the trainer to offset some of the deep seated guilt he felt for having lied about Charlie Soap's ownership.

Dennis had a page full of notes in front of him and was tapping them with his biro as he spoke.

'I'd like to suggest something. I know you three have tried to work out who the Meat Man could be, and why he would want you to fail to claim your inheritance. But I think you're wasting your time…'

'I'm sure it's Paul,' Clara cut in.

'Yes, we know,' Ruth replied, 'But as we've discussed - at great length - his motive is flimsy at best.'

Dennis continued, his voice raised slightly, 'Instead of running around trying to work out who, what, and why, you should be concentrating on simply finishing the task. You're already here on the yard, so the stable visit elements of the task will be done automatically. If we can perfect a plan for the two days at the races you'll collect your inheritance and it won't matter who tried to stop you.'

'It will still irk me,' Sophie grumbled.

Ruth and Clara mumbled their backing and Dennis tossed his pen onto the table and ran a hand through his hair, a gesture all three ladies took as a sign of his patience running out.

'Can we at least get Frankie to Redcar before you three play at being all-action detectives?' Dennis pleaded.

The ladies murmured their approval.

'Right. Good,' he said, drawing in breath, 'I want to use the fact that he, er… the Meat Man, needs Fun Boy Frankie or Charlie Soap to run.'

'What do you mean?' Ruth queried.

'He needs the horse to be at the races, and one of you three not to be. So far he's tried threats and warnings. From what you've told me about your trip up to Hamilton, he's also tried to sabotage your transport.'

'What about Ascot?' asked Sophie.

'I don't think he had enough time to work out a proper plan to stop you. I only changed the ownership into your names the day before the race, and you'd already travelled down there to stay in a hotel the night before. I think the torching of your caravan was all they could pull together in the time available.'

Ruth was shaking her head, 'I wish I knew who it was that told him we were staying in the caravan.'

'We've been through this,' Sophie said with a sigh, 'You'd told Gertrude we were there, which means all your family may have known. Paul and his family knew, and of course my Sister knew. Any of these people or their extended family and friends, or even other campers on the site could have inadvertently passed the information to the Meat Man.'

'It's best to concentrate on Redcar,' Dennis reminded them.

'You said we had an advantage over the Meat Man?' prompted Ruth.

'Aye, we need to use a combination of misdirection, camouflage, and almost certainly, dumb luck.'

Dennis smiled at each of the women. When he reached Ruth, he added, 'And after her exploits at Hamilton, your mother is going to be delighted to learn she has a role to play.'

It was the first time Clara and Sophie had seen Ruth scowl since arriving at Dennis's yard.

Thirty-Five

Ruth crossed her arms and began rubbing the tops of her shoulders down to her elbows in an effort to warm them up. It was surprisingly nippy. She challenged herself - what did she expect? She was trying to stand motionless in the centre of a small wood at the far end of Dennis's property and it wasn't even six o'clock in the morning yet; it was bound to be chilly, despite it being late July.

Sycamores dominated the wood, with the odd ash or elm dotted around too. Ruth had thought about leaning against one particularly large tree while she waited, but decided against it when she found the trunk layered with green algae. She'd been waiting twenty minutes before she heard a car slowly making its way around the country lane on the far side of the wood. It's brakes squeaked, the engine cut off and two doors slammed shut.

Ruth heard her mother before she spotted the trio of figures on the other side of the wood. Gertrude seemed oblivious to the fact that her voice was carrying into the wood and well beyond. Ruth called out softly to them. When this failed to attract their attention, she tried again. Realising that her calls couldn't be heard above the sound of her mother ordering the other two women about, she swore under her breath, stepped out from behind the trunk of an elm she was hiding behind and started to wave.

The early morning chorus of birdsong in the branches above fell significantly in volume as Gertrude, Alvita, and Marion tramped into the wood and started to make their way through the nettles, brambles, and clumps of bracken. Ruth felt like screaming at them to be quiet.

'Ah, there you are, Ruthy,' Gertude cried in a voice loud enough to scare a wood pigeon into mad flapping flight above her, 'Oh, dear, what on earth have you draped over yourself?'

Ruth's heart sank. Her standard placatory, self-deprecating reply to her mother's criticism was already bubbling up inside her.

'And what *have* you done with your hair, Ruthy?' Gertrude continued, cocking her head to one side and flaring her nostrils in disgust, 'Heavens above, you look like a boy. I never knew what Gregory saw in either of those women of his, but you need to return to Armitage Hall immediately. Being around them is turning you into a guttersnipe.'

Ruth opened her mouth, but then something clicked inside her and she caught her words before they were able to escape. She took in her mother for a moment; somehow Gertrude looked smaller and less formidable than she'd appeared only six weeks ago back at Armitage Hall.

'It's a cardigan, Mother. A rather nice lamb's wool cardigan. And my name is Ruth, not Ruthy. I'm not eight, I'm thirty-four, and I'll make my own decisions on how my hair is cut!'

Ruth didn't give her mother the chance to reply. She quickly gestured to Alvita and Marion to follow her and set off at pace through the trees towards her cottage. All three of the women were carrying bulky bags and Gertrude petulantly threw hers to the ground, thrust her hands onto her hips and opened her mouth in order to begin scolding her daughter. The bag landed with a soft thud, hardly the impact Gertrude was after, and when she looked up again Ruth and the other two women were lost between the trees.

'Ruthy?'

'Ruth?'

With no answer forthcoming, the old lady looped a hand around her bag, swept it up and set off at a canter after the three women, bewilderment etched into her face.

***

7-30am

It was as Dennis was running through the plan a third time, for the sole benefit of Gertrude, that he came to the conclusion that the old lady would find fault in whatever plan he presented to her.

'You are a decoy, Mrs Armitage. You'll just sit in the car,' he told her, desperately hoping this most basic explanation of her role would stem the tide of her petty qualms. From the expressions on the faces of the other five ladies sitting around his table, they all held the same hope.

'Mr Dennis…'

'It's just Dennis,' he corrected.

Gertrude didn't seem to grasp the reason for his interruption, staring wild-eyed at the trainer, 'Mr Just-Dennis, I am playing the role of my daughter, am I not?'

'You are indeed, Mrs Armitage,' Dennis replied, trying hard to muffle a sigh that had started to form in his throat.

'Putting aside the issue I have with the route, I fear your little sideshow is destined to fail, Mr… er… Dennis. We three are poor facsimiles of these women. Besides, my wig is too long! Ruthy… erm… I mean, Ruth has seen fit to chop her hair off since we were at Hamilton races!'

Gertrude pulled out the three foot long black wig from her clothes bag and shook it at her daughter. For a moment, Ruth imagined her mother might be strangling a long-haired Yorkshire Terrier..

'It won't matter, Mother,' Ruth insisted, having shaken the image

173

from her mind, 'Apart from the staff in the yard, no one has seen me with my new hairstyle. Besides, as Dennis had told you, you'll be inside the car at all times. You just have to be a *rough* facsimile of...'

Gertrude held up a silencing finger, 'I think...'

Marion had been rolling her eyes at just about every comment Gertrude had made and she'd now had enough. She silenced the old woman with her own waggling index finger.

'*I think* you're right, Gertrude,' she said with a dangerously sweet smile, 'You should stay here until Alvita and I get back. After all, asking someone of your standing to sit in a car wearing your daughter's clothes and a wig is asking far too much of you... we'll dress up a bale of hay and use that instead – it'll have the same effect.'

'Sarcasm never gets the job done,' Gertrude replied reproachfully.

'Perhaps,' Marion conceded, 'However, I was serious about the bale of straw. At least it will be quiet during the journey.'

'I'm merely pointing out that we should strive for a realistic look if we are to fool these criminals,' Gertrude replied huffily.

'Well, there's no time like the present, let's get you ladies ready. You have two hours!' Dennis said, energetically jumping to his feet in the hope the women around the table would follow suit, 'Sophie, Clara, Ruth, you know what to do, you need to be ready at nine-thirty. Perhaps you can spend a bit of time before then helping Alvita, Mrs Armitage, and Marion become erm... more like yourselves. '

Everyone got up except Gertrude.

'I'm still not clear on a number of...'

She was drowned out by a cacophony of groans.

Marion cried out, 'For pities' sake, someone find me a pair of scissors. That blasted wig is getting the chop.'

***

9-45am

Danny was edging the horsebox away from the gelding's barn when Martha appeared, ready to prepare Fun Boy Frankie for his journey to Redcar.

'Don't worry, I've already loaded him up. He wasn't any trouble,' Danny told her.

'I'd have done it,' Martha remarked, 'I'm not late am I?'

'No, of course not. I was down here with nothing to do, so I thought I'd save you the bother. He's our only runner today and I had the time.'

Martha gave the Head Lad a sullen nod. Frankie was her horse. It made no sense for Danny to be doing her job.

At ten o'clock the horsebox set off to the sound of Frankie happily kicking a hind foot into the box wall and making the whole vehicle shake. Danny was driving, with Martha riding shotgun. Both of them winced at the unexpected sharp, loud bang as an aluminium plated hoof met metal – it had sounded like a gunshot and there was a subsequent scrabbling noise from inside the box. Martha looked across at Danny with a questioning frown, which he ignored.

On a good run, Redcar was an hour and twenty minutes from Malton, so Danny expected to arrive at the track for about eleven-thirty, well before Frankie's six furlong nursery handicap at ten minutes to two. He glanced into his wing mirror and guided the horsebox out of the car park with the beginnings of a smile on his lips.

Dressed in the outfits they'd worn at Hamilton when attempting to pull off their impersonation, Gertude, Alvita, and Marion were standing self-consciously on the edge of the car park, their wide-brimmed hats purposefully placed at rakish angles. As the horsebox disappeared down the drive, Sophie, Clara, and Ruth's doppelgangers made a show of waving their racehorse off for twenty seconds, before immediately returning to the farmhouse.

The horsebox skirted around Norton and joined Amotherby Lane, a B road heading north towards Kirbymoorside. At Danny's request, Martha reported in to Dennis by text message to confirm they were making good, smooth progress.

Once inside the house, Marion caught up with Dennis, 'Was that worth it? Do we really think that these people will be watching the yard?'

'Just covering the bases,' Dennis explained, 'Middlefields is well named. We're half-way up a slowly rising hill and at the foot of a point where the hillside becomes steeper. We're surrounded by woods, scattered buildings and paddocks – most of them above us and overlooking the yard. There are a hundred different places for someone to spy on us if they had the mind to.'

***

11-45am

'I'll be right behind you,' Dennis assured them, 'But if we encounter the Meat Man, please remember that timing is everything.'

He received two nods and one verbal reply, but purposefully closed the door and tapped the roof of the car to avoid having to reply to Gertrude's latest snipe.

Clara's SUV pulled onto Beverley Road and trundled into Norton with the three ladies inside on high alert. The drivers of every approaching car were assessed in minute detail. Any vehicle coming up behind them was assumed to be the Meat Man until the driver came into view or the car peeled off down a separate route. It didn't help that none of them had ever set eyes on him.

When there were no cars around them, Marion, Alvita, and Gertrude peered over every hedge, gate and into every garden and side-road for anything and anyone that looked suspicious. The atmosphere inside the car was tense and fractious, especially when an Audi pulled out and followed them out of Norton and stayed with them through the village of Swinton.

'Gertrude!' Marion hissed through gritted teeth from the driver's seat. Will you stop looking out the back window! You heard Dennis, we have to string this out, or you'll have the Meat Man realising you're not Ruth in a trice!'

Gertrude chewed thoughtfully on the inside of her mouth, unable to form a viable argument. Eventually she muttered, 'It would be much better to actually catch this Meaty Man. I'd bring him down and give him a good thrashing.'

Alvita had hardly said a word all morning, preferring to listen and soak up everything around her. She had allowed Gertrude's pronouncements to wash over her up until now, rarely passing comment. However, she now felt compelled to speak.

'Nothing succeeds like excess,' Alvita pointed out in a calm, clear voice, 'But I doubt you would beat this Meat Man in a fist fight, Mrs Armitage. I would advise you against challenging him physically, and instead lash him with your tongue from a distance. Your command of spiteful and derogatory vocabulary is impressive.'

It took several seconds for Gertrude and Marion to digest Alvita's little speech. Marion reacted first, snorting a wispy chortle out through her nose before breaking into a hearty laugh. It was received by Alvita with a mildly surprised smile. Gertrude ran the young woman's words through her mind another time, unable to decide if she was being insightful or downright cheeky.

Two hundred yards behind the SUV, Dennis followed in his Land Rover. He watched in horror as the car slowly drifted across the white lines in the centre of the road and wobbled before being wrestled back into its correct lane with a sudden jerk. Concerned something was wrong, he called up Marion's mobile on hands free. She answered after a couple of rings and brightly assured him there was nothing to worry about.

'Alvita managed to tickle my funny bone and I was laughing so hard I forgot to drive,' she explained.

***

176

Danny had taken the most obvious, direct route to Redcar. So far, it had been an uneventful journey, for which he was thankful. Dennis had made it crystal clear that the cargo he was carrying today was far more important than any of the horses in the yard, and the Guv'nor had been deadly serious. It all sounded strange to him – wills, weird tasks, and millions of pounds in inheritance - but then he'd met plenty of owners with tons of money and all of them seemed to have their quirks.

He and Martha had been up since five-thirty this morning and, if this was a normal Friday afternoon meeting at Redcar, he'd be pulling into the big lay-by cum car park at Birk Brow. The small café kiosk there sold very decent fried egg sandwiches in lorry driver sized bread buns.

Danny grimaced as he watched the small white trailer with a British flag fluttering from its corner, flash past on his right hand side. There would be no egg bap and coffee on the way today. He sighed and his full concentration returned to the road ahead.

The occupant of a silver coloured Audi parked in the Birk Brow car park watched the horsebox continue past. Bates spotted the box immediately and didn't allow the vehicle out of his sight until it disappeared around a bend over a quarter of a mile away. Bates put his fried egg sandwich with hot sauce to one side, chose one of the two phones on his empty passenger seat and typed out a short text message.

BATES: Just the driver and lass in the Smith horsebox today?

A reply pinged back before he'd had chance to pick up his sandwich again.

DYLAN: Yes, why?

BATES: No other passengers?

DYLAN: Only the horse.

He read the messages back before deleting all of them. Retrieving the remainder of his bap he bit into it and groaned when it ejected a squirt of bright yellow egg yolk streaked with red hot sauce down his shirt.

***

Clara had been studying Ruth for the last few minutes and decided she must have lived a pretty sheltered existence in her teens and twenties. Ruth had worn a permanent grin since setting off and had all on to not giggle each time the horsebox went round a corner, pitching them all sideways as they perched on their bale of straw. Sophie had her eyes closed, but wasn't asleep. She'd stretched out in the straw, legs and arms crossed, rocking in unison with the floor of the horsebox, her head rolling

177

against one of the plastic coated woodchip bales stacked to the ceiling of the horsebox.

Dennis had built them a shady little den at the far end of the horsebox. A 'den' was the only way to describe it. It consisted of two parallel walls of woodchip bales with a few more laid across the top so that anyone looking in from the back of the trailer, or through the viewing grate in the cab, would see nothing but stacked bales. There were two straw bales and a thick layer of straw on the floor; the only compromise to comfort. If Jerry had seen them crawling into this woodchip baled paradise he'd have been straight up the ramp to investigate. It was the perfect child's playhouse, even though with the trailer doors shut, they were sitting in a gloomy half-light.

Apart from Dennis, Danny was the only other person that knew the No Regrets syndicate were travelling to Redcar in such close proximity to their racehorse. In fact, the three women couldn't be any closer – Clara could hear the gelding snort every now and again, and the floor of the box would tilt slightly as Fun Boy Frankie shifted his considerable weight from foot to foot.

'You're enjoying this, aren't you?' Clara whispered to Ruth, careful to do so under the sound of the throbbing engine and road noise.

Ruth's smile broadened and she nodded.

'I'm loving it.'

Clara paused, thoughtful for a moment, before asking, 'Why haven't you left Armitage Hall? It can't be any fun living with Gertrude.'

Ruth didn't answer straight away. She studied Clara for a long moment before concluding she was serious. Content there was no hidden barb in her query, Ruth answered in a whisper.

'Mother and Timothy needed me after Father died.'

When it became clear this was the full extent of her reply, Clara rolled her eyes at her, demanding, 'And..?'

Ruth shrugged, but under a steady stare from the two women, was pressured into continuing.

'Timothy was too young and Greg was just about to go to University. I've never come across a reason to leave since,' Ruth added, albeit a little defensively.

Clara thought for a moment, 'I remember a boy… now, what was his name…ah! David wasn't it?'

Ruth wrinkled her nose and the edges of her mouth turned down, 'It was a mistake. He was using me. It took me some time... and he wanted…'

Her face hardening, Ruth turned on Clara, taking her by surprise, 'Are you making fun of me?

'No!' cried Clara looking hurt. She immediately clapped a hand to her mouth, fearful she'd been too loud. Sophie opened an eye and all three of the women looked up towards the viewing grate that backed onto the cab, willing it not to be pulled back. They all held their breath as a muffled conversation took place in the cab. However, the box continued to travel at speed and they slowly began to breathe again.

'No, I'm not being funny with you. I'm not sure why, but I'm interested in *you*,' Clara whispered earnestly, 'It's just that you're enjoying Middlefield stables that much, I think you should consider staying away from Armitage Hall when all this is finished with!'

Ruth nodded and smiled apologetically.

'I'm… sorry. You… you could be… right.'

An awkward silence ensued. It looked like Ruth was going to add something, but instead she clamped her mouth shut and moved off the bale of straw she was sitting on. Getting gingerly down on her knees, she crept out of the den though a small gap Danny had left to one side. Once though, Ruth straightened and moved over to the partition at the back of the box. Speaking softly, she began running her palm down Fun Boy Frankie's nose. Within seconds her mind was elsewhere.

'You've got her thinking now,' Sophie told Clara quietly inside the den.

'Yeah, well, she'd be daft to go back to Armitage Hall.'

'Agreed.'

Sophie closed her eyes again and shuffled to get comfortable. Sitting on her bale, Clara stared into the half-light and wondered how Jerry was getting on back at the yard.

'I can't quite work something out,' said Sophie suddenly.

Her daydream disturbed, Clara aimed a frown at her friend and found Sophie with both eyes open, staring at her intently.

'I've worked with hundreds of bereaved people from all sorts of backgrounds, and yet I can't quite pigeon-hole your grief. I know you *are* grieving, and yet you don't fit any pattern I've seen before.'

'Oh, God,' Clara snorted, 'Now you're going to tell me I'm weird, or *unique* aren't you?'

'No,' Sophie said with a slow shake of her head, 'It's like there's a wall of… doubt, or anger that's stopping you from showing your true feelings for Greg. You've said you weren't getting on too well in the last couple of years, was it because you thought he was having an…'

'Yes, alright!' Clara hissed, 'He was having an affair. Happy now?'

Sophie remained serious, watching Clara. Waiting. Half a minute passed before she said, 'Chances are, that wall you've erected to suppress your anger will crumble at some point. When it does, you'll need to get help.'

The horsebox engine note dropped and they could feel it slow down. There was a sudden jerk forward, sending all three women off-balance and then it took a long corner.

'Roundabout!' Sophie whispered, clinging onto the edges of her bale, 'We can't be too far away now.'

Ruth was crawling back into the den when Clara started to speak. She kept her voice monotone and low, concentrating her unfocused gaze on a random spot on the floor of the horsebox.

'It went on for two years. I don't know who she was... I didn't want to know. Greg spent more and more time away from home, and I blocked it out and carried on. Every week he would visit his horses and he'd go racing once or twice, even when one of his horses wasn't running. He lost interest in Jerry and when he told me he was ill, I actually thought it was just another excuse to spend time with the other women.'

She blinked and looked from Sophie to Ruth, 'I didn't want him to leave us, so I said nothing. I refused to go racing on the odd occasion he invited me. I'd never met them, but I grew to hate his racehorses.'

***

12-08pm

Bates checked his phone again. Dylan still hadn't checked in with him. That was annoying, but not unexpected. However, it probably meant one of two things; he was mobile, and unable to report, or he'd gone rogue. Bates swore loudly, enough for the expletive to carry to the middle-aged woman sitting in her car parked alongside him in the Birk Brow car park. She stared disapprovingly at him through her drivers side window. He glared back, daring her to complain. The woman was travelling alone. Realising it had been a mistake to react to the horrid man's language, she quickly dropped her gaze, twisted the lid back onto her thermos flask and drove off seconds later.

Bates had worked with people like Dylan all his life and they were always a risky proposition. However, the risk could be minimised. The trick to employing damaged individuals like Dylan was to know your employee's motivation.

He could rely on Jimmy – the lad was an old-fashioned bully. He recognised that glint of excitement in the boy when he was dominating a fearful mark. Mostly due to his looks, Jimmy was useful. It helped if he didn't have to open his mouth. Like most bullies, Jimmy lacked confidence. He had limited uses beyond his penchant for intimidation, but made up for it with his dependability. Jimmy would follow instructions.

Dylan was very different. He needed to be directed, closely monitored, and controlled. Dylan's lack of a moral compass and failure to feel remorse made him a rare find. The boy was unimpressive to look at, although his skeletal frame did hide one or two surprises. Unfortunately, sometimes Dylan believed he could conduct himself with impunity, which meant he could easily become distracted, unaware of threats, and made him a liability in certain situations.

It had taken some time, but Bates had worked out how the boy ticked; Dylan was a frustrated electrician, a talented climber, and a pyromaniac. In fact, he was more than that, he was a talented arsonist. Behind those sunken green eyes lay a monster that rarely got the opportunity to indulge in its passion for wires, sparks, flames, and smoke, so Bates made sure he fed the monster every now and again – and in return Dylan remained within the lines of acceptability.

Bates had indulged him lately by allowing the Falworth woman's caravan to be targeted when they'd almost missed a new racehorse running for the No Regrets syndicate. Dylan had reported with some pride how he'd climbed a nearby spruce tree and watched as the caravan burned to the ground, the boy's enjoyment heightened by the arrival of a fire engine.

He'd asked for the caravan to be lightly singed, which was why when Bates had to rely on people like Dylan, it made him nervous. The boy had been due to report eight minutes ago. That meant he'd have to call him and expose a two-way link between them.

One of the three phones lying on the passenger seat buzzed and Bates immediately picked it up, feeling a mixture of relief and anger. It was Dylan.

'You're late.'

'The reception ain't great up 'ere. I had to walk up the hill to get a couple of bars.'

'Why call? I told you to text. All I needed to know is when they left.'

'Somethin' ain't right with 'em, Bates. I gotta feelin'.'

Prickles of heat wafted over Bates's neck, 'Don't use my name on the phone,' he growled. He took a breath and continued in a business-like tone, 'So what's up? What's so wrong?'

'They left a few minutes ago in that posh woman's SUV... but I've seen 'em before - at the races - an' they didn't seem right today. It could be my binoculars, but two of 'em looked smaller and the other 'un had put on weight.'

Once again, Bates swore loudly. Facing the possibility he'd been out-maneuvered, he quickly considered his options.

'Did you see the horsebox leave?'

'Yeah.'

'Did anyone get into the back with the horse?'

181

'Naa, not that I saw.'

'So no one got in? Tell me exactly what you saw.'

There was a short pause. Bates could imagine Dylan curling his top lip, or worse.

'The box reversed up to the barn,' Dylan related in a tired tone, 'The lad who was driving opened the back doors. They loaded some bales of straw, or something like it. Then the horse was led in, and they bolted it closed and set off a few minutes later. That was it.'

Bates shuddered and pinpricks of sweat started to appear on his forehead.

'Did you count the stable staff in and out of the horsebox?'

Dylan remained silent. By doing so, he'd answered his question. For the first time in the conversation Bates allowed real anger to enter his voice.

'You've blundered, and you need to…'

The line was already dead. Bates scowled, tossed the phone onto the passenger seat and immediately gunned his engine. Pulling his car haphazardly out of the car park at pace, he aimed the Audi north in pursuit of the horsebox. He ran the timings through his mind. If the No Regrets syndicate were hiding in the back of the box they had at least fifteen minutes head start on him. If they'd hit traffic they'd only be on the outskirts of Redcar by now.

Pushing his foot to the floor, Bates reckoned he might just catch them in time. As he drove, the conversation with Dylan kept forcing itself to the forefront of his mind and was making him sweat; he shouldn't have spoken to the boy like that, he was liable to react badly. Bates ran a palm over his forehead. Was that pepperoni he could smell on his hand?

***

Dennis cut off his call with Danny, the weight of worry pushing down on him with considerably less force than a few minutes earlier. The horsebox had reached the outskirts of Redcar and was now following the traffic into the north side of the racetrack. They hadn't seen anyone or suffered any interference and Danny expected they would arrive safely at the entrance to the racecourse stables in less than ten minutes.

Fifty yards in front of Dennis the SUV conveying Gertrude, Alvita, and Marion on their fake journey was, as planned, pottering along. They had reached the outskirts of Hutton-le-Hole, a small village on the southern edge of the North York Moors and Dennis was wondering whether he could tell Marion to stop at The Crown pub at the centre of the village and start back for the yard. He'd instructed his in-car telephone to make the call when a motorbike he hadn't spotted in his mirrors, zipped past him at speed.

He watched the rider weave expertly around another two cars in front of him and slow considerably in order to sit on the back bumper of Clara's SUV. Dennis swore, immediately checking he'd dialled Marion's number, fearing he was too late and too far behind them to influence whatever was going to happen next.

'Some idiot is right up our backside,' Gertrude noted, turning to peer out of the rear window. The rider was within a yard of the back bumper and began revving the trials bike's engine, filling the car with a rasping sound.

'I'm aware of that,' Marion barked, 'It's difficult not to be, given the fact he's almost on top of us. Now do as you're told Gertrude, turn around and get your blessed head down!'

Marion glanced over at Alvita. She was pressed against her seatback and held a tight grimace on her face, but otherwise seemed to be coping well enough.

Remaining ludicrously close to their rear bumper, the trials bike followed them through the village. Marion's phone began to ring again, but she ignored it, all of her attention on her mirrors and the small, wiry rider dressed in dark clothes and wearing an open-faced black helmet, and dark goggles. She tried to concentrate on the rider's eyes, but it was useless; the bike was weaving around so much she couldn't even work out if it was a man or a woman trying to intimidate her. Not sure whether to speed up or slow down, Marion settled for maintaining about twenty-five miles an hour, in the hope it was a silly kid showing off, and not the Meat Man.

Once they'd left the village behind and reached open countryside the rider veered into the right-hand lane and came alongside the car.

'Can you believe it!' complained Gertrude loudly over the noise of the bike, 'The cheeky little oik is taking pictures of me.'

Sure enough, when Marion stole a look out of her driver's window the bike rider was riding one-handed whilst the other held a phone out at arm's length, pointed inside the car. For a moment they locked eyes and Marion was surprised at how young he appeared.

Marion glanced back to the country road ahead. They had been following a shallow left-handed bend for a hundred yards, but now the road swept back to the right. From her elevated driving position in the SUV she spotted a car approaching around the bend, it's blue roof just visible above the hedge. She felt a wave of relief flow through her; the bike rider would have to accelerate and pass her. A check in the rear view mirror also confirmed that Dennis was now right behind her. Marion maintained her speed, waiting for the unwanted paparazzi to speed away.

Everything slowed for Marion. Her precious few seconds of

reaction time stretched, as realisation dawned on her that the bike rider wasn't going to move from the middle of the right-hand lane. Being on the wrong side of the road, going around a left-handed bend, and too low to the ground, the bike rider couldn't see the oncoming car, and the car wouldn't see him until it exited the bend... and it was too late.

'Hold on!' she shouted.

Marion tugged on her steering wheel, sending the SUV veering right-handed towards the biker. For a split second she saw the biker's eyes widen. It was only the lightest of touches, however it was enough to buffet the bike towards the right hand verge. Ignoring Gertrude's admonishment from the back seat, Marion watched as the bike wobbled, lost speed and the rider was sent somersaulting over the handlebars upon reaching the grass verge. A dry stone wall ran the length of that side of the road, but at his reduced speed the rider thumped safely into the long grass a few feet from the wall, his bike crashing awkwardly to the ground, sending up a spray of soil and turf.

Marion sensed the oncoming car before she could turn her head and focus. It suddenly loomed large in front of her, travelling at speed. Automatically wrenching the steering wheel to the left, and the safety of the proper side of the road, the SUV lurched. Her sudden jerk on the wheel was accompanied by the squealing of brakes from the oncoming car. Marion knew immediately she had over-compensated, and desperately tried to rectify her error. She was aware of a jolt, a thump that sent her head whipping forward, and to the sound of Alvita and Gertrude's screaming, the road disappeared from beneath her wheels.

***

Danny turned off West Dyke Road, into the stables car park at Redcar racecourse and made Martha jump by screaming 'Yes!'

He proceeded to bang on the back of the cab and slid the viewing grate open.

'We're here! We'll have you out of there in a minute!'

Martha jumped again when she heard whooping from the horsebox and the sound of several hands slapping the cab.

'What's going on?'

Danny grinned at her, 'Sorry, but Dennis and the ladies needed to keep this quiet. We think someone has been watching the yard. He even thinks there's a mole in the yard helping this Meat Man guy to stop the ladies collecting their inheritance. It's all a bit Dick Francis, but excellent fun – I built them a den out of woodchip bales and brought them here in the back.'

The girl stared at him open-mouthed and remained silent until

Danny had reversed the box up to the unloading bay in front of the stabling entrance. He pulled on the door release catch and made to get out, but Martha reached over and tugged on the arm of his shirt.

'What is it?' They've been cooped up in there for fifty minutes. I need to let them out.'

'I know, it's just a quick question. Do you remember Mr Armitage?' she asked.

'Yeah, of course.'

'It's just… well, he was quite nice to me. And you think these ladies are nice too…'

She lowered her voice and leaned toward him.

'I've been told these ladies aren't really interested in the horses and once they've finished this… task thingy in August the horses will leave Middlefield.'

Danny's brow furrowed.

'No, you've got that wrong.'

'But if they don't complete it, Dennis will get to keep Frankie and Charlie,' Martha added brightly.

She may be eighteen, but she's still as green as grass, Danny thought. Nice girl, who'd been through the wringer in the last few years when her mother died, but she was too easily taken in.

'Who told you this?' he asked gently.

Martha looked away, 'Just one of the err… work riders.'

She's also a terrible liar, thought Danny.

'Do you think the three ladies like Frankie and Charlie?'

Martha shrugged, 'Yeah, I guess so.'

'Well, I can tell you for certain that Ruth won't see the horses leave for another yard. And Clara's little boy has become very attached to them. I really don't think you should be too worried about either horse leaving Middlefield,' Danny assured her.

He pushed the cab door open with his foot, 'Come on, let's unload our precious cargo.'

He'd expected Martha to brighten, perhaps even flash a smile back at him. Instead, she bit the inside of her lip and adopted a thoughtful, pensive air. Danny got down from the cab and when Martha still hadn't moved called out, 'Hey! Come on!' before swinging his cab door shut.

They rounded the horsebox and together they started to unlock the back gate, receiving an impatient whinny from Frankie as it opened. Frankie gave the box a final kick before they led him out and speaking to him in soft tone, Martha walked the gelding towards the racecourse stables entrance. It was a good job Martha had been taken on by Dennis two years ago Danny thought as he watched her go. He couldn't have seen her surviving the cut and thrust of life outside the Middlefield family.

'All clear?' Sophie asked from the back of the box.

'It better be,' said Clara, crawling out from the den of bales and standing up. She wobbled and needed to lean against the side of the box , 'My legs feel like they've been at sea for the last hour.'

Following assurances from Danny that the coast was clear the three ladies clambered over straw and a dollop of horse muck Frankie had kindly left behind, and stepped blinking into the early afternoon sunshine.

'Thank goodness we didn't arrive this way at Royal Ascot,' Ruth said, pulling at several pieces of straw hanging from her cardigan and skirt.

'Don't worry, you'll fit right in,' said Danny handing out stable passes, 'Follow me, we'll see where Frankie has been stabled for the afternoon.

On the West Dyke Road, an Audi slowed to a crawl and the driver stared into the horsebox park for Redcar Racecourse as the No Regrets syndicate decamped and headed into the stabling complex.

***

There had been times, especially during the last few months, when Marion Armitage had questioned why she'd married into this family. Simon was a good husband, straight-forward, even loving… but surely these attributes were the base standard every women should expect? Why on earth hadn't she looked beyond the man and seen the car crash of a family around Simon? And now, as a result of being married into the Armitage family, she'd actually *experienced* a car crash.

'Is everyone okay?' she asked, peering into a wonky rear-view mirror.

Alvita had lost her hat, but seemed fine, nodding back. Gertrude's wig had slipped half-way off her head and a curtain of hair was shielding one eye. Sitting bolt upright in her seat wearing a glazed expression. She opened her mouth to speak but nothing came out.

With her mother-in-law finally speechless, Marion was on the verge of delivering a sarcastic comment, but the moment passed and instead, she twisted around in her seat to study Gertrude properly and check the old woman wasn't injured. She soon wished she hadn't, as a spasm in the back of her neck indicated she wasn't completely free of injury herself.

'Are you okay, Gertrude?' she asked, clamping a hand to the base of her neck and rubbing at the whiplashed muscles and tendons.

Alvita joined her in inquiring after the elderly woman's health, yet there was still no sign of a reply. Undoing her seatbelt, Marion leaned between the front seats and placed a soft hand on Gertrude's knee.

'Gertrude?'

The Armitage family matriarch blinked hard. She peered down through her one hooded eye at the hand on her knee and frowned as if questioning why a hand should be squeezing her just there. Blinking again, rapidly this time, Gertrude slowly lifted her head and met the gaze of her eldest son's partner. She ran a pale pink tongue around her teeth and finally swallowed.

'You... you... bloody idiot!' Gertrude screamed at Marion, shaking with such fury her wig slid off her head and fell into her lap.

'She's fine,' Marion reported dejectedly.

Thirty-Six

August 8th 2016

Ruth sauntered down the boys' barn stopping at certain stable doors to stroke an inmate, or peek in to check on a less sociable sort. It was just after one o'clock in the afternoon; her favourite time in the yard.

A summer shower drummed a familiar plinking tune on the steel roof and with the morning's work completed the barn was full of horses and devoid of people. Ruth had fallen into the habit of walking the barns and paddocks after her lunch. Even though she now spent most of her mornings working in the huge open-ended buildings, there was nothing she enjoyed more than being alone with the thoroughbreds. If she was in the mood, she'd wander up to the paddocks at the back of the yard and sit on a fence, or lean against a favourite gate, simply watching the magnificent animals as they mooched, played, and grazed.

As she approached Fun Boy Frankie's stable she quietly called to the gelding.

'Frankie?'

There was a scuffling noise and the clop of a foot on concrete. Frankie's head appeared over the stable door. A swallow looped over Ruth's head and dived into the young horse's box just as she held out a hand to the gelding. Frankie never even flinched; the barn was home to dozens of these summer visitors.

'You're more interested in whether I've brought you a carrot,' Ruth told him knowingly, scratching the two-year-old behind his ear.

This was an early afternoon ritual; providing her favourite horses with a treat. When Frankie began chomping hungrily on his carrot it only took a second or two for Charlie's head to poke out of his stable and snort for attention. Charlie Soap now occupied the box next door to Fun Boy Frankie, the colt and gelding having become the best of buddies. Charlie had gone through several partners in the paddocks before eventually hitting it off with Frankie, who was a much more relaxed character and managed to cope with Charlie's little tantrums and stood up to him when the colt's playfulness became too rough.

Ruth moved over to Charlie's door and scolded him for his impatience. The colt took the carrot and walked to the back of his stable before dropping, sniffing, and rolling the vegetable over with his tongue before biting the first chunk off.

'You're a funny onion,' Ruth told the colt, slowly shaking her head.

'He's not the only one around here,' said a female voice. Ruth turned her head and as she'd expected, Martha was walking down the barn. She hadn't heard her approach, the noise of the rain on the barn roof

188

masking her footfalls.

Martha joined Ruth at the stable door and she shuffled over so the two of them could watch Charlie playing with his carrot.

'Danny isn't too happy Charlie missed the Richmond Stakes last week,' said Martha in a neutral tone, 'But that's how it goes with racehorse feet. It was only a small abscess, but there was no way he could run.'

'Yep. I know. Dennis was spitting feathers the day you found him lame, but there will be other races for him. I think he mentioned an important race called the Middle Park at Newmarket near the end of September instead.'

They left Charlie to pick over what remained of his carrot and moved back to Frankie's box. The gelding was immediately at the door, nudging their hands with his lips in search for more food.

'Frankie would eat all day if you allowed him,' Martha said with a smile, telling the two-year-old, 'You'd be a pot-bellied blob if we allowed you to eat everything you want.'

'This boy had better win in two weeks' time,' Ruth said, playing with his mane, 'I was so disappointed when he finished third at Redcar.'

'I know, but it wasn't his fault.'

'I'm beginning to understand that winning a race isn't as easy as Charlie makes it look,' Ruth admitted with a small sigh, 'Poor old Frankie bumped into a really decent horse last week.'

Martha didn't reply immediately, instead pursing her lips and regarding the gelding thoughtfully. This was ground that had already been well trodden and discussed. Frankie had led from the moment the starting stalls opened and was still out front as they entered the final furlong. Until half a furlong out, he'd looked home and hosed. Looking back at the replay, it had been obvious the eventual winner had been waited with. Once unleashed, the flashy chestnut had run Frankie down under a tender ride and pulled away for a cosy victory. Poor Frankie had got tired trying to get to the winner, and lost second place when weakening in the final strides.

'He'll have his day in the sun,' said Martha positively, quickly adding, 'I hear all three of you might be leaving the yard after Frankie goes to Beverley later this month.'

Ruth wasn't sure how much Martha knew about Greg's task, so she simply nodded and said, 'Clara and Sophie will be going home once Frankie's run.'

She somehow couldn't bring herself to say she would also be leaving the yard. At present, it was a topic her mother delighted in dropping into virtually every conversation. Attending Frankie's run at Beverley would see the No Regrets syndicate accomplish Greg's task.

The two women watched Charlie finish off his carrot in an easy silence. As the colt was munching on his last mouthful, Martha turned to Ruth once more.

'Is everyone okay after the crash?'

Ruth gave a low rumbling laugh that made Martha smile, 'My Mother is still recounting her near-death experience, but actually it was more of a scrape than a crash. All three of them are fine apart from a bit of whiplash. Mind you, Clara's car has a nice dent down its side.'

'Dennis says they ran into the verge and the car skidded sideways into a fence. He said the man on the motorbike who caused it all fell off, but got up and sped away before he could collar him.'

Martha watched the older woman's face contort into a worried grimace and decided to change the subject.

'Well, I'm glad they're all okay. You must be really proud of your family.'

Ruth snorted, 'Huh! What makes you think that?'

Martha recoiled a little, surprised by this reaction.

'Well, they were all trying to help you, Miss Falworth, and Mrs Armitage. It must be nice to have so many people willing to put themselves in danger for you. I heard that the man on the bike was trying to make sure you lost your inheritance?'

Ruth pulled away from the stable door, ready to deliver a stinging tirade on how warped her family were and how wrong this nosey stable lass could be. But upon seeing Martha's frown, she hesitated, and thought better of it. She hadn't taken the time to drill too much into Martha's past, but Ruth was aware the girl had no family. To this young lass, even a family like her own had to be preferable to nothing.

'You're… er, right,' she stumbled on, 'I am… er, *lucky* to have a family like mine. They can be a little intense, and we have our moments, but I guess they're not so bad. Thanks for reminding me.'

This made the stable lass smile. Ruth couldn't help but smile back.

Thirty-Seven

August 27th 2016

He'd been crouched in the hedgerow for forty minutes before he seized his opportunity. He'd scared the girl half to death. Once the kitchen light had lit the back of the cottage up and he was sure it was her, he'd crept across the back lawn and waited patiently for his moment to strike.

It troubled him to think she'd literally jumped when he'd grabbed her from behind. She'd struggled intensely, dropping her bag of rubbish in order to tear at the arm he'd clamped around her neck. It was surprising how much strength she'd shown, given she was a strip of a girl. Riding horses daily must have made her strong – he made a mental note not to under-estimate horse riders in the future.

Her physical condition hadn't made any difference to the outcome. She had scratched, wriggled, and swore at him, but never seen his face. And once he'd told her he was her blackmailer and tightened his arm around her neck, she had quickly capitulated.

As he walked away along the country lane that ran behind Dennis Smith's property the thought of his dominance over the girl momentarily forced an amused sneer onto his face, and yet it was soon replaced by a sickly feeling of self-loathing.

As he'd been advised, the party had been a gift. There was no way you could monitor a property effectively with hundreds of guests roaming around the place, producing hits on your surveillance system every minute. He reckoned it had been switched off. It had made the job infinitely easier and he'd achieved his goal. Even so, he didn't feel triumphant.

He continued down the lane, then leapt over a gate and crossed a paddock, the moonlight strong enough to dimly light his route. He went over another fence and stood beside a small car, hidden by a high hedge, no more than twenty yards from the main road. He was fishing in his backpack for his keys when a phone began vibrating softly in his trouser pocket. He threw the backpack into the backseat of the car and fished the phone out, but missed the call.

Redialling the number, he was connected after a single ring.

'It's me,' he said into the silence that greeted him when the phone was answered.

'Why didn't you call? Has it been done? This is important. We only have one more opportunity.'

'I've been busy… The girl has been warned.'

'Did you have to hurt her?'

'Of course not. She was scared witless…'

'And will she do as she's told?'

'I don't doubt it.'

There was a few seconds pause during which he wondered whether his double negative had caused confusion.

'What about your other man?'

'I saw him. He's ready. We're *all set*, okay?'

There was a pause and the hint of a frustrated sigh.

'Thus far you have failed to deliver, so forgive me if I find your confidence uninspiring. Make sure they don't reach Beverley tomorrow. Use any means.'

He bit his lip, smarting from the rebuke.

'Well?'

Standing in the darkness beneath the oak tree, he slowly rotated his head until his neck made an audible click. It wasn't necessary, it didn't ease any ache, it was just pleasing; a physical affectation gifted to him as a result of a past injury.

'Hey, are you there?'

'You can rely on me. I'll make sure they don't reach Beverley... by any means,' he replied coldly.

Thirty-Eight

7-13am August 28th 2016

Clara waited behind her front door in the half-light of her cottage hallway and squinted at her watch again. At exactly seven fifteen she undid the latch. Clad in a Japanese print silk dressing gown, Clara opened her cottage door and with one eye closed and the other focused at the step, she bent down to recover the two bottles of semi-skimmed milk that stood waiting for her. The early morning sunlight was stinging her retinas but she didn't mind too much, there was something about having milk delivered to the doorstep that was rather novel and strangely homely. She didn't know why, it just was.

Slowly turning to re-enter the cottage, Clara was relieved when a voice called out. She spun around, ready to deliver her speech.

'Morning!' Ruth repeated loudly, ensuring she could be heard right across the yard and beyond, 'It's a good one isn't it!'

'Yes, lovely,' Clara replied, peering up at her beaming next-door neighbour atop a large bay mare. The horse had come to a halt on the walkway to the gallops, about twenty yards away.

'I'm still driving us to the races today aren't I?' Ruth queried in a voice purposely louder than was necessary.

'If you don't mind, I might still be over the limit after last night!'

'That's why I asked,' Ruth said with a half-laugh. Her mount snorted and pawed the ground with its front fore, keen to be off to gallops. She allowed the mare to step forward and complete a turn.

'What time should I be ready to leave for Beverley?' Clara shouted.

Ruth was joined by another two horses and their work riders and they started to move off.

'We need to set off at exactly eleven. No worries, I'll shout you!' Ruth called over her shoulder and departed with a wave.

With a bottle of milk in each hand, Clara waggled one back at the departing trio even though they were unlikely to see it. Behind her, Jerry emerged from the darkness of the thin hallway and shimmied past his mother. He was wearing a pair of wellies, and a dirt smeared t-shirt and jeans.

'Where you going, it's only seven-thirty?'

The boy grinned, 'Mucking out three boxes for Danny!'

'What about your breakfast?'

'Danny said I can eat with the lads and lasses at half-past eight, I'll have it with them,' he countered, jogging backwards down the front path. His mother returned an appraising stare but soon rolled her eyes and told him, 'Okay, but stay out of trouble and don't accept any money from either

193

of them!'

Jerry gave his mother a cheeky grin, 'I promise!' and swung around, running off in the direction of the barns.

Clara clicked the front door shut behind her, bustled down the hall and into the small kitchen at the back of the cottage where she busied herself with her breakfast, wondering what it was about dung that young boys found so fascinating.

'Anyone home?'

Clara peered through her kitchen window out onto the large rectangular back lawn that all the cottages shared. She found Sophie staring at her through the kitchen window. Her eyes were big and she was sucking her cheeks in and poking her nose out so it squashed against the window pane, pretending to be a nosy neighbour.

'These cottages don't half remind me of my Mum's old house in York,' Sophie called through the window pane once she'd dropped her pose, 'Everyone gets to know your business!'

She grinned and moved to the back door, waiting to be let in.

'Coffee?' Clara queried as she unlocked the door and pulled it open.

'Yes please!'

Sophie and Clara had fallen into a routine of sharing their morning's coffees together since moving into the line of four terraced cottages. The first one was occupied by two stable lasses, one of which was Martha. The second housed a couple of stable lads. Clara was in the third with Jerry, and Ruth and Sophie shared the end terrace with Bella.

'Have you done your announcement?' asked Sophie in a conspiratorial whisper.

'Yep, if there was anyone out there listening in, they'd have definitely heard us!'

Sophie grinned like an excited teenager.

'What're you so happy about?' asked Clara, 'Is your sister talking to you again now she's collected the insurance money on her caravan? Or is it because your new laptop turned up the other day?'

Sophie pondered this for a moment before replying.

'Oh, I don't know. Despite everything, I woke up in a good mood this morning. Isn't Jerry around?'

Holding a piece of buttered toast in her mouth, Clara plonked two mugs of coffee down on the sturdy, yet bijou breakfast table and sat down, crunching down on her toast as she took her seat.

'Nope, Danny has got him scraping up horse dung… which is apparently a greater draw than having breakfast with his mother.'

Sophie gave a small laugh and fingered the handle of her coffee mug nervously. She didn't know why it was so difficult to broach this subject with Clara, when she could happily discuss far weightier matters with her grieving clients. She'd tried several times, and been unable to breech Clara's defences. It was infuriating, and today was a big day. It would be nice to finally place this lost piece of the jigsaw and know what the full picture looked like.

Clara sighed heavily, 'What is it? You want to talk about something, don't you. If it's about me choosing the cottage that happens to have the double bed again, then…'

'It's not that,' Sophie assured her with a shake of her head, 'I want to talk about us… again.'

She regarded Clara steadily, trying to read her friend.

Clara took another bite of her toast, chewing the mouthful slowly, her eyes darting nervously around the table.

Sophie continued, 'We've been getting on well the last few weeks given the circumstances, and well…I wondered if we could talk about what happened after the wedding day.'

Her gaze never left Clara's face and a prolonged silence developed.

'This again? I don't know if that's such a great idea,' Clara eventually offered, 'Dredging up the past is never…'

'I've… *enjoyed* being with you, around you and Jerry,' Sophie interrupted, her embarrassed gaze now directed at her coffee mug, 'I realised this when we were driving back up from Ascot that… I've missed having you around. You can be the most annoying, blunt, and irritating women when you want to be, but…'

'Thank god there's a 'but',' Clara chipped in.

'But… Greg's task is almost over. We've been racing four times and we've visited the yard five times, although the fifth time has lasted over a month. Assuming today at Beverley with Frankie goes smoothly we'll have completed Greg's task and there will be no reason to stick around. The only thing left will be to attend the final confirmation of the will on September 1st.'

Sophie let this hang in the air for a moment before continuing, 'I'd like us to go on being friends, but I think we need to have a proper talk about what happened after the wedding… *my* wedding.'

'Last night was a riot wasn't it?'

Sophie pursed her lips, and stared at her friend, frustration and disappointment written across her face. Clara was grinning back at her over the brim of her coffee mug. Sophie sighed, realising she wasn't going to get anywhere with Clara in this sort of flippant mood. So, she mentally parked the conversation, reasoning it was too early in the morning for Clara to take anything seriously, especially after last night.

In fact, it had been a great Sunday evening. Dennis had thrown a party; a hog roast at the stables in celebration of reaching the five hundredth winner of his training career. One of the large turn-out paddocks had been turned into a small village of marquees and picnic tables, all festooned in bunting. A bouncy castle had been installed for the kids and from all over Malton and the surrounding area, hundreds of Dennis's friends, owners, trainers, stable staff and their children had attended, some drifting in and out through the afternoon and evening, others staying until the light began to fade, after which everyone crowded onto a makeshift dance floor in the largest marquee. It turned out that young or old, racing people really appreciated a good party.

Most of Malton's horseracing fraternity had been there, a community of trainers, jockeys and stable staff Sophie and Clara were slowly being introduced and integrated into, and to whom Ruth already seemed to be a paid-up member.

Ruth had taken to life in Malton like a duck to water, embracing the lifestyle, the people, and most significantly the racehorses. Once Dennis had discovered she had ridden as a teenager he'd hoisted her onto his favourite hack and given her ability as a horsewoman a thorough going over in the ménage. Suitably impressed, from that moment on Ruth had become a part-time stable lass and work rider, albeit Dennis had been careful, currently limiting her gallop work to hack canters on the easier rides in the yard.

'Ruth seemed to be enjoying herself,' Clara remarked, shifting the focus of their conversation even further away from the events surrounding her elopement with Greg, 'I saw her talking at length with that cute young trainer from the other side of Norton. He managed to get her laughing. You know that rumbling low laugh she has? It got a whole bunch of them going.'

'I saw them dancing together.'

'Really? I can't imagine Ruth dancing!' exclaimed Clara, pushing her lips out gleefully, 'Come to think of it, I don't think I've seen her pout, snarl, or scowl recently either. It's like she's a different woman away from Armitage Hall. Now that she's got her family at arm's length she's...'

'Blossomed,' Sophie offered.

'Yeah,' Clara agreed thoughtfully.

This caused a pause in their gossiping as both women considered this thought.

Presently, Sophie said, 'I actually like Ruth a lot. She's been fun to live with. Once you chip away all the sourness, she's got a sharp sense of humour and if you can get her to laugh, well, it's really difficult not to see the funny side.'

'I know! I heard her through an open window a couple of days ago. I had no idea what she was finding funny, but I had to giggle along with her. Her laugh is really infectious.'

Both women sipped at their coffee, enjoying their own private images of Ruth's laughter.

'We should try to convince her not to go back to Alnwick,' Clara suggested, 'If we can keep her away from that poisonous Mother of hers she'll stand half a chance of staying normal and bloom a bit more. You never know, she might even find a nice chap if she stays around here long enough.'

'I don't know,' Sophie said, sucking in air over her teeth, 'Our attempts at match making didn't go that well when we were younger. Besides, I'm sure Ruth won't want to go back to Armitage Hall.'

Clara looked doubtful, 'You don't know Gertrude Armitage like I do. She'll reel her back in somehow. She'll wrap her tentacles around Ruth, pull her back to Alnwick and turn her sour again - you just watch. We need to fix it so the old witch can't get her suckers clamped onto Ruth again.'

Sophie shook her head, 'Listen, if you're up for a bit of prying into lives, perhaps we can return to the night I came around to your flat and you attacked me. I still don't understand…'

Clara cut her short, holding up a palm, 'Will you let that go!'

'It's unfinished business.'

'We've both apologised and we're getting along okay, so why go into it?' Clara protested.

'I need to know why everything went crazy and you reported me to the police,' Sophie pressed, 'And then there was the restraining order you and Greg had slapped on me. It was just so… nasty and unlike you. What made you do all of that? I need to understand why.'

Clara became sullen and hard-faced, a twitch of her eyebrows the only sign of her inner turmoil. As the silence extended, so the simmering pressure grew inside her.

A staccato double knock on the front of the cottage made both women jump. They heard the door handle squeeze downwards and a young female voice said, 'Hello?' and both of them breathed again.

'Yes, we're through here, Martha,' Clara called shrilly, sounding like a kettle letting off steam. Then in a whisper combined with a hard stare she warned Sophie, 'Please, *just forget it*!'

Martha's smiling face poked around the kitchen door.

'Sorry to interrupt.'

'You're not. Come on in, you've timed your entrance perfectly,' Clara declared, giving Sophie a meaningful stare, 'Is everything ready for Frankie to win his race today?'

'Yep! Just checking in to make sure you're all still going. I'll be heading off to Beverley in the box with Frankie in five minutes.'

'We're not going to be long behind you. We want to get there nice and early.'

'Ah, well I'm glad I caught you. You might want to go out of Malton on the A64 and then go cross-country, as I've heard there are roadworks on the A1079.'

Clara blinked a few times and her brow furrowed as she tried to envision the route in her head.

'I'll remind her,' Sophie said, playfully rolling her eyes, 'Clara's got a mind like a sieve this morning,'

The young women looked from Sophie to Clara, as if waiting for further confirmation. When it became clear nothing else would be forthcoming she shrugged and smiled.

'Okay, just wanted to make sure,' she said a shade awkwardly and turned to leave.

'See you there,' Clara called after her, 'We're really looking forward to this run.'

The front door clicked shut and Clara turned to Sophie, 'Is it me, or was that a bit odd?'

'She's only eighteen. You and I did odd things at that age. If I remember rightly, you were going through your Goth stage, and I was busy pretending to have strong political views because I fancied Roddy Taylor in the upper sixth. You know he ended up being a Conservative MP down in the South West?'

'Never! Rod Taylor...'

Their conversation drifted into fuzzy nostalgic memories, the type that always ended with both of them trying to remember the names of old school friends and becoming confused with who did what to whom, and when. Before they knew it, Ruth was walking into the kitchen, hot and happy from riding out and smelling of saddle oil. She immediately stared at Clara's dressing gown and instructed both women to get a wriggle on because it was time to get ready to go racing.

'And time to catch a criminal!' Clara exclaimed.

'More of an arsonist, really,' Sophie corrected.

Ruth growled something unintelligible at the two of them and they grinned back at her, feeling like teenage girls. Another even harder stare from her had them hurrying off in different directions to change and prepare.

Thirty-Nine

10-45am

Dylan was enjoying himself. Trying to quantify his growing sense of anticipation, the closest comparison he could imagine was a prisoner incarcerated for many years but who knows for certain he is about to be released in a few short hours. The rush was exhilarating and he told himself that his decision to cease taking his medication had been the right one; everything was so much clearer, his senses heightened.

He could feel the tree branch bending against his back as the breeze got up a little stronger, providing him with a feeling of weightlessness. There was something about clutching the thick, lichen encrusted limb of an oak tree fifty or sixty feet up in the air that filled him with contentment. He'd climbed trees and made dens, hideouts, and nests in them since he was a small boy. No one bothered you up a tree, and it was usually quiet, except for the birds and the rustling of the leaves. In his experience, people tended to look down, rather than up.

And he'd been fearless growing up; there wasn't a tree in the woods around Blyth that he hadn't climbed as a youngster - right to the top. He'd never fallen, or at least, he'd never fallen and really hurt himself... he'd slipped a few times, but always walked away. It was odd, but he was sure that if he gave each tree respect, in return they would look after him.

He still climbed them now, aged twenty-one. Thanks to Bates he'd amassed some quality gear and could live in a tree for weeks if he wanted to, safe and secure in his all-weather hammock, never needing for his feet to touch the ground – a place where his world tended to be confusing and frustrating. He could have walked further up the hill to get a view of the paddocks and barns below, but where was the fun in that? Here he was - closer, shielded by the dark green leaves and the thick branches of this ancient oak. He'd tried a dozen or more different trees in this dense wood over the few months he'd been watching the yard and always returned to this oak. It seemed to call to him.

Dylan shuffled his shoulder slightly in order to avoid a knot that was digging into his shoulder blade. It was still tender since falling off his motorbike a few weeks ago. Secure in his new position, Dylan lifted the binoculars old Bates had given him weeks... or was it months ago? He couldn't remember, but then his memory wasn't to be trusted, he wasn't clever like that; he was clever in other ways. But they were good binoculars – he'd never imagined you could see so clearly from so far away... you never know, Bates might forget to ask for them back. Dylan smiled inwardly. After today, old Bates could sing for his binoculars.

199

Chances were he'd never see the old grouch again anyway. Besides, he'd have enough cash to buy an even better pair for himself. He'd been clever enough to find his own... what was it that Bates called them? *Clients...* that was it! He had his very own *client.*

He should be calling Bates now. Or rather, informing him by text message. The trainer had been busy in his bottom paddock for the last hour, and he'd also overheard an interesting conversation. Instead, he'd sent a text to his client... who had been really pleased with him.

Dylan inhaled a deep breath of the sweet summer air and released it slowly. Yes, his client was right, it was time to give Bates the boot. He couldn't help smiling. He had an ace pair of binoculars, his first ever paying client, and he was in one of his favourite places... alone in a tree. And he was being clever.

***

Dennis left the ride-on lawn mower on the edge of the field and leaving the paddock gate open, he walked the two hundred yards up the dusty lane. There wouldn't be any horses getting turned out in the front paddock today.

Striding along with purpose, he headed for the tack room and was pleased to find it bereft of staff. On the morning of a race-day he always preferred to prepare alone. It was a ritual his father had followed and Dennis had eventually become determined to maintain. He would close the door to his tack room and the lock would click into place. Then Dennis Smith the racehorse trainer would prepare the racing silks and equipment for the day's racing.

By the light of a single, naked light bulb he flicked through the silks on his Owners' rail and removed Greg Armitage's orange and green colours. Folding the shirt with care, he placed it into a small, immaculately maintained leather case, stamped with his father's initials. The cap was laid on top, above the collar, and then he adjusted four internal leather straps with old-fashioned buckles to hold the clothes in place.

Once safely stowed, he stared down into the open case. Often he would simply close it, collect the eye shields, blinkers, cheek-pieces, or tongue ties and be off. But every now and again he would conjure up a memory.

Today he reached into the case and laid a flat palm onto the silks. He closed his eyes, breathed in deeply, and was reminded of the man. A simple brush of the thin cloth with his fingertips had the ability to drive memories of his owner through his mind.

'Take a moment, lad,' his father had told him, 'The silks hold the hopes and dreams of your owners. You'll do well to take a moment to remember them every now and again.'

He'd been sixteen. It was only when he was twenty- eight and his father had been two years dead that he sought out his old race-day case, went through the ritual and understood what his father had meant. Without owners there were no horses to train, you needed to share your owners' dreams to make them happen.

Greg Armitage had been a complex, intelligent man who had shared his dream of conquering the bloodstock business with Dennis. Winning races had just been the start of the journey for Greg, he'd soon adjusted his targets and bought his bloodstock accordingly. The only factor he hadn't accounted for was the foreshortening of his own life and therefore the timeframe he had to achieve his goals.

When Dennis placed his hand into his father's case and touched Greg Armitage's colours he remembered the day his owner came into the yard and shared his dream. He recalled the time Greg asked a favour at the races, and the day he shared the news of his cancer and how his plans to fulfill his dreams had to alter.

His father had been a wily old coot. Dennis knew this ritual was hokum. It was there to remind a trainer that when you stripped everything away, horseracing wasn't so much about horses, it was about people.

Dennis clicked his race-day case shut, unlocked the tack room door, switched the light off, stepped into the sunshine and allowed it to play onto his face. His head and heart were now brimming full of hope for Clara, Sophie, Ruth, and Greg Armitage.

***

Dylan had been concentrating his gaze on the tack room for the last fifteen minutes and a knot of worry was starting to grow in his stomach. The door was usually left open, with staff constantly bobbing in and out all morning, but it had been closed by the trainer, the Guv'nor. When the wind was whipping up the hill he'd heard them calling him Guv'nor, as the breeze carried the staff's voices up to him. Dylan liked that. He'd like to be called the Guv'nor one day. But right now, he'd like the Guv'nor to come out of the tack room - he'd been in there too long.

He checked his phone for the time. It was a quarter past ten. He'd been told there was only one entrance and exit to the tack room, but the old man had been in there a good ten minutes, and he was beginning to worry there was a back door and he'd missed him. Or perhaps he'd already left... Dylan's forehead turned cold and he realised the breeze was cooling his sweat. When the trainer emerged from the tack room a minute later carrying a small tan coloured case by its leather handle, Dylan found himself quietly giggling with relief. He caught himself and concentrated.

He needed the trainer to leave with the horse… Frankie something-or-other it was called. Dylan willed the old man with his silly little suitcase to load up the horsebox and get going to Beverley races. But the trainer wasn't moving. He was just standing there outside the tack room, with his eyes shut and with his face pointed up at the sky. It looked like he was saying a prayer… Dylan shrugged.

***

Two hundred yards north-east and twenty-five yards further up the hillside, Bates bit into a cheese roll. He missed his meat sticks, but since he'd discovered they made his breath stink like rancid offal, they'd had to go. He munched through the last of his white cheese and pickle roll, licked his fingers one by one, and dried each digit with his handkerchief before training his binoculars onto Dylan.

Not for the first time over the last few weeks, Bates marvelled at how the lad managed to keep his balance and be comfortable on a branch that was no more than eight inches thick. The lad had an impressive camp set up, considering he was sixty feet up in the air and was being constantly blown around in the wind. He noted the positioning of the lad's bandy legs twisted around the bough he was currently straddling and idly wondered whether Dylan's wiry stature, a result of his father's complete disregard for his son's wellbeing as a child, actually provided him with extra gripping power.

Forty

The horsebox containing Dennis, Martha, and Fun Boy Frankie was long gone by the time Sophie, Ruth and Clara bundled themselves into Clara's dented SUV in the Middlefield stable car park. Apart from some short runs into Malton and a trip out to the caravan site to collect Bella, this was the first time since Frankie had run at Redcar that the three ladies had ventured out of Middlefield. With Jerry and Bella safely in the care of Danny for the afternoon – Jerry eagerly earning extra pocket money by doing odd jobs around the yard - everything was set for their day at Beverley races. Their final day at the races as the No Regrets syndicate.

It should have been something all three of them were looking forward to, but when Sophie climbed into the back seat of the car she sensed the tension. Her pulse was racing. The details of the plan they'd all worked on meticulously with Dennis over the last three weeks ran once again through her head. It felt she was listening to some sort of demonic audio book that endlessly played the same short story on auto-repeat.

Ruth started the car's engine, but didn't engage the automatic gears into drive. Instead, she swiveled in the driver's seat and shot concerned looks at Clara in the passenger seat and Sophie in the back.

'Are we sure we're doing this?'

'Yes,' her friends replied in unison.

'They will definitely try to stop us.'

'We know,' Sophie replied.

'That's why we've planned this journey for the last three weeks,' Clara said in an exasperated tone, 'Don't tell me you've got cold feet!'

'No. It's not that. Not that at all. It's just… Oh, it doesn't matter,' Ruth blustered, slamming the car in reverse. She glanced over her shoulder again and swung the car out of its parking spot.

'Spit it out,' Clara insisted, placing her hand on Ruth's as she messed with the gear lever looking for drive. Ruth applied the brakes.

'Alright, Alright! I've just realised that today might be the last day we spend together. If we don't make it to Beverley, that's it – we go our separate ways and we lose. We lose our inheritance and I lose all this and…'

Her grumbling trailed off, and she gestured with both hands to indicate the stables.

Clara and Sophie remained silent for a long moment.

'And?' Clara queried eventually.

'And I haven't had so much fun for… well, I don't think I've *ever* had this much fun!' Ruth said breathlessly, 'If we don't get to Beverley I just want you both to know how gratef…'

'Oh for heaven's sake!' Clara complained, 'What is it with you two today? Yes, we all get it. Never mind the odd couple, we're the odd trio, treble, triad? Oh, I don't know… Clever old Greg has managed to bind us together, but can we *please* stop all the navel gazing? We've got Frankie running, our super little horse, and I might add that he really deserves to get a win on the board.'

Sophie and Ruth nodded, slightly shocked, but also buoyed by Clara's outburst.

'We chose the right plan! So let's stop all the touchy-feely nonsense and get this done!'

By the time Clara's speech had come to its climax, she was shouting and Sophie and Ruth were grinning. An exasperated Clara shrank back in her seat, sucked in a big breath and holding out an arm and a flat hand, she pointed to the ribbon of dusty private road ahead of them and yelled, 'Drive!'

'One second,' Ruth said, quickly tapping at the dashboard whilst Clara sighed loudly. The sound of a synthesizer suddenly filled the cabin and the recognisable opening chords of 'The Final Countdown' by eighties pop-rock group Europe boomed out.

Ruth gripped the steering wheel with both hands, stamped on the accelerator and the ladies left the yard in a cloud of dust, and to the sound of inspirational soft rock.

***

Dennis pulled into the horsebox park at Beverley racecourse and felt some of the pressure lift from him now he and Martha were on racecourse property. He knew this racecourse like the back of his hand, so paid no attention to the rows of cars parked on the Beverley Westwood, the large expanse of common grassland that acted as the car park on race days. It was unlikely Fun Boy Frankie would be targeted by the Meat Man, as the ladies were the focus of their actions. Even so, Dennis took solace from achieving the first goal of the day; delivering Frankie safely to the track.

Win or lose, this would be Frankie's last run with the added threat of intimidation and interference. It would be a blessed relief once today was over and done with.

As soon as he turned the engine off, Fun Boy Frankie kicked the side of the box impatiently. Dennis checked his watch. It was a just after two o'clock and they were late, albeit purposefully late. Frankie was running at three o'clock. According to the British Horseracing Authority rules they should have been at the track for one o'clock at the latest, a full two hours before the advertised race time, but the ladies had thought it best to keep the Meat Man guessing.

Plucking his phone out of its holster on the dashboard, Dennis checked for the umpteenth time that none of the ladies had called, texted, or left a voice message. He was unsure whether he should be relieved or not when he found there was nothing from them.

'I reckon he wants to be out,' Dennis noted drily as Frankie's hoof walloped the side of the horsebox once again, 'We should try bringing him with a travelling partner next time, I might try that goat he seems to get on with. What do you think?'

Martha had been quiet during the thirty minute long journey. There was nothing too strange about that, the travelling lads or lasses would often snooze on the way to the races; she'd started work at half past five, and stable hands took their sleep whenever they could get it on race-days. However, they rarely sobbed.

Huge blobs of tears were coursing steadily down the girl's cheeks before being rubbed away by the heels of her hands to become wide red smudges that were making Martha's face glow. Dennis pulled a bunch of tissues from a box of travelling essentials he always carried in his driver's door and offered them with a soft, 'Here you go.' Martha took them with a pain-stricken murmur of thanks.

It wasn't the first time he'd had a stable lass start crying in the horsebox. When Dennis came to think about it, there had been plenty of lads too. When you were dealing with live animals linked to everyone's hopes and dreams, there were inevitably days of defeat, disappointment, and god forbid, injury. A young, largely single workforce also meant liaisons between the staff were often quickly made, and just as quickly dissolved. There was a gamut of reasons why a stable lass should be crying in the cab of Dennis's horsebox, but not Martha. If there was only one thing he'd learned about Martha over the last two and a half years, it was that she wasn't the sort to burst into tears.

Dennis didn't fuss. He sat in silence for a full minute, allowing Martha to regain her composure. When the flow of tears had been stemmed and her shoulders stopped jerking involuntarily he asked, 'Want to tell me about it?'

Martha looked across at her boss and felt a wave of shame and disgust wash over her. For a moment it threatened to consume her in further tears and despair, however she took a few ragged breaths, composed herself, and started to speak in a croaky voice.

It took only a few minutes for Martha to tell her tale, during which time Dennis remained still, grave-faced, and silent. When his stable lass ran out of words he remained tight-lipped for a long moment as he contemplated the ramifications of what he'd learned, staring out through the windscreen of the horsebox.

'Redemption is at hand,' he eventually muttered in consolation, continuing to inspect the view outside the cab, his mind whirling, trying to find connections and resolutions.

This statement was met with a confused frown from Martha and when a moment later Dennis suddenly whipped around in his seat she jumped in surprise. He fixed her with a sharp, appraising eye and demanded the answer to a series of short questions. Once he was satisfied with the answers, Dennis issued a set of instructions.

'Are we clear?'

'Yes,' Martha confirmed, her tears forgotten and hope now shining in her eyes.

Scowling when his phone told him it was now two-twenty-three, Dennis tried in turn to call each of the ladies, urging each of them to pick up as their ring tone sounded. Three times he was sent to voicemail and left short, urgent messages. On the third call he ended it by thumping the phone screen with his finger and swearing angrily under his breath.

Further instructions were issued to Martha as they began unloading Fun Boy Frankie, who snorted and stamped his feet testily as they opened the doors to the horsebox and lowered the ramp. Dennis grabbed his race-day case and hurried after Martha and the gelding into the stables and emerged two minutes later at a run. He leapt back into the horsebox and was on the road back towards Malton moments later.

***

Bates frowned and checked his watch again. Something was wrong. It was ten past two and the 'No Regrets' syndicate hadn't left the yard. Inexplicably, they were sitting together inside a car on the edge of a paddock at the bottom of the yard. They would now be cutting it fine to reach Beverley in time for their three o'clock race.

Training his binoculars onto the car he confirmed to himself beyond doubt that the three women were still there and it was definitely them; not their Armitage doppelgangers.

However, there was definitely something very wrong with this situation, and it wasn't the women's behaviour that led Bates to this conclusion. Dylan hadn't been in touch. His tree-loving apprentice had failed to send any text updates for the last hour. Three pre-arranged update times had come and gone and the lad wasn't responding to any of Bates's demands for an immediate reply.

Grumbling under his breath, Bates chastised himself for becoming disappointed in the lad, after all, he had to all intents and purposes, placed temptation in his way. Still, he'd harboured a half hope that the lad wouldn't let him down.

Bates turned forty degrees to his right and spotted Dylan in his tree. The boy was watching the yard through the binoculars he'd given him. There was still time for the lad to change course, thought Bates.

All hope of the lad altering his present course of action evaporated in the next fifty seconds.

Forty-One

2-15pm

The drive down Dennis's private track to the main road took twenty seconds. They hadn't even reached the chorus of 'The Final Countdown' when Ruth swung the SUV in a wide arc on the chalk dust lane and edged them through an open gate into the bottom paddock, a rolling grass field surrounded by a substantial wooden fence and high hedge running along the main road into Norton.

It was empty, save for Dennis's ride-on lawn mower parked up against the hedge. Ruth brought the car to a halt, killed the engine, and the three ladies sat in tense silence. Sophie couldn't help running their alternative plans - the ones to somehow capture the Meat Man and his accomplices -through her mind one last time, wondering whether they'd made the right decision.

The five weeks since Frankie's last run hadn't been solely spent whiling away the hours at Middlefield Stables each day. Sophie had done a limited amount of work with her bereaved clients, Clara had organised for her house in Durham to be placed on the market and investigated schools in the York area for Jerry, and Ruth had basically become a member of Dennis's stable staff. Sophie had also visited the local police station to garner some support for the idea that someone was trying to intimidate them out of their inheritance, with little success. The caravan fire wasn't being treated as suspect, as the attending fire crew had identified the seat of the fire was a heated blanket that had been accidentally left on and eventually sparked the fire. When Sophie had explained that as far as she was aware none of the women owned a heated blanket, the duty sergeant hadn't so much laughed, as smirked her out of his police station.

However, with Dennis's help they had formulated plans. Meeting around his kitchen table on the summer evenings when he didn't have any runners at night meetings, the four of them had worked out a slew of cunning ways in which they could catch, trap, or trip up the Meat Man and his associates. They had brainstormed plan after plan. Sophie and Dennis had worked out several intricate plots, however it had taken Ruth to point out that they were trying to solve a problem that would automatically disappear once Fun Boy Frankie had run at Beverley.

'We've completed every element of the task so far. If we turn up at Beverley in time for the race, take our photo in the paddock to prove we've been there for our race in August, the Meat Man automatically disappears from our lives doesn't he? Won't we have won?' Ruth had asked.

The four of them had wordlessly traded hopeful looks.

'Why take the risk of trying to trap him and reveal his identity?' Ruth had continued in her quiet, thoughtful way of speaking, and to which Sophie and Clara had now become accustomed. And so they had agreed; they would concentrate on their final visit to the race and nothing else.

'If we're talking about keeping it simple,' Clara had suggested, 'I've always wanted to...'

'It's coming!' squealed Clara excitedly.

Sophie's attention snapped back to the three of them, sitting in the SUV in the bottom paddock. The distant sound of something large and mechanical grew to fill the silence. Soon, the invasive noise reached fever pitch. Each of the women turned in their seats... and with their noses pressed to the car windows, looked wide-eyed up towards the crest of the hillside.

***

Bates swallowed hard and stared down the hill. There was no need for binoculars; it was clear how the No Regrets syndicate would be reaching Beverley in time for Fun Boy Frankie's three o'clock race.

The helicopter swung into view over the top of the hill behind Bates, sending the tops of the trees into a swirling rage. Seconds later it was touching down in the bottom paddock and with rotor blades still turning, the three women hurried across the paddock, tentatively stepped up, and after an element of initial confusion, took their seats.

Bates sniffed appreciatively. You had to admire the simplicity of their solution. He now realised what the trainer must have created on his ride-on mower earlier in the day. From where he was on the hill, the undulations in the paddock had made it difficult to pick out exactly what Dennis Smith had been doing, other than cutting the grass, but Bates could now recognise a circle with a large 'H' in its centre cut into the grass where the helicopter had landed. Dylan must have had a perfect view of it, being higher up in his tree.

When Bates trained his binoculars back onto the oak tree, the bough Dylan had been clinging to no longer held any of the tell-tale signs of human habitation. The lad was gone.

Forty-Two

'Phones off please, ladies,' Colin, their pilot said through the headsets he'd passed around, 'FCC rules I'm afraid. But the flight time to Beverley races is only fifteen minutes, so you'll not be out of contact for too long.'

The three women obeyed the instruction and without further preamble Colin lifted the surprisingly, and in Clara's case, worryingly small craft into the air.

***

2-25pm

Dylan waited in the shadows of a sycamore tree on the edge of the top paddock until the helicopter had departed. He sent a text message to his client and switched the phone off, stowing it in the side-pocket of his military grade backpack. Once the sound of rotor blades cutting through the air had dropped to a murmur he rolled under the paddock fence and laid up against one of the many undulations in the turf, scanning the land that rolled downhill for two hundred yards before reaching the outskirts of the stable buildings. Beyond a small group of horses half-way to the barns, he spied what he was looking for outside the ménage.

It wasn't difficult to spot the short, fit looking man and the boy. The yard was quiet now, and he'd been watching the two of them for the past two hours, wheeling barrows to and from the muck pile, sweeping the concrete walkways between the barns, and leading horses to and from the barns to the paddocks and walker. After almost two months watching the yard from his hammock in the oak tree Dylan knew every foot of the Dennis Smith stables. He knew when staff started, ate, and finished. He knew the busy times and when the yard would go silent. When he closed his eyes he could visualise the layout. He was confident he could walk around the yard blindfold, should the need arise.

Dylan had also spent enough time in these woods to know when someone was following him. He'd known from eight o'clock in the morning there was someone else in the woods with him, just like he'd known when his client came searching for him all those months ago. His senses really were on fire! As was the case then, he had a small surprise waiting for anyone who tried to sneak up on him.

Digging into his backpack, Dylan's spidery hands withdrew a black pouch with a Velcro fastener. Still lying on his stomach against the rise of the grassy hollow, he ripped the pouch open and withdrew a shiny yellow plastic device, hid it under his body, and waited for the footfalls behind him to reach the paddock fence.

Bates had thought about calling out to the boy, but he was fearful Dylan would run. Crouching down beside him and having a quiet chat seemed the next best alternative, and it would ensure no one on the yard would hear anything, especially from this distance. The lad hadn't heard him, being consumed with the view of the yard. Dylan was lying on his chest, flat to the paddock grass, no more than ten yards away from the fence. Bates scrambled between the horizontal wooden bars and started to approach him. He'd only taken two steps into the field when Dylan suddenly flipped over, onto his back. Both the lad's hands were clasped around what appeared to be a chunky yellow gun.

Bates hardly had the chance to raise his hands before the two electrode wires popped from the gun and embedded themselves into his chest.

'What the…' Bates managed to get out before his muscles endured five seconds of random contraction, sending him to his knees.

Holding the taser gun tight, Dylan grinned mirthlessly as his mentor fell forwards once the initial charge had finished confusing his muscular system. Bates groaned, but hardly had chance to collect his thoughts before he began convulsing once again as Dylan discharged another round of electronic pulses into him. Bates began straining to draw in air, only managing short panting breaths.

'Took me ages to get hold of one of these through the dark web, 'Dylan said conversationally, now sitting up and watching Bates with interest, 'Of course, I've powered it up a bit. That's why you're having trouble breathing. It should operate at two-hundred milliamps, but I've managed to take it to five-hundred. It starts to injure the muscles and means you stay incapacitated for longer between bursts.'

When the device had finished its second pulse, he cocked his head to one side and examined his prisoner as Bates rolled over onto his back and sucked in several huge lung-filling breaths.

'Don't try and pull the electrodes off,' Dylan warned, zapping Bates again.

While his captive writhed nearby, Dylan pulled a hand-sized black block from his backpack along with two steel tent pegs. He waited patiently until the five seconds of electricity had finished ripping through his mentor and Bates was left fighting for breath. Then he rammed the pegs through the cuffs of Bates's jacket, effectively pinning him to the turf in a crucifixion pose.

'I've work to do for my *client*,' Dylan lectured him, 'And I can't stay around here. That's why I invented this.'

The young man held up the black plastic block. Bates eyed it nervously, too busy pulling in air between the surges of electricity to waste precious energy trying to speak. The lad must have skipped his medication and no amount of talking would make him see sense now. Dylan was off the rails, inhabiting his own warped reality.

'It's clever,' Dylan announced with a imperfect gap toothed smile as he stood over Bates, turning the black plastic brick over in his hands, 'It's a lawn mower battery, but you'll be happy to know I've dialled its power down and added a timer. That means that once I plug it in, it will deliver a 500 milliamp burst every four and a half minutes or so. That'll keep you out of my hair long enough to do my work.'

Bates tried to lift his arms, but his muscles refused to respond, screaming at him to cease trying. The skin on his face felt taut and it rippled as he fought to control his breathing. As Dylan fiddled with the wires coming from the black brick, Bates sucked in an acrid smell of burning; the electrodes were singeing, or possibly melting the clothing where they'd attached to his chest.

'Won't be long now,' Dylan promised, still fingering with wires from the battery, twisting them together to create a circuit with the wires embedded in Bates's chest. He added a flick switch box close to the battery and set the whole makeshift contraption down on the grass a few yards away from Bates.

A minute had sped by without another shock coursing through Bates and he tried his legs and arms again – they were weak, but slowly regaining their strength. Whatever level of electricity the lad was sending into him was far greater than a standard issue Police taser gun. The lad wasn't to know, but Bates had some experience of tasers.

A few seconds of testing told Bates his arms were still too weak to pull the tent pegs out – he was strangely impressed with the lad for that move – but he tensed his legs and was about to attempt to flip himself over, hoping to pull one of the electrodes out, or break the circuit where Dylan had spliced the wires, when a new, nerve jangling shock ripped through him.

'There we go!' the lad remarked gleefully, looking around and smiling as Bate's body shook uncontrollably for five seconds, leaving him gasping for air and every inch of his body screaming in pain.

Dylan pulled a mobile from his backpack and switched it on, tapping a short message and stowing the device once again.

'Lots to do, so I must be off,' he told Bates, 'Not to worry, you're all set. It's programmed to shock you every four-hundred and fifty seconds – just enough to keep you helpless, but not kill you.'

Dylan didn't wait for the next shock from the battery to send Bates into spasm. He did a perfunctory scan of the stable buildings with his binoculars and began striding purposefully down the field towards the centre of the yard. Bates didn't bother to watch Dylan go. He was too busy counting.

***

Clara slipped ungracefully from her seat in the helicopter, delighted to reunite her sensible, yet stylish shoes with a flat, unmoving surface. She bent down and shuffled away from the aircraft, happy in the knowledge that by hook or by crook, she would get a lift back in the horsebox after the race.

The fifteen minute trip to Beverley had been a great adventure for Sophie and Ruth, the two of them giggling and pointing things out on the ground like fascinated schoolgirls. To Clara, every minute of the journey had been stomach-churning torture.

'Dear me, Clara. You look like death warmed up,' Ruth noted as the three ladies were being escorted by a member of the racecourse staff on a short walk from the landing area in the centre of the racecourse, around to the owners' entrance.

'I'm fine,' Clara lied, still a little wobbly on her feet, but determined to brazen it out.

In truth she'd have rather ridden Fun Boy Frankie back to Malton than spend another moment in that flying death-trap. She calmed herself with the knowledge that in less than half an hour Greg's task would be complete and there would be no more hiding out in Malton, or worries about being pursued by an unknown man, with unknown objectives, and who possessed a strong smell of meat.

Clara was accepting her Owner's badge from the clerks at the entry desk when she heard a shriek of delight from the owners lounge next door. It could only be Gertrude Armitage. Within seconds a flood of people had rushed the double doors and Gertrude, Simon, Marion, and Timothy descended upon the three women, full of smiles and in Gertrude's case, obvious relief. A few steps behind, Paul and Thomas waited for the flurry of smiles and kisses to subside before they both offered their own, less intimate greetings. Thomas produced a business-like, watery smile and explained he'd been asked by Mr Sedgefield to attend, as today was the final element of the task. After an officious doorman pointedly revealed the area beyond the door was reserved for racegoers with Owners badges, and they only had Premier badges the group moved outside.

'I'm guessing that was you arriving in the helicopter?' Paul ventured as soon as the group had left the Owners' and Trainers' foyer and stepped into the racecourse, 'Mighty fine idea, beautifully timed too – Gertrude was beside herself with worry.'

'Are you here to apologise?' Sophie asked abruptly.

Paul took on a hurt expression.

'I've said I'm sorry,' he sighed, 'Greg did ask… actually he *instructed* me to do everything I could to bring you three together.'

Ruth had heard his pained explanation and popped up beside Sophie.

'Come on, Sophie. There's no way he was involved in the car crash or burning the caravan down. Seriously, this is Paul we're talking about.'

'And what about the water in the petrol that meant we only just got to Hamilton on time?'

'My driveway gate had been tampered with as well,' Paul said, 'I promise I didn't know that would happen.'

'You never told us that when you picked us up,' Sophie queried.

'I didn't want you to be worried.'

Sophie fixed her gaze on Paul for a long moment. He stared back, breaking into a self-conscious sweat.

Clara joined them and asked, 'What's up?'

'Sophie's deciding whether we can trust Paul again.'

'Hmm… Sophie not trusting you. I've been there before. I don't rate your chances, Paul.'

Sophie was still staring into Paul's eyes when a women's voice called, 'Clara Armitage. Is there a Clara Armitage here?'

Fingers pointed and hurried shushing led to Clara being tapped on her shoulder by one of the ladies from the Owners and Trainers foyer.

'Mrs Armitage, there's a telephone call for you,' the women said quickly, she fiddled with her glasses as she spoke, a little flustered, 'Your mobile is switched off apparently and… the gentleman calling says it's extremely important you speak with him on an urgent matter. He's on our internal phone.'

Clara's face fell and she swapped worried looks with Ruth and Sophie. Without hesitation, all three of them hurried after the clerk, through the double doors and back inside the Owners and Trainers foyer. Seconds later Clara was standing at the Owners and Trainers reception, a landline phone in her hand, and with Ruth and Sophie at her shoulder. She took a quick, calming breath and said, 'Yes?'

'Is that Clara Armitage?' a brusque man's voice asked.

'Who wants to know?'

There was a pause, followed by a clicking in the background, 'Who am I? he said in a muffled tone, 'I'm the man who has your son.'

For the second time within a few minutes Clara's knees went wobbly and prickly heat washed over her.

'What's happened?' Sophie asked Clara, partly in mime, and fearing the answer.

'It's the Meat Man... he says he has... Jerry,' was all Clara could say in the moment. She was thinking, desperately trying work out whether to believe the Meat Man and how she should react. Ruth and Sophie gaped at each other, too many questions and horrible possibilities filling their minds.

'Phones!' Ruth whispered urgently to Sophie, 'I didn't turn mine back on, what about you?'

Sophie shook her head, but unlike Ruth she didn't immediately start rummaging in her bag. Instead, she placed a hand on Clara's shoulder and said quietly, 'Concentrate. Listen carefully. What words does he use? His accent. Ask to speak with Jerry. Insist on it! Now, breathe...'

She placed her hand onto Clara's chest and widened her eyes, encouraging Clara to fill her lungs and exhale slowly in time with her own breaths.

The man came back on the line.

He growled at Clara, his anger threatening to burst though in every other word, 'Leave the racecourse, Mrs Armitage. Miss the race. Leave now. Before three o'clock, or your son...'

'I want to speak to him right now!' Clara interrupted. She started to bite the end of her thumb and forefinger, willing the man to answer. Sophie gently pulled Clara's fingers away from her mouth and held her hand.

'No, you get out of the...'

'If I can't speak to him this minute, I'm going nowhere,' Clara insisted, frightened tears now cascading down her cheeks.

The line went silent. Clara slowly looked into Ruth and Sophie's faces. Ruth had her phone clamped to one ear, her palm over the other, concentrating on what was being said. Sophie was squeezing her hand, her eyes brimming with hope.

'Mum?'

The line suddenly had an enormous amount of crackling static. Jerry's voice echoed as he said, 'I'm here Mum. Danny doesn't feel too well, the man fired a gun at him...'

Clara waited until her little boy had finished speaking, but hadn't been able to concentrate on anything after the mention of a gun, other than the image of Jerry being held hostage at gunpoint. Anger fizzed inside her, the urge to rant at the Meat Man blunted by her sense of helplessness and fear for her son. She began saying a few calming words to Jerry when there was a sudden click and the man's voice returned.

'Will you leave now, Mrs Armitage, or shall I make your son scream for you?'

Clara gritted her teeth. She was desperate to tell the Meat Man exactly what she thought of him. A younger, more confident Clara would have done so, she'd have given this bully both barrels... and probably ruined her life... again.

A short announcement about a non-runner in a later race filled the racecourse for a few seconds and a fuzzy, warm feeling ran through Clara. She'd faintly heard the announcement echo down the line to her. He had to be here... the Meat Man was phoning from the racecourse!

She asked, 'How will you know if I leave?'

The man paused, eventually replying, 'I will know.'

'But *how*?' Clara demanded, her confidence building, 'I could leave and you wouldn't know. You might hurt Jerry even though I do leave!'

Was that a small sigh she heard? Clara pushed the phone even harder to her ear. The Meat Man cleared his throat. It sounded rough, and the image of the Meat Man, the acrid smell of his breath filled Clara's mind. She imagined he'd not only eaten too much processed meat during his lifetime, but also sunk too many bottles of hard liquor.'

'You're wasting time, Mrs Armitage,' he growled, 'Do you really want to gamble with your son's life? You have one minute, and don't let anyone try to stop you leaving.'

Sophie frowned. She'd been listening intently to Clara's side of the conversation, but now she stared at her with questioning eyes. Clara put her palm over the receiver.

'I think he's here on the racecourse. Look for someone on a phone who can see I'm in here!' she whispered urgently.

Sophie nodded, and pulling at Ruth's arm steered her a few yards down the foyer and issued updated instructions into her ear. Clara watched the two women stop, share another quick, but more earnest conversation which ended in the two of them nodding and then looking over at her. She waved them away.

Clara hoped her inner feeling of guilt wasn't too obvious. The Meat Man had already rung off. He'd been right, she couldn't afford for anyone to delay her or stop her from leaving. And there was a group of people on the other side of the double doors who stood to gain millions of pounds if she stayed. They wouldn't take the time to understand her little boy was in danger; they'd only be concerned with the money.

Sophie and Ruth moved closer to the racecourse door and peered through the reinforced glass whilst being closely studied by the doorman.

'Are you with them?' he inquired.

Ruth nodded.

'Well you can tell 'em that they can't use this door without an Owner's badge. I've already had to refuse entry twice to the loud elderly lady.'

On the other side of the door, the entire Armitage family, along with their entourage - including Paul, Marion, Alvita, and the young solicitor, Thomas - were standing together, no more than five yards away. Simon and Marion were trying to calm Gertrude down, and the others wore nervous looks and kept glancing at the double doors, presumably checking the foyer and that the three ladies were still visible through the thick glass of the doors. Sophie reminded herself that as long as the entire No Regrets syndicate remained in the racecourse for the next forty-five minutes and posed for one photo, it would provide the Armitage's with a meal ticket for the rest of their lives. Everyone outside the Owners and Trainers entrance had good reason to be concentrating on the three of them.

Ruth glanced over to her extended family. Almost all of them were staring their way or jabbing fingers at their phones. Beyond her family, she recognised no one. She couldn't locate anyone looking shifty or acting like a blackmailer...

'What use is this?' Ruth moaned, 'I've never met the Meat Man and neither have you. We saw He-Man at Ascot, and that was only for a few seconds at a distance. You've met one of his... gang, Skeletor didn't you – is he out there?'

Sophie took in the owners and trainers area that consisted of a dozen tables, each filled with a smattering of people. She scanned them, not so certain the Meat Man would be in an Owners-only area. Besides, there was no view into the foyer – the Meat Man would surely need to know Clara was still at the reception desk. Beyond the Armitage group in the general admittance area race-goers were milling around, and Sophie double-checked to see if any of the faces reminded her of the teenager she'd encountered on the Knavesmire.

'No. I can't see him. There must be at least half a dozen men out there and none of their faces ring any bells, even the ones without a phone. How about you?'

Ruth shook her head and glanced back at Clara.

'She's gone!'

Sophie swore under her breath and the two of them scampered back to the reception desk and hurriedly asked where their friend had gone. The clerk gestured towards the exit doors and would have liked to explain that the rude lady had slammed the phone down, swore a number of times, and then run out of the racecourse. However, she was robbed of that pleasure as Ruth and Sophie had already set off in pursuit.

Inside the racecourse, Gertrude peered suspiciously into the foyer entrance through the glass panelled doors.

'I can't see them,' she said hotly, walking up to the double doors. The portly gentleman manning the door wore a name badge on his chest and possessed a healthy air of scepticism as Gertrude approached. He pushed the door open a crack and asked if he could help, strategically placing his ample frame between door and frame.

Gertrude asked a couple of questions through the half-open door, turned to the Armitages, and as one, the family rushed the Owners and Trainers entrance. The doorman saw sense at the last moment, stepped back and allowed the rabble to stampede past him. Gertrude stumped up to the reception counter, slapped her palm down and demanded to know where the rest of her family had gone.

The Armitage posse soon spilled out of the exit, led by an anxious Gertrude screaming Clara's, then Ruth's name. They'd only covered forty yards when their little group was brought to a halt by two marshals who had created a cordon to allow the horses for the three o'clock race to cross the car park and enter the pre-parade ring. Four horses were led past, the last of them looking familiar. Paul recognised Martha and Fun Boy Frankie.

'Martha, have you seen them, Clara, Sophie, and Ruth?' Paul called out.

The girl had been concentrating on the horse, her head turned towards the gelding's shoulder. When Paul called again, louder this time, she kept walking but her head twisted his way and for a moment she faced the group before stable lass and horse disappeared behind a wall and into the pre-parade ring beyond.

Beside Paul, Marion stated, 'That stable lass was crying. Shouldn't we find out if she's okay?'

Paul didn't answer. He'd also recognised the tell-tale signs of unhappiness in Martha and as the marshal's cordon was dismantled and the group surged forward, he hesitated to follow them, his thoughts focused on the girl with tear-stained cheeks and a fearful expression.

'Paul?' Marion queried, demanding an answer.

Shaking the girls face from his mind, he shrugged at Marion as if disinterested, and moved off to catch up with the others. Marion paused to peer into the pre-parade ring as they passed the opening in the wall, but Martha was now pacing around the pre-parade ring and out of speaking range.

Seventy yards ahead of the Armitages, Clara ducked under the running rails and sprinted towards the helicopter. She'd long since lost any sense of decorum, allowing her light skirt to billow in the breeze and her horrendously expensive handbag to bounce against her body as she ran to the helicopter. She didn't care about the sickness inducing ride, all she wanted was to get back to Jerry as soon as she could. She could put up with another fifteen minutes of hell to be with her boy again.

Her hopes of an early getaway faded as she approached the

machine. The cockpit was empty and the helicopter was silent and lifeless.

'Pilot! Pilot!' Clara screamed between gasps for breath. She was about to repeat her appeal when a head popped up beyond the nose of the machine where a blanket and pillow had been laid out on the grass. The pilot scratched his head and stared at his client, bleary-eyed.

'Wake up, Colin! You're taking me home. Now!' Clara shouted irritably. She started to yank at the helicopter door and was pleased when it clicked and swung open. Shouting more hurry-up instructions at her pilot, she climbed in.

Ruth crossed the racecourse, ignoring the marshal's protests on the gate to the course enclosure and sprinted towards the helicopter, spurred on by its rotor blades starting to turn. She began waving her arms at the pilot as she ran. Behind her, Sophie struggled on at a slower pace, slightly jealous of Ruth's impressive speed, shouting, 'Get them to wait for me!' after her.

When Ruth reached the helicopter and pulled the door open, she found Colin doing his best to explain to Clara that he couldn't take to the sky when one of his clients was running and waving at him. In return, he was being berated by an apoplectic Clara. She looked down at Ruth, tossed her head back and shouted, 'For the love of... my son is being...'

Hardly able to get her words out, she clenched her fists, took a breath and screamed, 'I'm not staying, there's no amount of money that will keep me...'

'I agree. I'm coming with you. All for one and one for... well, you know what I mean,' Ruth shouted over the sound of the engine and rotor blades. She lifted a thumb over her shoulder and added, 'Hold up, Sophie's coming too.'

Ruth planted herself in the co-pilot seat beside Colin, careful not to kick any instruments, then she took a look over her shoulder and caught Clara's eye and shouted, 'She's missed you, you know. She told me yesterday at the hog roast.'

'Is this really the time to be...'

'Yes it is,' Ruth broke in, 'Before we set off running after you she told me it didn't matter about the money. She was for leaving straight away to make sure Jerry is okay.'

Clara covered her face with both hands and gave a long, agitated moan during which Sophie arrived red-faced, her hair flapping around in the downdraft.

Sophie's breathless arrival prompted Clara to press her lips together and wipe a tear from her eye. Ruth leaned over and helped pull Sophie into the seat beside her and clapped a thankful hand on her friend's knee as she fought for her breath.

'Get on then, Colin. Make this death trap fly!' Clara shouted. The three ladies each pulled on a set of headphones as the sound of the rotor blades quickening rendered normal conversation redundant.

The helicopter lifted into the air a few seconds later, leaving Clara's stomach on the ground. As it rose, she gritted her teeth, swallowed, and chanced a look downwards. Her attention was caught by a small gaggle of people in the Owners' and Trainers' car park. They were pointing upwards, and she soon recognised the Armitages. Even from two-hundred yards up in the air Clara could clearly pick out Gertrude, as she was the one shaking both her fists at the helicopter.

Forty-Three

2.45pm

The most recent five seconds of nerve jangling pain gave way to residual aching and once again Bates started to count. Once the involuntary convulsing had ebbed away, he tried again to lift an arm, a foot. They were unresponsive. Gravity seemed to have increased four-fold, pushing his leaden body into the grass. He remained pinned out, staked to the ground in a pose he imagined was reminiscent of Vitruvian man. Even moving an eyelid was a Herculean task. He blinked away his blurred vision and inspected his view of the sky. Wisps of perfectly white cloud sauntered by, on a deep blue background. This vista had one element spoiling its perfection; the lower branch of a sycamore tree. It hung tantalisingly close, but realistically too high to be of any use to him. Twenty-eight... twenty-nine...

Bates again cursed himself for being caught out. Not only had he underestimated the lad's ingenuity with electronics, he'd not checked on his medication, and most importantly, he'd not realised how badly the lad needed to prove himself. Well, he was certainly paying for his lack of man management.

Thirty-six... Thirty-seven. And it wasn't as if Jimmy was about to pitch up any moment and pull the wires out of his chest; he was deployed elsewhere. Also, he had a horrible feeling Dylan's timings were all to cock. That second shock had come far quicker than he had anticipated. It wasn't a huge surprise to Bates. The lad was reasonably adept when it came to fiddling with electronics, however his attention to detail became shot to hell without his medication. He'd said the shocks came every seven and a half minutes, that would be four-hundred and fifty seconds...

Forty-one... forty-two. Bates tried to relax. Fighting the muscle spasms only made the pain stronger. He had another four-hundred seconds to recover enough to... There was a familiar soft electrical tick nearby and Bates's chest burst into a hot centre of pain whose tributaries then coursed around his body in search of muscles to inhabit and disrupt.

Concentrating on his breathing alone, Bates only opened his eyes again when he'd reached twenty-two, more to test they were still working, rather than expecting to profit from the exercise. Dylan had got his numbers wrong, the shocks were coming every forty-five seconds, not four-hundred and fifty. That wasn't good. At this rate Bates reckoned he had minutes to live. Without that seven minute recovery time, his body would begin to shut down.

Thirty-two, thirty-three... The long, bay-coloured head of a horse hung over Bates for a few seconds, then dropped to investigate his chest, the gelding's lips rubbing against his t-shirt. As his count reached thirty-eight a second head descended from the sky and warm, grassy breath bombarded his senses. Bates was beyond being able to control his limbs, but as the electricity began to surge through him this time he made an effort to make the wires attached to the small barbed darts in his chest go taut. Wasn't flight a horses primary response to a threat? If they were scared enough, one of these huge animals might just kick the wires out, or bash the battery in their rush to get away.

Forty-four, forty-f… He endured another five seconds of agony, and it took a further ten seconds for him to open his eyes and check on whether the scuffling of hooves he'd heard had resulted in any improvement to his situation. It appeared not. His blurry sight cleared enough for him to see the two electrodes were still impaled into his chest with wires still intact.

However, some way off, a new set of eyes lowered themselves into his field of view. Bates recognised them immediately. He'd been following this dog's movements around the racing yard on and off for the last few months.

Kilroy approached carefully and sniffed tentatively at the man's hand. Behind him, a few yards away, Bella looked on. The German Shepherd ran his nose up Bates' arm, over his shoulder and his warm wet tongue took a prolonged lick at the meaty flavoured sweat on the side of the man's forehead.

Bates closed his eyes, waiting for a voice to demand what he was doing pinned to their paddock and hooked up to a battery emitting electrical torture. No such comment came; the dogs must have found him on their own.

His concentration fully on Kilroy, Bates had lost count, and so when the next shock sent his muscles into spasm, he wasn't ready for it. He gave a weak groan as the electricity took over. When it released him from its debilitating grip, Bates could smell burning. Clothes, plastic, or flesh… he couldn't tell. He pushed this query to the back of his mind, he had bigger troubles - it was taking longer for him to recover from each jolt; that meant it wouldn't be long before he lost consciousness. He had no idea how much damage was being done to his nervous system, or his heart… or his brain come to that, but being unconscious while his body was being fried every forty-five seconds couldn't be good for any of his organs.

He felt the dog's paws land on his stomach before he'd recovered enough to chance opening his eyes. It seemed Kilroy hadn't been frightened off by his agonised twisting and writhing. When he managed to focus, Bates found Kilroy staring at the wires embedded in his chest. The dog was emitting a low whine. For a moment Bates considered bellowing at the dog in the hope he would flee, pulling the wires out as he went. An attempt to speak killed that thought immediately, he was unable to get a single word out; his tongue felt like a slab of dead meat.

Kilroy now nosed his way between the wires and to the left-hand side of his chest, sniffing constantly. Bates suddenly realised what was going on. The dog was after his pepperoni. It had to be a combination of his own odour, plus a half finished pepperoni stick secreted in the breast pocket of his shirt; the dog could smell it and was after a snack. He'd had to wean himself off the spiced meat, rather than go cold turkey. The half-stick was his self-allotted afternoon portion.

Bates calculated the next shock was due in no more than fifteen seconds. He drew in a ragged deep breath, expanding his chest and held it, bringing the wires closer. With luck, the dog's muzzle would pass close to one of the wires and perhaps knock it, in order to win its prize.

With two paws on the man's chest, Kilroy looked down, his tongue lolling out over the mess of wire and bloodstained shirt. The meaty smell of the man was overpowering, enticing, and he was salivating. But a wire cord was tight across the cloth pocket where the smell was strongest. Kilroy would not be denied. He lowered his head, clamped his jaws around the wire and yanked upwards.

There was the slightest of tugs to his torso, however Bates couldn't be sure what this meant. He felt a scraping and a strong smell of dog wafted upwards. It didn't matter what the dog was doing, the next jolt was due any moment. He gritted his teeth, dimly aware that Kilroy had now dismounted his chest.

Bates's count had reached fifty when he blinked his eyes open and realised the dog had pulled one of the barbs and its wire out of his chest. With its circuit broken, there would be no more five seconds of electric mayhem. He turned his head to the right and though glassy eyes caught sight of a German Shepherd and Greyhound sharing a meal of pepperoni in the bottom of a nearby grassy knoll. He wanted to say, 'Good dog,' but didn't have the strength.

Bates breathed in another ragged breath, aware he was still counting. It took a concerted effort to stop. He closed his eyes and tried to relax, attempting to ignore the muscles all over his body that continued to randomly twitch, each creating their own piercing, individual needle of pain. He pushed the agony away by occupying his mind.

The recovery time from a single, standard taser shock could be, at best, a few minutes, but was more likely to be an hour or two. He calculated his recovery time from the higher, non-standard voltage shocks to which he'd been exposed and realised it could be nightfall before he had the strength to pull out the pegs pinning his arms to the ground. A faint smile graced his lips as he contemplated the revenge he would exact when he caught up with Dylan, the treacherous young weasel. The smile remained on Bates's face until he fell into a deep, dreamless sleep.

Forty-Four

2-50pm

Something was up. Mitch Corrigan knew as soon as he walked out of the weighing room and onto the soft grass of the parade ring. Despite hunting around the ring for the No Regrets ladies, he found no sign of Frankie's connections, and even stranger, Dennis was missing.

'Where is everyone?' he asked Martha, walking with her as she led Fun Boy Frankie around the Beverley parade ring.

The girl's face was wracked with a mixture of fear and regret. She replied, 'Gone. Dennis too, and it's all my fault.'

'Gone where? The syndicate had to be here for the race didn't they?' Mitch queried.

Martha rubbed her free palm across her cheek, adding another angry red smear to her pale, tear-stained face.

'They left in the helicopter. Their family was *so angry*,' she told him in emotional snatches of breath.

'They will lose… millions of pounds. I was scared to tell them that… that… it was me that was helping the Meat Man!'

Expecting her to break down and burst into further floods of tears at any moment, Mitch drew to a halt and allowed Martha to continue alone with Frankie on her next circuit of the ring. She needed time to collect herself, and he reckoned firing more questions at the young woman would only add to her problems. By the time she'd led the gelding around again, Mitch had retreated to the centre of the parade ring and was standing alone, head down, waiting for the jockeys' instruction to mount to be announced.

Mitch closed his eyes and emptied his mind of everything he'd just learned. Instead, he focused on the one thing he could materially affect in the next fifteen minutes: placing Fun Boy Frankie into a position that would allow the two-year-old to achieve the best possible finishing position in the upcoming nursery handicap.

***

Sophie and Ruth remained silent for the first minute of their flight, as did Clara, who spent the time staring listlessly down at the moving patchwork of fields below her filled with wheat, oats, and oilseed rape. There wasn't much to debate. They were heading back to Middlefield stables to ensure the safety of a young boy and a young man. What could they say to a mother who was suffering acute anxiety every second that it took to bring her son closer to her? So there was an element of surprise

225

when Clara cleared her throat and began to speak to them through the small microphone attached to her headset, her words being transmitted to the other two passengers.

'I'm grateful to both of you… and I'm sorry,' she began, her eyes remaining fixed on the fields below.

Ruth and Sophie's murmured self-deprecating replies that Clara waved away.

'Seriously, I'm sure Jerry will be fine when we get there, but I can't lose anoth…'

Clara's voice trailed away and she shot a nervous glance at Sophie and then Ruth before returning to her examination of the constantly changing landscape underneath the helicopter.

'You… *We* couldn't take the chance,' Sophie said with an air of finality. She tried hard to sound positive, despite her curiosity being spiked by Clara's words.

Ruth nodded, 'I agree. Jerry is far more important than Greg's stupid task.'

'Thanks you two,' Clara whispered gratefully after a short pause.

The conversation stalled. Ruth and Sophie joined Clara in allowing the scenery to drift by without really taking it in, nervously willing the helicopter to reach its destination and trying not to allow their minds to dwell on what they might find when they landed back at Middlefields.

***

Dennis pulled off the main road and into the lane leading to Middlefields. Flooring the accelerator, he rushed up toward the house and barns, a plume of dust following him. At the narrowest part of the track, between two paddock fences with tall hedges, he brought the horsebox to a brake-melting stop, effectively blocking access; if the Meat Man was still here, he wouldn't be able to leave by car.

Dennis was angry. Some of his anger was leveled at the Meat Man, but mostly, his rage was directed at himself. Having had time to think hard during his thirty-minute break-neck dash from Beverley, Dennis's first thought on learning that Martha had been groomed, manipulated, and then intimidated and threatened, had been to blame himself. When he really thought about it, there had been subtle changes in the girl over the last few months – her growing obsession with the No Regrets horses, complaining about the ladies moving into the empty cottages, and he'd ignored the biggest sign of all, the change in her attitude. When he re-examined Martha's behaviour in the last fortnight, her cheerful smile in a morning had been in short supply, tending to be replaced with a tired grimace. Her overflowing enthusiasm for the job had shrivelled to simply completing her duties - and he should have noticed.

Dennis had shuddered when he was reminded that Martha had lost her mother only two years previously. He'd known how deeply invested Martha was in the yard – it was her new family – and yet he hadn't protected her properly. He'd allowed these unscrupulous criminals to feed Martha with lies about him and the No Regrets syndicate, and once their hunger for information had been sated, they had moved on to intimidate, blackmail, and manipulate a vulnerable young woman.

It hadn't been the Meat Man that had visited Martha. She spoke of a young man, no more than a lad by the sound of it. Soon after the ladies had completed their first, bad-tempered visit to the stables, Martha had been approached by this lad whilst out on a walk. She'd become vague when relating how the lad gained her confidence, but Dennis could guess. The consequence of this meeting was that she had believed the No Regrets syndicate meant to remove their horses - her horses - and do harm to the yard. So Martha had started to pass information to the lad regarding the ladies: primarily their movements and race plans.

When it became clear the syndicate weren't a threat to the horses in her care, Martha had tried to blank the lad, only to find he started to blackmail her, threatening to expose her duplicity, which would surely result in the loss of her job and her home if she didn't carry on supplying the information he needed. The final pieces of information he had demanded from Martha on a particularly nasty visit to her last night, during the hog roast, was Clara's mobile number and where her son, Jeremy, would be at the time Fun Boy Frankie was due to run at Beverley.

Dennis hoped he was wrong. Connecting the two meant the Meat Man was about to target Jerry, and he guessed Clara was set to receive an intimidating telephone call any time soon, although he'd not been able to reach her on her mobile.

As he clambered down from the cab, Dennis could feel the rage building within him. Once his feet touched the ground he paused for a few seconds and took a deep breath, swallowing his anger, pushing it down. He needed a clear head. If the Meat Man was still here, he was going to need guile, not anger.

The yard was quiet, as it should be at a ten to three in the afternoon. Dennis jogged past the farmhouse and up to the first of the barns, peering into its dim interior and shouting, first for Jerry, then Danny. A couple of horses' heads popped out of their stable doors, and stared his way. Nothing was out of place. He strode down the barn's central corridor, checking in each stable, calling out for Jerry and Danny as he went. His voice produced a faint echo, but there was no reply.

Dennis stepped out of the colts' barn and, after giving the paddocks a cursory inspection, entered the bottom of the second barn, both ends of the barns being open to allow the light summer breeze to flow through them. Everything was pristine, tidy, and as it should be. A three-year-old whinnied at him as he passed, hoping to earn herself an early meal, otherwise the fillies' barn was quiet.

A single glance into the entrance to the juvenile barn made Dennis stop and stare. Something was out of place. A sweeping brush lay discarded in the central corridor, beside it an upturned plastic bucket was rolling in a small arc as the wind caught it, sending it one way, then the other. Breathing deeply, Dennis ventured into the barn. He tried calling out again, receiving no answer, and started down the wide corridor, checking every stable.

A rustling, scraping sound made him stop and listen. It was coming from a stable close by. The rustling ceased and a dull metallic thud from the same stable made his heart jump. He called for Danny and Jerry again and the thudding sounded once more. Running his tongue over dry lips Dennis quickly covered the ten yards distance to the stable and peered through the steel bars. Danny was lying in the corner, his mouth covered with tape, his arms and legs similarly bandaged and his eyes closed. A pair of thin wires were attached to his back. When Dennis kicked back the bottom lock on the stable door and pulled it open, Jerry fell out onto his feet. The boy was bound and gagged like Danny. Dennis now understood it had been Jerry, banging his elbows or even his head against the stable door, who had alerted him.

The boy lay on the floor, his relieved eyes fixed on Dennis as the trainer bent down to begin removing the thick grey tape from his mouth.

'It's okay, Jerry. I'll be careful,' Dennis whispered as he searched for the edge of the tape.

Jerry murmured something and Dennis caught his eye. The boy wasn't looking at him, instead he was focused over his shoulder. The relief in those young brown eyes had been replaced with fear.

Dennis turned quickly, but it still wasn't fast enough. The blow to the side of his head sent his eyes rocketing upwards into their sockets and a shrill whistling noise suddenly filled his head. As he fell, Dennis spent his last moment of consciousness berating himself for not realising that the brush and bucket had been missing a shovel.

Forty-Five

Clara swallowed back her nausea, trying to rid herself of the acidic taste tickling the back of her throat. She started to fiddle with the helicopter door as soon as Colin brought them to a rather uncertain landing in the front paddock. It had required two aborted attempts before they slammed onto the makeshift 'H' cut into the grass. In normal circumstances her pilot would have been the recipient of a severe ticking off. Not this time though, Clara held a single thought in her head; finding Jerry.

Initially pursued, but soon overtaken by Ruth, Clara struggled into a passable jog with Sophie matching strides. They were soon on the track up to the barns, all three of the ladies shouting out for Jerry and Danny.

Ruth reached the stranded horsebox first, noticing on passing that the cab door had been left open. She frowned at the two behind her, but maintained her speed. The same expression was soon gracing Clara and Sophie's faces after peering questioningly into the vacant cab. Ruth slowed upon her approach to the farmhouse, suddenly aware that the Meat Man could be lurking within, and she tried calling out Danny and Jerry's names towards the barns. With no immediate reply she changed direction.

'I'll try the farmhouse,' Ruth shouted over her shoulder and crossed to the hedge and opened the garden gate.

Thirty yards behind, Sophie and Clara came to a shambling halt, holding their backs and wheezing, red-faced. They watched between gasps of breath as Ruth headed silently down the garden path to the farmhouse door.

'Come on, the barns,' Clara said with purpose, and set off toward the mare's barn at a strong walk. Sophie gritted her teeth and ran to catch up.

Behind them the helicopter took to the air once more. The noise prompted Clara to glance around and wonder whether they should have told Colin what was going on. She'd been frightened he might not bring them back if he knew a man with a gun was holding her son hostage within a few hundred yards of his landing pad. It no longer mattered, he was airborne once again.

Instead of entering the barns, Clara passed each in turn staring down the long corridor of stables for any sign of life that wasn't equine, continuing to call out names and hoping the Meat Man wasn't waiting to pounce on them. The first two barns yielded nothing more than a few whinnies and the odd curious stare from the residents. The final barn produced a very different result. Clara's heart jumped and she immediately broke into a run down the corridor, screaming for Sophie to follow.

Clara knew from recent experience what a dead body looked like, and this body didn't disappoint. As far as she was concerned, it had all the hallmarks of being dead, even though she couldn't make out the identity, beyond it being an adult male. Both Sophie and Clara came to a halt a couple of yards away from the unmoving mound of awkwardly placed limbs and torso, and stared for a second or two.

The body was lying face down on the cool, dusty concrete, one leg bent at the knee, and folded over the other, one arm under the body, the other stuck straight out. His hand was lying palm up, and Sophie noticed two fingers were tarnished with a sickly yellow colour.

'Dennis!' Sophie gasped, surging forward and falling to her knees beside the body, pulling at his jacket to roll Dennis over. Clara followed suit, helping to untwist Dennis's limbs.

Several muffled cries of 'Mum!' came from inside the nearest stable. A deeper, rumbling voice chimed in with the lighter boyish one. Clara stood, ignoring the body at her feet - now lying on its back - her stomach flipping with anticipation. Between the vertical bars that started halfway up the stable front she saw Jerry and Danny lying in the corner of the stable among a few inches of wood chippings, inexpertly trussed up like Egyptian mummies with what appeared to be insulation tape.

'Jerry!' Clara exclaimed, rushing over to the stable door and kicking away at the bottom latch until she could pull it open and rush in.

From the floor of the corridor the body moaned. Sophie, who had been watching Clara, jumped backwards as if she'd been electrocuted. She swore loudly and then smiled in wonder at the newly resurrected trainer as he pushed himself up on his elbows and squinted at her.

'Has the shovel happy little sod gone?' Dennis asked, holding the back of his head in one hand and wincing as his fingers investigated a small area of hair matted with blood.

It took a moment for Sophie to catch on.

'Ruth!' she said, standing, 'She's in the farmhouse.'

***

'Boss?'

The lad hissed the call again at Bates as he ducked under the three-bar fence that separated the top paddock from the woods.

Bates stirred from his half-sleep and tried to open his eyes. It was as if using the muscles around his eyelids started a chain reaction. The whole of his body felt a wave of excruciating pain ripple from his eye sockets to every other muscle, the abused tissue communicating how unwise it was to start operating once again.

'Christ, Boss. You look like crap,' Jimmy told him matter-of-factly as he peered down at the older man.

Bates was pleased his young apprentice had bothered to come find him, nevertheless the lad's mindless comment and the fact he wasn't busy unpinning him from his crucifixion position on the ground, made his blood boil.

'Get me up you idiot,' he croaked.

Jimmy rolled his eyes and set to work whilst chuntering sarcastically, 'Nice to see you Jimmy. Good of you to pop over and rescue me. If it wasn't for you, Jimmy…'

Bates failed to reply. With teeth gritted, he was helped up to a sitting position on the grass and remained hunched over, trying to breathe. Every lungful of air, no matter how small, sent pain spiralling around his chest and into his back. Using his nerves as transport, the jangling agony then travelled into his arms and legs.

Jimmy stood back, eyeing his boss. He wasn't used to seeing Bates like this; ashen, crumpled… and looking old. Someone had done a proper job on him.

'Want a hand up?'

Bates would have loved to have barked at the lad, but instead he settled for a hoarse, 'Get down!'

Jimmy fell to his knees.

'There's no-one around at this end of the yard,' Jimmy assured him, 'I waited until they'd gone into the barns.'

'No dogs around?'

'They're with the women in the barns. There's a few horses at the other end of this field, but that's it.'

Jimmy watched Bates put a hand onto the turf and make to get up. He crawled forward and helped haul his boss to a shaky kneeling position.

'What now, Mr Bates. We're done here, aren't we?' Jimmy asked

231

hopefully.

Bates tried not to allow the pain to show through his grimace.

'Not quite. I gave Dylan… too much rope,' he rumbled, 'We've got a couple more jobs to do before we're finished.'

Jimmy curled his lip.

'Yeah…,' he agreed with a weary sigh, 'I had a feelin' you'd say that.'

Throwing an arm around Bates' waist the two of them struggled to their feet and Jimmy guided the older man to the fence. He rolled his fragile boss through over the lowest horizontal bar and helped him to his feet again. Locked together, they staggered into the wood.

Bates started to think about the dogs. He could have been dead if the German Shepherd hadn't pulled the wires out of his chest. Once they were under cover of the trees, he ordered Jimmy to give him a minute to catch his breath and they collapsed onto a fallen tree.

'Do I smell of pepperoni, Jimmy?' Bates asked after his breathing had flattened out.

Jimmy's eyebrows dived downwards and Bates noticed the lad was suddenly finding the leaf litter on the floor of the wood to be of immense interest.

'I'll take that as a yes,' Bates noted sourly.

Forty-Six

3-02pm

Mitch had been relieved when Martha released Frankie and the two of them were left to hack up the Beverley straight together. There was definitely something odd going on with that girl. As Frankie walked forward and slotted into stall ten at the five furlong start, once again Mitch tried to empty his mind and concentrate. Besides, he'd soon be back with Martha - the winner of this race should be crossing the line in a little over a minute.

'Two to go,' a stalls handler cried behind him.

Mitch gave the gelding a final stroke down his mane, gripped the reins in his left hand and got himself poised to break and get a position. The stalls sprang open and Fun Boy Frankie put his race experience to good use by shooting forward. After half a dozen strides Mitch eased the gelding across to the inside rail and sat at the front of the twelve runner field, hardly moving on the two-year-old.

3-03pm

It wasn't until Ruth had entered the farmhouse and investigated all the downstairs rooms, calling out Jerry and Danny's names, that she heard a floorboard creak above her and considered checking the upstairs. She'd never had the need to venture upstairs before and stood at the bottom of the oak staircase considering the possibility that Dennis may not want her to be wandering alone around his bedrooms.

Another unnatural noise from above decided her. It sounded like something wooden being scraped across the floor. Despite not answering her calls, Jerry or Danny could be up there, so she had a duty to investigate. All the same, she stepped lightly up the deep maroon carpeted staircase, alert for any further noises.

Ruth stepped onto the landing and allowed herself a quick look to her left down the corridor. A tastefully decorated hallway with fancy cornices and wall-mounted lighting led to three closed doors. To her right the staircase gallery gave way to the other end of the corridor and contained five evenly spaced doors, three on the left, two on the right. The last one on the right was ajar.

'Jerry? Danny?'

She saw no point in being silent, having called their names several times as she went through the ground floor. If there was someone up here, they would already know she was searching the house.

'If there's anyone there, it's time to show yourself!' she called as forcefully as she could.

The thought of bumping into the Meat Man was worrying, yet the indignation she felt for the threats against Jerry and being forced to give up the task at the last moment was strong enough to send her down the corridor, ready for whatever she might face. She stopped outside the barely open door and pushed it with a forefinger. It didn't move. Ruth looked down and could see the door hadn't shut for some time. The bottom of the door was grounded on a thick, dark blue carpet inside the room. Expansion or warping of the thick old door, or perhaps the weave of carpet itself being too deep had caused the issue.

Taking a breath and holding it, Ruth gave the door a firm push and fell forward into a pleasant bedroom with the same high ceilings and beautiful cornices. A simple but elegant light fitting hung from the centre of a white ceiling rose, although there was no need for artificial light, as the afternoon sun was streaming in through two large sash windows. She gave the single bed, pale blue floral wallpaper and various sideboards and cupboards a glance, having already decided this room wasn't lived in. It had the air of a spare room. Motes of dust sparkled in the sunlight, and with bare surfaces and the lack of personal effects, Ruth turned to leave.

A photograph on the bedside table caught her eye. Dennis had dozens of photos downstairs, almost all of them contained horses. This one was of a couple. She was only two strides from the bedroom door, and told herself she really should continue her search, but curiosity compelled her to examine the photo in greater detail. There was a younger Dennis, probably mid-thirties, looking amused, alongside a stout woman with a joyful smile, and a weathered face. She was holding the reins to a pony, upon which a young girl sat giggling.

As Ruth bent over to take a closer look, a floorboard squeaked in the corridor. She swung around in just enough time to catch someone flashing past the door, heading towards the landing. The shock was enough to make her gasp and lose a valuable second before setting off in pursuit.

Whilst screaming for the trespasser to stop, she shot out into the corridor in time to see a small, thin man slip through a door at the far end. He was dressed in green and black army fatigues. She followed, noting he'd left the door open in his haste. Upon reaching the room and stepping tentatively into another bedroom, she knew why he hadn't bothered to barricade the door – a sash window was wide open, curtains billowing, and providing a view out onto the back garden and the trees beyond. She quickly scanned the room to make sure this wasn't just a ruse. Satisfied, Ruth crossed to the window and leaned out.

Fun Boy Frankie was bowling along. His gallop was almost mechanical, eating up the undulating ground as he led the field up the Westwood. Mitch sat motionless, simply ensuring the gelding didn't over-exert himself.

At the two pole, he took a sly look over his shoulder, as he couldn't sense anything coming to his flanks, none of the usual stomp of hooves as they slapped into the turf, or the crack of a whip. All of that noise was still distant. His glance confirmed he was a good two lengths clear of the nearest challenger, and his competitors were busy trying to chase him down.

Mitch allowed another furlong to fly by before he eased the rein out and pushed down the gelding's neck for the first time. The Beverley crowd reacted to his motion, a wave of noise crashing over the Westwood and the approaching runners. Frankie gave a squeal of excitement, pointed his nose at the rising ground and dug his toe into the turf.

Stealing another look to his left, Mitch ceased pushing. Today, right now, was the gelding's moment, his owner's time. Frankie's maiden victory. His adversaries were toiling in his wake. Four easy strides lay before horse and rider until they would flash past the winning post in glorious isolation.

3-05pm

Despite screaming at the top of her lungs for the boy to give himself up – for Ruth was now sure it was a teenage boy who was shinning down the ancient drain pipe – he did no such thing. She now noticed the army clothes hung off the wiry young lad as he descended cat-like to the ground. Jumping down the last few yards he looked up at her, and his drawn features contorted.

Dylan smiled. This was his domain, his sport. He'd climbed up and down drainpipes for years and never been caught… apart from that one time with Bates. No middle-aged woman was going to follow him down the forty feet of aging iron piping. He lazily retrieved his backpack from a nearby bush, aimed another broad grin upwards as he slung it over his shoulders, and jogged down the back garden and off into the woods to where his hidden motorbike lay.

Ruth watched him go; his jaunty open gait and bandy legs jolting a memory from months before. Where had she seen him before?

She considered the drainpipe, no more than two feet away from the window ledge… and told herself to stop being so fanciful. Even if she managed to make it to the ground in one piece, she would be chasing a much younger man alone through woods.

Ruth dejectedly made her way back downstairs and as she reached the hallway, Jerry burst through the front door, his mother, Sophie, Danny, and Dennis bustling down the front path after him, desperately calling for the boy to wait for them.

'Auntie Ruth! I was tied up, and Danny was shot with wires that fizzed, and Dennis got shovelled, and Mum came to...'

'Slow down!' Ruth laughed, being equally relieved and amused by the boy's antics.

Jerry pursed his lips, trying hard to contain his excitement. Before Clara could land a restraining hand on his shoulder, he offered, 'I could go and find the Meat Man, couldn't I?'

Forty-Seven

'No one is going to hospital. No one is calling the police,' Dennis insisted.

He tapped his index finger repeatedly on the large table in the farmhouse's back room. It made a dull knocking sound, effectively calling their impromptu meeting to order. The No Regrets syndicate glared at their trainer.

'For heaven's sake, Dennis,' Sophie complained, 'Danny and Jerry were kidnapped and held to ransom. You've been burgled and assaulted, not to mention the fact that we've all lost several million pounds of inheritance.'

Dennis leaned both elbows on the table, closed his eyes and energetically rubbed the bridge of his nose. His headache relented slightly.

'I'm fine. Danny and I have had worse kicks from horses.'

'All the same, to be on the safe side you should get checked out and I'm sure the police...'

'I promised your husband I wouldn't involve the police in anything to do with your syndicate,' Dennis interrupted curtly.

In turn, he gave each of the women a resolute stare.

'Why would Greg do that?' asked Clara.

Dennis shrugged, 'He was adamant. Under no circumstances was I to contact the police, no matter what happened to your syndicate.'

'And going to the hospital with your injury might ring alarm bells?' Sophie ventured.

'I imagine an officious nurse might find a blow to the head with a shovel worthy of reporting.'

'By the way, where is Danny?' Ruth queried.

'He insisted on checking the barns again, just in case our burglar left anything behind.'

He saw the concern in her face and added, 'He was only hit with the taser once and then wrapped up in tape. The Meat Man got Jerry to do the taping, then he did a poor job on Jerry before locking them in the stable.'

From the other end of the room Jerry piped up from the sofa, 'Mine was better than the Meat Man's!'

Clara shook her head, 'That wasn't the Meat Man. He was far too young.'

'So who was he?'

'It sounds like Skeletor,' Sophie said quietly, 'The lad who tried to bully me on the Knavesmire.'

A contemplative silence descended on the table.

'So we've lost our inheritance because of me,' Clara said grimly.

'But Jerry is safe, and Greg's task is over,' Sophie responded firmly.

Ruth nodded her head slowly, 'And my Mother is going to have to learn she can't always have it all her way.'

'You'll have the opportunity to tell her that on Thursday,' Clara pointed out with an amused smile, 'We have to be back up at the solicitors in Alnwick.'

'Is it really worth going?' Sophie wondered out loud.

Ruth snorted a small laugh, 'It's Greg. He loved his surprises. It'll be worth being there to discover exactly what he had in mind. Someone is sure to get a shock.'

The three women started to get up from their seats but Dennis waved them down.

'I have to tell you about Martha…'

'I was wondering what you were doing back here,' Sophie said, already a step ahead of the others.

Dennis gave a quick synopsis of Martha's horsebox confession from earlier in the day, but was at pains to stress the stable lass had been coerced.

'Martha was tricked and then blackmailed into providing information about your movements,' explained Dennis, 'I blame myself. She was vulnerable and I didn't keep a close enough eye on her.'

Dennis spent the next few minutes explaining how a careful set of lies had led to Martha becoming a spy for a lad who sounded very much like their burglar, and how she was blackmailed into providing him with further information, even when she knew his intentions were to hinder the No Regrets syndicate.

'Speaking of Martha, what's happened to Frankie?' Ruth suddenly blurted.

As if to order, Dennis's landline phone rang out. It immediately went to answer phone and seconds later Martha's voice filled the room. It became apparent her words were being fuelled by strong emotions.

'Dennis? Dennis, this is Martha…'

Ruth got up to answer the phone, but Dennis shook his head, 'Let's let the lass speak.'

'I really am so sorry about what's happened. I've been trying your mobile, and the No Regrets ladies phones but they all seem to be switched off….'

The three women rolled their eyes at each other and started to dig in bags and pockets. In the rush to return to the yard, they'd not switched them back after the helicopter had landed.

'I know it means I'll have to leave Middlefield,' continued Martha between sniffs, 'But I want you to know that I'm ever so grateful. It was... hard after my Mum died and you gave me a great job with lovely people and magnificent horses.'

There was a pause where the girl appeared to be breathing heavily or catching her breath.

'I'll come home and apologise to the ladies - I treated them ever so badly. I think I got too attached to the horses and it blinded me, you know, with my Dad owning them originally.'

Clara's jaw fell open and she stared in utter confusion at the old-fashioned tape answering machine on the top of Dennis's desk. She whipped around and stared at Dennis, but he was leaning forward, head bowed, examining the table.

Martha's message continued, 'I'll leave tomorrow, if that's okay. I can go tonight if I have to. I'm sure Racing Welfare will find me a bed.'

There was a pause. When Martha began speaking again her voice was breaking up. She sounded so young, embarrassed, and so very sad.

'He won, Dennis,' her words catching in her throat, 'Please let the ladies in the syndicate know that Frankie won... It was glorious, he just ran away with the race from the front. There was no interference today, they never got near him.'

Martha mumbled a few more words of apology and rang off.

An awkward silence followed the beep on the yellowing tape recorder. Ruth and Sophie locked eyes, completing a conversation with just a variety of looks, facial expressions and darting their eyes at Clara. She was leaning over, her hand over her mouth, partially covering her face. Dennis was watching all three of them with a deadpan poker face.

Eventually Clara removed her hand and looked around the table.

'I did hear that right, didn't I...' she remarked. Before anyone could construct a comment, she added, 'Martha referred to my Greg... as her *father?*'

She straightened and appraised the people around the table like a teacher waiting for the first hand to go up in class.

'She's a nice girl. It sounds like she's been set up,' Ruth offered.

'Of course she was set up!' Clara replied hotly, 'By Greg! She's helped to scare the daylights out of Jerry and I, making us flee from our home, burned a caravan down, and rounded it off nicely by taking my son hostage!'

'Martha is not directly responsible for any of those things,' Dennis said gently.

Clara sprang to her feet and rounded on the trainer, 'Did you know? Did my two-timing, rat of a husband tell you he had a daughter?'

Dennis remained seated and replied calmly in a measured tone, 'No, he didn't. He was instrumental in finding her a job here with lodging when the girl's Mother died, and I admit I was curious about their relationship, but I didn't know anything, not for certain. Until now she's been a perfect employee and a credit to herself, and her Mother.'

'Well that's just peachy!' Clara raged, 'I bet you're all going to tell me next that she's forgiven for losing us a small fortune as well.'

She didn't wait for an answer, stalking out of the farmhouse via the back door, an unhappy Jerry following on her command.

'She'll calm down and come round. I've seen her flounce out plenty of times,' Ruth said once she was sure Clara was out of earshot.

'I'm not so sure,' said Sophie, her gaze held by the sight of Bella and Kilroy sitting together on the grass in the back garden, bathing in the last of the heat in the afternoon sun, 'Clara's lost her husband to cancer and now their entire relationship is tarnished. It was one thing to suspect Greg may have been having an affair for the last couple of years, but quite another to discover it's been going on for all seventeen years of your life with the man.'

'She may have lost a husband, but Clara's gained two good friends,' suggested Dennis.

Sophie broke off from gazing into the garden and examined the trainer's wrinkled and weather-worn face for a long moment.

'You're right,' she agreed eventually, 'Have you got any champagne?'

Forty-Eight

With a chilled bottle of Moet in one hand and a trio of fluted glasses in the other, Sophie led Ruth to the cottages. Striding up the garden path in single file Sophie entered Clara and Jerry's little terraced cottage without knocking. They found the subject of their mission moping in her bedroom. The lock was long-since inoperable, so they walked straight in.

'I'm not in the mood,' Clara informed them irritably.

Sophie ignored her, popping the cork on the bottle while Ruth lined up the three glasses.

'You forgot to celebrate Frankie's win!' Ruth declared happily.

'Come on, Tinkerbell,' Sophie said warmly, 'Everything looks better with a glass of champagne inside you.'

As soon as Clara took her first sip of the champagne, Sophie knew she had her on the road to recovery. If there was one thing Clara enjoyed more than anything, it was an impromptu champagne party. They toasted Fun Boy Frankie several times and Ruth produced a second bottle.

Clara knew full well what Sophie was doing. She'd done it many times before, commiserating with her by avoiding the issue and plying her with alcohol. It was a ritual that worked well; they would eventually both reach a point of inebriation where she could talk through the issue and Sophie would offer funny, off-hand, and sometimes wild or outrageous suggestions to help solve the situation. Tonight, however, on a day of high drama and revelation, Clara decided the time was right to share her biggest secret.

The three of them were lying half on top of each other on Clara's bed, champagne glasses balanced, when she sat up and said, 'It's not so much the fact Greg had a daughter that bugs me. What I can't understand is why he spent seventeen years with me, knowing I couldn't.'

Ruth frowned at her, 'You couldn't what?'

'Give him a daughter. Or a son for that matter.'

Sophie recognised a particular tone in Clara's voice. It was a subtle change. A change that immediately put her on edge. Something important was coming.

'We did wonder whether it was you or him with the problem. Greg always said he wanted kids,' Ruth admitted, 'But Jerry is one of us. He's an Armitage. We love him, and Greg loved him.'

'I suppose so… I was pregnant once you know.'

Sophie studied Clara's face carefully, desperately trying to understand which direction her friend was heading.

Clara swallowed hard before she continued, 'I was three months pregnant on the day of your wedding to Greg. If you're wondering whether that was the reason he chose me instead of you, don't – he never knew I was pregnant.'

She slowly turned and locked eyes with Sophie. Her eyes were glassy, filled with tears about to burst out and stream down her cheeks.

'I'm telling you this because… well, because I might not get another chance, and I might not be strong enough again…'

She dabbed a tear away with her knuckle.

'I hated being at your wedding. I genuinely thought Greg had made his decision, and left me. I was okay with that, you were good together. I told myself that my relationship with Greg had just been a silly fling.'

Clara took a ragged breath, composed herself and continued, 'You need to know that I didn't force him to change his mind and choose me instead of you. He always was a ditherer when it came to making big personal decisions. Strange really, he could make business decisions in a trice…'

'He actually told you before me, you know,' Clara added as brightly as she could, 'Then he came to find me and insisted we leave the wedding reception immediately.'

'Clara, you don't have to…'

'Please, Sophie, let me finish,' Clara pleaded, 'You wanted to know why I was so upset with you, why our relationship needed a seventeen year gap before it could be repaired? Well here it is… The day after the wedding we argued on the stairs outside our flat in Newcastle. Do you remember? Things got heated and we started pushing each other and you shoved me out of the way to get to Greg and I tried to push you back… but ended up tumbling down a few steps.'

Sophie suddenly felt cold and hugged herself. She'd somehow sobered up the instant Clara started to tell her story.

'Yes, of course I remember! Greg took you to the hospital. But it was just cuts and bruises.'

Clara, still sharing a wide-eyed stare with Sophie, gave her the faintest of sad smiles, 'You tend not to stay in hospital overnight with cuts and bruises.'

She took another faltering breath and blinking away the tears, said in a flat tone, 'I lost my baby. I lost Greg's baby.'

Ignoring Ruth and Sophie's horrified expressions, Clara quickly continued, 'When I arrived back at the flat the next day you were there again, sorting something with Greg. I was so angry with you… I blamed you. I told myself you had caused me to lose my baby. I quickly lost my temper and said some hateful things.'

Sophie remembered that second encounter with Clara clearly. It was seared into her memory. Clara had been inexplicably unapologetic and bloody-minded. Sophie had never felt anger like that between them before and the two of them had torn into each other with the savageness of lionesses protecting their cubs. After seventeen years of the closest of friendships, Sophie could not believe Clara had no compassion, nor any remorse for ruining her wedding and stealing her husband. The turmoil of her wedding day, the loss, the embarrassment had still been so raw. Yet Clara had turned up in a foul mood and became intensely vitriolic. It was the day Sophie decided she and Clara could never be friends again.

And amongst all of this bad blood, Greg had been no more than a bystander. He'd remained in the background, listening to the two of them trading insults, watching them tear their friendship apart. Yet Sophie hadn't blamed him... it had been Clara. Clara had been the architect of her sorrow, she was the catalyst that had brought insurmountable pain to her life. The blame lay squarely with Clara.

Opening her mouth to speak, Sophie was soon silenced by Clara's raised flat palm and a shake of her head indicating there was more to tell.

'And then two days later I started to get stomach pains. They were so bad, I had to go back to hospital.' Clara continued to in a low, monotone voice.

'I doubt you even knew I was ill, you'd disappeared back to York with your family. The doctors at the RVI tried their best, but the miscarriage had caused too much damage. I'd started bleeding and caught an infection. Soon, the only option was to perform a hysterectomy...'

'Oh my God, Clara,' Sophie gasped, resisting the urge to fling her arms around her friend. Tears now flowed freely down her own cheeks. Ruth looked on, stunned.

Clara hugged herself and said, 'I've held onto my anger for far too long. Even when we adopted Jerry I couldn't think of you without an all-consuming anger flooding into me.'

'Why didn't you *tell me*?' Sophie asked hoarsely.

Clara paused before answering, choosing her words carefully. She was staring, unfocused, at the wall of her bedroom, Sophie and Ruth motionless and slack-jawed as she spoke.

'I don't really know,' Clara said in a low, faraway voice, 'I've tried to work out why I remained quiet. It was probably a defence mechanism... when I was angry with you, I didn't blame myself. Perhaps I needed that. It was my secret, my pain, no one else's. I never told Greg. It was enough that I'd lost the ability to give him a son or daughter. Sometime I'd kid myself into thinking I kept my secret in order to protect you and him... but if I'm honest, I don't think I'm that wholesome. On the rare occasions I can bear digging deep inside me, I tend to conclude I kept my loss to myself because I was grieving. For the little girl I lost, and for the children of my own I could no longer have in my life.'

She blinked, turned to face her friends and gave them a brave, hopeful smile.

'But… the anger has gone. And I've told you now…'

Forty-Nine

It had taken forty minutes to walk the streets of Wallsend. They'd been asking questions in shops, snooker halls, and amusement arcades, in order to track him down. However, Bates was feeling confident. One of lads they'd met in the local bookies obviously held a grudge and had been only too pleased to point someone of Jimmy's size in the right direction. Parking up opposite the Duke Of York on Wallsend High Street, he and Jimmy had a short conversation whilst they watched both entrances to the public house.

Pulling their collars up against the squally wind and spitting rain, they crossed the busy main road and entered the pub in unison, one man through each entrance.

It didn't take long to find him. He was nursing a half pint of lager in the back room, busy watching two heavily tattooed men play pool for money and with obvious hopes of sharking a few quid from them. As Bates and Jimmy converged on the small young man he glanced toward the door to the men's toilets and made to get up. Bates shook his head and all hope of escape drained from the boy's face.

Sitting either side of him, Bates joined the boy in watching the next few shots on the pool table while Jimmy never took his eyes off the boy.

'Remember me, Michael?' Bates asked eventually.

'Blummin' difficult not to,' he grumbled.

Bates nodded, 'Remember that favour I granted you five months ago down at The Bridge?'

'Aye?'

'It's time for you to show your gratitude.'

The boy's cheek twitched and he looked from Jimmy's intent stare to Bates, who was still focused on the red and yellow balls being fired around the green baize a few feet away. Michael lowered his voice.

'I ain't doin' nowt serious or, y'know nasty, like.'

Bates turned and steadily regarded the young lad for a few seconds. Then he smiled.

'That's good, Michael. I'd never ask you to do anything outside the law. I simply wish you to put your... *street talents*... to use for the benefit of a good cause.'

Michael's eyelids quivered, uncertain whether this was good or bad news.

Showing a modicum of amusement, Bates continued, 'I'm not asking you to do anything you haven't already done a hundred times before. I need you to acquire two mobile phones for me. Two very specific mobile phones.'

The boy breathed out and a smile broke out across his face, 'That, I can do Mr... er...'

'Bates,' said Bates.

The game of pool was drawing to a close in front of them. One of the players who had been chasing the black ball around the table for the last minute and a half, finally ended the game by potting it accidentally with a lucky rebound. Michael watched the players slip away, and with them, his chance to snaffle a few quid from them.

'Want a game, Mr Tyson?' Bates inquired with a nod at the table.

'It's Mike. Sure, we can play. But I ain't playin' you for money, Mr Bates,' he assured him.

Bates gave a thin-lipped smile, 'No problem, we shall play for bragging rights.'

Mike Tyson frowned, having no idea what Bates meant. He shrugged it off. The bloke and his muscle-bound teenage mate seemed to be on the level.

'One thing though,' Mike said, leaning over the pool table as Bates racked up the balls.

'Oh yes, what's that?'

Mike cocked his head towards Jimmy, 'Can yer stop 'im lookin' at me like that?'

Fifty

Thursday 1st September 2016

The sombre mood in the Sedgefield Solicitor's office was darkened further by the arrival of Gertrude Armitage, accompanied by Timothy and Alvita. The No Regrets syndicate had arrived early and the three ladies had chosen to sit together in the front row. They were in the same room the original will reading had been heard. Gertrude made a point of walking down to the desk at the front where Mr Sedgefield was already sitting, gave him a glare and then transferred it to the ladies on the front row. Her steely gaze drilled into anyone who made the mistake of catching her eye, and she wore an expression that dared you to lock horns with her. The fact she remained silent was actually more intimidating than her usual ranting.

Timothy gave Ruth a disdainful look and remained silent when she said hello to him. Alvita smiled apologetically and was immediately treated to a scowl from her boyfriend.

'I imagined we wouldn't be flavour of the month with my family, but this is ridiculous,' Ruth whispered as the remainder of the Armitage family seated themselves in the row behind.

'I'm so happy to hear you say that,' Clara replied, leaning across Sophie and tapping Ruth's hand, 'Five months ago you'd have been the one making vicious comments and sneering. Now you're one of us!'

Ruth raised an eyebrow, 'And you would have been biting back at me. Instead you're sitting here beside your arch enemy!' All three members of the No Regrets syndicate tried to stave off smiles.

Behind her, Gertrude let out an overly dramatic sigh in response to the smallest hint of levity coming from the row in front.

'Greg got what he wanted, didn't he,' commented Sophie quietly once the novelty of giggling even louder in order to rile up Gertrude had subsided.

All three women contemplated this for a moment and it prompted Clara to twist her head and check up on Martha, sitting quietly at the very back of the small room with Jerry. The three of them, but especially Clara, had made up with the young woman. Having apologised profusely to the syndicate once she'd returned from Beverley with Fun Boy Frankie, the troubled teenager had been amazed to discover that none of the syndicate apportioned any blame to her.

'We've discovered a few things today that have helped put your actions over the last few months into perspective,' Sophie had told the stable lass without elaborating.

'And you're an Armitage now,' Clara had added, 'That alone is punishment enough for something that wasn't your fault in the first place.'

'It also makes me your Auntie,' Ruth had added with a comic grimace.

With all three of them still reeling from the day of high emotions, it had been gratifying to see the teenager brighten, and they'd all sat down to watch Frankie's winning race in the farmhouse, Martha cheering up enough to give them a stride by stride commentary. They'd then decamped to the juvenile barn where Danny was already back to work, having fully recovered from his tasering and incarceration. He'd led Frankie out to the paddocks and Martha and the syndicate had fed Frankie carrots whilst making a fuss of him, all under Dennis's watchful gaze.

Simon and Marion were the next to arrive, offering rather subdued hellos to the three women before sitting down. Marion turned to look questioningly at Martha, but passed no comment. Thomas came in and without introduction, took up a position standing in the shadows in the back of the room. Sophie noticed the young solicitor glancing around the room and for some reason his face drained of all colour when his gaze landed on Jerry and Martha.

Paul was the last to arrive. He entered, nodded his apology to Mr Sedgefield for being slightly late, took a seat well way from any of the Armitages, and didn't make any attempt to acknowledge anyone else.

'Charming,' Clara said in a low voice.

Sophie tried to catch Paul's eye, but without success. He was concentrating all his attention on the plump, balding solicitor behind the desk at the front of the windowless room.

Mr Sedgefield looked up from the small piles of paperwork spread out over his desk, sparkling cufflinks catching on some of his papers, his jowls wobbling. He received a nod from Thomas, and cleared his throat. It was a long, phlegm enhanced act that ended with him producing a satisfied hum. It made Clara feel slightly queasy.

'The Armitage family, Ms Falworth, Mr Corbridge, and other interested parties,' Mr Sedgefield began, aiming a business-like glance at each group at he said their names, 'Thank you all for attending. This is the final reading of the will of Mr Gregory Armitage. I, as the executor of the said will, have been charged with determining whether the, er… *task* Mr Armitage set out five months ago has been completed as per his instructions.'

He cleared his throat again and Clara winced.

'I see we have a member of the public present here today,' Mr Sedgefield said, eying Martha, 'Can I suggest she leaves before I…'

'Get on with it,' Clara cut in, 'She's with us.'

The solicitor removed his glasses and rubbed his eyes, adopting a mournful expression which he turned towards Clara. Realising from her expectant stare it would be useless to protest, Mr Sedgefield chewed on his bottom lip for a second before picking up a document from his desk. He began to read.

'Ahem… I have to report that Ms Falworth, Ms Clara Armitage, and Ms Ruth Armitage failed to complete Mr Armitage's task. As such, the conditions of his will state that I must now provide you with Mr Gregory Armitage's revised instructions pertaining to the distribution of his estate.'

As the solicitor drew breath to continue there was a single, sudden movement and all eyes were drawn to Paul, who was sitting with his open hand waving above his head.

'I wish to object,' Paul began.

There was a general groan around the room. Since the race at Beverley there had been representations made to the solicitor's office from virtually everyone present. Sophie had represented the No Regrets syndicate and three days of intense discussions with Mr Sedgefield had resulted in no significant progress. The solicitor's hands were tied. Greg had been annoyingly specific when laying out the rules of his task: unless photographic evidence was provided of all three members of the syndicate inside the parade ring after every run and each stable visit, the task was deemed to have been failed. There could be no excuses under any circumstances. Sophie was at least relieved that none of the syndicate had become seriously ill over the five months. She wouldn't have put it past Gertrude to wheel any of them into the parade ring, quite literally on their death beds.

Paul had been actively pursuing the solicitor and speaking with everyone else involved at length, to the point where he'd become something of a pest. But the will was explicit and Mr Sedgefield had remained apologetic, but firm.

Paul continued, 'The decision to fail the No Regrets syndicate is not in the spirit of Greg's will. He would never have considered foul play when…'

'Mr Corbridge…'

'I insist you…' said Paul in a whiny voice.

Mr Sedgefield removed his glasses, gave Paul a hard stare, and began speaking over him, 'Mr Corbridge! We have exhausted every avenue over the last three days. As you are aware, the Armitage family may contest the will if they wish, but Gregory Armitage was instrumental in the construction of his will and was incredibly careful to be specific. There are no allowances for failure for *any* reason.'

Paul's hand dropped and he became mute.

'I only have nine pieces of photographic evidence in front of me. I required five stable visit photos and five race-day photos. The race attendance in August is missing. Ladies, do you concur?'

The corpulent solicitor peered expectantly at the three women sitting in the front row. Ruth and Clara refused to answer so it was left to Sophie to murmur a hardly decipherable reply in the affirmative. If it wasn't for the fact that Greg had insisted on all his beneficiaries being present for this final reading, or else forfeit the smaller sums paid to them five months ago, Sophie doubted either Clara or Ruth would have attended. By comparison, the fifty thousand Greg had earmarked for her was embarrassingly large. During the last few days she'd read the will over and over and found nothing in its pages that gave her, or the Armitage family any real hope of salvaging anything other than these meagre sums. Sophie had come to the conclusion that if anything, Greg had written the task requirements in such a way that the odds had been stacked against the three of them from the start.

'I understand that there was some… ah, now how was that put?'

The solicitor shifted his paperwork around and adjusted his spectacles, 'Ah yes… a third party *causing interference.*'

A few members of his audience leaned forward a little, wondering if salvation was at hand. Mr Sedgefield immediately quashed this glimmer of hope.

'Whilst I personally have the greatest sympathy for your situation, I am merely a conduit between yourselves and my client, Mr Armitage. I am bound by my position as executor to follow his instructions according to his wishes - and he was determined that his task should be completed in line with his expectations.'

As this statement was greeted by a round of grumbling from his audience, Mr Sedgefield added, 'Quite what this third party would gain from their interference is anyone's guess. I admit to being at a loss to see why anyone would even bother, unless there is someone out there who simply wants to see the Armitage family suffer.'

A number of people turned their disgruntled gaze onto Gertrude, including Ruth, whose relationship with her mother had cooled significantly in the last week. Sophie and Clara had been particularly pleased when they learned that Ruth intended to stay on at the stables indefinitely as a part-time work rider and bookkeeper. The two of them had been in the background, encouraging Ruth when she finally found the courage to call Gertrude and inform the Armitage matriarch of her decision. Her mother's reaction had been predictably self-righteous, topped off with a generous serving of emotional blackmail.

Noisily clearing his throat yet again, Mr Sedgefield cast an attentive eye over his audience. Clara understood the solicitor was using the mannerism as a warning he was about to speak. Nonetheless, she was unable to avoid shivering with distaste. It really was disgusting. The hubbub in the room dropped until Gertrude's voice was the last to still be complaining. Even she was eventually silenced.

Sedgefield picked up a single piece of paper that had been kept separate from the rest, and began reading, 'I, John James Sedgefield, as executor of the will of Mr Gregory Alan Armitage, can confirm that on the first day of September 2016 I will carry out the...'

Sophie's mind wandered and eventually centred on Martha as the solicitor continued to deliver his stream of legal garbage in such a way to render it impossible to follow. She reflected on how grief took on many shapes and caused a sufferer to be extremely vulnerable. Once the teenager had explained that she had only discovered Greg to be her father when meeting him for the first time by her mother's death bed in 2014, and then losing him less than two years later, Sophie had understood why Martha's vulnerabilities had been easily stoked by her unknown blackmailer with his string of carefully crafted lies.

The young man, who Sophie had decided was almost certainly one of the Meat Man's associates, had ingratiated himself over the space of a few weeks and proceeded to fill Martha's head full of lies about, in particular, Ruth and Clara, and stoked worries about her future at the yard and the wellbeing of the horses in her care. All of this had started just after the poor lass had witnessed the bickering between the ladies on their first visit to the yard. As with all clever manipulators, once Martha had passed on that first piece of private information – in her case, the fact Paul was driving the syndicate up to Hamilton for Frankie's second run - she was subsequently blackmailed into continuing to give up inside information on the syndicate's movements or face being exposed to Dennis as an informant, and potentially losing her job.

Sophie had spent a number of hours thinking back over the last few months and kicking herself for not recognising the warning signs. The girl had been suffering, and it had gone unnoticed. She knew both Ruth and Clara felt the same, and Dennis had been very self-critical, voicing his opinion that he had failed Greg, who had specifically requested the trainer look out for the girl.

Martha's personal story had brought a mixture of sadness, bonding, and strangely, some relief for one member of the syndicate.

Greg had met Martha's mother, Joanne, in his first year of university, a year before Clara and Sophie had landed in Newcastle as freshers. Their two month relationship had ended amiably; Joanne explaining to Greg she was leaving Newcastle for an alternative course in Leeds. In fact, Joanne had gone back to her home town of Darlington where Martha was born seven months later. Martha had never received a satisfactory explanation from her mother as to why she didn't involve Greg, however she believed it was linked to her mother's own troubled upbringing. Sixteen years later Greg had discovered he had a daughter when Martha phoned him out of the blue from Darlington Memorial Hospital, explained her story, and tearfully reported her mother was dying. Joanne had finally relented when she realised her sixteen-year-old daughter was going to be taken into the care of the local authority without Greg's assistance.

Clara had been partially placated upon learning that Greg's affair in the last two years of his life had been nothing of the sort; he'd been visiting Martha. Discovering her love of horses and riding, he'd secured a job and lodging for Martha in Dennis's yard, and then bought racehorses for the yard on the pretext of visiting them and going racing, when in truth he had been spending time with his daughter.

At a most sensitive age, Martha had lost her mother and newly found father in quick succession. Jerry had lost the same father. However, in doing so, they had found each other, discovering they were sister and brother.

Sophie became aware of Clara lurching in her seat and glaring a warning to the back of the room. A joyous sound was coming from Martha and Jerry in the back row; they were both trying to suppress a fit of giggling. Jerry was holding a finger over his top lip and had blown his cheeks up, pretending to be Mr Sedgefield as his droning legal babble continued. Martha had a hand over her mouth, trying to keep her mirth under control. Clara turned back and gave Sophie and Ruth a shrug whilst grinning from ear to ear.

Sophie smiled back at her friend. Clara's revelatory speech regarding the tragic consequences of their argument after her disastrous wedding had now had time to sink in. She had since spent many hours trying to understand why Clara hadn't told her. If anything, the mixture of sadness - for her friend's loss, the years spent apart, and the damnable unfairness of it all, had helped bring her closer to Clara. Sophie had come to the conclusion that maybe the years apart had been necessary, given the healing they both needed to happen. Perhaps Greg had known.

Sophie's attention was jerked back to the present by the solicitor listing people's names and balancing amounts of money. Mr Sedgewick then listed the good causes to which Greg's money would now be directed.

'Trust funds will be created to ensure a steady, reliable flow of money to Mr Armitage's choice of ...'

'This isn't right!' protested Paul, getting to his feet and waving his index finger at the solicitor, 'Greg would never...'

Mr Sedgefield glanced down at his page. With only one final paragraph to finish, he ignored the interruption and continued to speak over Paul's words, desperate to conclude his role in the meeting.

'...Greg didn't give money to charities!' Paul continued, 'He insisted they spent too much on administration and chasing government grants, he preferred to...'

'I've also heard enough,' boomed a male voice from the second row, 'Sit down, Paul.'

Timothy Armitage was on his feet. He tapped the face of his mobile phone once and pocketed it, slowly raising his eyes and silently signalling to Paul to retake his seat. A dozen frowning faces locked on the stern young man who was now radiating confidence.

This isn't like Timothy, Ruth thought. She noticed his girlfriend Alvita obviously thought the same, as she was staring up at him with a mixture of shock, and possibly, pride.

Sitting beside Timothy, Gertrude slapped her son's thigh.

'Sit down, Timothy, we're almost done,' she snapped.

'Be quiet and listen, Mother,' he replied without looking down. His unblinking eyes were still concentrated on Paul.

In a clear, steady voice Timothy said, 'It's time to reveal who has stolen our inheritance.'

Fifty-One

Where on earth has Timothy's new, deep, demanding tone come from, wondered Clara. She realised with a start that the youngest Armitage sounded a lot like… Greg! As Paul's nerve collapsed under Timothy's glare, he slumped back in his seat and Clara decided that this was indeed very un-Tim-like behaviour. Clever underhand comments and snide looks were more his stock in trade, not this commanding presence. However, it was quite enjoyable. Timothy's interjection was proving to be better value than Paul or the solicitor's contribution to the morning.

Still seated, Mr Sedgefield waved a finger at Thomas, standing in his usual place against the back wall. Via a mime the solicitor indicated for him to do something about the source of the interruption. Thomas snapped out of the stupefaction affecting the rest of the room, moved towards Timothy and requested he sit down, intoning darkly that, 'Mr Sedgefield is about to close his summary of Mr Armitage's last will and testament.'

Timothy refused, and waved the young man away.

At the back of the room, Martha broke into a sweat.

As Thomas repeated his instruction to Timothy, a single knock came from outside and the door to the room burst open, allowing the sound of an argument between a man and a female member of the solicitor's staff to filter into the room. The secretary's high-pitched insistence that she would call the police had little effect as a moment later a medium sized, bald-headed man in a well cut black suit strode confidently into the room.

'I'm sorry, sir, this is a private meeting,' Thomas spluttered, parking himself in the small gangway between the lines of chairs in an attempt to halt the man's progress.

'Speak to my secretary,' the man growled, hoisting a thumb over his shoulder. Behind him a large young man's frame filled the doorway.

Clara's mouth went dry and her chest began throbbing to the beat of her heart.

'That's the Meat Man,' she told Sophie and Ruth, hardly moving her lips. She stared at him, unable to take her eyes off the man for several seconds. Finally, she came to her senses and jumped to her feet.

Bates scanned the room as Thomas continued to remonstrate by poking a finger into his chest, noting that Clara Armitage was already out of her seat, and Mr Sedgefield was patting the pockets of his suit, presumably searching for his mobile phone. He checked over his shoulder, and was reassured to find Jimmy had closed the door and was presently standing cross-armed, blocking all entry and exit to and from the room. Finally, he concentrated on Timothy Armitage. They traded a fleeting, joyless stare and Bates was pleased; he only detected minimal nervousness. Perhaps Greg had been right to give the lad so much responsibility.

'Remain seated and listen!' Timothy demanded as across the room the volume of discontent increased once the intruder's identity had been shared among the family. The noise level dropped immediately and Timothy added, 'This is Mr Bates. He has been working for me for the last five months.'

The room dropped silent, apart from Thomas, who was still attempting to engage with Bates. He was barking a continuous flow of babble about private meetings and involving the police. Bates leaned forward and whispered two words into the young solicitor's ear. Thomas stopped speaking, his eyes wide and jaw slack. He made his way to the back of the room, reached out for the nearest chair, and slid into it, unable to take his eyes off Bates.

'There's no need to panic, you're not in any danger,' Timothy continued, moving along the row of chairs as he spoke.

'What's going on, Tim?' challenged Ruth, 'This is the Meat Man. *The Meat Man!* He's responsible for intimidation, arson, kidnapping and blackmail, not to mention ensuring all of us didn't benefit from millions of pounds of inheritance!'

Clara had quietly moved to the back of the room to protect Jerry and, in particular, Martha. She appeared to be taking the latest developments badly.

Now that Clara had put herself between them and the Meat Man she watched every one of Bates's movements like a hawk. Desperate to scream at the man she opened her mouth but whether it was shock or fear, no words would come.

Gertrude was out of her seat and on her way toward Bates. Now she understood who this gruff, but well-dressed man was, Gertrude wanted her pound of flesh. Sophie and Ruth lunged forward in unison and managed to halt the surprisingly strong old woman's progress. Instead, Gertrude aimed a torrent of expletive-ridden hate at Bates. He appeared not to hear it, escorting Timothy to Mr Sedgefield's desk and blocking the solicitor's only exit route up the alleyway to the door. Sedgefield was blustering complaints, however, a heavy hand from Bates on his shoulder pressed the solicitor back into his chair and a word in his ear zipped his mouth. Bates nodded at Timothy and the young man faced the room, confident and serious. As Timothy began to speak, Marion glanced at Alvita and saw she was smiling broadly, transfixed by her boyfriend.

'Mr Bates works for the Newcastle Constabulary. He is attached to the Young Offender's Unit, responsible for crime prevention and offender rehabilitation. He and Greg have known each other for many years and he's been helping us, outside his day-to-day duties, to deliver Greg's plan.'

Clara found her voice, shouting from the back of the room, 'Greg planned to have his Mother involved in a traffic accident, did he? He wanted his son to be kidnapped? I suppose you'll tell me next he ordered Dennis Smith to be clobbered with a shovel!'

Supportive cries rolled in from several members of the audience. Timothy held up two flat palms, trying to calm the room once more. As the volume of complaints rose, several wrinkles of frustration appeared on his forehead.

As the dissent grew louder, he sighed and reached into his back pocket, removed a small memory stick and holding it between thumb and forefinger, showed it to the room and waited. One by one, the Armitage family fell silent as their curiosity got the better of them, apart from Gertrude, who had no idea what a memory stick was.

'Shut up, Mother!' Timothy bellowed.

With his audience stunned at his outburst, Timothy continued.

'I accept this is a bit of a shock. Mistakes were made, for which I'm truly sorry. If you will just shut up for a minute I can explain.'

He inhaled a deep breath through his nose before continuing.

'This is a memory stick containing Greg's final video message. It's not been played – even I don't know exactly what's on all of it. Greg asked me only to play it to everyone at this final confirmation of his will.'

'As most of you know, before he died Greg spoke to each of us. Some of you have shared what he said, others haven't. I'm ready to reveal what he said to me.'

'Really! This is most irregular!' Sedgefield remonstrated, 'If you must continue, I must insist you allow myself and my colleague to leave this room!'

Timothy's demeanour altered markedly. Slowly, he swivelled his head and gave Mr Sedgefield a disdainful look. The large man' cheeks flushed as Bates, now standing behind the seated solicitor, increased the pressure on his shoulders.

'Greg asked each of us to complete a request of some sort,' continued Timothy, returning to face his family, 'My task was to co-ordinate Greg's plan to expose a fraud that has successfully defrauded the Armitage family of millions of pounds.'

This revelation managed to silence Gertrude, who had been chuntering complaints from her seat. She was now all eyes and ears. Ruth released her grip on her mother's arm, marvelling at the dramatic effect words like 'fraud' and 'millions' had on the old lady.

'I'll let Greg fill you in,' Timothy said with a genuine smile.

Snatching the controller from Mr Sedgefield's desk, Timothy activated the flat-screen television on the back wall above the solicitor's head. He pushed the memory stick into the side of the television and fiddled with the controller for a few seconds until a small highlighted box with an image of Greg's head and shoulders appeared on a black background. Bates removed his hands from Mr Sedgefield's shoulders and moved to stand to the right of the screen, his eyes never leaving the solicitor. Timothy stood to the left and theatrically pressed the play button on the controller.

Greg's image grew to fill the entire screen.

From the back of the room Jerry's cry of, 'Daaaad!' floated over the Armitage family.

From the television screen, Greg was smiling, although there was a hint of pain and an unfamiliar resignation behind his eyes. Clara squinted at the television. This recording wasn't like the one the solicitor had played five months ago, this was Greg much closer to the end.

'Hello everyone,' he said warmly, 'Before I start, you should see who I'm with.'

The camera that had been tight in on Greg, now zoomed out. He was sitting at his desk in his home office once more, Clara's back garden visible over his shoulders. Previously he'd occupied the desk completely, whereas he now seemed small, being dominated by the large oblong slab of larch his hands rested upon. Alongside him, two men were standing, one either side. It was Timothy and Bates.

'These two men have been charged with an extremely difficult and complex task. If everything went smoothly, you may not recognise Mr Bates. If it hasn't, you need to understand that neither Timothy nor Mr Bates are to blame… they were following my instructions.'

Greg winced as he adjusted his position in his seat. The smile was gone, replaced with a serious, almost pained expression.

Seeing Greg like this again brought Clara to the edge of tears. The final fortnight with her husband had been difficult – beyond any suffering she'd experienced. She stole a look down at Jerry in the seat beside her, and then across at Martha. They were both mesmerized by the image on the screen, their faces exhibiting the same mixture of heartbreak and anger she was feeling. The room was perfectly silent. Even Mr Sedgefield and Thomas were glued to the video.

'Five months ago, I told you I had a couple of regrets, which was why I sought to thrust Ruth, Clara, and Sophie together on a fun task to be racehorse owners for a summer season. That much was true, and I hope the three of you have benefitted from being…'

A fleeting, wry smile graced his lips as Greg paused for a moment.

'… in such close quarters, and having to trust and rely on each other. However, I had an equally pressing reason to send you on that escapade.'

The camera had been slowly zooming in as he spoke. Greg's face suddenly took on a sickly yellowish glow as the desk disappeared and only his head and shoulders remained. The close-up revealed sunken eyes and the tightening of his skin, making it appear paper thin.

'The Armitage family has used the services of Sedgefield Solicitors for three generations. They have been a trusted company, indeed the current Managing Director, Mr Sedgefield himself, helped me raise the initial funding and helped incorporate my company. So when it came to writing my will, I started by digging out my Father's will from twenty years ago, in order to get an idea of what was possible in terms of setting up Trust Funds. The documents left me disillusioned and hollow.'

Greg rocked slightly in his seat and took a few seconds to compose himself.

'I do hope Mr Sedgefield is watching this with my family,' said Greg conspiratorially, 'If my mother is there, I don't doubt she will tear you apart. You see, the reason the Armitage estate has dwindled to nothing more than a large dilapidated building and a few acres of land over the last twenty years, is entirely due to Mr Sedgefield systematically stealing from our father, and therefore, from all of us.'

Greg paused, allowing this bombshell to percolate.

He took a breath and continued, 'Because he had a young family, Mr Sedgefield advised my father to create a trust fund and place him in the position of Trustee. This allowed Mr Sedgefield to determine where the trust's money went. For example, the amount of my mother's monthly stipend, the running of the estate, and all the investments.'

'In fact, some of the investments made on the trust's behalf are so obscure, I had difficultly tracking them down. Sedgefield favours small companies that make a large capital investment with the trust funds money… and then go bust and write off the investment as worthless.'

Greg's eyes narrowed.

'By means of a variety of underhand methods I estimate Sedgefield has salted away over seventeen million pounds from the original twenty-five million pounds fund. And not satisfied with this level of dishonesty, every time the fund ran dry Sedgefield would suggest to our Mother that she should sell part of the estate - and plough the proceeds from the next parcel of land into the same trust fund.'

Mr Sedgefield shook his head contemptuously whilst firmly muttering, 'No, no, no!'

The action made his blubbery cheeks wobble. This greatly amused Jerry who grinned at Martha, pointing gleefully at the solicitor.

With Sedgefield talking over Greg's words, Timothy paused the video.

'This is fanciful poppycock,' Sedgefield declared immediately, his hard grey eyes assessing the Armitage family. His comment gained precious little traction with them. Apart from the young boy at the back of the room, he was receiving a battery of accusatory glares.

'It's untrue!' he insisted, 'Greg... Mr Armitage is mistaken. Sedgefield's is an honest, hard-working practice. We would never do anything *illegal*, and all the actions of the trust are recorded and...'

Timothy had heard enough, he rewound and slapped the play button with his thumb. Once more, Greg's voice crackled with intensity from the television screen.

'I should have realised earlier,' Greg cried, 'I didn't take an interest in the estate or the hall. All my effort and concentration went into my business. And at the same time my business was growing, Sedgefield was bleeding the Armitage estate dry.'

Greg paused, thoughtful for a second, then added, 'I imagine Sedgefield is denying all of this, isn't he? I bet he's trotting out some excuse that nothing illegal has gone on...'

This drew smiles from a number of the audience, who then glared at the solicitor.

'The trouble is, he's right,' Greg said with a grimace, 'On the face of it, all of his underhand mismanagement of the Armitage millions has been conducted within the law. It is infuriating. Sedgefield had covered his tracks, always being a step or two away from the disappearing millions.'

The air of expectancy in the room deflated and the Armitage's began to shrug and frown at each other, uncertain what this meant. Ruth and Sophie shared a few words and slipped from their seats to join Martha, Jerry and Clara at the back of the room.

Greg had been staring from the television for half a minute, as if allowing his audience to consider his conundrum. As the silence extended, Sedgefield made to get up but was pushed back into his chair by Bates and Timothy together. Finally, a very tired Greg closed his eyes and breathed in deeply.

'So if there's no smoking gun, what are you to do?' he asked.

Swiftly and smoothly, the camera operator zoomed out to frame Greg sitting at his desk and to reveal Timothy and Bates still standing either side of him. Both of them had their arms crossed and wore serious, determined expressions. Greg looked slowly from one man to the other and returned to face the camera with a faint smile and an eyebrow raised.

'You set a trap.'

Fifty-Two

Timothy paused the recording and nervously assessed the room's atmosphere. He glanced over at Bates, receiving a firm, reassuring nod in return. The initial silence following Greg's final words on the video was soon broken by several conversations striking up at once. Based on the number of frowns and heated discussions, Timothy placed the current state of his audience somewhere between bewildered and oddly hopeful.

Behind him, Sedgefield was demanding to be allowed to leave and being studiously ignored by Bates who continued to root the solicitor to his seat with a single hand. Standing against a wall at the back of the room, Thomas kept glancing nervously at his boss, then to Jimmy, who was still blocking the only exit like a man mountain. Simon, Marion, and Gertrude were engaged in a fiery argument and all three members of the No Regrets syndicate were whispering to each other whilst firing sour glances at Bates. Paul, sitting alone, waited patiently for the meeting to resume, whilst Alvita... Timothy did a double-take. His girlfriend was oblivious to Gertrude and Marion's raised voices around her. She was staring up at him, mouth slightly open, eyes large, drinking him in. He flashed her a quick smile and her face instantly lit up, sending an intense quiver of longing down his spine. In that moment Timothy Armitage realised he no longer had to walk in the shadow of his elder sister and brothers.

He took a second to suck in a deep breath. His job was only half-finished. Greg had laid out exactly how this should go – it was now Timothy's job to reveal how Greg's plan had worked out.

'Enough!' Timothy ejaculated.

The room fell silent.

'Greg set up his will through Sedgefield in order to catch him out, and with Bates's help, that's what we've done,' Timothy announced in a commanding voice, despite being sure he was quivering with nerves. He'd never spoken in front of an audience before today, but then he'd not done *any* of the things Greg's plan had demanded of him over the last five months - and yet he'd managed them.

'Greg pretended that he wanted this thieving piece of detritus to set up a similar trust fund,' he said, spearing Sedgefield with a scornful look, 'The fund would only be enacted if Sophie, Ruth, and Clara failed their task.'

'And we did fail, thanks to Bates!' called Clara angrily.

'Okay,' Timothy said with a sigh, 'Let's get something straight. Bates was not responsible for the car crash or Jerry being taken hostage!'

He shot a plea for help Bates's way and the older man, still with a hand pushed firmly onto the solicitor's shoulder, began to speak. Rather than the harsh Northumberland twang Clara was expecting, Bates spoke in a smooth, soft, almost beguiling Scottish accent.

'I was introduced to Greg Armitage five years ago when his company joined our young offender re-training scheme, for which I am responsible. He was a fine man and when I learned he and his family had been cheated, I offered to help. He had several aims among which the primary goal was to expose Mr Sedgefield and seek reparation.'

Sedgefield snorted his derision at this suggestion and muttered something condescending under his breath. Bates paused to give the solicitor a piercing cold stare and tightened his vice-like grip on the man's shoulder. Soon the solicitor's sneer had been transformed into a plea for mercy.

Bates relaxed his grip and continued, 'Timothy ran the operation. Myself and two of my associates…'

'Associates? Is that what the Meat Man calls them?' Ruth interrupted, her voice dripping in sarcasm, 'One of your *associates* caused a serious accident, held a young boy hostage, and tasered another one!'

The accusation was received with a volley of muttered agreements from the Armitage family.

Bates paused, momentarily confused, 'Meat Man eh?' he said with a wry smile once the reference to his eating habits had struck home, 'I like your style ladies!'

It started in the pit of her stomach. Bates was relaxed, in control, and horribly normal… even charming. How dare the man she and her friends had demonised over the last five months have the temerity to stand there and be amused, and be amusing - like butter wouldn't melt in his mouth. Sophie felt the kernel of pent-up anger begin to grow, double, then swiftly re-double until her fingertips, ears, and toes tingled. A heady mixture of anger and frustration soon filled her. And she had to let it out. Sophie sprang to her feet.

'This summer you have intimidated us, committed arson, kidnap, and blackmail,' she said in as measured a tone as she could muster, given she was shaking with rage, 'We have lived in fear, and the whole of the Armitage family have been placed in danger… and you think an amused smile is going to win us over?'

With eyes blazing, and arms outstretched, it was only as her little speech drew to a close that she registered how much venom she'd injected into her words. The wry smile was immediately wiped from Bates's face and a muscle in his cheek twitched as the room roared its approval.

Bates hadn't taken his eyes from Sophie. He continued to gaze thoughtfully at her until the room settled.

'I didn't do those things. He did,' Bates replied, dropping his eyes to the solicitor.

'And with his help,' Bates added, pointing an accusatory finger at Thomas who crossed his arms petulantly and stared at a spot on the floor, 'Allow us to explain, then you can judge who the villains are in this room.'

Unable to argue with such a straight-forward request, Sophie took her seat once more, her rage somewhat sated.

'Thank you for your patience,' said Bates. He paused a couple of seconds, to allow the room to return to silence, then began to speak.

'I had a team of two. Jimmy over there at the door provided the intimidation. He looms perfectly, but is also a skilled fork-lift operator now he's going straight.'

Jimmy's fixed scowl transformed into a cheeky smile for a few seconds as people twisted in their seats to regard him. He soon returned to his default scowl, which he wholly concentrated on Thomas.

'Greg had to move quickly once he uncovered what Sedgefield had done. Despite being short on time, he was determined to achieve his goals, even though he'd never know whether he would be successful. He was desperate for the ladies over there to be reconciled, and in the case of his sister, Ruth, her horizons broadened. Everything we did in the first few months of the task was with the goal of bringing you three together and driving you towards the Dennis Smith racing yard. We saw to it that you were never in any danger and every single hurdle we placed in your way was carefully choreographed. Each time you left your house or the Middlefield stables, we were there to make sure you would come to no harm. We promoted the three of you working together as a unit, and ensured you would always reach each racecourse on time.'

Bates settled his eyes on the No Regrets syndicate.

'Consider this. Who waved you through the accident close to the bridge outside Ripon so you got there just in time for the first run by Fun Boy Frankie?'

Bates caught Clara's eye.

'How do you explain an Uber taxi appearing within a minute when Mr Corbridge's car broke down on the way to Hamilton Park, even though you were in the middle of countryside, miles from the nearest town?'

'Mr Corbridge, who was it that helped release you when you found your driveway gates locked?'

Bates now looked at Ruth, 'You might not realise it, but we suggested to the Head Lad you travel in the horsebox to reach Redcar. Ask him where the idea came from… you'll find he overheard a drunken, bald old man not so much different to me telling a remarkably tall story in his local pub.'

Bates paused, taking time to scan an appraising eye around his rapt audience.

'Some of our actions were carried out to drive you ladies together, others to protect you, and sometimes to force Mr Sedgefield here to show his hand. Greg was sure that if you all spent time together, sometimes in a state of apparent jeopardy, the three of you would bond. We carefully placed hurdles for you ladies to overcome, and only by working together, would the three of you succeed, build trust, and turn to each other for help.'

'We managed to get you to share Sophie's flat for a night, and when you all disappeared together it took us two days to track you down to the campsite – thanks to Paul. By the way, you should be in no doubt that Greg set Paul up as a fall-guy. He was told to offer his help, then on your first outing to a racecourse, tinker with Clara's car to ensure the three of you spent time together by convincing Sophie to pick Clara and Ruth up from Scotch Corner services. Greg hoped the three of you would eventually suspect he was working against you and that would help to draw you together.'

Bates addressed Paul now, explaining in greater detail how Greg had set him up. He was initially bemused, but brightened once he realised he'd made a valued contribution. Bates concluded, 'You played your role to perfection, Mr Corbridge.'

Paul spun his head around to face the No Regrets syndicate, 'Greg always did use me as his stooge. I didn't mind, I enjoyed it,' he said happily, 'A few days before he died he gave me specific instructions, and also said I was to be honest and come clean with you three about what I'd done, but only after two runs from the horses.'

Ruth and Sophie exchanged groans, kicking themselves for believing Paul was anything but the most loyal of Greg's friends. Clara scrunched her face up, remembering how horrible she'd been to Paul that day at the caravan. She looked over at him and mouthed, 'Sorry!' when she caught his eye.

'It all helped to drive the three of you together, and send a clear message to anyone who might want to try and stop you from completing the task that you were a stronger unit than anyone other than Greg could have anticipated,' Bates concluded with a acknowledging nod at Paul, 'But we needed you to be at the Dennis Smith yard for the other part of the plan to work – catching Mr Sedgewick in the act.'

Beside him, Sedgewick registered his displeasure by sighing loudly.

'The other member of my team was Dylan. Ms Falworth, you met him on the Knavesmire at York. I must congratulate you on completely befuddling Dylan by taking pity on the wretched young man and offering him money to get a square meal and see a doctor,' Bates said, allowing his wry smile to return for a moment.

'You gave that terrorist money?' Clara asked in an incredulous whisper.

'I genuinely thought he was a desperate teenager who needed help. I meet a lot of them in my line of work!' Sophie replied testily, 'It wasn't until afterwards that it struck me he'd been trying to intimidate me.'

'Dylan was compromised by Thomas over there, on his first visit to the stables,' Bates continued, indicating the young solicitor with a pointed finger, 'You may remember, Thomas made some lame excuse to leave the rest of you during the first yard visit. I followed his progress from my position on the hill behind the yard as he poked around the stables for twenty minutes. He scanned the woods above the stables and went up there straight after leaving the yard. I'd situated Dylan in a tree above the yard and I believe Thomas spotted his binoculars reflected in the sunlight. Once he'd tracked Dylan down, he bribed him to help ensure you failed your task. Greg purposely mentioned there would be someone keeping an eye on the three of you. I'm guessing Mr Sedgefield thought that having that person in their pocket would ensure the failure of the task and allow him to plunder another trust fund.'

Bates shook Sedgefield's shoulder, 'What you didn't know, Mr Sedgefield, was that I set it up. We *wanted* Thomas to find Dylan. It's why I specifically chose Dylan for this job - he's depressingly easy to predict, as he's a lying, double-crossing little swine and always will be.'

Thomas had been shifting uncomfortably against the back wall throughout Bates's story. Seemingly unable to lift his head, he stared sullenly at the carpet and remained mute when several questions were fired his way.

Ruth called out to Bates, 'Why was it so important to get all three of us to Dennis Smith's?'

Bates's gaze rested on Ruth for a second or two before he answered, allowing his line of sight to momentarily travel beyond her to where Martha and Jerry were sitting. It was the smallest of flickers of his irises, but all three women picked up on it and resisted the urge to turn to the girl.

'I can answer that,' said Timothy confidently.

'You really don't have to,' Clara warned him with a hard stare.

Timothy locked eyes with his sister in law, 'I think it's time,' he replied levelly.

Clara rolled her eyes, 'Whatever!'

Gertrude, Simon, and Marion all looked at Timothy, and then swung around to inspect Clara, their confusion evident in their creased brows and narrowed eyes.

Timothy said, 'We needed a concentrated area where we could monitor Thomas and Sedgewick trying to affect the outcome of the task. Greg had paid to install security cameras all around the yard. Once we got you all there, we waited for them to make their move... and they did, by bribing Dylan and blackmailing a member of Dennis's staff into revealing your plans each time you went racing.'

'So why didn't it stop there? You could have reported them to the police and we'd not be in a situation where our inheritance has been stolen by Sedgefield,' Simon piped up.

'I am *here*!' Sedgefield moaned defiantly, 'And I've not stolen *anything*!'

Ignoring Sedgefield, Timothy replied, 'Greg knew that if the police became involved and the case wasn't strong enough, Sedgefield would ensure it took years, and a huge amount of money to bring any action against him. I don't know if you've noticed, but none of us have a huge stack of cash to fight a prolonged court case.'

Since asking her question about the racing yard, Ruth had been following the conversation, but watching Sedgefield closely throughout, wondering whether he really was the architect of a plot to rob her family of its money. Or had her father simply made bad investment decisions and Greg, in his weakened state prior to his death, simply got it wrong and read far too much into some will paperwork that after all, was twenty-five years old? However, when a malicious glint appeared in Sedgefield's eye upon Timothy's mention of a potential lack of money to pursue a court case against him, Ruth was sure Greg hadn't been mistaken. But she also wanted confirmation of something just as important to her.

Catching Timothy's attention again, she asked, 'Apart from this blackmailed member of staff, was anyone else involved...'

'To answer your *real* question, Ruth, I can tell you that Dennis Smith was not made aware of Greg's plan beyond training the two racehorses,' confirmed Timothy, 'We owe Mr Smith a great debt for taking you all in, although Greg did ask him to offer you lodging at the yard if you ever needed it.'

Ruth gave her brother a tight smile, pleased to have it confirmed that Dennis wasn't involved. In all this confusion, she couldn't have coped with finding out Dennis was one of the bad guys.

'Okay, let's wrap this up,' Timothy said, clapping his hands together and turning to face Mr Sedgefield. The solicitor had given up trying to leave, and was now leaning back in his seat, his hands clasped together over his stomach mound. He regarded his young accuser with an amiable tolerance, as a headmaster might approach a conversation with a naughty seven-year-old who had been sent to his office for the third time that day.'

'Good. I'm pleased you've seen sense,' Sedgefield said with a crooked smile, 'This has gone on long enough. Greg Armitage has made a huge mistake, and I know you won't have any evidence of wrong-doing by this company or its employees, because… we've done nothing wrong.'

He leaned forward and opened his arms, 'Perhaps Thomas shouldn't have contacted this… *Dylan* person, but he's young and inexperienced, I'm sure he was only trying to *help* the ladies achieve their goal. He certainly can't be held responsible for the unfortunate acts carried out by an employee of Mr Bates!'

Bates almost cuffed the solicitor around his fat head. Instead, he settled for giving Sedgefield a disarmingly rakish smile which to his delight, clearly managed to unsettle the man enough to make him sit up in his chair and force pinpricks of sweat to bubble up on his forehead.

Bates was still feeling the effects of the electronic torture. In the three days since Dylan had staked him out in the paddocks, his stomach muscles ached and the tingling still hadn't left his fingers, the inside of his legs, and his toes. He was having trouble sleeping, and when he did manage to drift off his dreams were filled with Dylan's skeletal sneer and pain. Lots of pain.

He hadn't told anyone. Only Jimmy knew, and he wouldn't tell a soul. But even Jimmy didn't know he was probably still alive thanks to the trainer's dog and his spicy cooked meat fetish. As far as Timothy was aware, he'd not been able to catch up with Dylan before he captured the Head Lad and Clara's son.

Bates guessed Sedgefield and Thomas had paid Dylan handsomely to ensure the No Regrets syndicate would fail. As well as being a world-class tree climber and an accomplished tinkerer with homemade electronic torture devices, the boy was no fool. For Dylan to risk committing a criminal act while doing private work for his police handler, Sedgefield must have promised a big pay day. The lad had also disappeared since leaving him for dead, another sure sign that the payoff must have been substantial - big enough to keep Dylan away from his usual haunts long enough for the final reading of the will to take place.

Bates leaned over Sedgefield, intending to pull the lump of a man to his feet. As soon as he bent over his stomach pulsed, sending spears of pain across his chest and into his ribcage. He winced and gritted his teeth to stem a cry of anguish that was burning its way up his windpipe. Sedgefield inspected the policeman, and for a long moment the two men stared intensely at close quarters.

Sedgefield broke into a grin, apparently amused. He whispered, 'What's the matter Bates? Feeling run down? You look like you could do with re-charging your batteries…'

Bates straightened, his eyes never leaving the solicitors smug face.

'You paid Dylan to do your dirty work and you didn't care how he did it, as long as you could get your hands on Greg's money,' accused Bates.

Sedgefield shook his head and pushed himself up and out of his chair, 'I think we're finished here,' he announced, 'These accusations against myself and my staff are frankly preposterous and you don't have a shred of evidence.'

'Oh, but we do,' said Timothy crisply, adopting a maniacally large smile, 'You'd better sit yourself down.'

Bates didn't need to be told twice. He stepped forward and eyeballing Sedgefield from close quarters, ordering him to take his seat. The solicitor took a moment to consider his options… and sat down. He now understood why Greg Armitage had been so insistent that his will be read in this particular room, being sound-proofed and boasting a single, easily barred exit. He could scream at the top of his voice and not be heard and there was no way he was going to force his way past the huge, muscular lad guarding the door. If only he could find his blasted phone. He must have left it in his private office, but patted his suit pockets once more, just in case.

'Lost your phone, Mr Sedgefield?' Timothy queried.

He spun around, 'Thomas, why don't you lend Mr Sedgefield *your* phone?'

With his head bowed, Thomas continued to stare at the floor.

'Thomas?'

'I don't have it,' he replied without looking up, 'I think I must have left it at home.'

Timothy waved his index finger, 'No you didn't. And you're not going to believe this… *both* your phones were handed to me this morning. Before he ran off this chap…'

'Or was it a woman? I couldn't tell…' he added mischievously.

'Anyway, he or she told me to look at certain text messages and phone calls made on the day Fun Boy Frankie was running at Beverley, and at the time a Head Lad and young boy were being held hostage.'

Timothy was enjoying himself, but kept his voice serious and business-like. He dipped into his jacket pocket and removed the two smart phones Bates had managed to acquire that morning. A resourceful associate of his, with the memorable name of Mike Tyson, had managed to accidently bump into Sedgefield as he crossed the company car park, and was unfortunately pushed into Thomas as he'd queued for his early morning coffee, purloining both phones from the solicitors pockets once they were distracted. Timothy examined both phones carefully.

'Give me those at once, they're company property!' protested Sedgefield, starting to get up. Bates held him in place.

'You two spoke with each other and shared a phone line with Beverley racecourse. There's also several text messages where you, Thomas, complain to Mr Sedgefield that your 'contact' can't reach any of the No Regrets ladies' phones in order to 'make the warning call'. And you, Mr Sedgefield then proceed to tell Thomas to, 'Calm down. I'll call the racecourse. Get your man at the yard on the line now.'

The room went deathly quiet.

'The ladies had their phones switched off because they'd been travelling by helicopter,' Timothy explained, 'So Dylan couldn't deliver his kidnap message and force the ladies to leave Beverley before the race. The two of you had to think fast because the race was due off in a matter of minutes… and this was your last chance to ensure the syndicate failed their task.'

Timothy had been switching his gaze between the two solicitors as he spoke. Sedgefield remained pokerfaced, but he was tiring of Thomas's refusal to show his face, almost bent double on the back wall. Striding forward without warning, Timothy kicked the chair in front of the young man. Thomas jolted straight, as did Marion and a few others.

'It was you blackmailing Martha, wasn't it? You were there the night before the race, getting Clara's mobile number so that Dylan could call her. Come on Thomas, it's time to tell the truth.'

Thomas peered up, bleary eyed. He looked scared, conflicted… and then he opened his mouth.

Come on, just nod or say, 'Yes', and admit it, Timothy said to himself, willing Thomas to break down.

'He has nothing to say,' Sedgefield called out. Thomas's mouth closed and his chin dropped to his chest.

'Besides, this is all academic,' Sedgefield continued, 'You stole the phones and probably placed incriminating evidence on them. I've never met a 'Dylan' and neither has Thomas. Now do yourselves a favour and allow us to leave. It's unfortunate your family has lost its inheritance to a number of charities, but I did warn Greg he was being fanciful with his 'task', especially when it relied upon four women, three of whom spend most of their time arguing, and the other being his bastard daughter!'

Sedgefield became immediately aware he'd made a mistake, and it was a mistake that was going to involve immediate pain. Clara tore towards him, leaving a wake of upturned chairs behind her. She dodged around Bates and swung her fist. Mr Sedgefield's nose exploded with a sickening crack and a spray of blood that immediately rendered his shirt and tie fit only for the bin. He let out a high-pitched shriek and covered his face with his arms, fearing another strike.

Bates pulled Clara away, telling her to calm down.

'I'm perfectly calm,' she replied, straightening her designer jacket and rubbing her knuckles, 'I learned in the children's homes that anger isn't helpful in a fight. Accuracy and an upward swing are far more important.'

Fifty-Three

Ruth and Sophie arrived at Clara's side, congratulating her and proceeded to shout further threats at Sedgefield. Jerry followed, wrapping himself around his mother's waist. Timothy stood beside the solicitor, fending off his family's advances and their questions. Paul watched on from his seat, as did Alvita. Bates took the other side of the solicitor who was back in his chair behind the desk, holding a white, blood-stained handkerchief to his nose.

Martha had slowly made her way down a row of chairs and was now standing a few feet away from Thomas, her head cocked sideways, trying to get a good look at his down-turned face.

'It's you, isn't it?' she said quietly to him, 'You're the one who walked Kilroy with me, made those horrible phone calls, and told me all those lies about my family. And...' her voice almost broke, '... and you came and frightened me on the night of the party.'

Thomas stared resolutely at the floor.

Unaware of Martha's words, Timothy held up both hands and asked for quiet.

'I can confirm that Martha is indeed an Armitage. She is Greg's daughter. Mother, you have a new grandchild.'

Gertrude wasted no time. She beetled straight across to Martha and introduced herself. When the girl offered her a handshake the old woman pushed the proffered hand aside and stepped in to hug her new granddaughter and wouldn't let go.

'Until a few months ago, the only person who knew Martha's secret was Greg,' Timothy said in a loud voice that quelled the conversations that had sprung up around the room, 'However, in setting up his sting, I believe Greg may have inadvertently revealed to his solicitor, Martha's importance to him and his family, leaving her to be used as a valuable pawn in Mr Sedgefield's plot.'

Sedgefield dabbed at his nose and remained silent.

'I have, or rather, Greg has a proposition for you,' Timothy continued, 'Before he died, Greg recorded another will on video. It splits his fortune equally between the Armitage family. It cancels his previous will incorporating the task, so Mr Sedgefield, you won't get your hands on any of Greg's money.'

Timothy faced Sedgefield as a small cheer went up from virtually everyone in the room.

'Greg estimates you stole between eight to fourteen million pounds from his father's estate. Bates and Greg have looked into your finances, and they reckon you can afford to pay my mother back four million in cash straight away and another four once you've sold the various properties you own here and abroad, no doubt bought through your crooked investment company.'

Timothy produced a document from his inside pocket and slapped it on the desk in front of Sedgefield. Still holding his handkerchief to his nose, the solicitor peered down at the single page of print.

'In exchange, we will return all the evidence we have amassed that implicate Thomas and yourself in criminal acts,' Timothy stated.

Sedgefield placed a finger on the page, tapping it a few times, then rolled his eyes upwards until they settled on Tim. Pushing the agreement back across the table with a single fingertip he said, 'A kind offer, but no thanks.' When he removed his finger Timothy noticed there was a bloody fingerprint left on the pristine white page.

'You've got nothing,' Sedgefield said with a half laugh, throwing his balled-up bloody handkerchief towards Tim. It bounced harmlessly off his chest.

Timothy's eyes narrowed, 'We're trying to make this easy for both of us. A court case will be costly and would drag our family and your business through the wringer. You can avoid all of that with this simple agreement. You know you acted improperly with my father, and you've become embroiled in intimidation, bribery, and kidnapping in your pursuit of my brother's estate.'

Sedgefield laughed again, this time it was a deeper, full bodied laugh that ended in a snort of derision, 'I don't think so... your brother shouldn't have sent a washed-up policeman and a kid to do a man's job. I think I'm going to double-up! You have no capital... none of you have any money! That house... Armitage Hall, is a money pit and worth nothing. Feel free to take me to court, I can keep you all tied up in expensive red tape for *years*! In the meantime the trust funds will continue to operate. Your grandfather was an idiot too – he made me the executor! There's not a court in the land who will convict me! And by all means bring charges against me for intimidation... your phone evidence is shaky at best. Thomas might get a few months, but only if you can find Bates's employee and he's willing to talk! *I'm untouchable*! Bates knows it, which is why I'm being offered this crazy deal.'

Sedgefield was on his feet, stabbing a finger around the room as he spoke.

'And *you* can expect to have the police charging you with common assault!' he cried in the direction of Clara, before pushing his way past Timothy and stumping up to the door where a cross-armed Jimmy resolutely blocked his path.

'Get out of my way you oaf!'

Jimmy sniffed, regarded the solicitor with minimal interest for a moment and looked towards Bates for instruction.

'You're not going to let this thief just leave, are you?' Ruth cried out at Bates, 'He's admitted he's defrauded us once and he's going to do it again!'

Everyone was on their feet, the Armitages had created a small gathering around Sedgefield and were currently watching Gertrude harangue him. Meanwhile Martha and Jerry had sat down either side of Thomas and started to speak with him. He was still hunched over, staring at the floor.

'It's your last chance, Sedgefield,' shouted Timothy, 'Walk out that door and you're risking your business, your reputation, and your family.'

The solicitor turned his back on Jimmy and studied the ring of people around him. A hush fell on the group as they waited for Sedgefield to speak.

He sniggered, 'The Armitages! You're all the same. Not one of you can see beyond that estate of yours. I warned your grandfather. He could have sold to developers, I put deal after deal to him, but all he cared about was the house and the land. It was the same with Greg. He only realised what a self-obsessed idiot he'd been when he had weeks to live – and tried to put it all right. Look at the mess he made of that!'

From behind the huddle around Sedgefield, a high, young female voice cut through the hub-bub.

'My dad wasn't an idiot,' said Martha. She was standing on a chair, peering over the heads of the Armitage family and addressing Sedgefield directly.

'Look at what he's achieved for me,' she continued, 'Two years ago I didn't have a father or a family when my mum died, and thanks to Greg, my dad, I've got an adopted brother, a stepmother, aunts, and uncles, and even a grandmother. What have you got, apart from our money?'

Sedgefield shook his head and frowned at the teenager, 'You're as daft as your father.'

'My father didn't make me intimidate, bribe, steal, and blackmail people,' Martha fired back.

Several heads began to switch between this strident young woman, whose words and style of delivery sounded unerringly like Greg, and Sedgefield, whose eyes had narrowed as he stared back at Martha. A hush fell on the room once more.

'When I met Thomas for the first time we talked for over an hour. I liked him. We had stuff in common. He told me his mother had a new partner and his father had two daughters, but that he wasn't really a proper part of either family. I told him about my dad, and then Thomas said his father could never treat him the same way he treated his other children. He said we'd both been rejected by our families. He made me feel angry and bitter… I didn't understand what Thomas was trying to do at the time, but now I do.'

Sedgefield frowned, 'What on earth are you…'

'But I think Thomas shared a bit more than he intended in order to win my trust,' interrupted Martha airily, 'Because I soon realised I hadn't been rejected. My father didn't know I existed for sixteen years, but when he found out, he made me part of his life. Clara and Ruth were exactly the same when they found out who I was. Whereas, you, Mr Sedgefield, have known about Thomas for nineteen years and you still won't treat him like your son.'

Sedgefield's face turned crimson.

'This just got interesting,' Sophie whispered behind her hand to Clara and Ruth.

'Sedgefield is your father?' Timothy asked Thomas.

Thomas nodded gloomily and slowly got to his feet.

'I hated it. I hated it all! I was scared of the horses and the dogs made me feel sick to my bones.'

He looked up at Martha, still standing on her seat.

'I was careful to keep clear of you on my visit to the yard, so I could…' he took a shaky breath, 'I'm sorry I lied about your dad and forced you to eavesdrop on your family. Mr Sedge… My *father* said I…'

'Thom-as!' snarled Sedgefield.

Marion, Simon, and Gertrude all rounded on the solicitor, warning him against another outburst. A downcast Thomas pushed between Clara and Ruth, quietly telling them he was, 'So, so sorry,'. He looked up at Jimmy, tear streaks marking both cheeks and asked if he could please leave.

'Let him go,' called Tim.

Jimmy opened the door a crack and allowed Thomas to slip through.

'Not so fast, Bub,' Jimmy told Sedgefield when he tried to follow.

Timothy checked with Bates, who shrugged. There was little point in keeping Sedgefield in the room any longer. They'd tried everything Greg had suggested, and failed. He despondently twirled two fingers at Jimmy, who started to move aside.

Sophie watched Sedgefield stride arrogantly past Jimmy and was suddenly reminded of her first visit to this office and a very different side to the solicitors personality. She was reminded of the woman in Sedgefield's office… his wife.

'It seems you and Greg had more in common than you imagined,' Sophie said, running her eye up and down Sedgefield thoughtfully.

'I'm nothing like Greg,' he growled.

'Oh I didn't say you were *like him*, I said you had something in common.'

Jimmy placed a hand on the doorknob and pushed it ajar. Sedgefield turned his back on the Armitage's and made towards the exit.

'I've often wondered why Greg didn't tell his wife about Martha. I guess she would have gone crazy.'

Clara frowned questioningly at Sophie and received a stern shake of the head and a quick hand signal that told her to button her mouth.

'Or perhaps she would have divorced Greg. What do you think Clara? How would you have reacted to discovering your husband had an adult daughter he'd kept quiet about for years, and been seeing on a daily basis?'

Sedgefield pushed the door open and a shaft of noonday sunshine penetrated the room. The intense, stagnant air suddenly sparkled around him.

'I suppose you'd want to know whether the other woman was still on the scene too... That's got to hurt her, when she looks back over twenty years of lies... wondering where you were that night you were working late or that long weekend with clients. It could shatter her world.'

Sedgefield halted inside the jam of the door, his back to the gaggle of people watching him leave.

Sophie paused as long as she could dare before adding, 'You know, if I was her, I'd divorce him. After all, I know how it feels when a man makes a fool of you. It's taken seventeen years for me to forgive him.'

Sedgefield swayed slightly.

'Yep, half of all his worldly goods. That's what I'd take off the cheating wretch... perhaps more if I could get it. I'd have all the power of the courts behind me as well. Oh yes! I'd screw up his finances good and proper.'

As soon as Sedgefield swung around, Sophie she knew she had him. His eyes were full of hatred. She could almost feel the heat radiating from his face, see the sweat dampened patches on his shirt, and she could smell his fear.

'I've met your wife,' Sophie said, with an eyebrow raised, 'Now there's a woman to be reckoned with. I'd certainly think twice before crossing her... she doesn't come across as the forgiving type.'

Smiling sweetly, Sophie beckoned to him with a single finger and said, 'Come back inside the room, Mr Sedgefield. I'm sure Timothy can work something out for you that means your wife never needs to know about your infidelity.'

Fifty-Four

24th September 2016

Sophie aimed a bright smile at Jerry and was pleased when he returned it with an uncertain, but brave smile of his own. The boy was nervous, holding his mother's hand tightly but with eyes wide, taking in everything that was happening in the huge, sun drenched parade ring.

She feared the clothes Clara had chosen for her son were at the root of Jerry's nervousness. With hair slicked back, his three-piece tweed suit was topped off with a purple bow-tie that made Jerry resemble a tiny Winston Churchill. She'd not passed comment of course, but she felt for the boy as he stuck to Clara's leg like a limpet, staring at the three-man camera crew that were currently interviewing Dennis.

'Only three runs from Charlie Soap so far this season, but all of them were impressive. And he ran a corker at Royal Ascot to finish second to today's favourite,' stated the mousey haired lady in an overly flamboyant ostrich feather hat, 'Have you been aiming your colt for today's Middle Park?'

Dennis rubbed his chin, 'It's just the way things have worked out. We'd have loved to have gone for the Richmond Stakes, but things didn't quite feel right for the horse, and the owners felt today's race suited him better.'

Seizing the opportunity to broaden the appeal of her interview, the lady stated, 'And I believe I have the owners here,' she said, checking her racecard as the cameraman framed Clara, Jerry, Ruth, and Sophie, 'The No Regrets syndicate, are here today, so what are Charlie Soap's chances?' she asked, nodding at Clara.

'Dennis says he will win, so we're expecting nothing less,' Clara said primly.

'Really!' exclaimed the lady, 'Then we should all back him, he's a thirty-three-to-one shot. And what do you think?' she asked Jerry without drawing breath.

Jerry looked blankly at the black sponge on the microphone she'd just thrust into his face, then at the ostrich feathers waving around on top of the woman's head.

'So how is Charlie Soap going to do today?' prompted the lady, raising her eyebrows encouragingly.

Jerry swallowed, let go of his mother's hand and dug his hands into his suit jacket pockets just like he'd seen Danny do at the yard when he was asked his opinion.

'The colt needs to get away cleanly and then take a position close to the leaders because the six furlongs at Newmarket doesn't suit closers,' Jerry told her confidently.

The woman peered at him with her mouth slightly open for a moment.

'If Charlie can track the favourite and kick on a furlong from home he'll have a cracking chance,' Jerry added, believing the woman's silence meant he was supposed to talk again.

'What's your name,' she asked.

'Jerry Armitage,' he fired back proudly, 'I'm going to be a racehorse trainer.'

The woman straightened, flicked her eyes around the highly amused owners of Charlie Soap and slowly came back to Jerry, drawing the microphone back to her own mouth, 'I don't doubt that, Mr Armitage.'

Dennis crackled with laughter as the presenter and her crew moved on.

'That was priceless,' Ruth cooed.

'Don't swell with too much pride,' Sophie warned Clara, 'We don't want you to pop!'

Clara was beaming down at her son, bathing in the reflective glory of his performance, 'Where on earth did that come from, Jerry?'

The boy found his mother's hand once more and looked up at the four adults, pleased they seemed happy with him, but bemused too, 'It's okay, Mum. It's what Danny said when I asked him about Charlie Soap's race.'

'I'm sure Danny will be right,' he added.

The adults quickly agreed and congratulated Jerry once more on his first ever media interview.

'The first of many, I'm sure,' Dennis told him.

Jerry wasn't listening; he'd noticed Charlie Soap and Martha entering the parade ring, 'Look, Charlie's here!'

The colt joined the line of horses and handlers touring the outskirts of the huge parade ring. When she came close enough, Martha waved to Jerry. He waved back.

Sophie gave both Clara and Ruth a nudge when she spotted Timothy, Alvita, Marion, and Simon waving from the parade ring rails.

'It's good of them to come,' Sophie commented.

Clara agreed, but Ruth's smile was a little forced as she waved back.

'They're probably here to try and convince me to come back to Armitage Hall,' she said through gritted teeth, 'My mother is calling me daily and won't take no for an answer.'

'I thought you'd decided to stay in Malton?' queried Sophie.

'She has,' Dennis cut in, 'She's on the payroll now, doing my admin, riding out and secretarial stuff...'

He paused, coughed, and added, 'I've asked Ruth to move into the house. The place has missed a woman's touch for far too long.'

Dennis was expecting a reaction, but not quite the strength of feeling Clara and Sophie displayed as they grabbed hold of Ruth and excitedly congratulated their delighted friend.

'There's nothing inappropriate going on,' Dennis said firmly.

Ruth rolled her eyes at the trainer.

'We get on, and I love being around the horses. It seems right,' Ruth told her friends.

'I can have a word with that lot if you want,' Clara said, sliding her eyes towards the trio of Armitages leaning against the railings, 'My right hook gets mentioned every time I meet them.'

Ruth shook her head.

'No, it's down to me,' she muttered, 'The one thing the last five months have taught me is that I have to take control of my own destiny. Greg isn't around to force me into taking the correct route anymore.'

The three weeks since the final reading of Greg's will had been filled with change for the No Regrets syndicate. The new will gave each Armitage, plus Sophie and Martha, a deposit in their bank accounts of a touch over seven-hundred thousand pounds each. Greg had seen to it that Clara and Jerry had been left three times as much, along with the house and everything else.

Ruth's decision to stay in Malton completed the final piece in the jigsaw for the three women. Sophie and Clara had feared Ruth would crumble and return to another decade or more of being maligned and bullied by Gertrude back at Armitage Hall. It had looked worryingly possible for a while, as Gertrude had become far less confrontational and easier to speak with recently.

Clara had sold her house in Durham and settled on a smaller, three-storey town house just outside the centre of York, not far from where she'd grown up. She and Jerry had already moved in and Martha also had a bedroom she used a few days a week when she wasn't needed at the stables in Malton. This development had come as a bit of a surprise to Sophie, who had imagined Clara might want to distance herself from the girl.

Clara had told her, 'I grew up without any sisters or brothers, but I had you. Jerry has a sister and Martha has a brother, I'd rather have them together than apart. Besides, Martha reminds me of Greg... and a little of my younger self.'

Sophie had returned to her flat in Acomb with Bella, spent a few days looking at the still unopened removal boxes stacked against the living room wall and finally spent an entire day taking them to the local recycling centre. She'd bought bookcases and discovered she had enough floorspace to dance in when all her paperbacks were neatly stacked away. Then she'd invited Clara and Ruth out for a meal in York and announced she was going to take the summer of 2017 off work and spend some of her money hiring an eight-berth camper van.

'I intend to embark on a five month tour of Europe,' she told them, 'And as we had such a nice time at my sister's caravan, I wondered if you'd both like to come with me? Kids and dogs are welcome!'

It had only took her thirty minutes and another bottle of wine to convince them it was a brilliant idea.

Mitch Corrigan crossed the parade ring and found the No Regrets syndicate engrossed in a conversation about Fun Boy Frankie. So much so, he wasn't noticed until he sidled up and stood beside Dennis.

'We felt on top of the world,' Clara enthused, 'And Carlisle racecourse treated us like queens after he'd won!'

'I'll remember that day for a while,' said Mitch with a broad smile, 'I've never been kissed and hugged as much after a winning ride in my life!'

The gelding had followed up his Beverley win by running in the second week of September and effectively cemented his place in the hearts of the three ladies and Martha by winning a ten-runner nursery handicap at Carlisle. Getting up to win by a head in the last stride, the two-year-old had a prolonged battle with the runner up in the final furlong that had made the victory even more thrilling for his devoted owners. Thankfully, this time the stewards didn't announce an enquiry into the result despite the two horses coming close together in the closing stages.

Mitch and Dennis soon disappeared to mount up on Charlie Soap and the ladies left the parade ring and walked around the huge stand to watch the race on the rails.

'It's funny isn't it, about Charlie Soap and Frankie,' Clara mused as they waited for the race to go off.

'What's funny?' asked Ruth, peering up the Newmarket straight to where a small line of stalls had a number of tiny stick-like horses milling around them.

'This doesn't feel the same as a Frankie race. Even though Charlie's running in what Dennis says is a really important race, I'm still more attached to Frankie, even though he's not as talented.'

'I know what you mean,' Sophie agreed.

Ruth gave the two of them a disbelieving stare, 'Frankie is lovely, but this is one of the top two-year-old races for colts. Some owners would give their right arm just to have a horse able to hold its own in this race.'

'I dunno,' Clara pondered, 'Frankie's just got more about him I guess. It doesn't matter that he's not a… what does Dennis talk about again? A 'Grip' or a 'Grape' horse?'

Ruth's cheeks reddened and she burst into one of her long, low, rumbling laughs that always ensured the other two women would be laughing with her within seconds.

'*Group* horse, you clot!' Ruth said, squeezing Clara's arm.

From below, Jerry asked with a frown, 'What's a clot?'

Clara beamed back at him, happy to have caused smiles to crease the faces of her friends, 'Erm… an amusing idiot, I think.'

Jerry thought hard about this for a moment, wrinkling his nose with the effort. Then the boy turned his face upwards once more and said in a serious tone, 'Yes Mum, you are a clot… but a nice one.'

Clara was still recovering from a complex mixture of pride and maternal bonding when the race went off, eventually transferring her attention to the racetrack. Fifty seconds later Charlie Soap hit the front at the two pole and went two lengths clear, Mitch angling the colt to the right, grabbing a pitch on the far rail. Only one other opponent could live with Charlie's pace, a flashy light chestnut ranging up on his outside over a hundred yards out and easing into the lead. By this stage, the three women and the little boy on the rails were bellowing Charlie's name.

There was a tussle between the two horses and they swiftly pulled several more lengths clear of the horse in third. The two of them duelled for the last half a furlong and passed the winning post together to a huge roar from the crowd, and exasperated screams from the No Regrets syndicate, knowing Charlie had missed out on a win by only a head.

The aftermath in the winners' enclosure involved a melee of people and cameras. Short, excited comments were made by Mitch, Dennis, Martha and then Dennis again as the magnitude of Charlie Soap's achievement was analysed, debated, and raked over. Those minutes skipped by quickly, punctuated by Dennis being interviewed by newspaper journalists and the racing television channel.

'That was an enormous amount of fuss for a second placing!' Clara commented as the syndicate travelled up the grandstand lift to the Owners and Trainers rooms.

Sophie looked to Ruth, half expecting her to shake her head and begin explaining to Clara how important that run had been, but she hadn't heard, or had decided not to hear her friend, preferring to breathe deeply and pitch her unfocussed gaze on the wall of the lift.

They managed to find a recently vacated table and cleared the half empty coffee cups and glasses to one end, barely having time to settle themselves before Dennis rushed in, frenetically scanning the room, standing on tiptoes. He spotted Ruth waving at him and immediately hurried over to their table.

'What is it? Is Charlie okay?' Ruth demanded.

'Yes, yes. He's absolutely fine,' Dennis said with a dismissive wave of his hand. He realised his heart was racing and took a calming breath, although it did little to lift the concern from the faces of his owners around the circular table.

'I've... well, *you've* been approached by the Japan Racing Association. They're interested in syndicating Charlie as a prospective stallion.'

Dennis received a ring of frowns that varied from pure confusion in Clara's case, via a querying doubt from Sophie through to Ruth's expression of worried concern.

'They want to buy into fifty percent of Charlie now, run him through to the end of this season and then as a three-year-old, they want to have a bash at winning the Guineas, or an alternative Group 1 race with him before he transfers to them one-hundred percent and goes to stand at their stud in Japan.'

'He's not for sale,' Clara declared indignantly.

Dennis locked eyes with her and slowly raised an eyebrow, 'They've started with an offer of eight million pounds.'

Clara gulped, 'Oh...'

Fifty-Five

2nd*22nd October 2016*

Those final meetings had seen Greg spend time, sometimes over several days, and many meetings, simply listening to his brothers, sister, and their partners. Then he'd given them each a task which he'd made them promise to complete and not reveal to anyone until after the final reading of his will in September.

He'd asked one question of each of them, 'Where do you want to be in five years time?' Then he had leaned back in his armchair and waited, never speaking until he was sure they had nothing else to add, or they asked a direct question of him.

Once he'd listened to their answer he'd told each of them he would consider what had been said and get back to them. Without fail, he returned to Gertrude, Simon, Ruth, Timothy, Marion, Alvita, and Jerry with an agreement to help them achieve their goals with his money. He did the same with Martha.

In return he asked them to fulfil one promise. Sometimes it was linked to their answer to his question, for others their promise seemed completely at odds with how they saw their life unfolding.

Ruth had promised Greg that should the need, or opportunity arise, she would not hesitate to leave Armitage Hall. She should not worry about her mother, Greg would deal with her care. But she had to promise to leave, even if the options of where to go were limited and meant placing herself at the mercy of someone for whom she had little respect. She promised, and never thought for a moment a situation would occur that would necessitate her leaving the hall.

When Simon had gone into detail about his idea for a retirement village using the old stables, the east wing of Armitage Hall and other outbuildings and grounds, Greg made him promise to organise architects, builders, and suppliers in order to cost and plan such a scheme. Marion had promised to attend a twelve week course aimed at covering all the aspects needed to start a business. Greg thought it best not to share these promises between the husband and wife.

Timothy had been handed the job of seeing through Greg's No Regrets plan. Having been introduced to Bates and briefed about Sedgefield, Greg had instructed his younger brother to see to it that the solicitor was held to account for cheating their father, and themselves, out of his legacy. Initially Timothy had refused, puzzled by the complexity of the plan and worried about the weight of responsibility being placed upon him. Greg had warned him that Sedgefield could potentially tie up the proceeds of his will for months, if not years, if he wasn't effectively cornered. It emerged it had been Alvita who proved to be the one to change Timothy's mind, convincing her boyfriend he should take on the management of Bates.

Alvita had impressed Greg enormously. In the end, without giving details of Timothy's task, he had asked the teenager to simply encourage, support, and stand by her boyfriend for the next five months. Greg had warmed to the girl after issuing a warning that Timothy would be taking on more pressure than he'd ever known, to which Alvita had replied, 'Good. It could be the making of him.' Greg had made it clear to Timothy that he thought Alvita had hidden talents and he shouldn't under-value his girlfriend.

Paul was given a small, but important part to play in the first few weeks of the No Regrets syndicate's task, and he promised willingly and wholeheartedly to his lifelong best friend, despite knowing he might be cast as the villain of the piece, at least for the first few months. Meanwhile, Martha had promised to keep her identity secret until she could meet her new family properly in September.

Greg had asked Jerry not to be sad when he passed, and to look after his mum for him when he was gone. Jerry had told his father what he wanted in the future. It was not to be left alone. In return, Greg had promised his son that he shouldn't worry, as before the summer was finished, he would organise for him to have a new sister. The boy had cocked his head to one side and giggled, telling his dad he was being silly.

The story of the desires and promises made by the extended Armitage family had been swirling around the hall's reception room for the last twenty minutes. Ruth brought the meeting to some sort of order by tapping a spoon against her coffee cup.

'Please sit down, Mother. You don't have to dominate the room for every gathering we have as a family. The rug in front of the fire has two marks where you usually stand!'

There was a ripple of kind-hearted laughter as Gertrude sat down.

'You've changed,' the old woman grumbled quietly.

'For the better, as have *you*.' Ruth replied, low enough so that only Gertrude could hear.

Ruth took in the group of family and friends variously sitting, standing, or in Alvita's case, draped over Tim. As well as every member of the Armitage clan, Sophie, Clara and Jerry, Martha, and Paul were present, making eleven people in total.

She thanked everyone for coming and quickly got down to business.

'You will know that Sedgefield has released Greg's money, as you should have received your payment last week.'

There was a general nodding of heads and hum of appreciation.

'Sedgefield has also agreed to make payments of fifty thousand pounds per month into a new trust fund set up by myself, Timothy, and Simon that will support my Mother and help to begin restoration of her rooms here at Armitage Hall. It will take us four years to get back everything he stole, but I think that's a great result in the circumstances.'

Again, the room echoed to the sound of agreement and a number of thankyous were issued toward Timothy and Simon.

'However, the reason for calling you all here is to announce that we haven't quite finished with the good news.'

Gertrude and Timothy shuffled to the edge of their seats. No end of questioning, and even a little light-hearted blackmail had been able to elicit a reason from Ruth for today's meeting.

'As you all know, Greg created a task based around horseracing in order to bring Sophie and Clara together, and to… well, I think he was aiming for me to discover a life outside these walls, allow me to regain my confidence and lose some of what he told me was downright cattiness.'

To her surprise, Alvita began to clap excitedly and Marion soon joined in. Sophie and Clara, giggling, added to the applause and Jerry clapped and whistled. Ruth studied them each in turn, puzzled but also amused.

'Was I really that bad before I left?' she asked with a self-deprecating smile.

'Yes,' Simon and Timothy said in unison.

Ruth rolled her eyes comically and keen to move on, started to speak again as soon as the clapping began to subside.

'As you're all aware, we have two racehorses that Greg placed in the name of the No Regrets syndicate that consisted of Clara, Sophie, and myself. What you won't be aware of – and we certainly weren't - the way horseracing works, meant Greg had set up an entirely separate bank account with Weatherby's, the people who manage all the paperwork and administration for racehorse ownership. He bought both the horses from that account, and then placed it in our three names.'

'So there's a bit of prize-money that's yours? Is that it?' Timothy asked.

'Yes, there's some prize-money. However, thanks to our trainer, we've managed to cut a deal with a large breeding operation. It allows us to race Charlie Soap next season, and then he will be syndicated as a stallion, or rather, a sire.'

Simon leaned forward, his interest piqued. Even with his light grasp of racing related matters, he knew that being a sire was only for those horses who reached the pinnacle of race-winning achievement. He thought hard for a moment; hadn't one of Ruth's horses recently finished second and then won?'

Ruth paused before delivering her final words, 'Following his second in the Middle Park at Newmarket and his subsequent win at Leopardstown in the Group Three race we signed an agreement seven days ago for our horse, Charlie Soap, to race again next season and then become a stallion in Japan. The contract is worth fourteen million pounds...'

She allowed this news to sink in for a long moment.

'...And Sophie, Clara, and myself have decided to share the proceeds from the sale among everyone here. You will all receive a million pounds. Our trainer, Dennis Smith, will receive the same, and we would like the remainder to be given to an adoption charity.'

Over the top of the wave of gasps and exclamations, Ruth continued, 'If it's okay with everyone, the No Regrets syndicate would like to keep the other racehorse, Fun Boy Frankie, as he's basically become Martha's and my pet.'

Gertrude got to her feet, and crossing to the fireplace took up her familiar position with her back to the fire, legs apart, dogs at her side. She warmed herself for a few seconds and then announced, 'I can live with that!'

***

The drive back to Yorkshire found the three ladies, Martha, and Jerry all in ebullient mood. Dennis's plan to run Charlie Soap once more in order to bag a Group race in October and increase the price from the Japanese consortium had been a masterstroke and Ruth especially couldn't wait to tell him of his windfall. Having received their share of Greg's inheritance, it was Clara who first suggested they share the Charlie Soap money with her extended family. Ruth and Sophie had agreed immediately. It was what Greg would have done.

'Simon and Marion will have their hands full, renovating all those buildings and creating a brand new business,' said Sophie as Clara turned the car onto the Beverley road, only half a mile from Middlefield Stables.

'He'd been secretly planning it for years, but never expected to have the money to fund it,' pointed out Ruth.

'And Timothy starting his own business... something to do with art isn't it?'

'He and Alvita seem to know their stuff,' Clara noted, 'He's another one who has changed as a result of Greg's task.'

'What will you do with your money, Martha?' Ruth asked.

'She's going to invest ninety percent of it!' Clara said sternly.

'And I'm going to splurge with the rest,' Martha added, 'Clara's words, not mine!'

'What about you Jerry. What do you fancy doing with your share?'

Clara sighed heavily and looked into the rear view mirror to where her son was sitting between Martha and Ruth in the back seat, grinning from ear to ear.

'I'm going to the sales with Danny and Dennis and we're going to pinhook a yearling!' the boy stated positively.

Clara shook her head. Sophie looked across at her from the passenger seat and mouthed 'What's that?'

'Don't ask,' she groaned, 'I've already travelled down that rabbit hole with him and he had an answer to every single one of my objections. I have an awful feeling this horseracing bug he's caught isn't going to disappear overnight.'

Fifty-Six

October 31ˢᵗ 2016

A thin smile curled its way onto Bates's lips. There were tell-tale signs on the forest floor. An area of flattened earth here, a trail of broken branches there. He stopped dead in his tracks and slowly tilted his head skyward to peer through the gathering darkness up into the forest canopy. Six weeks of painstaking tracking in his spare time had led him to this small, unkempt corner of Kielder Forest and now he'd reached his journey's end.

Dylan really had gone to pains to keep off the grid. Whatever Thomas and his father had paid him, or threatened him with, had worked. It had taken sustained pressure on a number of Bates's contacts to finally get a reported sighting of the teenager in Otterburn. From there he'd had to go door knocking at sheep farms and canvass forestry workers and land workers at pubs and cafes for news of anyone sleeping rough in the forest. His luck had changed when he popped into a pub close to the Scottish border on a Friday night and when asking a local whether he'd seen or heard of anyone living in the trees, he'd been pointed in the direction of a local farmer. The said gentleman, a portly chap with a flabby face riddled with small red veins had trouble clambering up and planting his backside onto his bar stool, but once there managed to down three pints before revealing that 'Some young lad was hangin' around Deadwater, 'an livin' aff the land.'

Bates spent two hours casing the area and returned the next evening. He'd had to step lightly at he approached, carefully locating several trip wires set up to warn his quarry. Bates had no wish to chase his ex-employee through the forest, as the lad would no doubt set off spidering his way across the canopy at the first sight or sound of him.

Dylan was encased in his hanging cocoon over thirty feet from the forest floor, his living area anchored to three substantial trees. As Bates drew closer it sounded like there was a television, phone, or radio playing. Good; it meant the boy had been on his own long enough to let his guard down. He clambered along fallen trees for the last twenty feet and after attaching his safety rope, hung off the trunk of the tree, getting his breath back.

The outline of Dylan's spine pushing against the thick, waterproof material that encased him was easy to pick out, and Bates had enough time to pick his spot before he fired.

The two tiny steel hooks tore through the cocoon and buried themselves into Dylan's bony back with a satisfying thunk. Immediately, there was a scream, the television sound cut off and the body in the bag juddered.

'Missed me?' Bates enquired conversationally once the pulse from the taser had stopped coursing through his victim. He waited a few seconds, imagining the confusion the boy must be feeling, rather pleased with the irony of Dylan being shocked by his own homemade taser. He was about to send another shock through the wires when the boy groaned, rolled tentatively in his sack, and answered him.

'Oh crap! Is that you, Bates?'

'Dylan! It's good to hear your voice again.'

There was a string of muttered expletives before the boy asked, 'How'd you find me?'

Bates grimaced, but forced his voice to smile back, 'Sooner or later you had to make a mistake, and yours was to give in to your craving for a kebab in Otterburn.'

The lump of human inside the cocoon wriggled, sending out another flurry of swearwords as Dylan tried to extract the barbed hooks from his back. Bates sighed happily and zapped him again.

'Alright!' screamed the boy once he'd recovered from the jaw tensing shock a second time, 'What do you want, you crock of...'

Bates pressed the trigger again, wondering when the boy would realise bad language would get him nowhere. His query was answered only seconds later when Dylan pleaded with him for the pain to stop.

Ten minutes later Dylan had returned to the forest floor. Bates had Dylan sitting on the trunk of a fallen tree. He examined the teenager, noting the bloodshot, sunken eyes that darted here and there seemingly of their own accord, the unhealthy pallor of his skin, and the bluish strip than ran around his lips.

'You're looking really well!' said Bates sarcastically.

'So would you if you were livin' off rabbit an' beans for five weeks,' Dylan replied sourly.

'Have you been taking your medication, Dylan?'

The boy scowled and looked away.

Bates shook his head sadly.

'You know it keeps you balanced. Stops you from making bad decisions,' Bates pointed out, 'When did you stop taking them?'

'Two months,' he eventually replied.

Bates waited patiently, his eyes never leaving the boy.

'Alright, three then,' Dylan spat.

'About the same time you decided to risk people's lives on your motorbike, pin me to a field and continually shoot me with electricity, and then kidnap a young lad and blackmail his mother?'

Still unable to meet Bates's gaze, Dylan snorted a short laugh and grinned.

Bates gave a heavy sigh, 'Stop grinning, Dylan. I could have died.'

The boy jerked his head up and stared, a little colour re-entering his cheeks, 'Naa, Mr Bates. I had that timer set to come on once every seven and a half minutes. Just enough to keep you…'

'It sent a shock through me every forty-five seconds, Dylan! My muscles were in danger of rupturing after fifteen minutes!'

'Oh,' Dylan said, lifting his chin and staring with glassy eyes off into the trees, 'I must 'ave got the timer a bit… off.'

Bates didn't know whether to scream at the lad or give his shoulder a friendly cuff and tell him not to worry. He settled for glaring at him. The boy had inadvertently missed a zero, he thought. It was an error that had sent a pulse of electricity through him every forty-five seconds instead of every four-hundred and fifty seconds… a blasted nought had almost killed him!

Bates watched as the boy's face contorted in anguish as the seriousness of his mistake registered.

'You got a shock every forty-five seconds…' he said slowly, swallowing hard, 'I'm really sorry Mr Bates. I didn't mean to… I just wanted… Oh, God.'

Bates regarded the boy stony faced. He was pleased, but wasn't about to reveal his true feelings to the lad, at least not just yet. He'd never had Dylan pegged as a killer. He was thoroughly mixed up, but he wasn't a killer. Bates had met a few killers…

He pushed the memories back and refocused his concentration on Dylan, sitting mournfully on his log, staring at the forest floor. He flicked his eyes up to meet Bates.

'You okay then, it must have been…'

Dylan swallowed, searching for a soft word to describe such a horrible experience, and came up dry. He'd tested his homemade taser, and had once shocked himself twice in a minute; the tingling and feeling of unworldliness had lasted for an hour afterwards.

'It was challenging,' Bates said drily. He watched the lad wince and bite the inside of his lip. It was a relief to see the lad showing some empathy. It wasn't a trait common in someone with Dylan's background – virtually ignored by his parents and forced to fend for himself until he was taken into care at the age of five.

Bates leaned against the trunk of a tree opposite the boy and sighed, 'It was my fault Dylan; I pushed you into it.'

The boy shook his head, 'When I think what might of 'appened…'

'No Dylan!' Bates said forcefully, 'Listen to me. I chose you specifically for this job, and I set you up so you *would* be compromised.'

Bates checked to see whether the boy understood, and was glad he hadn't blundered on; a heavy confusion was written deep into the frown on Dylan's face.

'I made sure Thomas saw a pair of binoculars reflecting in the sunlight from the woods on that first day at the stables. That's what first drew him to you. I was behind you, Dylan, further up the hill, making sure Thomas wouldn't miss such a glaring opportunity. I wanted him to find you and coerce or blackmail you to work for him. Do you understand?'

Bates waited patiently, watching the boy intently as he struggled to make sense of this new information. It took time for Dylan to reply.

'You tricked me into working for the solicitors so that you could catch… the solicitors?'

Bates debated how to answer, quickly deciding the boy needed absolutes rather than rambling explanations.

'Yes.'

'You knew I'd double-cross you?'

'I hoped you might report it to me, but wasn't surprised when you didn't.'

Dylan frowned and pushed his bottom lip upwards until he was pouting like a disappointed schoolboy, 'Huh, that young solicitor made it sound like I was bein' clever, like.'

'And you were. Only, I let you down. I didn't account for your tenacity.'

'My what?'

Bate's gave the boy a generous smile, 'Tenacity, Dylan. It's a compliment. You used your skills and brains to catch me out.'

A half-smile worked its way across the boy's face and suddenly Dylan's shoulders weren't as hunched and his eyes brightened.

'I planned to walk into the stables with you, explain what was going on and help you fake your call to Jerry's Mum and draw Thomas and Mr Sedgefield out into the open. As it was, you did it all for real without me.'

Bates took a deep breath, letting it out sharply, 'I know you were easy on Jerry and the Head Lad, but you could have really hurt the trainer with that shovel.'

'I did it like you taught me! I made sure I used the shovel handle and was careful to aim for the bundle of nerves at the base of his neck, not his head… is he okay?'

'Yeah, he's okay. You were lucky though. An inch either way and you could have done some lasting damage. Violence is always…'

'…the last option after all others have been ex… ex…'

'Exhausted,' Bates finished for him.

'I'm sorry, Mr Bates.'

'I'm also disappointed you burgled the trainer's farmhouse.'

'Window was open when I went past. No-one was in. Was an easy climb. Couldn't 'elp myself,' Dylan muttered.

'I'll need his watch back by the way,' Bates replied, nodding at the large silver watch hanging from the boy's bony wrist.

Dylan sniffed, 'Yeah, okay. Don't fit me anyway.'

'You know we caught Sedgefield and he admitted to what he'd had you do?'

The boy looked up and saw from Bates's expression that he wasn't lying.

'That was over four weeks ago. You've been eating rabbits for a month for no reason.'

Dylan frowned, 'I was hidin' from you.'

'No need. As long as I get that watch back to its rightful owner there will be no police involved, and if you're wondering, you can keep the money the young solicitor gave you. I would have given you double as a bonus for completing the job.'

Dylan's face brightened for a moment, then became glum. He stood up and eyed the older man suspiciously.

'Really?'

'Yup,' Bates sighed, 'You really have to start trusting people, Dylan. Otherwise you'll keep losing your friends, jobs… and places to live.'

Dylan was reminded of the small terrace house out at Byker in Newcastle where he and Jimmy had been living rent-free for the past six months thanks to Bates. The three of them had rubbed along happily enough. Come to think of it, he'd actually missed the big, daft lad over the last few weeks alone in the woods.

The boy stared at his ex-boss, trying to understand what was going on behind his blank eyes and expressionless face. He shivered, suddenly feeling the nip in the evening air and looked away, still none the wiser.

'You taking me to the police, Mr Bates?'

Bates sniffed and lifted his eyes to stare at the moon, now clearly visible in the darkening sky, 'You did some bad stuff, kid.'

'I'll collect my stuff and we can get goin' then,' Dylan mumbled.

Bates remained silent and didn't move from his seat on the tree trunk, watching with interest as the boy expertly retrieved various ropes, pulleys, and climbing equipment from the trees above him. Within a few minutes they'd all been packed carefully into a backpack that appeared far too bulky for the boy to manage on his own. However, Dylan swung it onto his shoulders with only the slightest suggestion of a grunt and stood before him. Bates waited.

'I'm sorry I screwed up, Mr Bates.'

Bates met the boy's gaze for a long moment before closing his eyes and accepting the apology with a silent nod. Dylan hitched his backpack up on his shoulders and turned to leave, expecting Bates to follow.

'My car is parked by the side of the track, down the hill. I'll meet you there in a few minutes. I'm going to watch the sky for a bit – it's so clear out here,' he said, tossing his car keys to the boy.

Dylan caught the keys and tried to hide the shock mixed with exhilaration he experienced when a way out of his mess was handed to him on a plate.

'It's okay, I trust you, Dylan,' Bates called after him.

Bates followed the boy's outline until he was soon lost between the trees. Still sitting with his back against the tree he pulled a pepperoni stick from his jacket pocket and took a bite, chewing the bright red meat thoughtfully. He was half-way through it when a quiet voice behind him asked, 'Could I get a second chance?'

Bate's turned and locked eyes with Dylan, careful not to show the boy how impressed he'd been with his silent approach through the forest. He took another bite of his pepperoni stick and studied the boy's hopeful face as he chewed.

'Want a bite?' he asked, indicating the bright red stick with a flick of his eyes.

The boy pondered the offer for a moment, trying not to show his disgust before answering.

'If it means I can get another chance.'

Bates began to chuckle, pocketing the meat stick and gestured to the boy to sit down beside him.

'You know something, Dylan. I doubt you've been aware, but we've been working for a man called Greg Armitage for the last five months. I met him fourteen years ago when I was still in the force. I took kids like you to Greg – kids who had records as long as your arm, kids who'd got pulled into crime and couldn't see a way out, or were robbing their neighbours because they didn't know any better – and he would give them a chance.'

Dylan looked up at the older man. Bates was examining the evening sky.

'I'd do the paperwork and take the boy or girl to his offices in Newcastle and sit them in front of him in a grand office with a huge desk and he'd wheel his chair around the desk and sit beside them. It wasn't a small company, still, Greg would interview every single one of them personally. He'd immediately toss my paperwork aside without even giving it a glance, look them in the eye and ask one question; He'd say, 'What's your passion, kid? '

Dylan's brow dived into a frown and Bates chuckled.

'Yeah, you're thinking exactly the same thing most of the kids did. Who is this idiot? It's not the sort of question you get asked that often, most people aren't that interested in finding out what really makes you tick. But Greg was. He'd get them talking about whatever got their blood pumping, or filled them with excitement. He was a clever man. He took on thirty-five of my kids and twenty-two of them are still working in his business, everything from security guards up to fully qualified software programmers.'

'Sounds like they were the lucky ones, Mr Bates.'

'The point is Dylan, Greg Armitage believed in second chances, and for some of those kids that's all they needed. And it's why I'm going to give you a second chance.'

'You're not taking me to the police?'

'Nope.'

'Where then?'

'Before I tell you, answer the question.'

Dylan remained quiet for a moment.

'The what's my passion question?'

Bates nodded, still studying the stars and the faint outline of a spiral arm that had started to emerge from the night sky.

'Electronics, Mr Bates… I seem to have a flare for it. And trees, I love trees,' Dylan said, looking up through the black branches silhouetted against the glittering cosmos.

Both men stared upwards into the night sky and a silence settled on the two of them.

Presently, Bates pursed his lips and nodded sagely up at the moon before turning to Dylan, 'Come on, kid. Let's get you home and get some decent food into you.'

'Home being…?'

'Byker. You've got your second chance, Dylan. Besides, Jimmy's missed you.'

Dylan produced a gap-toothed smile.

'Oh, but there's one thing you need to agree to,' Bates said as he pushed himself off the tree and stood over the boy, 'You need to see a doctor about your health, and medication.'

Dylan grimaced.

'I don't like 'em interfering with me,' he complained.

Bates compressed his lips into a rueful grin and placing a hand onto the boy's bony shoulder. He gave it a gentle squeeze.

'You know, Dylan. Sometimes, causing interference can produce a positive outcome.'

Enjoyed this story?

I do hope you have enjoyed reading this horseracing story. If you have, I'd *really* appreciate it if you would visit the Amazon website and leave a rating and perhaps a short review. Your ratings and reviews help new readers find my books, which in turn means I can dedicate more time to writing.

Simply visit **www.amazon.co.uk** and search for 'Richard Laws'.

You can also register for my book alert emails and news on upcoming books at **www.thesyndicatemanager.co.uk**

Many thanks,

Richard Laws
August 2022

Other Racing stories by Richard Laws

The Syndicate Manager
Gimcrack
An Old-Fashioned Coup
A Run For Your Money
The Race Caller
A Stable Full Of Winners (A collection of short stories)

Printed in Great Britain
by Amazon

46614732R00169